ALL THE KING'S MEN

RETURN OF THE ASSASSIN

Return of the Assassin

Published by Phoenix Press

Copyright © 2013 Donya Lynne

ISBN: 978-1-938991-25-7

This book is a work of fiction. References to historical events, real people, or real locales are used fictitiously. Other names, characters, places, and incidents are the product of the author's imagination, and any resemblance to actual events, locales, or persons, living or dead, is entirely coincidental.

Cover art by Reese Dante.

Licensed material is being used for illustrative purposes only and any person depicted in the licensed material is a model.

ACKNOWLEDGEMENTS

With every AKM book I write, the cast of helpers grows ever larger, and it becomes impossible to keep track of everyone and have enough space to thank them all. Special thanks go to my incredible, totally awesome group of beta readers in Traceon's Dungeon. I couldn't deliver these books at the level I do without each of you.

To those in my AKM Reader Group, I want to thank you for the laughs, the camaraderie, and the man candy that helps inspire me to create more characters, books, and scenes for this series. You all are very special. Keep being you.

To Caterina V. from Italy and my merry band of Italian fans, I want to give you a big hug and say *grazie* for your Italian translations that appear in this book. I specifically included that Italian conversation for you and all my fans in one of the most beautiful countries in the world. It is my dream to one day visit you all and see the magnificence that is Italy with my own eyes.

And lastly, thank you to Laura, my editor. We've taken this journey together from the first step. Look how far we've come, and imagine how much further we can go. I trust you implicitly with my manuscripts and know that when you have them, my babies are in good hands.

Books by Donya Lynne

All the King's Men Series

Rise of the Fallen
Heart of the Warrior
Micah's Calling
Rebel Obsession
Return of the Assassin
All the King's Men - The Beginning

Strong Karma Trilogy

Good Karma
Coming Back to You
Full Circle

Hope Falls Series

Finding Lacey Moon

Stand-Alone M/M Titles

Winter's Fire

Collections and Anthologies

All the King's Men Vol. 1 (books 1-3)
All the King's Men Vol. 2 (books 4-6)
Strong Karma Trilogy Boxed Set
Whispered Beginnings - A Romance Sampler

ALL THE KING'S MEN
RETURN OF THE ASSASSIN

DONYA LYNNE

DEDICATION

For you. You've been alone and suffering silently for too long. It's time you got your happy ending.

CHAPTER 1

GINA LAY PRONE ON TOP OF THE MIAMI HIGH-RISE, her eye to the scope on her rifle. Waiting. It seemed like waiting was all she did these days. But at least tonight she wasn't waiting for her mind to fritz out the way it had been for the past month. Tonight she was on a job. Hopefully, a job that would get her head back in the game.

Since leaving Chicago a month ago, Gina's life had begun to unravel. She had learned firsthand that she was her own worst enemy. Almost killing an innocent vampire had shoved insecurities, doubt, and that crap known as guilt front and center. They were her constant companions now. She slept with them, showered with them, and felt their ghostly tentacles fondle her mind twenty-four seven.

But her tormented psyche was only half the problem. The other half was Malek…maybe even more than half.

Warmth dashed through Gina's veins at the thought of Malek, who she had left in Chicago. She frowned at the traitorous flutter in the pit of her stomach.

She needed to get her shit together. This was no time for fear, sorrow, guilt…or love. Someone like her didn't love. She couldn't allow herself that emotion. Not anymore. An assassin who felt anything—who *loved*—was an assassin with a weakness. She knew that better than anyone. After her brother Gabe's death a year ago, her love for him had almost been her undoing…and maybe it had been. The jury was still out, but if the past few weeks were any indication, the verdict wasn't looking good, especially with Malek in her rearview mirror. She felt like he was always there, watching her, closing in.

"They're on site." She blinked back to awareness as Trevor's voice came through the transmitter in her ear. Trevor was a fellow assassin and longtime family friend. He was also one of Gabe's ex-boyfriends.

"On it," she said as a bead of sweat tickled the back of her neck and slowly slid across her skin. Damn Miami. Only the end of April, and already the humidity was uncomfortably high.

Gina pressed her eye to her scope as the light came on inside the laser-tagged apartment. A male with long, white-blond hair entered the room alone. Gina narrowed her eyes, pulled back, frowned, and then settled her eye behind her scope again.

Dacians? No way.

Gina drew her eye away and shook her head in disbelief. Full-blooded Dacians hadn't shown their faces in public in decades. In fact, some thought Dacian vampires were extinct. That's how long it had been since anyone had seen one.

But this guy? If he wasn't a Dacian, she was human.

There went the neighborhood.

She looked through her scope again and stretched out her senses to verify what her eyes had already told her. Sure enough, the acidic fragrance of ancient, Dacian blood reached out and touched someone. Her. And not in a good way. The stench was enough to make bile rise in her throat, and not just from the smell. Old memories—*bad* memories—snared her mind, and a shiver rippled up her back.

"Dacians, Trevor?" she said.

There was a pause, as if Trevor was considering her question, and then his voice broke through the silence. "Ah, shit. I didn't think—"

"You didn't think that was something I should know up front?" Gina's ex-mate, Armand, had been half-Dacian, one nasty sonofabitch, and as abusive as they came. The bastard had a right hook that would have knocked out Foreman, Tyson, and Holyfield in one punch. And that was being conservative.

Escaping Armand had almost killed her. Literally. Trevor knew this. He had seen Armand's handiwork firsthand. And even though it had been over a century since she—*ahem*—parted ways with the asshole, she never quite got over what she called the Armand

Effect. His beatings still left a nasty mark on her mental state. Yeah sure, kind of like a guillotine only just *sort of* removes a head. Who was she kidding? The mark Armand had left on her soul was more like a gouge that resembled the Royal Gorge in Colorado. A giant monstrosity of a wound that not even duct tape and Super Glue could fix.

Trevor's frustrated sigh broke through her earpiece. "I'm sorry, Gina. I wasn't thinking."

"Clearly." She rolled her eyes then squinted through her scope. "I'll make you pay for the nasty reminder of my past later. For now, where's the second target? I only see one."

She couldn't think about Armand now. She was working and couldn't afford another distraction, because enough of those already sat tapping their fingers in her psyche, waiting for her to let down her guard so they could righteously bungle her world to hell and back. She couldn't let that happen. Not now. Not on her first job since *the incident*.

"Mark Two is on his way," Trevor said. "And go easy on me, Gina. I'm still not myself, either. I miss him, too, and—"

"Forget it, Trev." Gina didn't want to hear what he was about to say, because she knew it had to do with Gabe, and she could only take one upsetting reminder of her past right now. "We've both been through hell."

But it hadn't always been that way. Once upon a time, she and Trevor had been happy, and Gabe had been part of that happiness. Back then, the three of them had worked as AKM enforcers in Atlanta. Now Trev ran an independent agency in Florida called the Knights of Justice, or KOJU. King Bain had never sanctioned KOJU, but their mission was similar to that of All the King's Men, just without the royal credentials.

Gina kept her eye glued to her scope. Her neck ached, her arms burned, and every muscle begged to be stretched. A shallow smile curved her mouth for a split second, and then was gone. Before Gabe's death, during happier times, the three of them had gone on a lot of stakeouts together, just like this one.

Poor Trev. He had taken Gabe's death hard. Even though they had broken up decades ago, Gabe had still been his best friend, and they were like family to one another. Two males, once lovers, who discovered they were even better friends. Trev had been swallowed by grief and heartache after Gabe was gone.

Gina, on the other hand, had turned her grief into something darker. Something vengeful and dangerous that spurred her to hunt down every person involved in the factory raid where Gabe was killed. Including Severin.

Severin had been Gabe's boyfriend at the time, and Gabe died thinking Sev had turned on him. He hadn't known Sev was a deep cover agent with Vampire Dreck Affairs. No one had known, and Gina hadn't taken the time to get the facts...just went after him with guns blazing. Sev had been as much a victim as she, Trevor, and Gabe, but she had been too hung up on vengeance to see his innocence, and she had almost killed him.

Thank God she had failed, but now her confidence was shattered. She was full of doubt and that enemy called emotion. It was as if she no longer had a place in the world. For the past month, she had drifted through her existence as a shadow, a wraith. Aimless and hollow. She didn't just feel empty, she felt rattled. All the pieces no longer fit, and she was a fractured projection of the female she had once been. And not just because of her attempt to assassinate Sev. Malek was partly to blame, too.

She closed her eyes and tried to push away Malek's memory, which was becoming harder to do. Malek was the male who had saved her when all she had wanted was to die. The male who promised to be a whole lot of holy-hell-I'm-in-trouble if she let him.

"Mark Two is on site." Trevor's voice came through her earpiece, startling her.

Gina shook herself out of her reverie and pulled her thoughts back into the present. A moment later, her hands trembled. Then her heart fluttered and began to race.

No, please no. Not now. She tried to ignore away the crackle of panic. "I don't see him." Her breath came harder in quick, shallow breaths, and sudden pressure tightened her chest.

Oh God, no. Please no. Not again.

"He's not in range, yet," Trevor said.

Gina's heart beat in her ears, suddenly frantic. *Thu-thump, thu-*

thump. Like a thoroughbred leaping from the starting gate in the Kentucky Derby, her heart raced and pounded against her rib cage.

This can't be happening now!

Damn it. She didn't need this shit. Not when she was minutes or even seconds from pulling the trigger and making society a better place by turning two Dacian vampires into worm food.

Ever since parting ways with Armand, she had suffered from occasional panic attacks, but never like this. Never this crippling, and certainly never this prolific. What had been a rare nuisance before had, in three weeks, become debilitating. And the attacks were steadily growing worse and more frequent. As if she were repressing some deep-seated emotion and this was her body's way of trying to get her attention. But what was she repressing? She had already dealt with the aftereffects of Armand's abuse a long time ago, and she wasn't repressing anything where Severin was concerned. On the contrary, she lived the guilt and shame of those actions every single godforsaken day. Through the process of elimination, that left Malek.

Nope. Not gonna think about him.

Too late. She already *was* thinking about him and couldn't stop.

She kept her eye on her scope and watched for the target, even as every muscle tightened and her chest constricted as if a python were putting the death squeeze on her.

"Gina? You okay?" Trevor said.

"Uh-huh. I'm f...fine."

"You're such a lousy liar." He paused. "Stand down."

"No. I'm fine. I c...can do this." She *needed* to do this to prove she wasn't falling apart and becoming an invalid. That she wasn't losing herself in the pot of rancid stew her life was turning into.

"I said stand down. I can hear you practically hyperventilating into your transmitter."

She frowned and listened to herself. Shit. She was. But she wasn't going to let Trevor down. Or herself.

"I can do this, Trevor." If she didn't, she may as well hang up her assassin's hat right now, sell her rifles, and off herself. If she couldn't perform, she couldn't work, and then what would she do? Knit? Yeah right. She'd rather poke herself in the eye with one of those foot-long knitting needles than use it for its intended purpose.

"Gina, I'm not going to argue with you. Stand down. I can take care of this. I just need to wait for Mark Two to enter the frame from the bedroom, and I can take them both."

The bedroom was on her side. She checked her scope again and saw Mark Two standing at his dresser, removing his cuff links. "I've got a shot. You take out One. I've got Two." Determination surged within her. She would not be an invalid. She would earn her keep or else.

"Gina...don't!"

Pphht! Pphht! Too late. She had already depressed the trigger. Twice.

The bullets strayed, and marble shards splintered from the side of the window.

Damn it!

The Dacian spun toward the window, and his hand shot to the waist of his pants for his gun.

Trevor cursed. "Gina! Abort, damn it! We're blown!"

No, she wasn't going to let this target get away! Especially since he was a Dacian. At this point, this shit was personal. "Take down One, Trev. I've got Two." She took aim again. Her finger trembled on the trigger, but she was able to fire off several shots. Surely one would hit.

"It's too late," Trevor barked. "One's gone!"

The bullets sprayed more marble from the wall then shattered the window. The target lurched to the side and ducked just as the last bullet zipped past where his head had been.

Shit!

Failure.

Trevor was going to kill her. She knew better than anyone that when it came to Dacians, you were lucky to get a second shot if the first shot failed. Dacian vampires were slick, wily, and cunning, and they had incredible hunting skills, finely developed and tuned to match their overly aggressive nature, which meant she and Trevor needed to beat feet. Missing this hit was a major fail, and if the Dacians weren't already on her and Trevor's trail, they soon would be.

When Trevor formed from the cloud of mist that blew up on her, she was already dismantling her rifle. But her hands trembled so violently she could barely unlock the pieces of hardware from each other. She was in a full-on panic attack. She never should have taken that shot. Hindsight was always twenty-twenty. Too bad foresight wasn't.

"What were you thinking?" Trevor was pissed, and rightfully so. He spun and snagged his gun case from midair a second after appearing, and then dropped it to the roof as he knelt and jerked Gina's gun from her hands. He finished taking it apart and hastily dropped the pieces into her case. "We've got to move!" He sealed her case shut, shoved it under his arm as he picked up his, and grabbed her wrist. "Now!" With a jarring yank, he pulled her to her feet and practically dragged her to the ledge of the roof, which overlooked the alley where their getaway vehicle waited.

"I can't breathe." She clutched at her vest. *Too tight. Too tight.*

Trevor cursed, shook his head, and threw a desperate glance over his shoulder. "Your breakdown is just going to have to wait until we're out of here. We're in deep shit."

No joke. They had just messed with Dacians. If shit wasn't already critical, it soon would be. Her past with Armand had taught her that much.

In all of three seconds, Trevor threw their gun cases over the side of the building, grabbed her, and sucked her into his vapor tunnel as he shot them to the ground.

"Get in and release the back hatch." He pointed to the SUV and looked back toward the sky. "Do it now!"

On shaky legs, Gina staggered to the passenger side of the SUV, nearly doubling over as her chest constricted and she gasped for air. She planted one hand on the side of the vehicle, jerked the door open, and crawled into the front seat. Trevor caught their falling gun cases as if they weighed no more than bags of potato chips, then hustled toward the SUV.

"Now, Gina! Goddamn it! Open the hatch."

Thrashing her hand toward the dash, she finally managed to swat the button for the back hatch, which clicked and hissed open so Trevor could toss the cases inside.

The SUV shuddered as he clunked the hatch closed, and a second later he was in the driver's seat, shoving the key into the ignition, foot already on the gas. With a shrill of squealing tires, they shot out of the alley and bounced into traffic, nearly sideswiping a passing car.

Ding...ding...ding.

The seat belt indicator signaled that neither she nor Trev were buckled up, but with her in a shivering heap halfway on the floor, lost in the grip of another panic attack and facing the seat instead of the windshield, fastening her seat belt was the least of her worries.

"Fuck!" Trevor slammed his hand on the steering wheel and checked the rearview mirror as he cranked the wheel to the left. Gina crashed into the passenger door then flung back toward the center console as Trevor straightened the wheel and shoved his Bluetooth in his ear. Then he jerked his seat belt one-handed over his shoulder and fastened himself in.

With shaky hands, she ripped open her jacket and released the vest. Goddamn, that thing was tight. She groaned, relieved to reduce the pressure, then pulled herself into her seat. Her arms gave out just as she turned to the front.

"This shit needs to stop, Gina." Trevor hit a button on the console and the sound of digital dialing mingled with the still dinging seat belt indicator. He reached across her chest, pulled the seat belt around her, and shoved it into place with an angry *click.*

Harsh, wheezing breaths burst from her lungs, and she doubled over, clutched her chest, and then slammed back against the seat as a sharp pain speared her sternum. She hardly noticed Miami's bright lights as they flashed by as she and Trev raced down the highway.

I'm dying. I just know I'm dying. Something's wrong with me. What's happening to me? The lights swam around her, and she felt like she was spinning out of control as a thousand disjointed thoughts attacked her mind in no particular order. *Is this my punishment? Is this the price I have to pay for my carelessness? For all my sins? For dishonoring Gabe by trying to kill Severin? For killing Armand? My own mate, for God's sake? Is my life ever going to be normal again? It was an accident. I swear! I never meant to kill him, but he was hurting me. He always hurt me. Who am I kidding? Killing him was no accident. Only Gabe knew. He tried to make him stop. Gabe...oh, Gabe. Help me. Please! I need you. I miss you. You were the only one who ever understood...the only one who knew the truth. Malek!*

The tumble of chaos in her head screeched to a halt on Malek's name as if he were the solution. Huh-uh. He was more likely the problem. Or at least part of it. Because there was no way she would ever let him be the solution.

Trevor barked commands into his Bluetooth. "Colby, get to my place. Grab Gina's things and grab my two black duffels from the closet and meet me at the airport in thirty." Trevor made a sharp right, cutting off traffic. "And don't fold her shit. Just toss what you can in her bag and go!"

Gina gasped, and her stomach rolled. "I think I'm going to throw up. Pull over." She grabbed for the door, but Trevor kept going.

He reached behind his seat, and his arm flailed until he found what he was looking for. Then he shoved an empty shopping bag at her. "You'll just have to puke in that, because I'm not stopping." He gunned the gas and flew around another corner, turning his conversation back to Colby. "No, I'm taking evasive action. They're probably tailing us. Gonna drive around Miami and lead them away from my house so you can get in and out with our stuff. Then I'm hightailing it to the airport. Call Axe and get him over to prep the jet."

Gina eyed the bag then closed her eyes and willed herself not to vomit. She just needed to talk herself down and she would be okay. Her panic was all in her head, but knowing that didn't stop the tumble of self-defeating thoughts from hammering away at her soul.

She had messed up in Chicago. She had almost killed an innocent male. What kind of assassin was that careless? She had ignored her gut and hadn't obtained all the facts? She had flown off half-cocked and made an incredible error in judgment. This was her fault. These panic attacks were her doing. But what if she never recovered? What if they continued to get worse until she could no longer function? Her life would be over. No one would hire her, and she would have no way to survive.

At one time, she had been a revered assassin...cool, calm under fire, and stable. Now she was anything but, and her body reminded her of that every day. Even worse, she never knew when a panic attack would strike. Their rhyme and reason made no sense.

Tonight was supposed to have gotten her back on track. She'd been meant to redeem herself and become the badass bitch she had once been. Instead, she had failed. Again. Failure was becoming a trend.

Tears streaked her cheeks, and she bit her thumbnail as she looked out the window and tried to get a grasp on something— anything that would ground her. This was the worst panic attack yet, and fear jolted her heart that she might never gain control over the demons that assaulted her sanity on a daily basis now.

A sinking feeling dove through her gut, and a chill cut through her as she thought back to what Malek said to her in Chicago. She was beginning to fear his words that day were more to blame for what was happening to her than she first realized.

She'd been thrown in a holding cell at AKM to stew in the mix of guilt, shame, and wounded conscience creating a hole in the middle of her soul like battery acid. She'd been inconsolable, but Malek had refused to leave her. He had been a presence in her cell as constant as her pain, appointing himself her personal guard. Eventually, she became grateful for his company, even when they only sat in silence. He'd comforted her simply by being there.

On the day in question, she had been in lockup for maybe four or five days, laying in bed and trying not to think about how badly she had screwed up. But after blowing two holes inside an innocent person's chest, it was hard not to think about it... and dwell on it...and regret every stupid, careless, misguided decision that led to the moment she pulled the trigger.

She lay on her side in the dark, facing the wall, and exhaustion finally began to win out over the litany of self-deprecating thoughts parading through her mind, and she drifted toward sleep. Malek was there...behind her on the other bed.

She was just on the brink of sleep when Malek sighed. The rush of air was tinged with the telltale hint of frustration, and a moment later, the quiet rustle of the other bed told her he'd sat up. But she was too near sleep and too wrapped up in her own problems to pay him much attention.

Silence followed for another few seconds, and then Malek whispered so quietly that his voice sounded almost like breath. "I know you're asleep, but…" He trailed off, and the blankets stirred again as he uttered a quiet groan, as if he were frustrated with himself. "I don't know what's happening to me."

Curiosity pulled her from the brink of sleep, but she refused to turn around. She didn't want to talk about whatever was bothering him. She had her own shit to deal with. He thought she was asleep, so if she kept up the act, maybe he would leave and take his frustrations elsewhere.

"How did this happen?" he whispered, as if to himself. "I can't take another mate. I can't."

She frowned, eyes closed. A mate? Surely, he wasn't talking about her.

"I don't know how this happened." He reflected aloud. "I shouldn't be feeling this way, but I am." He moved, and Gina felt his gaze prickle the hair on the back of her neck. "God forgive me, but the connection is there, and I feel it growing stronger every hour. I don't know what to do. Why do I want you when I haven't even…?" From the tone of his voice, he didn't sound happy. Then he continued. "I can't let go of my past, Gina. I want to, but I can't. How will this work if I can't let go of…?" He trailed off with a sigh.

Whatever was on his mind was serious. Bad serious. And she hoped whatever it was, it was strong enough to overcome whatever mated male biological body chemistry he had going on—or *thought* he had going on—because the last thing she wanted was another mate. She didn't do relationships. Not since Armand.

When he spoke again, his voice was even softer and right behind her, as if he were staring at the back of her head, maybe even studying her. The warmth of his breath caressed her neck. "How did you become my mate, Gina? I'm not worthy of you."

Gina's thoughts bounced back to the present as Trevor took a turn too closely and jumped the curb. That was it, wasn't it? Malek had royally freaked her out by declaring she was his mate, and like a startled deer, she had bolted. Just up and ran like a chickenshit as soon as she was released. Was that the kind of thing assassins did? Did they flee at the first sign of trouble? Hell no! They stood and fought, or at least laid down the law. She hadn't done either. She should have turned around then and there and told Malek that he could want to be her mate all he wanted, but that didn't mean she reciprocated.

But there was one catch. She was attracted to Malek. As in really attracted to him. A revelation she had refused to admit to herself for days after leaving Chicago, and which she still didn't voice aloud. But just because she found Malek attractive didn't mean she wanted him for a mate. Hell no!

Trev was still throwing out instructions to Colby, and his gaze danced up to the rearview mirror every few seconds. "Okay, call me when you're on your way to the airport." He disconnected and shot her a look. "You okay?"

She threw the bag he had given her behind his seat with a vicious swipe of her arm. "Do I look fucking okay, Trev? Huh?" She shouldn't have yelled at him, but right now she was about to implode, and she still trembled like a wet dog in the snow as adrenaline broke through her system. "Shit!"

Trevor ignored her outburst and gunned the SUV down a winding road that circled one of the hundred or so lakes in the area. Sometimes South Florida seemed like one big lake with islands all around. "We've got to get out of here."

With Dacians on their ass, the safest thing to do was to hightail it out of town for a while and make it harder for them to follow. And based on Trev's conversation with Colby, hightailing it involved flying.

"Where are we going?" she said as she wrung her hands, the attack beginning to wane. Her foot bounced on the floorboard like she was playing "Chopsticks" on a hi-hat.

He shrugged. "I don't care. Anywhere but here. Any suggestions?"

She stared down at her shaking hands. All this had started in Chicago. Whether Malek was the catalyst or not, her panic attacks started after she left Chicago. This was her chance to man up, go back, face the situation, and be the hard-ass she had been trained to be. And maybe going back would finally put an end to the incessant e-mails she kept getting from some jackass named Micah, who worked at AKM. Micah wanted her to return to Chicago, too, and she could only imagine it was because Malek had fallen into mated male *suffering*. But she refused to reply.

To be honest, she was surprised no one had come after her, yet. Mated males didn't do well without their mates, and the king's law went to exceptional lengths to protect them, even if it meant hunting down a female and dragging her kicking and screaming back to her mate. Not that many females resisted a mate's call. Statistics would probably show that 99.99 percent didn't. Gina just happened to be in that .01 percent who did.

The agony must be unreal for him. One more layer of guilt wrapped around her as she thought of what Malek could be going through right now without her.

Damn it, she didn't need to develop a conscience. She didn't want another mate. Period. End of story. Malek would just have to find a way to cope...the same way she had after dealing Armand the eviction notice from her life...because that shit hadn't been easy, and she wasn't going back there. Ever.

Unfortunately, Malek had already reawakened her despair with his damn declaration that he had mated her. Why couldn't he have kept his mouth shut? Because then she wouldn't be in such a mess now. She wouldn't know he had mated her, and she wouldn't be harboring even more guilt than she already was.

She liked Malek. He seemed different. Sweet. That was why her conscience ate at her now. Malek didn't deserve to be in such a pickle, suffering God only knew what agony, because of her. He had said that day in her cell that he wasn't worthy of her. Ha! He got it backward, because *she* wasn't worthy of *him*. If only he knew the truth, he would see that mating her was a mistake, and maybe that would be enough to ease the suffering and help him heal from her absence and go on without her.

She knew most males weren't like Armand. But enduring such violent trauma at Armand's hands had left her shattered and unable to fathom ever getting that close to a male again. The thought that history would repeat if she took another mate was irrational, because Armand was the exception, not the rule. But she couldn't help herself. Not after all she'd suffered. Armand had been like an IED she'd stepped on…only all the damage from the blast was on the inside, and she had the PTSD to prove it.

Still, desperation made people do strange things, and she was desperate for these mind-numbing anxiety attacks to stop before they killed her. Like it or not, only one solution seemed evident. She needed to go back to the source. To Malek. So she could face him and put an end to his fantasy that they were supposed to spend the rest of their lives together.

Fuck biology. Fuck the physiological bond that tethered him to her. She wasn't having it. All she wanted was to be done with him. Discussion over. If it killed him, it killed him. Not her problem.

She frowned at the thought. She didn't want to hurt Malek, but her number one priority had to be herself. She had put others' needs before hers for too long and needed to take care of herself this time.

"Well?" Trevor prompted her again. "Thoughts? Suggestions? New York, maybe? We could go to—"

"Chicago. We need to go to Chicago." She glanced across the seat at him.

"What?" He looked surprised. "I thought you said you never wanted to go back to Chicago."

She hadn't told him much about what happened in the Windy City—only enough to give him an idea of how bad the situation was. Now it was clear that running away from the past was a fast track to hell, and if going back to Chi-Town could release her mind and her heart, then the sooner they returned, the better. And maybe that would get that Micah asshole off her back, too. Right now, Micah's constant e-mails were making the situation worse, even though she no longer read them.

"I changed my mind," she said. "I need to go back to Chicago."

Reluctant acknowledgement tainted Trevor's expression. "Okay, Chicago it is, but I hope you know what you're doing."

Gina chewed on her thumbnail again as she glanced out the window. "Yeah. Me, too."

Several silent minutes later, Trevor's phone rang and he picked it up. He listened then said, "Good, I'm on my way. Tell Axe we're going to Chicago."

Looked like Colby had their things and was on his way to meet them.

Trevor shot to the highway and made a beeline for the airport. They arrived in record time. Axe already had the jet prepped and the engines fired as she and Trevor tossed in their luggage and rushed to their seats.

"Go!" Trevor called up to Axe.

Without a word, Axe pulled the jet away from the terminal and taxied toward the runway.

Before she knew it, the jet lifted off, Chicago bound.

When she looked down at her hands in her lap, she realized that for the first time in forty-five minutes she wasn't shaking. The pain in her chest was also gone.

For some reason, she didn't think that was a good sign.

SEARCY'S BOOTED FEET LANDED WITH A THUD a moment before his son, Vaydon, appeared beside him. Wind blew their long, pale hair off their faces as their yellow eyes, sharp with hunting sight, turned up in tandem to watch the private jet take off. Dark malevolence shrouded them like poison.

He cursed, and the sound came out like the spit from a cobra despite his calm demeanor.

Their prey had gotten away. For now. But that male and his female friend with the anxiety problem wouldn't get far. Searcy imprinted their scent, panic and all, and he knew it was only a matter of time before he caught them. He swirled the fragrance of the two assassins around and over his sensory glands, embedding their essences into his memory. Familiarity touched him from the female, but he couldn't recall where he had scented her before. It would come to him. Such things always did.

Without taking his eyes off the private jet, which grew smaller as it climbed, Searcy took a deep, steadying breath and said, "Find out where that jet is going. Kill whoever you have to."

Without so much as a nod in Searcy's direction, Vaydon strode toward the edge of the building, calm, collected, and unhurried.

His long hair billowed on the wind. His broad shoulders stretched the calf-length, black trench across his back, and his boots thunked with measured heaviness over the surface of the flat-topped roof. Then, as if falling into shadow, Vaydon disappeared into mist.

Searcy stared at the small pinpricks of light blinking from the jet's wings.

So, the Knights of Justice were finally onto him and Vaydon. It had been inevitable. What did he think? That he and Vaydon could continue their treacherous dealings and illegal transgressions forever and go unnoticed? But he hadn't counted on King Bain's royally disbarred Knights catching his trail so soon.

Impressive.

But futile.

His plans were already well under way. It wouldn't be long before he shook things up in the vampire community, and by then, King Bain's AKM enforcers and the KOJU vigilantes would have to play catch-up. And by the time they did, the throne would be his again. Back in his bloodline where it belonged.

Vaydon reappeared from the ether and strolled toward him, a smear of blood on his chin. "Chicago," he said, turning his gaze toward the jet as it disappeared behind a cloud.

Ah, Chicago. The king's backyard. How perfect. Searcy issued one final glance toward the jet that held those who had just tried to kill his son. No doubt he had been in their sites, as well, but they were either too inept or poorly trained to finish the job. Now he and Vaydon were kicked dogs, sleeping giants awakened, and it was their turn to become the hunters.

"Chicago it is then," he said, turning one perfectly arched brow toward Vaydon as his eyes shifted back to silver.

His son's thin mouth curved into a loose, crooked grin. Vaydon loved the hunt as much as Searcy did. Like father, like son. They thrilled over the kill...the pain...the suffering of others...especially when it came to the blasphemous vampire clans who had overthrown Dacian rule countless millennia ago. He would teach them. Searcy would show them the error of their ways. After all, he hadn't spent centuries in exile without a plan to take back what belonged to him. The traitors would pay. He had been patient for what seemed like forever, but the time for patience was almost over.

The fact that this hunt for his would-be assassins would take place in King Bain's backyard made it all the sweeter. And once he recalled where he knew that bitch who had taken a shot at Vaydon was from—and he *would* remember—killing her would provide the icing on the cake.

As if teasing him, a memory flashed, and then vanished in a blink. Ah well, soon enough. He would remember how he knew her soon enough.

"Let's go. We have a trip to get ready for." Searcy turned on his heel and paced away with measured steps, disappearing into ether as he went. Vaydon followed and faded into the night with him.

Those two Chicago-bound assassins had just fucked with the wrong Dacians. And he would see them both dead before the next full moon.

CHAPTER 2

MALEK GASPED AND JOLTED UPRIGHT IN BED, drenched in sweat.

Another nightmare about Carmen. Dead. Lying broken on the floor. This was why he hadn't slept more than a few hours in the past two weeks. When he did, the same nightmare stole into his dreams and he awoke torqued, gasping for air, soaked with sweat, and ready to put his fist through a wall.

Slamming the heels of his hands over his eyes, he shook his head. *No, no, no! She's not dead. She's only sleeping. She's only—*

She's dead.

Malek threw his hands away from his face and scowled. *Shut up.* The Voice had riddled him for over a week, but he wasn't in the mood for its antagonism right now.

She. Is. Dead.

Malek growled at The Voice, but a moment later he hung his head. It was right. Carmen *was* dead. On some level he knew that. He just hadn't accepted it. Not entirely. But he was beginning to, which was why the suffering throttled him harder each day. Why he was such a mess. Why he wasn't eating or feeding. Why he was buying whores every night and fucking them to within a brink of insanity. Well, the last he wasn't doing because of Carmen. That was Gina's doing.

Gina... The Voice sighed.

The Voice liked Gina. No, it loved her. But Malek couldn't give her to it. For one, she was gone. Secondly, Malek refused to disrespect Carmen by taking another mate, and since The Voice lived in his mind, to give Gina to it meant he would have to accept that he had mated her. Still, his body broke a little more each day with the need to claim her. His *calling* urged him to find her...to complete the mating and bind himself to her...to fulfill his biological obligation to procreate.

Yeeesssss.

Malek threw off the covers and jumped out of bed, pissed off, wound tight, and about to explode. His cock throbbed. Hard. Again. It was always hard now. Always ready to betray him. All he wanted was Carmen, his beautiful first mate. But she wasn't here. She never would be again, no matter how hard he denied it or tried to reason otherwise.

In the bathroom, he cranked on the shower and hopped in before the water grew hot. The blast of cold stung and quieted his mind for a few seconds, and then the water warmed. Then the mental shitstorm began again. All he could do was hang his head, let the hot water saturate him, and breathe. If he could. Every breath he dragged into his lungs made his chest ache. Just like his traitorous dick, his chest ached all the time now.

Heartburn.

He blew out a derisive breath as he pressed his knuckles against his sternum and rubbed. This wasn't what humans referred to when they said they had heartburn, but the expression was accurate. His heart definitely felt like it was burning, and the inferno only seemed to worsen every day.

Rub-rub-rub.

He worked his hand over his chest until the water began to grow cold again. Then he turned off the faucet and grabbed his towel as he stepped out of the shower. The bathroom was filled with mist, and the mirror was covered in condensation.

What did the night hold? He should report to work but didn't have the energy. And wouldn't Micah love that? In the past few weeks, Malek had excelled at getting on Micah's shit list.

From the corner of his eye, he caught movement and a flash of wild, auburn hair and spun to follow it.

"Carmen?" He looked over his shoulder then turned around again, but no one was there. He was alone.

This wasn't the first time he thought he'd seen Carmen in his periphery. He'd caught glimpses of her numerous times in the past few days, but every time he looked, she was gone.

A reflection of auburn hair in the foggy mirror brought his attention back around, but once more, when his gaze stole into the area where he thought he'd seen her, she was gone. No one was there but him.

Alone.

The word held new meaning for him. While Carmen had been dead for centuries, he had never really felt alone...until now. Now the solitude encroached and bound him, clawed at his insides, and made him mad with desperation.

He was in the in-between...Switzerland between two adversaries. Except he was being forced to choose a side. Either he stayed with Carmen's memory and died, or he joined Gina and lived. Each side had pros, and each had cons. If he chose Carmen, he would die, but at least he would hold Carmen's memory intact. If he chose Gina, he would live but forever disgrace his first mate.

Rock, meet hard place.

He got dressed, snagged the keys to his truck off the dresser, and headed out. There was no sense in denying himself. He knew what he needed, and he knew where to get it. Fuck Micah. Malek would just have to suffer another tick mark on Micah's list, because work didn't appeal to him tonight.

AN HOUR LATER, Malek was settled at his favorite booth at Four Alarm, head hung over his drink like a vulture. Heavy bass throbbed the darkened, sweat-scented air, and techno dance beats pumped through the club's speakers, jarring his already flayed nerves.

Four Alarm was packed tonight. Wall-to-wall bodies. Men trolled for action, and women who wanted to give it—for a price—eyed potential clients, as well as the size of their wallets. It's why Malek was here. He needed what these women offered. And his wallet was very thick. All the better since his needs had grown more depraved every night since

Gina left.

Gina.

She was what he really needed. She was the only one who could fulfill his body's urgings. Good thing she was gone, because he wasn't sure he could handle her presence if she were still around.

Gina. The Voice whispered her name inside his brain as if pleased he was thinking about her.

He slammed his eyes shut and hunched farther over his shot glass as if he had been punched in the gut.

So this was what it felt like to lose a mate. This despair and agony. A knife to the chest would have been less painful. The problem was, Malek hadn't just lost one mate, but two. After hundreds of years, he was finally dealing with Carmen's death. Mating Gina had ripped open the wound he had successfully tucked away for centuries—one he had avoided facing—and now Carmen's death pummeled him as if she had only died yesterday. So, not only was he suffering the loss of Gina, but also the death of Carmen. Maybe he should just walk into the dawn come morning and end his misery.

Not a bad idea.

Malek opened his eyes and scoffed into his glass of whiskey. And this wasn't the fancy shit, either. This was burn-off-your-tongue, stab-yourself-in-the-eye, cripple-your-liver rotgut.

Nothing but the best.

But the liquid sewage helped quiet The Voice.

She's dead, moron. Deal with it.

Or maybe not.

He pinched his eyes shut again and grimaced at the vision of Carmen lying on a dusty wooden floor worn smooth by his boots and her dainty slippers. Their home. He saw the home they had shared long ago in the European countryside during the Middle Ages. That simple cottage had been the sanctuary he'd shared with Carmen. His mate. His life. His reason for being.

In his mind's eye, her body was bent at an unusual angle, her head turned toward the door, her eyes open and lifeless.

One arm lay outstretched beside her, as if she had been reaching for something, or maybe putting something away on the shelves. A jar of fruit preserves lay shattered nearby, and the footstool was toppled beside the table.

The sour taste in Malek's mouth intensified as he broke out in a sweat, the mental image looping over and over from the moment he opened the door until he saw the preserves.

No! She's not dead. He forced the image back and replaced it with another. One that was more acceptable. Carmen was lying in bed, eyes closed, body peaceful. Her chest rose and fell, rose and fell. The rhythmic pattern of sleep. *See, she's just sleeping.*

Fine, buddy. You just keep telling yourself that.

Malek glanced down at the shit-brown liquid in his shot glass. *Fuck you. Just fuck you, asshole. She's not dead. And I'm not your buddy.*

He waited for a retort. Anything to contradict him and piss him off even further, but The Voice silenced and left Malek alone. Finally, blessedly alone with his drink. Maybe The Voice had finally gotten the hint that he wasn't interested in dissenting opinions. There was only one right answer to the question of Carmen's whereabouts. She was sleeping, damn it. Just sleeping. She was human and needed her rest, for God's sake. Couldn't everyone see that? And yesterday she had been away washing his tunics and trousers in the stream that ran through the woods by their cottage. And the day before that, she had been out in the fields, chasing the vermin from the garden. There was an explanation for where she had been all this time.

Riiiight.

I thought you were gone.

Nope. And I won't be until you see.

See what?

That Carmen is dead.

Malek slammed back the whiskey as if he had a fire in his belly and wanted to fuel it. Maybe he could burn The Voice out of his head. Little fucker. Another glass, another swallow. Another, and still another. One after the other, he kicked them back, the bottle in one hand and the shot glass in the other. Pour, drink, pour, drink, until…

His bloody knuckles stopped him cold. How had that happened? The flesh was ripped, and dried blood filled the creases of his skin. Oh, that's right. He had gotten into a fight on the way here. With a brick wall. The wall won. But his hand should have healed by now. Why hadn't his injuries healed? He dismissed the question with a bemused chuckle.

Hitting the wall had felt good. Almost purifying. And it had shut up The Voice for a while. Not long enough, but any reprieve from the heckler in his head was welcome. Because The Voice didn't have anything good to say. Just shit, crap, and lies. Pain seemed to silence it, though, so Malek would need to keep up a steady supply to fill the demand.

Suicide Economics.

He snorted in amusement from the new term as it popped into his mind. Maybe somebody should create a class and teach all male vampires about suicide economics. That way, they would be prepared for losing a mate, because when a male lost his mate, his body would demand a kind of pain he would have to supply or else, even if that pain led to suicide. Hence the name of the course.

Perhaps he could teach suicide economics to young males hitting their transition into adulthood. The class could be a prerequisite for vampire sex education, because all males needed to know what they were getting their balls into by going down Happy Lane with a pretty, young female who could turn out to be their mate, and consequently, their downfall. Heck, maybe he should petition his commander, Tristan—oh wait…no. Micah was in charge now, wasn't he? Well, maybe he could petition Micah to talk to his good buddy, the king, about funding for a class in suicide economics for all the young males. Hell, he had plenty of firsthand experience with the subject matter. He would make a fine instructor. The perfect teacher.

If he survived the week.

He chuckled almost maniacally at his ludicrous musings before somber melancholy settled into his heart once more, and he stared down at the brown, high tech plastic table that supported his arms.

Carmen…Gina…Carmen. He was lost without them. Without *both* of them, but he refused to see Gina for the savior she was at the sacrifice of Carmen's memory. He couldn't take a new mate when his heart still clung to the memory of another. Tears threatened the lower rims of his eyes as pain, sorrow, and something darker—something forlorn that reeked of self-loathing and defeat—ate away at his soul and burrowed deeper into the recesses of his gut.

Growling out an exhale, he blinked away his emotions and leaned back in the darkened corner. He caressed the lip of his shot glass with his fingertips as if it were the pristine nipple of the woman he wanted. Gina's nipple. Her lovely, perfect, heavenly…

No! He winced and jerked his fingers away from the glass as if it were, in fact, Gina's breast and he had committed adultery by touching her.

What kind of male was he to cheat with Gina when he was already mated to Carmen?

You fool. Carmen's dead. Gina's alive. Get on with your life before you lose your mind.

He groaned. *Before* he lost his mind? He felt like he already had.

Every bone ached, every muscle protested. Even his eyes felt weary, his eyelids heavy from lack of sleep. When was the last time he'd actually slept? Really slept? He couldn't remember, and his brain hurt when he tried to.

He would figure it out later. Right now, he needed only one thing other than the vile liquid he kept pouring down his throat.

Four Alarm's crowd was target rich tonight. As it was every night. But the way he had been burning through the whores the past couple of weeks and building a reputation as a depraved sex addict with a thing for kink, he would have to find a new source soon. Perhaps he might eventually be forced to venture into the seedy Underground, a place enforcers like him were more inclined to raid than visit for recreational purposes. But the clientele at The Underground was better suited to fill his debauched needs. He would keep it in mind, but for tonight he eyed a few good prospects at Four Alarm who, as yet, still seemed oblivious to his degenerate reputation from the way they eyed him from their perches.

He hungered, his cock hard. The damn thing had been hard since Gina showed up in Chicago a month ago.

He slammed his eyes shut, refusing to think about Gina anymore tonight.

"Hey, baby. You look lonely."

I am lonely. He lifted his gaze to the leggy blonde who slithered up to his table like a snake, stealthy and cunning. She smelled of another man's semen, but it didn't matter.

"I do, huh?" He sprawled against the red leather seat of the booth, legs open, arms slung over the back.

He looked her up and down, and the corner of his mouth kicked upward. For a whore, she dressed nicely. Classy leather skirt, sleeveless silk blouse. Or maybe it was fake silk—polyester that wanted to pretend to be more expensive and sophisticated than it was.

She placed her leather clutch on the table and took a seat beside him, and her gaze dropped to the bulge in his pants. "That for me?" Her hand crawled up his thigh.

"You'll do."

She smiled, showing perfect teeth behind full, sparkling lips. This one's pimp definitely took care of his girls.

"How much?" He might as well cut to the chase. He didn't have the time nor the inclination to play games when it was clear he wanted what she offered.

"That depends." She tilted her head to the side, and her eyes danced flirtatiously up and down his body as if she were sizing him up as boyfriend material.

Why did she have to play like that? Didn't she know it was a waste of time to be coquettish? He wasn't looking for romance, and he wasn't trying to find a girlfriend. He wanted to fuck. Hard-and-body-punishing-stick-it-in-and-abuse-it fucking. That was all.

"On what?" *Let's get the negotiations done and get out of here.*

"What you want," she said.

Now they were talking. And he already knew what he wanted. "You. My house. I'll pay for the entire night."

"The entire night?" Her manicured eyebrow arched.

He nodded. He wouldn't need her all night, but after he was finished with her, she wouldn't be fit to take another customer.

Her perfectly shaped eyebrow quirked as her tongue peeked out and wet the seam of her mouth. She hazarded a look to her left, and he followed her gaze to a man at the bar. Her pimp.

"You need to get permission?" Malek leaned forward, closing off his cock to her probing hand as he refilled his glass.

She stiffened. "I'll just be a minute." She slid out of the booth and swished her way around tables and other patrons until she reached her boss. The two glanced back at him, spoke briefly, and then she prowled her way back, jacket in hand. That was a good sign.

"One thousand dollars," she said, sliding in beside him once more.

"Done." He swallowed his shot and dropped the base of his glass to the table with a finality that said the conversation was over and it was time to go.

With a nod toward her pimp, she scooted aside and stood back up. He followed suit, adjusting his hard-on as he pushed himself off the leather seat.

Without a word, he took her hand and led her to the back exit, out into the brisk night, and to his truck.

You sick bastard.

Shut up.

He wasn't above paying for what his body needed, and if it kept Gina off his mind, so much the better.

But it doesn't keep her off your mind, dickhead.

I said shut up.

He got behind the wheel, determined to make Gina's memory disappear, even if it meant losing his mind.

I can arrange that.

I bet you can. Hell, he already *was* losing his mind, holding whole conversations with himself like he was jockeying between split personalities.

Pulling away from Four Alarm, he kept his gaze to the front. "What's your name?"

"Trina."

Eh.

"What's yours?" she said.

"Malek."

"Pleasure to meet you, Malek." She settled into the passenger seat and took a mirror out of her purse to check her lipstick.

If only she knew, in thirty minutes, the state of her lipstick wouldn't be important. She had the right equipment, and that was all that mattered. And by the end of the evening, he'd make her question whether hopping in his car *had* been a pleasure.

And just the thought of what he needed to do to her to find relief filled him with disgust. He hated himself for what he did to these women, but he couldn't stop himself. It was out of his control now.

"I hope you like it rough, Trina." He stabbed a guilty, sideways glance at her.

She froze and looked across the seat at him as if he'd grown a horn out his forehead.

He'd been prepared for that reaction and didn't miss a beat, jumping in before she could protest. "I'll give you two thousand dollars to like it rough." He hit the gas and pulled out onto the main road. "And you won't even have to tell your boss about the extra thousand."

That settled her down a bit. "How rough?"

"You'll see."

Oh yes, she would see just how far into hell he had fallen since Gina left town.

Inside Four Alarm, Lorena's gaze lingered in the direction the handsome, obviously tortured, dark-haired vampire had disappeared with Trina. Lucky girl. Bitch, more like. That male looked like he would make a worthy bedroom adversary.

He appeared to be working through major demons, all angsty and ready to snap. How delightful. Lorena did enjoy a male who could give her the harsh, physical working she yearned for, which other males—human, dreck, and vampire alike—often failed to deliver. But that was what it meant to be a Thracian female. The last of her kind, no less, which meant she was often unsatisfied in the bedroom, since there were no Thracian males left to please her.

Lorena glowered toward the back exit. She had been about to move on that sexy beast of a male when Trina cut her off. Now she seethed at the loss.

"Thank God he's gone." Jess heaved a sigh of relief beside her.

"Who?" Lorena regarded Jess through narrowed eyes.

"That asshole who just left with Trina."

With one brow raised, Lorena glanced back at the empty shadows that led to the exit. "Why? What's wrong with him?"

Jess fluttered her hands as if chasing away a swarm of gnats. "He's a creep. Took me home one night. Super sweet. Next night, though?" Her face screwed up with disgust. "The asshole choked me. As if I'm in to asphyxiation." Jess licked salt off her hand before downing a shot of tequila.

Lorena's brow flicked with interest as the corners of her mouth lifted. "Asphyxiation, huh?"

"Yes." Jess gasped from the shot then quickly sucked a lime wedge. "You'd like him."

Lorena tapped her long, manicured fingernail on the table, brooding further over her loss. She wasn't a working girl like Jess and Trina, but only because she didn't charge the men she sought for sex. She had a healthy appetite for rough sex and kink in all its forms, and when Bishop didn't have her on some task or another, or on her back himself when he visited, she took advantage of the downtime to play. Figured she'd waited ten seconds too long and lost what promised to have been a very good time.

"Know his name?" She uncrossed and recrossed her legs, leaning toward Jess and tucking a long, stray curl behind her ear.

"Marek, or maybe…no. Malek. That's his name. *Creeper Malek.*"

Malek? She recognized that name. He was one of the AKM vampires. But *this* guy—the defunct trophy of male hotness Trina had just stolen away with a bat of her fake eyelashes—hardly resembled the male she had seen on various surveillance assignments. This male looked lost and desolate, full of danger and deadly aggression, while the Malek she had seen in the past had seemed reserved—a male who had his shit together. One who kept his head when everyone around him lost theirs. If this was the same Malek, what the hell had happened to him?

And when could she steal a trip into his bedroom?

With a gleam in her narrowed eyes, her bloodred lips slowly crept into a smile as she gave one last look toward the exit. She would definitely have to keep an eye out for that one. A member of AKM *and* a rough rider? Luck had just smiled down on her.

CHAPTER 3

BISHOP SET HIS SOBRANIE IN THE ASHTRAY on the bathroom counter and leaned closer to the mirror. The scent of the brown, gold-tipped cigarette wafted up in a thin line of gray, wispy smoke.

"How much were you able to salvage?" The voice of his boss, Premier Royce, the leader of the drecks, rose from his cell phone on the counter.

"Enough," Bishop said as he poked at the new, sensitive fangs peeking out from the roof of his mouth. He had finally been able to take an inventory of everything brought from his Arizona lab. There was a lot left to recover, and they had suffered a major setback, but they had what was important.

"But not all." Royce sounded perturbed.

Bishop swung his gaze down at his phone with an air of irritation. "Given the circumstances, I think we've recovered efficiently from our little break-in, Royce. We salvaged most of the data, had fail-safes in place to destroy incriminating evidence"—so that *his precious royal highness*, the premier, couldn't be implicated in the nefarious goings-on he sanctioned in private—"and managed to evacuate a few of our best test subjects so our experiments can continue with minimal disruption." Bishop's mind flickered to the female locked away and chained to the bed in an isolated cabin in a wooded area a few miles from his new underground lab in northern Indiana. He was eager to get this business trip in Chicago over with so he could get back to her.

"You should have been more careful," Royce said. "You should have had better safeguards in place, Bishop. I pay you—"

Bishop slammed his fist on the counter. "You pay me nothing I can't obtain elsewhere!" Who was Royce to question him? He was merely a figurehead. The ruler of their race who hadn't the spine to unzip his fly and flop his cock on the table for all to see what his true intentions were. He hid behind masks and spent his time negotiating falsehoods with the vampire king, pretending to adhere to the truce between their races while going behind the vampires' backs and making others—like Bishop—do his dirty work. How dare that sniveling *politician* criticize him?

"I don't like your tone, Bishop."

"And I don't like your interference, Royce."

"You will address me with the respect I deserve."

"Or what?"

Not even a month ago, Bishop wouldn't have spoken so candidly against the premier, but he was different now. Maddox's blood, his venom—his genetic *donation*—had seen to that. Bishop was no longer merely a dreck. He was something more. Something stronger and more powerful. The new fangs in his mouth—both the uppers *and* the lowers, just like Maddox's—proved his personal experiments were working.

He still looked like a dreck, with his blue-tinted skin and blue-black hair hanging down the front of his body, but the new dental work, as well as his more muscular and taller body, indicated he was changing. Before long, he wouldn't need Premier Royce, his funding, or his pesky interruptions.

Too bad he had lost Maddox in the raid on his Arizona lab a week ago. Bishop still had Maddox's blood samples, as well as samples of his venom, which was enough to conduct more experiments, but there was so much he couldn't do without his prized, Slavic vampire. He had only just obtained him, and now he had been stolen away. By his son, no less. That hairless vampire named Trace. A prize in his own right, to be sure. That bastard had been powerful enough to destroy his lab with no more than a wave of his hand.

Bishop actually drooled at the thought of having both Maddox and Trace in his possession. Just think of all he could accomplish with their genes, especially if he could get Maddox's other son, the mysterious assassin his keepers referred to as the phantom.

Royce sighed, which brought Bishop out of his reverie. He glared at his phone. "Or what, Royce?" he said again.

"Bishop, let's not argue."

In other words, Royce didn't have the spine to punish him for his insubordination. He was a useless puppet. Nothing more than a mouthpiece. A token where a commander should be. The race needed a strong leader, one who wasn't afraid to show King Bain and his AKM lackeys that drecks were a race to be reckoned with. A leader who would shred the peace treaty and throw it in King Bain's face. One who would exploit the vampires' growing addiction to cobalt to quash them under his proverbial thumb.

Wasn't that why cobalt had been manufactured in the first place? Cobalt production had been Bishop's first assignment. He had formulated cobalt in the eighties, using deadly dreck venom to create a drug that vampires could get high off of, something they couldn't get from human drugs. But then Royce had all but pulled the plug on the experiment. At the time, it had been enough for him that vampires easily overdosed and died on the stuff, but that hadn't been enough for Bishop. Behind the secrecy of his lab, he had continued to tweak and experiment with the formula, searching to fulfill the original objective: To use cobalt to trip vampires into mutancy. Mutants were deadly, and they had short lifespans. What better way to exterminate a race or control them than by triggering their own demise from the inside out?

Yes, Royce had finally come back around to Bishop's way of thinking, but he needed to be ousted. He didn't have the stomach or the drive to make the ruthless decisions necessary for the drecks to overcome the vampires.

In time, Bishop would take over. He just needed to be patient. A way would present itself.

"Fine, Royce. Let's not argue." Bishop grinned at his reflection and pressed the pad of his thumb against the tip of one fang. He winced, both as the young fang pierced his skin and pain shot through the roof of his mouth, triggering fluid to leak down and drip from both fangs. He smacked his lips. Mmm. Vampire venom. He was producing vampire venom. How sweet.

Royce sighed again. "So...what now? Grotek and Chane were arrested by King Bain's men. Those two could lead the king's enforcers back to you, and consequently back to me. And after you and Apostle got Princess Miriam involved, the king will be out for blood. What do you plan—?"

"Grotek and Chane will be dealt with by morning," Bishop said, his voice flat.

Grotek and Chane were the two cobalt dealers he and his brother, Apostle, had set up to take the fall if things went south with the princess's abduction. Good thing, too, because shit had gone way south. Grotek and Chane were loyal, but it was time to cut ties. Besides, the two dealers were a loose end, and Bishop didn't like loose ends. They were messy. It was better to snip them off and ensure nothing was left to unravel.

Royce paused, and Bishop felt his doubt through the line. "How? They're locked inside the king's dungeon. No one can get in or out without Bain's authority."

"Oh, ye of little faith. I have a secret weapon," Bishop said with a smirk. *A secret weapon that might come in handy when I'm ready to oust your ass.* "Remember the two vampires who sold Maddox to me?"

"Yes. What of them?"

"Remember how I told you they held prisoner Maddox's other son, an assassin who can leave his body, use a totem to hunt down his victim—no matter whether he's out in the open or locked in a dungeon cell—and kill him?"

"Yes." Royce sounded like he was beginning to see where this was going.

"Well, I've sent Apostle to retrieve totems from Grotek's and Chane's homes."

"So you plan on using the assassin to kill them inside King Bain's dungeon?" Royce chuckled. "Clever, Bishop. But how did you manage such an arrangement with the assassin's keepers?"

"Part of my arrangement with Jacob and his partner, Haslet, was that their precious commodity never learn that they sold Maddox to me. Using Maddox is how they keep the assassin compliant. And the other part of the arrangement was that I be allowed to use their assassin's services any time I need them."

Royce made a thoughtful noise. "And now we need them."

Not "we," asshole. Me.

"Yes." Bishop lifted his abandoned Sobranie and took a healthy drag, letting the exquisite smoke fill his lungs before exhaling through his nose.

"When? Time is of the essence."

Bishop rolled his eyes at his own reflection in the mirror. Nag, nag, nag. And bitch. That was all Royce did: bitch and nag.

"Jacob is arriving tonight to personally claim the totems Apostle brings from their homes. Then it's just a matter of returning to West Virginia and giving them to the assassin."

"Very well. Have them call you when the job is done, and then I want you to call me. I don't want any surprise inquiries from King Bain about how two drecks implicated in his daughter's abduction ended up dead while locked in his dungeon."

Blah, blah, blah. Bishop flapped his fingers as if mimicking a puppet. "Of course. You'll be the first person I call."

Bishop disconnected and settled his cigarette between his lips as he admired his reflection. True, the destruction of his Arizona lab had been a setback, and months of research and advances had been destroyed, but at least his personal experiments were coming along, and he still had his precious plaything, the petite, blond mixed-blood who captivated his thoughts even now, so all was not lost. Once he replenished his store of test subjects—which would be easier now that his new lab was so much closer to Chicago, as well as to several prime East Coast cities like New York—he could get his research back on track. And once he accomplished that, he could formulate his plan for taking Royce's place as the drecks' new ruler.

Now, where was Apostle with those totems?

APOSTLE PARKED AND GOT OUT OF THE CAR he had purchased with the money he'd finally hacked out of his old bank account. Being pronounced dead over two months ago had made accessing his funds a bit challenging, but not impossible.

He locked the Mustang's door and tucked the felt bag that held Grotek's and Chane's badges inside his jacket, and then headed toward the entrance of the hotel. The local news had been running stories about the missing Chicago police officers for days, but they would never be found. Not with what Bishop had planned for them. Grotek and Chane would end up in the unsolved crimes file, and there they would remain for eternity.

Apostle hated losing two of his dealers, especially since these two used the common cover of being police officers, which granted them all kinds of special access to places Apostle needed access to, but such was the casualty of doing business according to Bishop's rules. Rules Apostle questioned more and more every day.

As he rounded the corner and entered the hotel's lobby, he scratched his chest through his shirt and jacket. The latest round of punishment—stings from Bishop's genetically altered scorpions—still itched like a bitch and put Apostle in a foul mood. Too bad the vile creatures hadn't been lost in the destruction of Bishop's old lab. But noooo, Bishop just had to save his precious nasties so he could continue subjecting Apostle to their deadly stings and the horrid side effects.

Apostle wasn't sure how much more he could take of his brother, his moods, and his whack-o experiments. The fucker was altering his own genetic makeup, for Chrissakes! Bishop couldn't hide the changes taking over his body. Apostle saw the fangs. He had noticed the recent growth spurt and the way Bishop's facial features took on those of Maddox's, as well as the way he had begun to crave blood. Those were things Bishop couldn't hide. He was becoming the enemy, for God's sake! The goddamn enemy! Apostle hadn't signed on for this. Bishop was going down a path Apostle didn't want to follow.

Perhaps Apostle should start consolidating assets. If he made a run for it, he wanted his resources easily attainable and within reach. He had enough trusted followers that he could start over elsewhere, as long as he flew under Bishop's radar, which meant dealing cobalt would be out.

Sigh.

If he ran, he would have to go back to catering to human drug needs. But there was good money to be made in heroin. Right now, the New England area was a veritable paradise for heroin dealers. He could easily sell a gram for forty dollars north of Boston. In New York, he'd only get eight bucks for the same amount.

Not that he'd been doing his research or anything, which showed how seriously he was considering striking out on his own. But those plans were best kept to himself.

He hit the button for the elevator and squirmed against the maddening itch of his torso as he stepped in and rode up to their floor.

"It's about time." Bishop glared at him from the bathroom in their shared suite. "Where have you been? Jacob is due any minute."

Apostle pulled the felt bag out of his pocket and handed it to Bishop. Then he shucked his jacket, tossed it on the bed, and yanked off his shirt. The damn material irritated the angry, swollen sting marks that dotted his chest and stomach.

"I got here as fast as I could." He glared at Bishop as he scratched his torso.

Bishop arched a warning eyebrow at him. "Do not test me, brother, or I shall punish you further."

Apostle shuddered and stepped back. Just the thought of one of those arachnids crawling over his skin was enough to stomp out his bravado.

Bishop plucked his cigarette from the ashtray on the

bathroom counter and walked past Apostle, back into his bedroom. He fingered the felt bag with his free hand as if the contents held the remnants of the Holy Grail. Not that the drecks were religious, but even Bishop could appreciate the value of ancient Christian artifacts.

"So, you got what we need?" Bishop set down his cigarette, opened the bag, and slid the two badges onto his palm.

Apostle stood to the side, his blunt nails constantly scratching, ever scratching. Was this how humans covered in poison ivy felt? Because this shit sucked. "Those are their badges."

"Perfect." Bishop slid them back into the bag. "Finally, something you didn't fuck up. Perhaps there's hope for you yet, my brother. Not that you'll ever live up to Deacon's memory."

Deacon. Their other brother. Apostle's twin. The one who died when Apostle had been the intended target. Bishop was never going to forgive him for Deacon's death. Deacon had been the prodigal brother. The pinnacle of evil in Bishop's eyes...and the perfect manager of Bishop's operation. A title Bishop wanted him to take, but in which Apostle had no interest. For obvious reasons. He glanced down at the dozen or so welts on his belly to remind himself of just one of those reasons.

Apostle turned for the bathroom. He wanted to shower. Cold water helped lessen the miserable burn and itch of his wounds.

"Where do you think you're going, brother?" Bishop said. "Get dressed. Our guest will arrive soon and I can't have you looking like...that." Bishop raised his hand and gestured toward Apostle's marred stomach.

"Maybe you should have thought of that before *punishing* me, dear brother." Apostle started for the bathroom again. "And clothes irritate the stings."

"You insolent fuck!"

Apostle turned to find Bishop already on him, his eyes flashing red. With a violent shove, his back crashed into the wall as Bishop pulled a dagger from his sleeve and sank the blade into the side of his abdomen. Bishop's other hand gripped his throat in the mother of all choke holds.

"You do as I say, you miserable fuck." Bishop got nose-to-nose with him, and he cringed and grunted as Bishop twisted the knife. "Not that you'd notice or be grateful, but my pets gave you a gift. And now you'll see just what that gift is, not that you deserve it. I almost wish I could take it back." He yanked the knife out and stepped away, anger and frustration seething through his clenched teeth. "Your appreciation is for shit."

Apostle looked down at the wound and clutched his side as he stumbled forward and fell to his knees. "What the fuck? What the hell's wrong with you?"

"Just watch, brother." He nodded toward the knife wound. "See?"

Apostle peeled his hands back and gasped. The wound was already healing. Before his eyes, the edges of the wound pulled together and closed as if on a time-lapsed recording. What had taken days before now took only minutes. "What the—?"

With a casual turn, Bishop entered the bathroom, rinsed the blood off the dagger, and dried it on the towel as Apostle stared after him. "The scorpions were genetically altered with vampire DNA. And not just regular vampire DNA, because not even vampires heal that quickly." He returned to the room. "My bio-hackers made a few modifications, and we found that using scorpion venom enhanced those alterations exponentially. So..." Bishop offered a crooked grin. "When they stung you, they implanted their designer DNA into your own genetic makeup. The aches, the lethargy..." Bishop picked up his cigarette and settled it between his lips before continuing. "Even the itching." He waved his hand in an arc as if encompassing all Apostle's symptoms. "They're all part of the changes taking place in your body, Apostle."

Apostle stared openmouthed at him. What was Bishop saying? That he had not only begun altering his own DNA, but he had also done the same to Apostle? Without his permission? Apostle didn't want to become a hybrid. He wanted no part of the vampire gene code in his body.

Damn Bishop! And damn his bastard Frankenscorpions!

Bishop sauntered away, that goddamn cigarette leaving a sickly sweet trail. "Even now, you probably don't feel much pain, do you?"

Apostle frowned, then shook his head. "No. Not really." But so what? Real warriors felt pain. They lived for it. The pain kept them sharp in the field of battle. It kept them from getting careless. And Apostle was a warrior, not some glorified lab rat.

Someday Bishop would pay for what he had done. Apostle was nobody's fool and nobody's bitch, least of all Bishop's. Fuck him. Decision made. Maybe not tomorrow, and maybe not next week, but soon Apostle would have his revenge. A day would come, and he would get payback for the sin Bishop had committed against him in the name of science, and then he would be gone. Out of there. On his own again. Just the way he liked it.

"See?" With a flippant wave, Bishop turned away and fondled the felt bag on the bed, obviously unaware of the mental battle raging inside Apostle's head.

"See what? That you're psychotic." Apostle stood and stalked into the bathroom. He flipped on the water and grabbed a washcloth from the rack.

Bishop turned an exasperated glance Apostle's way. "Dear brother, there is a fine line between psychosis and genius."

"Uh-huh. And you're walking it." Apostle stepped into the bathroom doorway, dabbing the wet cloth over the wound, which was already nearly halfway healed.

A knock came at the door and Bishop sneered. "That's right. And you'll do good to remember that, little brother. Now, get dressed while I let in our guest."

Stalemate. For now. But one way or another, this conversation wasn't over.

Apostle watched his Malcolm-McDowell-*A-Clockwork-Orange*-demented brother leave the bedroom. All Bishop needed was one set of fake eyelashes, a cane, a glass of milk, and a white suit with what looked like a large diaper strapped to suspenders on the outside of it, and Bishop would be the star of his own Stanley Kubrick film.

Whack-o!

Voices came from the main room, so he finished wiping the blood from his torso and inspected the mostly healed wound before grabbing a fresh shirt from his suitcase.

When he entered the main room, Bishop was handing the felt bag to someone Apostle had never seen before. This must be Jacob, the vampire traitor who owned Maddox's son, the assassin who could do with his mind what others couldn't even do with their hands.

"Here are the items you asked for," Bishop said. "When can I expect the job to be done?"

"As soon as I get back, I'll put our phantom on it."

Bishop caught Apostle out of the corner of his eye. "Ah, there you are. Finally." Bishop turned toward the vampire. "Jacob, this is my brother Apostle. I'm grooming him to take Deacon's place."

Apostle noted the disdain with which Bishop spoke, and anger bubbled inside him like water about to boil. So, Bishop could consort with vampires like they were his best friends, but when it came to his own race, his own flesh and blood, Bishop treated him like he was the enemy. That was fucked up right there.

He stepped forward and barely restrained a snarl of disgust from the smell of vampire in their hotel room.

"Apostle, this is Jacob." Bishop gestured to each in turn.

He shook his hand but remained back, wary of him. It didn't matter that Jacob held the key to eliminating the last remaining tie between Princess Miriam's abduction and him. Apostle didn't like Jacob. And he didn't like putting his fate in the vampire's hands. Not one bit.

He had a bad feeling about this. At least that's one thing the Frankenscorpions hadn't altered: his gut instincts. And his gut told him shit was about to get real.

And this time, Apostle had no intention of sticking around to experience the fallout.

CHAPTER 4

MALEK SETTLED DEEPER INTO THE EASY CHAIR and brushed the woman's blond hair aside. He growled and dropped his head back at the sight of her lipstick-stained mouth bobbing up and down on his cock. *That's right, Trina, how do you like your lipstick now?*

Every muscle in his body strained, and his chest heaved for breath as his fingers fisted Trina's hair. She had been at it for over twenty minutes, and he was no closer to coming than he had been an hour ago. His orgasm took up shop in his nuts and drummed its fingers as if a warm mouth and slippery tongue weren't a good enough reason to come out and play.

Bruises covered Trina's arms from where he had held her down and fucked her earlier, and her hair was a bird's nest of tangles compared to the perfect coif she'd sported after leaving Four Alarm.

Still, as hard as he had taken her, he couldn't come.

He knew what the problems were. Yes, problems, because he didn't have just one. Malek was monumentally fucked up and only getting worse with each passing hour. He longed for two females. One dead, one alive. A war of wills battled within the confines of his skin, and his flesh and his mind were the battlefield. Talk about your split personalities. Right now, Malek was his own worst enemy, with one-half of his psyche rooting for Carmen while the other cheered for Gina. In the middle was indecision and torment, and that's where Malek lived.

The rational part of him that knew the truth dimmed a little more each day. It withered away like drought-stricken grass, its roots dying and lifting from the soil. Before long, there would be nothing left that made sense. He was on borrowed time, a male on the path of self-destruction. But there was enough of his rational side left to comprehend at least on a very small level that he was in serious trouble. As in, he was losing the battle with his mind and would eventually implode. And most likely die. But he was powerless to stop the out-of-control freight train that felt more like a sun getting ready to supernova.

Pushing Trina off his cock, he pointed across the room. "Get on the bed. Now."

She wiped her mouth with the back of her hand and regarded him for a second, and then got up and did as he said, crawling onto the bed then turning over to lie back. The extra thousand dollars he'd promised kept her compliant.

"No," Malek said, stepping to the foot of the bed. His aching cock jutted out like an antenna. Only it wasn't receiving. Or transmitting. The damn thing was practically useless. "This way." He pointed at the foot of the bed. "Lie this way and hang your head off the side."

With fearful hesitation, Trina turned and settled onto the bed so that she was face-to-cock with him. With a subtle shift, she hesitated but wrapped her arms around his hips, knowing what he wanted. But the nervous look in her eyes made it clear she wasn't overly eager in the new position that had her staring up at his erection as if it were a demon.

"Open up."

Like a good girl, Trina opened and pulled him closer, taking the head of his cock into her mouth again. Her teeth grazed his flesh as she fought back the urge to push him away. That extra thousand was certainly doing its job to keep her manageable.

Bending over and planting his fists against the mattress on either side of her torso, Malek began thrusting his hips forward and back, pushing his cock deeper with each stroke. In no time, he was pounding his cock down her open throat. He'd never done this to a woman, but then, he was doing a lot of shit he had never done. Before long, if he didn't actually die from his internal torment, he would be as bad as Micah and have a whole BDSM theme in his bedroom. How about that? Floggers, maybe even a St. Andrew's Cross. Would Trina look good strapped on the cross? Would that get him off?

Ah, yes. Now his orgasm lifted one interested eyebrow. It liked this, both the visual and the deep throating, as well as the gagging sounds Trina made as she pushed against the front of his thighs to keep him from driving so deep. But still the little bastard wanted more.

A bead of sweat dripped off Malek's nose and splattered on one of Trina's jiggling breasts. He needed to come, damn it.

He would have come three times over by now if Gina were the one doing the honors, but then again, Malek wouldn't have been fucking Gina's mouth. He wouldn't have been *fucking* her period. You didn't *fuck* your mate. You made love to her. You adored her. You cherished her.

Shit! What was he thinking? *Get that thought out of your head, Malek.*

But the wick had already been lit. His balls liked the image of Gina on her back, her arms holding him as he made love to her. His nads drew up and tingled, ready to blow, but damn…it was taking forever.

Frustration rose inside him, and he doubled his efforts, pumping harder against Trina's mouth as he gripped her breasts and squeezed, allowing the briefest of fantasies about Gina holding him against her body to play across his mind in hopes just the thought of her would hurry his orgasm along.

It didn't matter that Trina gagged, choked, and pushed against the front of his thighs. He was oblivious to everything except getting his goddamn orgasm to let go, for the love of God. He couldn't take much more of this.

Apparently his stubborn orgasm liked the small gift he had given it with the idea of Gina making love to him and decided to be nice, because literally out of nowhere, his release shot through his body and dribbled down Trina's throat as he slammed his hips against her face one last time.

Not that he felt much relief. It hadn't been that big of an orgasm.

Great. A consolation come. Now he would get to walk around with a semi for a few hours and feel all coiled up and ready to pounce on anything with two legs.

Trina pushed him backward and came up choking, spitting, and gasping for air, gagging for good measure. After coughing through her gag reflex and swallowing his itty-bitty dribble of semen, she glared at him, but otherwise kept her mouth shut, probably for fear that if she bitched, he would revoke the extra grand.

No need to worry about that. He sauntered over to his bureau, his hard cock bobbing and dripping out one final pump of semen— as if his orgasm thought that would make things right with him— and grabbed his money bag. After pulling out a stack of hundreds, he counted out twenty then looked over his shoulder.

"Get out." He held the money toward her.

"Fine by me." She flung herself off the bed, snatched her clothes, and marched toward him. Without so much as a thank you, she swiped the bills from his hand. "Do me a favor next time you see me."

"Yeah? What's that?"

"Ignore me." She grabbed the rest of her things and headed upstairs.

Malek heard her call for a cab, and a few minutes later she was gone.

He heaved a sigh, although not one of relief. With his dick still hard and his orgasm laughing after teasing him with a Smurf-sized release, how could he feel anything close to relief?

His own behavior sickened him. He was supposed to be the nice one. The guy who never forgot his manners and offered a polite smile to everyone he met. But now he was a bastard. He had abused Trina's body without a care for her feelings or whether or not he was hurting her. He had paid for her services, and in the same way someone rents a car and drives like a bat out of hell without caring if they nick the paint or dent the bumper, he had driven poor Trina until her proverbial wheels had nearly fallen off.

He knew what he had done was wrong. Even a working girl like Trina deserved respect, but lately he couldn't seem to muster anything but degradation and contempt. Not for anyone, even himself. Every night, he brought his latest trick back to his home and abused the living hell out of her, all for his selfish need to beat the despair from his body. And every morning—if she lasted that long—she left tousled, bruised, and deflated, which left Malek to mentally flog himself for his crude and abhorrent behavior.

The way he was now.

God, he was such a bastard.

Like an alcoholic, he promised every morning to clean himself up, but every night he discarded his oath and returned to the streets to troll for more. No matter what he did, he couldn't lift himself out of this pit of destruction sucking him into the bowels of purgatory, and the vicious cycle did nothing to ease his already torturous inner dialogue.

Full of pent-up frustration and self-loathing, Malek spun on his heel and barreled to the bathroom. Clenching and releasing his fists, he paced outside the shower, ready to snap, and then whipped forward to flip the shower on with an abrupt jerk of his hand.

Every day he felt himself losing his grip on reality, as well as his sanity. He knew he was monumentally fucked up. At some basic level of his awareness, he understood that The Voice was a product of his own making. But knowing he was his own worst enemy didn't stop him from arguing with himself on an almost daily basis. Daily? Try hourly. The Voice antagonized him relentlessly to give in to Gina's pull, but he refused, willing to sacrifice himself in the conscious realm for the sake of keeping Carmen's memory intact.

He knew Carmen was dead. Within the belly of his soul, he knew she was gone, but on the surface he refused to accept it. And by denying the truth, he kept her alive in spirit, alive in his soul.

And that was where agony erupted like a blown blood vessel, only on a volcanic scale. Now that his soul yearned to mate with Gina, there wasn't enough room for both females to set up house inside his heart. He had to choose one or the other but couldn't. The result was an extinction level event that rivaled the fiercest battles in all of history. The Octagon of death between the Romans and Saxons.

Was this what Micah had gone through after losing Jackson? Or Katarina, for that matter? If so, he had a new respect for his old friend.

Malek threw himself under the shower of water, which hadn't fully heated up. The cool flow spilled over him, matting his long, black hair to his face, neck, and shoulders as he leaned against the cold, tiled wall on outstretched arms and turned his head up into the falling water.

He and Micah had been best friends once, a long time ago. In the Middle Ages, they had trained together and grown up side by side as warriors. They had been more like brothers than friends. No, their friendship ran much deeper than that. He and Micah were kindred souls, so close that their lives practically mirrored one another. What happened to one happened to the other. That was how it had always been between them. And it was a testament they proved over and over, even when they both took mates at the same time. Micah had mated Katarina and Malek had mated Carmen within months of one another. But the magic connection between them was also a curse. When Micah lost Kat, it had only been a matter of time before Carmen died, too.

Malek had feared her time was coming and petitioned King Bain the First to allow him to change her. But that was before the laws regarding human mates had been changed to allow for such a contingency, and the king refused his request. Within days of receiving the king's reply, Carmen was gone.

At least in Micah's case, Katarina had been a vampire. She'd had a chance of survival. Carmen had been human, which meant she'd had no chance. The stroke that took her life was an ailment she could have avoided had she been immortalized through his venom.

If he had been allowed to turn Carmen, she might well still be with him today. Perhaps he should have done what Tristan had with Josie. Josie had been human, and Tristan had broken the law to change her. And she wasn't even Tristan's bonded mate. Tristan had been punished, but look at him today. He still had Josie, and she was pregnant with his young.

That could have been his life. He could have had that with Carmen. If only he hadn't been such a stickler for following the law, Carmen would still be alive today, and he never would have mated Gina, which meant he wouldn't be where he was right now.

In hell.

Malek sneered and ran his palm over his trimmed goatee as he recalled how many times he had been told how lucky he was that he wasn't a statistic for not dying after Carmen's death. Lucky? How could anyone call what he had gone through—as well as what he was going through now—lucky? If anything, he was cursed. To have to endure life without his mate was hell, even if he had avoided the worst by refusing to accept her death. But life has a way of catching up with you when you refuse to acknowledge it, and Malek's time had come.

And it was Gina's fault. If she hadn't come tearing into his life, sniper rifle blazing, he wouldn't be in this fucked-up mess right now. She had shown up like a whirlwind of temptation, and Malek had immediately felt the connection between his soul and hers. He had been enthralled with her, unable to take his eyes off her or even leave her side while she had been held prisoner at AKM, but now he wished he had never met her at all.

He gasped and bent forward, trying not to succumb to the calling—and to the suffering—he knew was destroying his nerves. He was without his mates—both of them. One he could no longer have, and another he refused to accept.

But who was he kidding? He hungered for Gina in a way that traced back to the dawn of the vampire race. A male needed his mate as much as he needed blood, oxygen, and the darkness to survive.

He was fucked. Any way he sliced it, he was way fucked. Not just a little, and not even a lot, but on a scale so large there wasn't a way to encompass its enormity.

It's all in your head...it's all in your head.

That thought was more accurate than he wanted to admit, because try as he did, the time he spent with Gina weeks ago in her cell never left his mind.

For an assassin, she had looked so small. Almost frail in stature. But beautiful beyond description. With slim hips and a trim waist, she was a diminutive force of nature. How could someone so petite be so deadly?

He had sat for hours, simply staring at her. Her neck beckoned him. Gina's neck was amazing, a stretch of flesh and bone to be worshipped. He wanted to lift her short hair away with his fingers and simply revel in her neck's erotic beauty.

His body grew hard all over from the sight and her scent, and he wanted to bury his nose into the delicate curve below her ear and press his lips against her nape as he spread her open and sank inside her from behind...to taste and smell her wild fragrance as his body rejoiced in her fragile depths.

Make love.

Fate had delivered him an angel for a mate. An angel with a neck worthy of Aphrodite.

With a shake of his head, Malek slammed his eyes shut, grimacing at the memory as his body shivered, despite the now scalding water that spilled from the showerhead. Still supported on his outstretched arms, he bent his head down. He struggled to contain his emotions as his shoulder-length hair slid across his neck and washed forward to hang on either side of his face.

"Carmen." Heartbreak tortured his voice as he uttered her name, and a harsh sob wracked his shoulders. "I miss you." He choked back another sob. "I miss you so damn much." Without her, he was only half, and the bad half at that. Look at what he had done to Trina tonight. And to the others in the weeks before. He was the worst version of himself without Carmen.

Without Gina, too.

He shut off the shower. Hollow pain ranged through his muscles and deep inside his bones. He pushed open the glass door and swiped the towel off the rack as he stumbled back into the bedroom, running the towel haphazardly over his wet skin and hair before wrapping it around his waist and heading upstairs.

In the kitchen, he pulled a bottle of water from the refrigerator. That, a couple of apples, and half a block of cheese were all he had left in the fridge, not counting the molding two-week-old leftover spaghetti sitting on the second shelf. But he wasn't eating, anyway, so who cared if his fridge and cupboards were on empty and growing science fair projects?

Twisting the lid off the water, he let the door close and turned toward the barren kitchen counter and the dining room table beyond, piled high with books. A shopping bag from the local bookstore sat on the floor, by the leg of the table, discarded there days ago after he had returned home from wherever he had been that day. The days all blurred together now. Between the lack of sleep, no food, all the extracurricular sex that left him feeling like a lecherous heathen, as well as the ache that throttled his chest twenty-four seven, he was lucky to remember his own name.

With a sigh, he set the bottle of water on the counter, rubbed his thumb up and down his aching sternum, walked to the table, and picked up the bag. He set it on one of the stacks, and, one by one, pulled out each carefully chosen book. He had spent hours in the bookstore, selecting what he thought Carmen would like. Even past closing time, he had wandered up and down the aisles until one of the employees told him point-blank it was time to check out. Only then did he mosey up to the cash register and make his purchase.

In the past couple of weeks, he had bought at least two hundred books, as if each one was a token or vessel that would lead Carmen back to him. As if the more books he bought, the greater his chances of seeing her again.

As carefully as if the books were made of antique paper or delicate crystal, he set each on top of a pile and meticulously lined up the edges as he caressed the covers with all the love Carmen deserved.

She had loved to read. Not many could in those days, but she could. She had been his breathtaking, educated beauty. He often found her sitting in the rocking chair on the porch of their cottage, her nose buried in one of her leather bound books. She read and reread each one and never grew tired of them. What would she think of his gift to her now?

For an instant, he thought he saw Carmen out of the corner of his eye, but as soon as he glanced up, she was gone.

Malek...

Was that her voice or just the wind rustling the branches against the window? He closed his eyes and heard his name again.

Malek...

"Carmen?" He opened his eyes and stepped toward the opposite corner of the table, where he thought he had seen her a moment ago. "Are you here?"

Malek...

He turned, and through watery, bloodshot eyes that hadn't seen sleep in days, he saw a filmy image of Carmen shimmer and disappear just as he reached for her hand. His hand closed over empty air.

He stared at his loose fist, suspended in front of him as if he grasped her fingers, but there was nothing there. Just emptiness, a void of sorrow, his limbs robbed of movement and his soul ripped of the momentary joy he had felt by her brief presence.

Carmen had been nothing more than a sleep-deprived hallucination. A waking dream sent to torture him.

Every muscle in Malek's body tightened, and his fist clenched so forcefully that his arm shook.

"No!" Agony rent his heart, which shuddered then raced as he lunged forward into the space where Carmen had just stood and drove his fist through the drywall. If only he could die.

Images of Carmen's death threatened to overtake his mind, but he pushed them away as he pounded against the wall again, showering the floor with plaster and chips of paint.

"Stop it! STOP IT!" He turned, slammed his back against the wall, and covered his face with his hands before sliding to the floor. "Carmen, oh God, Carmen!" With his eyes squeezed shut, he sobbed into his hands. His chest pumped with each hiccup of breath, and his torso contracted with every strangled wail until he threw his hands to the sides and screamed up at the ceiling, "WHY?"

Silence was his only reply.

He drew his head down and blinked. Tears splashed to his cheeks. "Why?" He withered into a fetal ball on the floor, curled into himself, and covered his face once more. Hopeless despondency overwhelmed every base need and instinct. If the blinds and drapes had been open, and the sun rose, he wouldn't have been able to move to save himself.

CHAPTER 5

GINA POURED ANOTHER SHOT OF JOSE CUERVO and her body relaxed into her seat on Trevor's private jet.

Trevor walked back from the galley holding two bottles of Corona with lime wedges sticking out the tops.

"For me?" she said, taking a bottle.

"Yep."

"But what about Jose?" She lifted her glass.

Trevor took the glass from her and placed it on the table. "I think you've had enough of him." He sat down across from her, so that he faced her, and leaned back in his seat.

Trevor was one of those strikingly handsome males, with dark hair, dark eyes, and a smoothly shaved, square jaw. Clean-cut and refined, he oozed sex appeal and success, and drew a person in the same way a perfect sunset made you stop and stare in awe. You just simply couldn't look away and had to admire God's exquisite craftsmanship. And Trevor was a damn fine work of art.

Too bad he and Gabe had never been able to make their relationship work. They had looked good together. But sometimes things just weren't meant to be. And if Trevor had mated her brother, he might not have survived Gabe's death. And then she would have lost two brothers that night instead of one.

The two sat in silence for a few seconds, then Trevor said, "You know Searcy and Vaydon are going to come after us." Their targets had graduated from being Mark One and Mark Two to Searcy and Vaydon. This was serious.

Talk about a buzzkill. The temporary light mood the

tequila had created whooshed out of the cabin. "Yeah, I know." Her gaze dropped to her lap. Not even Jose could cut through the guilt that riddled her. "I'm sorry, Trevor. It's my fault for—"

He raised one hand and cut her off. "No. That's not what I'm saying, Gina. I'm not trying to lay you with a guilt trip or anything. I'm just…" He paused then shook his head. "I'm worried about you." He sat forward. "What the hell happened to you tonight? What's with you and these panic attacks?"

Tonight hadn't been the first time she had broken down in front of Trevor since arriving in Florida. With the attacks coming more frequently, he had witnessed a few of them in one way or another. Either right before, right after, or during—like tonight.

For several long seconds, she silently held his gaze, trying to put into words the mess of thoughts in her head. But it was like a stew in there. All the filing cabinets of her mind had been opened and the contents blown around until she couldn't make sense of the chaos. It felt like a tornado had whipped through her thoughts. But then, that's what these panic attacks did to her. They destroyed any semblance of mental order.

Maybe the panic attacks were a result of the forced order she tried to impose as she picked up the mental pieces and tried to reorganize them. Maybe her anxiety was trying to tell her she wasn't compartmentalizing her thoughts correctly… that she wasn't putting the pieces back in the right places as she pulled herself together and re-filed her thoughts. Because every time she thought she had everything where it belonged, she flipped out again, and then the process of cleaning up started over.

Except there was one piece she refused to file away. Malek. For weeks, she had fought finding a place in her mental structure for him. There was no place for him in her life.

"Gina? Talk to me." Trevor's deep, gentle voice pulled her from her muddled thoughts.

"It's Malek, Trev."

His brow furrowed in confusion. "Who?"

She breathed out a frustrated sigh. She hadn't told Trevor about Malek, so she quickly recapped for Trevor what Malek had said to her in her cell when he thought she'd been sleeping.

Trevor looked almost shocked. "You're mated?"

"No, of course not." She clenched her jaw, blew out a heavy sigh, and looked away. "I mean, hell...I don't know. Shit, Trev, I just..."

"Are you going back for him? Is that what this is about?"

"No. I just..." What? Just what? Now that she was on her way back to Chicago, she was more confused than ever. "I need closure on this, Trev. I just left him there. He never knew I had been awake. Or that I'd heard him. What if he tries to come after me? I need to make it clear I can't have that. I just can't accept a mate. Not after−" Her mind turned toward Armand, because Malek wasn't the only cause of her panic attacks. In a way, Armand was, too. The two males were tied to one another in her mind. "Not after Arm−"

"I know, Gina. Relax. Calm down. Don't think about him right now. That's only going to make things worse."

She shook her head and looked up as if the overhead held the answers she needed. "What if Malek was wrong? Could he have been mistaken about mating me? I mean, maybe I'm getting worked up over nothing."

Trevor shrugged, a look of sympathy on his face. "I've never mated anyone, so I can't speak from experience, but I doubt it. I suppose it's possible that he was simply caught up in the moment, that there's a slim chance he was wrong or made a mistake, but I'm pretty sure a male knows when his instincts have fired up over a mate."

"But there's a chance?" She nibbled her thumbnail.

"There's always a chance, Gina." He didn't look like he believed it, though.

Great. The odds were stacking up against her.

After a moment's silence, Trevor shifted forward. "Does this have anything at all to do with Severin? Or Gabe's death?" He paused. "Or is this all about Armand and what he did to you?" He paused and held up his hands as she jerked her gaze to his. "I'm sorry. I hate bringing him up, especially since I just told you not to think about him, but I can't help thinking he's the cause of all this. Your anxiety. Your fear of accepting Malek." He sighed. "If Malek has mated you, you're going to kill him if you don't accept him, Gina. You have to know that. Whether he actually dies physically or only dies spiritually, you're going to kill some part or all of him if he's your mate. Maybe your panic attacks are your body's way of dealing with the guilt of that, because you know what a mated male goes through. And even though you pretend you don't care, I know you've got a conscience that's got to be eating you up."

Maybe Trevor was right. Sure, she was terrified of being mated, but she also hated the idea of hurting an otherwise nice guy like Malek. Perhaps her panic attacks were caused by a one-two punch. Fear and guilt.

"Yes, I know, Trev. God, I know. But I just can't be with him. Okay?" She glanced down. "And maybe what I did to Severin plays a part, because God knows I fucked up that whole incident beyond repair. And then there was Sev's father, Lakota." There were so many pieces to the puzzle. So many components that could be to blame. Malek and Armand were at the heart of them all, but she couldn't forget about Sev, Lakota, and all she had done to everyone involved.

"Who?" Trevor frowned.

She had never told Trevor about Lakota, either. "Lakota is Severin's father." She held up her hands as if to ward off the guilt brought on by remembering how she seduced Kota to get to Sev. "He showed up. Things happened."

Trevor leaned forward and touched her wrist. "What really happened in Chicago, Gina? You've told me bits and pieces, but I don't think you've been level with me. All I know is I've never seen you so fragile. You're not the same Gina I knew two years ago. Maybe talking it out will help."

Gina's mind bounced from thought to thought. Where did she start? She heaved a sigh and looked out the window. "Aside from what Armand did to me, everything regarding why I went to Chicago started with Gabe's death," she said.

"I was there you know? When he died." She glanced over to see him shake his head.

"No, I wasn't aware of that." His gaze dropped to the floor, and his hands fumbled with his bottle of beer. "I, uh...I didn't want to know too much about what happened." Trevor's voice fell to nearly a whisper as he spoke. "So I ignored the news for a while...kind of kept myself isolated so I didn't hear about it."

Clearly, he still missed Gabe.

Gina reached out and took his hand, squeezed it, offered him a compassionate smile, then let go as she leaned back in her seat again. "Gabe died in my arms, Trevor. It was a raid on a cobalt distribution center. Shit went bad. Way bad. And this vampire showed up. A mixed-blood, it turns out." She looked over to catch Trevor's reaction. "It was Severin."

"No shit."

"Exactly. I thought he was a traitor. I thought he had used Gabe and was working with the drecks. After Gabe's death, I vowed I'd see every last one of those fuckers die." She dug her fingernails against the bottle of Corona and tilted her head down so that her short, dark hair fell over her face. "I was so bent on revenge that I got careless."

"And chased Sev to Chicago and nearly killed an innocent male," Trevor filled in, figuring out the puzzle by the pieces she had already revealed to him.

She nodded and took a swig of beer. "Yes."

"So, how did Sev's father factor in?"

She took a steadying breath. "As luck would have it, Sev's father came to town, trying to track Sev down. They were estranged from one another." She spit out a staccato laugh, remembering how Lakota had poured his heart out to her over what had happened between him and Sev and how he desperately wanted to set things right. No wonder she had never told Trevor about Lakota, because even now, just the mention of Lakota made her want to crawl under something. Like maybe a mountain or a falling meteorite the size of Texas.

Trevor shook his head. "And...? What happened with him?"

She bobbed her head to the side then looked down. "He was staying at my hotel, if you can believe that. I thought I'd fallen under a lucky star." She mocked herself and kicked back another heavy drink. Then her cynical grin faded. "I used him." She scrunched her upper lip and crinkled her nose in self-loathing. "Lakota. Sev's father. I used him to get close to Severin. I did things with him, made him trust me. I made him like me." She looked away again, biting back the tears that stung her eyes. Even now, after all this time, thinking about what she had done sickened her and filled her with self-hatred. She was nothing but a whore who had used a good male, Lakota, to get to an even better one, Severin. Poor Sev had been the hardest hit by Gabe's death, because he'd had no one to mourn with, and here she came, with her high and mighty, self-righteous, revengeful idiocy, thinking she could do no wrong and had all the answers. She had nearly added insult to injury by almost killing him, almost taking him from a father who wanted to make amends, as well as from his new mate, Arion, who would have died without him.

"You slept with him? Lakota, I mean?" Trevor spoke quietly, breaking her from her painful thoughts.

She nodded and winced, wiping the back of her hand under her nose as tears stung the backs of her eyes. "Yes. I slept with Sev's father. I made him think I was available. I made him think I was in it for him." She paused and frowned. "And then I almost killed his son."

Trevor changed seats so he was sitting next to her. "But you didn't kill him, Gina. He lived."

"No thanks to me." She sat forward and cursed. "Damn it, Trevor, I've never been that careless, but I was so hell-bent on my own revenge and my own selfishness I took shortcuts. I ignored the voice in my head that said something wasn't adding up. And an innocent male almost died because of it, his only crime being that he had loved my brother and had wanted to save him. That's why he showed up at that raid the night Gabe died. He'd gone there to try and protect him. But like me, he was too late. Gabe was already dead. And here I'd thought he was there to finish him off." She dropped her face into her free hand. "I'm such an idiot."

Trevor touched her arm. "You're not an idiot."

"Well, I'm reckless then, which is even worse."

"Quit beating yourself up, Gina. You're better than that, and we both know it. You're a badass bitch who had a bad day. We all have them sooner or later. We just need to figure things out. That's all."

She shot him a dubious look.

The two sat in silence for a minute as Gina pulled herself back together. Finally, she took a deep breath and brushed her blunt-cut bangs out of her eyes as she straightened. "After nearly killing Severin, I wanted to die, Trevor. The guilt alone nearly killed me."

His dark eyes softened when she glanced at him, and he caressed her arm, trying to comfort her.

"I was locked up in that cell for days, tormented by guilt. All I could see was the bullet tearing into Sev's chest, like the memory was on a looped recording, replaying in my mind over and over and over." She circled her finger in the air several times. "But Malek was there. He guarded me and watched over me." Her eyebrows scrunched together briefly. "While he was there, I felt…okay." His presence had made her feel safe, secure, even comforted. "I thought at first that he had been assigned to guard me, but when he made that statement about being my mate, it became clear that he had chosen to be there. He wanted to be there. He was so nice to me." She grinned reflectively, thinking back on the gentle male who had stayed by her side and calmed her mind.

Another time, another place, and she would already be his. He was worthy, and she liked him. Since leaving Chicago, she had often thought about Malek in ways she shouldn't have, but never for long. She couldn't let herself go down that path, because no matter how nice he had been, or how attracted she was to him, she couldn't trust herself with any male ever again. He could turn in a blink and hurt her. Just like Armand had.

The corners of Trevor's mouth lifted knowingly. "He

sounds really nice."

Gina narrowed her eyes. "Don't give me that look. You know how I feel."

Trevor nodded, and his eyes narrowed back at her, as if he could see right through her. "Yes, I do. And I know why. But you like Malek. I can tell. And that scares you, doesn't it?"

She scoffed. "Why would I be scared?"

"Why indeed?" He eyed her and she felt her face heat. "Remember, I know how Armand abused you, Gina, and what that abuse did to you. You can't hide from me. And you can't hide from yourself, either. Not forever. Maybe that's what all this is about."

She broke her gaze from his and looked down. *Guilty.*

Trevor's voice dropped and softened. "Gina, you don't need to be afraid of falling in love again. I think it's silly that you keep yourself guarded like you're in prison because that asshole did what he did to you. The only thing you're guilty of is having an innocent heart and being played by the Fates. It wasn't your fault that a half-Dacian turned out to be your mate, or that he was such an evil bastard. But you got out. You freed yourself, Gina. Don't forget that. You were strong enough to get yourself out of a bad situation before it killed you. Not all mates are good mates, doll, but none are as bad as Armand. He was the exception, not the rule, all because of his Dacian blood. You know the Dacians are bastards. You know that the other vampire clans don't treat their mates the way Dacians do.

"Don't let that bastard inflict you with a lifelong sentence that prevents you from ever loving again. So help me God, if I wasn't gay, I'd show you just how wonderful love could be, Gina. You deserve it more than anyone I know. Any male worth his name and the parents who birthed him would be honored to have such a female as you as his mate. If Malek has chosen you, then he's chosen well. And if you like him, maybe you need to think about giving him a chance, because I'd bet every cent I own that he would be the kind of mate you deserve. The kind of mate Armand never was but should have been."

By the time Trevor finished, Gina was fighting tears again. She wasn't usually this emotional, but lately, with the panic attacks, the guilt, the nightmares, the lack of sleep, the bad memories of what Armand had done to her, as well as her frayed nerves over Malek, she was an emotional mess.

Trevor was right. She wasn't the same person she had been two years ago. She wasn't even the same person she had been two *months* ago. She was used to being in charge of herself and her environment. Calculated and sure of herself, full of confidence, able to make snap decisions in a single millisecond and shoot a fly between its multifaceted eyes at one hundred yards. Now she was lucky to hit the trash can from ten feet. And decisions? Forget it. She couldn't trust herself to decide between Coke and Pepsi right now, let alone a life with or without Malek.

All she knew was that Armand had left her with a case of post-traumatic stress disorder multiplied by a hundred. She hadn't even been with him a year, but what he had done to her had defined the rest of her life in the worst possible way. No wonder Malek's proclamation of being her mate had awakened anxiety attacks handed down by Satan himself, because it reminded her of what being mated the only other time in her life had been like. Who could blame her for being terrified of walking down that road again?

"I don't know, Trev. Maybe you're right." She sighed, and her thoughts returned to Malek and how nice he had been to her. So handsome and sweet. Could she get over her fear to give him a chance, as Trevor suggested? She wasn't sure. "I just don't know. Even if I did, what could I offer him? Huh?" She absently slid her palm down her belly.

Trevor eased back with a sigh, his eyes sharp, yet compassionate. "You have plenty to offer him."

She scoffed. "Not what matters."

"How do you know what matters to Malek?"

"Because it's the same thing all males of our race want, Trev. It's what they yearn for during their calling. Their desire for young drives them."

Trevor tsked. "And yet I'm gay and will never mate with

someone who can bear me a child."

Gina ricocheted backward in her seat. "That's different. And you can still have a child. There are ways. You can—"

Trevor held up his hand. "No, Gina. There will never be a way for me to have a child with the male I eventually mate, if I'm so blessed to take one. My mate will never be able to carry my child. His belly will never be able to grow with what I give him during my calling. And yet, I know that when I mate him, whoever he is…" He waved his hand in a wide arc as if casting a spell over the land for his mate to magically appear, "I know I will love him with all my heart and won't give a damn that he can't have my young. Just as Malek won't give a damn you can't have his. All that matters to a mated male is that his mate is *with* him. Do you understand?"

Gina huffed and drew in several tight breaths. "Yes but…I mean…" She held her hands out in front of her, palms up, as if they held the common sense she was trying to find to counter Trevor's words of wisdom. "But Trev, that's different. It's not the same—"

Trevor leaned forward and tapped his finger against the side of her head. "It *is* the same, Gina. It's only different in your head." He tap-tap-tapped her noggin again. "You make it different in your mind, just as you've convinced yourself you're not good enough and that what Armand did to you is proof that you have to stay unmated for the rest of your life. It's all in here, Gina." He cradled her head and curled the tips of his fingers into her hair. "It's all in your mind."

For a moment, they sat in silence, and then Trevor offered her a compassionate smile as he pulled his hand away and settled into his seat and crossed his legs. "Let me tell you a story."

She scowled. "I don't need a story—"

He held up a hand. "Just hear me out."

"Fine." She sat back and crossed her arms.

He leaned forward. "There's a footrace held in Colorado every year called the Leadville 100," he said.

Say what? Was he really going to tell her a story about a

human footrace? Gina frowned curiously. "What does a race in Colorado have to do with me?"

He tilted his head and arched an eyebrow at her. "Just hush and listen."

"Fine." She adjusted her crossed arms and got comfortable.

"So, the Leadville 100 is a grueling one-hundred mile trail race over rocky terrain, steep inclines, and at altitudes where no sane human would dare to run." Trevor's face relaxed, his gaze thoughtful. "Runners come from all over to compete. Thrill seekers or just people who enjoy seeing how far they can push their bodies."

Gina nodded, willing him to get to the point. But Trevor told his story at his own pace, ignoring the impatient tap of her index finger on her arm.

"By the end of the race," he said, "nearly half the runners have dropped out from exposure, fatigue, injury, altitude sickness, what have you." He chuckled. "They say in Leadville that this is the one time each year that all the beds in the hotels *and* the hospital are full at the same time."

"I'll bet," Gina said, watching him. What was his point? Because he clearly had one.

Trevor smiled and swallowed his last gulp of beer. "Several years ago, this guy brought runners up from Mexico to run the race. They were called the running people or something like that, and they had never heard of the Leadville 100. These were people who lived in such remote places that there weren't even any roads to get to them." He eyed her. "These were people who had never competed in a race. Running was simply a way of life. They didn't know about strategy, training, or how to compete. And they weren't told about altitude sickness or how brutal the course was." Trevor uncrossed his legs, sat forward, and rested his elbows on his thighs. "Gina, these runners broke records, and they broke them because…well, they broke them because they didn't know any better. No one told them they had to beat anybody or that they would fight the elements or run in darkness so pitch black they wouldn't be able to see a foot in front of them without a flashlight. These 'running people' had no preconceived notions about how to dress or what shoes to wear or that their feet would become bloody with blisters. They had no expectations. They just knew they needed to run. And run they did."

Gina was beginning to understand where he was going with this.

"Point is, Gina, those who don't have any expectations about the race are the ones who do the best in it." Trevor reached over and tapped the tip of his index finger against Gina's temple again. "It's all in here, Gina. It's all in your head. You just need to run. That's all you need to do. Run and feel the wind on your face and your hair flying back." He skimmed his fingers through her hair then paused, took a deep breath, blew it out, and grinned with his whole face so that his breathtaking dimples creased his cheeks. "The folks who organize the Leadville Trail 100 and participate in it have a motto: *You're tougher than you think you are. And you can do more than you think you can.*" Trevor cupped her cheek, leaned forward, and kissed her forehead. "You *are* tougher than you think you are, Gina. And you *can* do more than you think you can. Don't limit yourself because of the past or because you had one monumental asshole try to steal your thunder. Don't let Armand win by getting inside here." He tapped her head again. "Don't let him clip your wings, Gina."

She stared into his eyes and cherished the warmth of his hand as it caressed her face again, and she mulled over what he had just told her.

"You're a good friend," she said, cupping his face with her palm. "And I know Gabe is looking down smiling right now."

"I hope so." He turned his face into her hand and kissed her palm. "You two were my best friends, and now you're all I've got left. You're family to me, Gina. I want to see you happy, and it sounds like you really like this Malek guy, but you're just scared to let yourself get close to him. I saw your eyes twinkle when you spoke about him. Maybe you should explore that when you return to Chicago. Throw caution to the wind. Take a chance." He paused and offered her an encouraging smile. "Run free without any expectations or preconceived notions. Just run. And see where things go."

She bit the inside of her bottom lip. Could she unlock her heart and let Malek in? If only she didn't have Armand hovering in her memory, the decision wouldn't be so hard. Even so, she wasn't sure she was good for any male, anymore. Her hand slid to her stomach once more. Ever since Armand, she had thought of herself as damaged goods. In a way, she blamed herself for Armand's abuse. Was it her fault? Had she done something wrong to deserve his foul treatment? She knew that was nonsense, but in the corners of her mind, she couldn't completely rid herself of the notion that she had brought Armand's wrath on herself.

Even if what had happened wasn't her fault—and she knew deep down it wasn't, and that her illogical thoughts to the contrary were just rubbish—what male would want a mate who couldn't birth him a son or daughter? The damage Armand had inflicted had left her as infertile and barren as a desert. Her womb was a brittle, drought-stricken wasteland. Not even her immortal vampire healing powers could fix the damage Armand had left inside her body. Even in vampires, some things were simply too fragile to heal once broken.

"I'll think about it, Trevor," she said, caressing her abdomen before taking her hand away.

Just then, Axe's voice broke over the intercom. "We're approaching Chicago. Prepare for landing."

Trevor squeezed her hand then took their empty beer bottles to the galley and discarded them. Then he returned and fastened himself into his seat.

She turned her gaze toward the window and the lights of Chicago. It would be dawn soon, but they had just enough time to seek cover at a hotel, where they could hole up until sundown.

"We should probably check in with the local AKM branch tomorrow night," Trevor said. "Let them know we're bringing Dacians to their turf."

With a nod, the irony wasn't lost on her. Micah had been after her relentlessly to return to AKM. Looked like he had gotten his wish. She would just have to make it clear once she saw him that her reasons for returning weren't for him. Facing and overcoming the demons that had haunted her since leaving Chicago were first and foremost. The fact that yet another failed job had brought her back here was purely coincidental.

"That'll make Micah happy." She had told Trevor about Micah's e-mails. "Now maybe he'll stop e-mailing me."

"Well, that's one way to look at it."

"I guess." With a roll of her eyes, she looked out the window again as all the ingredients of her anxiety rolled around her thoughts like tumbleweeds. Micah, Severin, Lakota, her brother Gabe, and Malek and Armand. *Most of all*, Malek and Armand. Was she really doing the right thing by returning? Was this really going to solve her problems? Three hours ago, this seemed like the right answer. Every bone in her body had told her coming back here would make everything right again. But now, doubt crept in and the second-guessing began, mostly because Trevor wanted her to run with the wind in her hair and give Malek a chance.

She felt like a student at exam time, who had known the material in, out, and sideways right before the test began, but once faced with the questions, the answers vanished inside a vacuum. While returning to Chicago had, at first, seemed like the solution, now she just didn't know. She could be making matters worse by coming back, not better. Or, according to Trev, this could end up being the best decision she ever made.

Could it really be that simple?

Tucking her hair behind her ear, she looked down at her lap and bit back her worries. Whether coming back was the right decision or not, and whether allowing Malek in would be a blessing or a curse, she was here now, so there was nothing she could do about it.

Trevor was right, though. She did like Malek. More than she should. Malek was a good male, and he deserved better than she could give him, but she couldn't deny her attraction to him. But what male wanted damaged goods?

For decades, she had used what happened with Armand

in her favor and had become one tough bitch of a fighter, enforcer, and assassin. Instead of becoming a frail, weepy victim, she had erected a hardened exterior and become the type of female no male would ever hurt again. She had even learned how to use her feminine wiles to her advantage, as she proved when she seduced Lakota to get to Severin. But now she wondered if she had only fooled herself all these decades. Was she as over Armand as she wanted to believe? Or had she merely tucked his memory away and now found herself forced to deal with him as Malek pushed his way into her life?

Malek. He really was a handsome male, with long, dark hair, a mouth with seductively curved lips, and eyes that were dark windows of sex appeal. And he was only a few inches taller than she was, which was rare for a male vampire, who usually towered over her. If she was being honest, Malek was her ideal type. At least what her ideal type used to be, pre-Armand.

Heat filled her cheeks, and she kept her gaze averted toward the window so Trevor wouldn't see how just the thought of Malek affected her. Her heart beat faster just thinking about him.

Right choice or wrong, she would see Malek soon, and maybe she would give him the chance Trevor suggested. Or maybe not. She so didn't want to open that can of worms again.

For the first time in years, a glimmer of hope flickered in her heart. Hope for a future she thought she would never get another chance to have. Did she dare let that seed of hope blossom?

A gentle, secret smile curved her mouth, and she bit her lip. Was such a future possible? Could she put her fear aside and take a chance? Could Malek be the one who would set right all that Armand had destroyed?

Why did that speck of hope burn a little brighter at the thought? And yet scare the shit out of her at the same time?

CHAPTER 6

MICAH SCOWLED AT THE SCREEN ON HIS TABLET. There was still no reply from Gina, and he was running out of time. Malek was on the verge of sinking. Screw that. He was all-out drowning.

A knock on the doorframe brought his gaze up. Stryker loomed as wide as the doorway, military straight, just outside his office.

"How's it going?" Stryker said.

"Good. A few scheduling challenges, but we'll manage."

Liar, liar. Things were beyond challenging. More like catastrophic. With Tristan on house arrest for his part in duping the king during the Io-Miriam fiasco, Micah had been put in charge of the team—the growing-smaller-every-day team. Io was still in his calling with Miriam, so he wasn't going anywhere that would take him far from her and his bed for more than a few hours, which meant Io was off the schedule until he could endure an eight-hour shift without getting a hard-on. Trace was locked up in the king's dungeon—damn that mess all to hell and back—and Arion had quit a month ago. That left Micah, Severin, and Malek, who was about as useful as a bucket of water in the ocean with his hormones raging between his mating call to Gina and his desire to continue denying Carmen's death. The fidiot. Which meant it was just Micah and Sev. An army of two.

"I can spare a body or two if you need it." Stryker scratched his thick, black buzz cut.

"Who do you have in mind?" Micah leaned back and waved Stryker in.

Stryker sat down in one of the chairs, his back Marine straight, his expression all hard-ass and full-on business. "What about Lakota?"

Micah chuffed. "And have Severin kill him? You sure you want that?"

Sev still hadn't warmed up to his father, and Micah suspected it would take time before those two could coexist in tight spaces together, say, inside a crater-sized canyon, for instance. After what had gone down between Lakota and Sev's mother ages ago, Micah couldn't really blame Sev for holding a grudge against his father. If Micah were in Sev's shoes, and his father had raped his mother to get her pregnant with him, he would have been pissed beyond forgiveness, too. But apparently Lakota had found God or some shit by marrying a human who taught him the meaning of true love and gave him a gaggle of mixed-blood children. How 'bout that for a vampire who hadn't officially mated or had a calling? His testicular soldiers were potent little critters to give him multiple progeny without ever going into a calling.

Too bad all male vampires couldn't drink Lakota's Kool-Aid and be as fertile with *their* mates. Micah would give his left nut for one night with that kind of semen power. He wanted nothing more than to see Sam swell with child. But that was not to be in the immediate future. He had already experienced his first calling with her, but Sam's newly immortalized body hadn't been strong enough to accept a pregnancy. Maybe next time. *Definitely* next time. He was ready for children of his own.

Stryker shrugged. "Maybe putting them together will quicken the kiss-and-make up stage." He laced his fingers over his torso. "I couldn't care less, to be honest. As long as they're not killing each other it's no sweat off my back, but I know others are complaining about the tension. If shoving them into a room together and locking the door will help break the bad blood between them, I say we try it."

A cockeyed grin broke across Micah's mouth. "Damn, Stryke, I didn't know you had it in you."

"What? A brain?" Stryker gave an uncharacteristic smile, which was about as far as the guy went toward laughing.

"Well, that too, but I was referring to your sadomasochistic side."

Stryker blew a puff of air through his lips and rolled his eyes. "Hell's bells. That's your arena, not mine."

By now, everyone knew the kind of lifestyle Micah lived, but he still got the impression that many misunderstood exactly what his tendency toward Domination was about. He wasn't into giving pain for pain's sake. He did it because those who received pain from him enjoyed it, needed it, or otherwise simply wanted it. For him and those he had Dom'd in the past, it was about pleasure and providing a service. By definition, he was not a sadist, who simply gave pain for the fun of it. Still, he wasn't about to go into a lecture with those who didn't know better, Stryker included.

"Whatever, Stryker. You're well on your way toward 'my arena' with ideas like putting Sev and Kota together. But I like it."

"So I'll send him over when he comes down?"

Lakota still lived on site in one of the dorms upstairs.

"Sure. I can put him to good use."

Stryker nodded. "He's good. Strong instincts and excellent in hand-to-hand."

"Just like Sev," Micah said thoughtfully.

"Like father like son."

"Don't let Sev hear you say that."

Another of those rare grins cracked Stryker's serious expression. "Good point."

Micah regarded Stryker through shrewd eyes. Should he tell Stryker about Gina? If she eventually chose to show up or reply to his e-mails, Stryker had a right to know about it since he was giving Lakota to him. Not only did Lakota have bad history with Sev, but his more recent history with Gina was even worse. If she came back—and it was beginning to look like she wouldn't, so this might be a nonissue—her presence could compromise Lakota's joining his team.

What the hell? He would cover his bases and let the chips

fall where they may.

"There's a chance Gina could come back," he said.

"Gina?" Stryker's eyes narrowed and his brow crinkled as if he had no idea who Gina was.

Micah found it surprising that so few people remembered Gina's name, but remembered all too well what she had done to Lakota and Severin. Micah leaned forward and rested his arms on his desk. "The female assassin who used Lakota to try and kill Sev."

Realization dawned on Stryker's face and he nodded. "Okay, I've gotcha. Her. Why would she come back? Wouldn't that be suicide?"

Micah huffed and shifted uneasily. "Because I asked her to."

"You what? Are you trying to get her killed?"

Micah was fully aware that his plan could backfire all too easily, but it was Malek's only chance, so he had no choice. "She might be Malek's only hope."

Stryker leaned back, crossed his arms, and tilted his head. "Man, you've lost me."

"She's Malek's mate, Stryke."

That got his attention. "Hell no. Are you sure?"

Micah nodded and sighed, exasperation and frustration battling for dominance inside his head. He tapped his temple. "I can see all, remember? I'm sure."

"How exactly does that work? I mean, I know he's fucked up over Carmen, but...now this? Is this why he's been walking around like a pissed off walking time bomb for the past couple of weeks?" Stryker rubbed his palm over his black buzz cut and shook his head, obviously trying to imagine the hell Malek was going through.

"Yep. That would be the reason." Micah drummed his fingers on the desk for emphasis. "The shit flowing through his thoughts right now is lethal as fuck, too. The guy is majorly losing his mind. It's like there's two of him in there: the devil who's sucking him further into hell, and the angel trying to get him to embrace his call to mate Gina. He knows Gina is his mate, but it's like he feels as if he's cheating on Carmen or disgracing her memory or some shit by taking another mate, so he refuses to accept Gina. I mean, Stryker, the guy is holding conversations with himself, for God's sake. The couple of times I've picked up on them...?" Micah rolled his head and blew out a low whistle. "Let's just say his shit is fritzing out, and it's getting worse every minute. If I can't get Gina back here and get him to accept her, we'll be putting Malek in a body bag within the month. Maybe the week." He felt about as helpless as a dry log in a forest fire. No matter what he did, Malek was going to go up in flames. It was just a matter of time.

Stryker closed his eyes and dropped his head back with a groan. "God. I had no idea."

Micah was picking up a lot of *I'm glad I never have to worry about this* from Stryker. Clearly, from the thoughts racing through Stryker's mind, he wasn't in to the whole mating thing and this just provided one more piece of evidence as to why he kept himself away from females, in general. The less exposure he had to them, the better his odds that his biology would never fire up to claim one and thus send his heart and soul into precarious waters. If Stryker never took a mate, he would never find himself in the same shithole Malek was now in, and for Stryker, that was fine and dandy.

Micah wanted to tell Stryker that the risk was worth it. Being mateless, he was only half. If he knew what taking a mate felt like, he would be begging for his as-yet-unclaimed mate to hurry up and find him already.

Stryker would just have to learn that on his own, and Micah had a feeling the guy wouldn't be able to run forever. Especially since AKM was in the middle of a mating boom.

Micah had seen this a couple of times during his lifetime. He couldn't explain it, but there seemed to be some mystical vampire phenomenon which occurred at irregular intervals, where large numbers of matings occurred in a short span of time, as if some bizarre polarity pulled mates together and led them to one another at a time when the race needed to propagate. It usually—but not always—happened before another war broke out between the drecks and vampires or during a time of growing calamity, so this newsflash wasn't exactly good news.

His parents had simply called it the *preparing*, while others referred to the mystical force as a pull phase or *pulling*. Whatever it was, if they were in the midst of a pulling, Stryker might not have a choice. His mate would simply show up, and he'd fall. Hard.

Only time would tell. Not all unattached males succumbed during a pull phase, so it wasn't like there were any guarantees or anything.

He shook his head and clapped his hands on the desk, snapping out of his thoughts. "Yeah, well, she might not even come back. This is all speculation at this point. She isn't answering my e-mails, and short of sending out resources I don't have, I'm not sure I can drag her back here in time to save Malek from going down and never coming back up." He eyed Stryker. "But if she does come back, it could put her and Lakota at risk. You still want to give him to me?"

One of Stryker's eyebrows arched. "Could be risky. I mean, if she does come back. But..." Stryker paused and made a face that looked like he couldn't believe he was thinking what he was about to share with Micah. "If what you're telling me is true, Lakota could be really helpful to your cause."

Micah's brow popped high on his forehead and he blew out a low whistle. He could see Stryker's thoughts and honestly couldn't believe the guy had drummed up such a plot. "You're not doing anything to eliminate your growing reputation as a sadist, Stryke."

With a sigh, Stryker rubbed his hand over the back of his neck. "What better way to spark a male's protective mating bond than to put his mate in harm's way? Say...by putting someone who wants to kill her in the same room with her?"

"Damn, remind me never to get on your bad side." Micah leaned back and laughed. "But, man, I like how you think."

Stryker was proving to be full of surprises today.

A twinkle sparked in Stryker's eye, and he shook his head. "What can I say? I haven't always been a nice guy."

Micah chuckled and rubbed his palm over his thickening beard. He really needed a shave. "You'd better be careful or people will start to think I'm rubbing off on you."

Stryker sat back and relaxed as much as the guy could. "Like I said, I wasn't always such a nice guy." He tilted his head to one side. "So, do you like my plan?"

"I think it's genius. As long as it doesn't blow up in our faces." But really, did he have any better ideas? "It's all we've got, though, and I need to get through to Malek somehow. This might be it. *If* Gina shows up, that is." And that was becoming a very big *if* with each hour Gina didn't contact him. Micah leaned forward. "Okay, so send Lakota over at nightfall. I'll arrange the schedule to put him in."

Stryker issued a sharp nod and stood. "Will do. Hit me up if you need anything else."

"Thanks."

The big, broad male stopped in the door and turned around. "By the way, I got word earlier that quite a few of the victims from the lab in Arizona that Trace and Io penetrated last week had family in the Chicago area. Survivors and the bodies of those who didn't make it are being brought here. A couple in pretty bad shape just arrived an hour or so ago." Stryker nodded in the direction of the medical ward. "Once they're more stable, they'll be moved to the new facility."

The new underground facility was only a couple of weeks away from being fully operational, but the transfer of certain functions, particularly those in the medical wing, were already being migrated to the new location.

Micah checked the clock. "An hour ago, huh?"

"Yep. And more on the way. Looks like we'll be making quite a few upsetting phone calls to area families in the near future, once we have everything in order."

"Fuck me." Micah blew out a heavy sigh and shook his head. He had a bad feeling about this latest news. If a large number of the victims were from Chicago that meant that the drecks in Chicago were collecting vampires, which would explain all the recent reports of vamps gone missing. This held all kinds of implications, none of them good. "How's it going out there, anyway? In Arizona, I mean? I've been so busy dealing with Malek, Gina, and having no bodies on my team, I haven't heard the latest."

Stryker's expression grew grim, but true to his militaristic demeanor, he didn't mince words. "It's bad. Real bad. Several victims have already died. Most of the others are strung out on cobalt. Some can't even be described." With a shake of his head, he sucked his teeth then pursed his lips. A moment later, he continued. "One of the vics brought in earlier was just a boy. Looks like he was filleted. I don't know how he's even still alive. Our people are trying to learn what they can from what little was left behind out there, but there's not much. This was a professional operation, well-funded. Whatever Bishop and Apostle were doing with those vampires and mixed-bloods, it was fucked up. And I think we're going to have our hands full real soon. This shit could go all the way to Premier Royce, and I'd bet my ass it does."

Premier Royce, who swore he had no knowledge of any funny business or illegal behavior being perpetuated by his people. Yeah, right. Sure. That bastard was a master at keeping his ass clean. *Too* clean. What Micah wouldn't give to be in the same room with Royce just once so he could dipsy-doodle into his mind and capture his secrets.

"Keep me posted, will you?" Micah said as he stood.

"Sure thing." With that, Stryker spun on his heel and marched out the door, his boots thunking like a perfectly timed drumbeat as he headed toward his own office.

Something wasn't right, but Micah couldn't put a finger on it. His instincts told him there was a tie between cobalt distribution and what was going on in Bishop's lab. Were the drecks using cobalt as a lure to draw in victims, or was there some darker, more sinister purpose to the drug? If the victims coming back from the lab were strung out on cobalt, it meant that Bishop was dosing them with the blue shit. Logically then, the question was why? Obviously, the drecks were using cobalt against the vampires, but to what end?

Agitated and needing to move, Micah left his office and went to the medical ward. He wanted to check on Maddox anyway, so while he was there, he would look in on the two victims Stryker had referred to.

He stopped at the reception desk just inside the double doors. "How is he?"

Everyone knew by now who he was referring to when he stopped in.

"He woke up," the nurse behind the desk said.

"He did?" This was a new development. "Why didn't someone come and get me?"

She shook her head. "It wasn't pretty, Micah. The docs didn't want any interference."

Well, shit on a stick. This didn't sound good.

He brushed back his hair. "Can I see him?"

She offered a crooked grin, dipped her head to one side as if she already knew there was no way he would take no for an answer, and waved him back.

"Thanks." He hurried down the hall and made his way to Maddox's room, where he quietly opened the door. Maddox's imposing form lay on a bed they'd brought in special for him. The normal medical beds weren't big enough, but even with the bigger bed, his feet came right to the bottom edge of the mattress.

A heart monitor *beep...beep...beeped* beside him, but what surprised Micah were the wrist restraints. And the leg restraints. And the thick leather and iron binding around his waist, as well as one around his neck. He was strapped down to the bed like a serial murderer about to receive death by lethal injection.

What the fuck? What in the hell had happened when Maddox woke up to warrant such treatment?

He approached the bed and noted that Maddox's pale eyes—so like Trace's—stared straight up at the ceiling. The mammoth male didn't even seem to notice Micah was there.

"Maddox?" Micah peered closer but got no response. Not even a blink. And what little he got from Maddox's mind didn't make much sense. But then, the guy had apparently been in some kind of hibernation or some shit, so his hardwiring was probably going through a reboot.

"Can you hear me? Maddox? I'm a friend of Trace's. Your son?"

Maddox blinked, shifted his eyes toward Micah, and with a deathly quiet hiss, drew back his lips to expose two impressive sets of Slavic fangs.

Micah narrowed his eyes at the unusual reaction. "So, you *can* hear me."

Another hiss, this one louder.

"I'm not your enemy, Maddox."

This time Maddox growled, and the muscles in his arms corded as he clenched his fists.

"Okay, so you're not ready to talk." Micah backed away.

He wasn't scared of Maddox, he just didn't want to upset him.

The door opened, and Micah turned as the doctor entered.

"Why is he restrained?" Micah asked, not at all pleased that Trace's father was being treated like an animal at the zoo.

"Our guest became a bit *agitated* when he woke up." The doctor gestured around the room.

That's when Micah noticed the broken glass in the cabinets, holes in the wall by the door, and a couple of snapped shelves.

Ooohhh. Okay. "I see." He glanced back at Maddox, whose gaze was locked on the doctor. And not in a good way. More like a you're-dead-if-you-get-any-closer kind of way. Talk about your evil stares. Maddox could have turned Medusa into stone.

"He went crazy. Tossed two of my nurses aside like they weighed no more than feathers."

Micah didn't know what to make of this. What had they gotten themselves into with Trace's father? "Any idea why?"

"No." The doctor shook his head. "He just went berserk, yelling in some odd language as he tore up the place."

"He's an ancient." Micah looked back at Maddox. "He was probably speaking in his native language."

"Well, whatever language he was speaking, we couldn't understand him, and we weren't about to call for a translator. We finally subdued and tranquilized him. I'm here to give him another so he doesn't rip out of his bindings."

Micah shook his head. "You can't keep him tied down like that."

The doctor waved his arm around the room. "Tell it to my staff, Micah. We can't have him running around like a savage, tearing up the entire building and killing God only knows how many in the process, either."

Frustration didn't begin to describe how Micah felt about the situation. Maddox didn't seem intentionally dangerous. Scared? Wary? Absolutely. But they weren't going to acclimatize him to the new world he'd awakened to by treating him like he was a prisoner in a barbaric dungeon. Maddox needed to trust them, and strapping him down wasn't the way to go about gaining his trust.

"I want him taken to the new facility then," Micah said. "Place him inside one of the new Plexiglas rooms, but I don't want him tied down like this." He pointed at the restraints. "Do you understand me? Fuck, but a prison cell would be better than this bullshit. He's Trace's goddamn father and an ancient who's been in hibernation for God knows how long. He's not a fucking animal." The more he talked, the angrier he grew. "I don't care about your busted up room, and I don't care if your staff is afraid of him or that you think he's a savage. I will not come back here and see this shit again. You got me!"

An amused chuckle rumbled from the bed, and Micah turned to see Maddox grinning from ear to ear, his gaze trained on Micah.

So, Trace's father could understand English just fine, could he?

"You ass." Micah smirked and shook his head. He liked this guy.

Maddox's reply was to chuckle louder.

Stepping to the side of the bed, Micah met Maddox's gaze. "Fine. Don't talk. But I know you can understand me."

Maddox stopped laughing, but a shit-eating grin stayed plastered on his puss as his eyes narrowed. He looked almost insane. And who knew? Maybe he was.

"I'm going to have you transferred to another facility," Micah said. "Someplace where you won't be restrained like this." He tapped his fingers on the heavy leather binding around Maddox's wrist. "But I won't tolerate any more outbursts. No more making like a gladiator and busting shit up. This is the twenty-first century, not medieval times. We clear?" Until he got answers about how long Maddox had been hibernating, he would have to assume the worst about the last time Maddox had set waking eyes on the world. "You deserve better treatment than this."

Maddox frowned and looked away as if he was uncomfortable with Micah's compassion.

How strange. But then, for a vampire as old as Maddox, who had obviously been someone of power and influence at one time, he might still hold old codes of honor. One of which could include shying away from pity.

Mental note made. No more pity for the big guy. He turned toward the doctor, who remained a few steps away. "Get him out of these goddamn restraints and moved to the new facility now or, so help me God, I'll see you on shit duty for a month."

Without another glance toward Maddox, he marched out the door and down toward the trauma unit. No doubt the two victims from the lab had been taken there, where they would be under constant surveillance.

He passed through the double doors and stopped at the front desk. "I want to see the two vics brought in from Arizona earlier this evening."

With a nod, the nurse on duty buzzed for a doctor.

This was the wing where enforcers went when shit got bad in the field. Severin had done his time here after Gina shot him, and Sam had started out here after he changed her into an immortal. Princess Miriam had even paid the unit a visit after her first cobalt overdose, before she stabilized and was moved to a room where she met Io. Hell, was it some kind of requirement that relationships had to start inside the walls of the trauma unit? Did death have to seem imminent for a mating to take place? It sure looked that way if recent history was any indication, but damn, there had to be a better, easier way.

One of the doctors who had treated Samantha through

her transformation approached him. "Hello again, Micah," she said. "How's Sam?" Her name badge read Dr. Fae Snow.

"She's good."

"I'm glad to hear it. I hear you want to see our two new guests, is that right?" Dr. Snow was all business. Efficient.

"Yes, please."

She was already leading him down the hall. "We've got them in induced comas," she said as she walked briskly through a set of doors, along a short hall, and into a round room. In the center sat an array of desks, personnel, and monitors. The patient rooms were situated on the periphery, with nothing but windows facing the nurse's station so that each patient never lacked eyes on him or her.

Dr. Snow led him to a room on the right. "This is Kieran. That's as much as we know about his identity."

"What the hell?" Micah stared at Kieran's exposed arms and torso. His beige skin was covered in dark—almost black—tattoos. As if they had been burned into his skin.

"I know," Dr. Snow said. "That's some impressive artwork he's sporting, isn't it?"

"I'll say." He peered closer and cocked his head to one side. These weren't ordinary tattoos. If he wasn't mistaken, they were warnings, but in a primitive language he'd only seen a handful of times. But clearly, Kieran was marked as an outcast. Ostracized from his clan.

Micah needed to do some research, but it looked like Kieran held some interesting powers that had spooked his clan badly enough to brand him.

Dr. Snow checked his vitals. "He was belligerent when they brought him in, suffering from hardcore cobalt withdrawal like nothing I've ever seen. We're keeping him in the coma until we've cleansed his tissues of the worst of it." Dr. Snow placed her hand on Micah's shoulder to get his attention. "Let me show you the other one. He's much worse."

Micah followed her to the next room over, and his heart broke. This one was merely a boy, not even through his transition to adulthood. He was tall and lanky, with dark hair and tender features. He couldn't have been older than nineteen or twenty and looked like he was being held together by a thick, white bandage. Crimson bled through from what appeared to be a gaping wound that started at his sternum and ran down his torso. He imagined the wound extended to the boy's groin, but the sheet was drawn up to keep him covered.

"What happened to him?"

Dr. Snow shook her head and bit her lip. Clearly, whatever the boy had endured was gruesome. "It looked like they had begun to dissect him or something. He had been cut open. I have no idea how he survived this long, and it will take a miracle for him to live."

"I believe in miracles," Micah said. "What do you need to make sure he makes it?"

With a huff of frustration, Dr. Snow shrugged. "Blood, and lots of it."

"Done. I'll donate some now and tell everyone on my team to come and do likewise."

Vampires didn't have blood types. Theirs was universal, even for the mixed-bloods, which this boy was.

"Do you have a name for him?" he asked.

"Intel matched up facial indicators to a record of a kid attending the University of Chicago named Savill Hawke. Real loner. Not a lot of friends. The file says he's a musical prodigy. He's in the music program and hasn't been to any classes in about a week. One of the day staff checked out his apartment but no one answered. I'd say he's our boy, but I'm not positive."

"Have you contacted the parents to see if they can confirm ID?" Micah said.

"We've tried, but we can't reach them. They're in Europe on some kind of tour."

"Keep trying. In the meantime, let's go pull some of my blood."

They left the broken boy behind, and she led him to a small room in back, slipped on gloves, and prepared him.

As his blood flowed through a tube into a collection bag, Micah stared up at the pocked, white ceiling. He had a lot to chew on. Malek, Gina, Lakota, Sev, and now it looked like Chicago had been used as a collection center for lab rats in Bishop's experiments. He thought about the broken boy, Savill, hooked up to machines, traumatized so violently he had to be placed in an induced coma. In the very next room, a mysterious, marked male recovered from God only knew what. And more victims were on their way, and who knew what ailments and afflictions they would bring with them. On top of that, Trace was still sitting in the king's dungeon, and Micah had no idea whether he was surviving or if his power was slowly eating him alive.

As Dr. Snow removed the tube and bandaged his arm, he sat up and combed his fingers through his hair.

"Thank you, Micah," Dr. Snow said as he slipped out the door.

Micah was a tough-assed male, but even he had limits. He pulled out his phone and called Sam. She was his anchor. His life's blood. The one person who aligned his mind, body, and soul in the midst of chaos. Just her voice would make everything right, even if only for a few minutes.

"Hi, baby. I was just thinking about you," she said.

"Hey you. Anything good?"

"It's always good when I think about you." She laughed that effervescent laugh that was uniquely hers.

In an instant, his heart mended, and he took his first real breath all night.

And that was what a mate did for a male. Made him whole. If only Malek would realize that.

CHAPTER 7

LED ZEPPELIN BLASTED THROUGH THE SOUND SYSTEM in the seven-thousand-square-foot basement Brak had called home for the past twenty-six years, four months, and nine days. But who was counting? He had no windows or exposure to the outside world, and the basement was more a prison than a home, despite its luxury accommodations, but it was better than the last hole he had been relegated to by his keepers.

Jacob and Haslet were two vampires who, if Brak was given the chance, he would love to destroy. And that was saying something, given that he hated killing. Ironic since that was exactly what his keepers made him do whenever they felt the whim. He didn't have a choice, though. If he refused, they would hurt his father, and Brak wasn't about to lose the only family he had left. If using his power for harm was what it took to keep his father safe and hope alive that one day they would be free again, then he would do it, even though it mentally and physically devastated him.

Brak set down the set of one-hundred-seventy-five-pound dumbbells he'd just shredded his last set of biceps curls with, snagged his towel off the bench, chugged the last of his bottle of water, and shut off "Kashmir." As he crossed the room to the kitchen, he wiped the sweat off his chest and arms. He grabbed another bottle of water from the fridge, which was growing empty. No worries, though. Another delivery of groceries was due in a couple of days.

He'd downed the water by the time he kicked off his shoes and made his way to his studio table. A grand piano rested in the open space a few feet away, and a pair of guitars sat on stands along the wall. He sat down behind his massive studio table, with its computers, mixers, and equipment, and slipped on his headphones. The only thing that made his isolated imprisonment tolerable was his music, his art, and books. And surfing the Internet.

The world sure had changed since he'd been captured and made into a slave, and he often fantasized what it would be like to see with his own eyes the cities that had sprung up like lighted forests all over the planet. All he knew of this new world, besides what little he saw while he was set loose to work for his keepers, was what he had learned through reading books or on sites such as Wikipedia. Well, and what Cynthia told him. Cynthia was his friend. She watched over him while he recovered from his servitude.

He was lucky his keepers even granted him access to this new thing called the Internet. For over ten years he had surfed and learned like a sponge, enraptured by the wondrous images on his monitors. He even watched movies. Real movies. His favorites were science fiction and romance, which he had learned from Cynthia was strange. *Most men don't enjoy romance,* she'd said. But Brak wasn't like most men. He was innately gentle, with simple wants, and a desire for the kind of companionship the men in the movies he watched found with their women.

Sadly, that wasn't meant to be his life.

For an hour, he got lost in his music before checking the balance of the bank account Cynthia had helped him set up. She shouldn't have, but she was always helping him do things his keepers didn't want him doing. *Sshh. Just between us,* she would say, holding her index finger in front of her lips. Brak got the distinct feeling Cynthia wanted to help free him, and when she talked about the outside world, she always seemed to be teaching him what he needed to know to survive. She browsed the Internet with him, showed him maps of the world, taught him the names of all the states, and explained that all the different lines were roads or what she called highways. She showed him pictures of cities, and how they had grown up from before he was imprisoned. And she had taught him about banking and investing, which he was able to do online.

Brak thought her instruction was odd, given that he was locked in enslavement for God only knew how much longer, but he loved talking to her. He felt like they were conspiring to break him loose, even though he knew there was no way that would ever happen. He would never leave his father behind and in danger like that, so as long as Jacob and Haslet had his father, Brak was relegated to be their puppet.

"Brak." Jacob's voice barked over the speakers in his cell, loud enough to be heard even though Brak was wearing headphones.

He slid the headphones back on his head so they rested around his neck. "Yes?" Oppression weighed down his voice. There was only one reason why his keepers spoke to him. They had a job for him to do.

"Time to earn your keep," Jacob said.

Burden weighed on his heart, but Brak set the headphones aside and pulled his long hair back before securing an elastic band around it. He had his father's features, built tall and muscular, with a strong angular face and wavy, dark brown hair. But Cynthia said it was his smile she liked best. Not that he smiled much. He didn't have much reason to smile, except when Cynthia was around. She made him laugh. When she was in his prison home, he felt his spirits lift. The only good thing about these jobs he performed for his keepers was that he got to see her.

But that was the only good thing. Talk about a Catch-22. To receive a little ray of sunshine, Brak had to go through hell.

"Fine. Send her in." Brak sat down on his bed, and he rubbed his sweaty palms up and down his thighs as he mentally fortified himself.

His powers had never been intended for this purpose. Trace was the destroyer. Brak was supposed to be the healer. And together they were yin and yang. Two halves that made a whole. But now Brak had to play destroyer, and his other half was gone. He had never learned what had happened to Trace after the death of their mother. All he knew was that after she died, Trace was gone and Father fell into suffering that led to a coma induced by their mother's magic.

The door opened and Cynthia walked in and smiled, her brown eyes twinkling. She was a sweet girl, the daughter of his last attendant, who had retired from her role of service.

"Hi, dahlin'." Her Southern accent brought an instant calm over him.

"Hi." Brak rubbed his hands over his thighs again. He hated that he had to do this.

Jacob's voice came over the speaker. "The usual protocol."

The usual protocol: Kill the targets and return in thirty minutes or less...or else his father would be hurt.

He exchanged glances with Cynthia, who sat down next to him, her face the picture of compassion. She knew how much he hated the way his life had turned out.

Brak held out his hand as he usually did and waited for her to give him what he needed.

She opened her canvas satchel and pulled out a wrapped bundle, which she unfolded until she set two metal badges in his palm. They looked like officer's badges. "Chicago Police" was written on both.

Brak sighed, lay back, and closed his eyes as he caressed the first badge with his thumb and forefinger.

His mind raced across the miles, so fast he couldn't focus on the blur of trees, cars, houses, buildings, and past doors. Within seconds, he was standing outside a dark cell in what looked like some kind of modern-day dungeon. Inside, a dreck lay on a small, lumpy mattress.

At least the target was a dreck. His keepers usually sent him after vampires or humans. Still, his power was meant to heal, not kill, and he would suffer the consequences of abusing what his mother had bestowed upon him in the womb. He always suffered from using his power, but misusing it made the sickness worse.

With a sigh, Brak's spirit form passed through the bars of the cell.

The dreck sat up, suddenly alert. "Who's there?"

Whoever this dreck was, he couldn't see or hear Brak,

but as with most of his victims, he sensed him. Much like humans sensed ghosts or when they were being watched, Brak's targets often felt when he was near.

He didn't know what this dreck had done to deserve the death sentence, and as much as it pained him, Brak pushed forward, knowing that if he didn't do this, his father would suffer. So, Brak suffered for them both.

With the ease of air passing through a door, Brak's invisible hand plunged into the dreck's chest and wrapped around his heart.

The dreck—Brak saw that his name was Grotek—jolted with a grunt, and his eyes shot wide as he clutched his chest. He clawed at Brak's ghostly, invisible hand, trying to grab it or push it away, but it was useless. Brak had Grotek in his grip, and once a victim was in his grasp, there was no escape.

Wincing, Brak squeezed harder. His instincts fought and nagged him that this wasn't how his gift should be used. Nausea roiled in his stomach, and pain shot through his head, but still, he squeezed harder as the dreck struggled. He had no choice.

"Sshh, it will be over soon," Brak whispered, more for himself than the dreck. Trying to comfort those he killed made him feel less like a monster.

Grotek's heart vibrated as if putting up one last surge of fight, and then it finally stopped beating. The dreck slumped forward and Brak let go and pulled out his hand. Grotek fell backward on the bed.

Brak didn't have time to mourn the death—and, yes, even drecks deserved to be mourned. He had to find the next target. He concentrated on the second badge, and within a split second he flashed to one cell over in the same dungeon, where another dreck—he saw his name was Chane—paced near the front of the cell. Clearly, he had heard Grotek's struggles next door.

"Grotek?" Chane called out in the dark as he stopped and peered through the bars. He stood directly in front of Brak.

"I'm sorry," Brak whispered. He reached through the bars and gripped Chane's heart.

Chane shrieked and tried to pull back, but it was too late. He gripped the bars of the cell and pushed, but Brak held strong and pulled him back, inadvertently slamming him against the bars with such force they rattled.

"Don't struggle," Brak said. "It only hurts more if you struggle."

If only his victims could hear him, he could ease them.

Unfortunately, Chane fought to free himself, causing his heart to rupture. Brak lost his grip and tore into Chane's lung as he tried to keep the dreck from falling, but all he did was create a bigger mess. Brak grimaced as Chane fell backward and crashed against the floor, his body arching in a violent show of muscular spasms as he coughed up blood. And then he fell still.

Sure, they were drecks, and they had obviously broken some law against the vampires to be locked up, but causing such horrific injuries when he should have been healing them left Brak feeling empty and horrid. He was an abomination. A freak of nature.

"Hello?"

Brak turned toward the voice that echoed quietly through the narrow aisle. Something about the voice sounded familiar.

"Who's there?" The deep male voice came from another cell.

Brak's ethereal spirit drifted, curious now about who else was in the dungeon with him who had a voice that touched him in a way that felt right...familiar...so like his own.

With a frown, Brak stopped. No. It couldn't be.

"Hello?" The male spoke again, more quietly, as if he sensed Brak, too.

With anticipation driving him, Brak whipped through the darkened aisle and around another corner until he reached the cell where the voice had come from. He peered in, and there, in the shadows...he could see...

"Traceon?"

Trace sat on the floor, his back against the wall, his pale eyes frantic as he clawed his own forearm. "Who's there?" Traceon's eyes darted back and forth, and then narrowed as he strained to see through the darkness. "I can f...feel you."

He seemed agitated, and both forearms were streaked with scratch marks, as well as remnants of what appeared to be self-induced bites.

Brak passed into the cell. Was this possible? He had thought Trace lost. Dead. But here he was. His brother. His twin. His other half. The one who balanced him.

"Traceon." Brak touched his brother's face.

Trace visibly calmed, and the agitation left him as he sighed. This was what they did for each other. They brought balance to each other's power. Brak allowed Trace to heal his deep-seated depravity, and Trace allowed Brak to embrace something darker without the nasty side effects he would no doubt experience as soon as he returned to his body. But he and Trace needed to be together for the fusion of their power to be effective. Together, they were more powerful than any creature known on earth. Mother had seen to that from their conception. It was her way to protect them.

"I'm here. You can't hear me, but you can feel me, can't you?" Brak brushed his hand down one of Trace's forearms, and then the other. The cuts and fading scars disappeared. How perfect it felt to heal, not hurt. Kneeling down, he placed his invisible hand on Trace's forehead. "Find peace, my brother."

Trace's power required constant maintenance to keep from blowing out of proportion and tipping the scale toward mutancy. How had Trace survived this long away from him? Without Brak, Trace should have been dead by now. Unless he had found another way to control his power.

The idea of what it took for Trace to stay under control sent a shiver through Brak's ethereal manifestation.

"Brak?" Trace lifted his arm and stared at his now-healed skin.

Brak had to hurry. His time was running out. With a leap, he entered Trace's body. Trace sucked in a loud gasp, and his body jerked violently as he accepted his brother's spirit inside him.

It had been too long since they had joined like this, and in Trace's weakened condition, the fusion was hard on his body. But it was the quickest way to collect information.

What Brak found hurt his heart.

Sorrow...pain...suffering...loneliness. Trace had spent the last two hundred years in a living hell. He blamed himself for Mother's death. He tortured himself and lived in constant agony, and his power was a scourge to his existence. God! The depraved acts Trace had subjected himself to in order not to lose control of his power made Brak sick. He had failed his brother by not being there. How had Trace survived?

Brak pushed forward into the present and saw friends. Close friends. One named Micah and another named Sam. They were important to Trace. Very important. Especially Micah. They saved him. Somehow, they kept Trace safe now.

So, where was he? Where was this dungeon Trace was held in? Brak dug deeper and saw Chicago. Trace was an enforcer in Chicago and had been arrested. Why? What had happened? This didn't make sense. What had Trace done to deserve this punishment?

He invaded Trace's mind further in an attempt to find the answer, but his search ended abruptly as he hit a memory he hadn't expected to find. What the fuck? Fury rose like a violent storm. So fierce was the rush of outrage that Brak was flung from Trace's body, and his ghostly visage slingshot past the walls of the dungeon and away from his brother as he careened out of control in a whirlwind of rage.

He might be the gentle twin, but that didn't mean he didn't have his moments. And as soon as he found Jacob and Haslet, they would know just how bad shit got when he had a moment.

They had lied to him. His father was no longer in their care. Trace had found him in some kind of lab and stolen him back to Chicago.

Which meant Jacob and Haslet were as good as dead.

TRACE GASPED AND SUCKED IN RAPID GULPS OF AIR as Brak's presence shot from his body.

"Brak!"

He was alive. His twin was alive. For so long he had tried to find him, and even though he had still been able to feel Brak's life force on occasion, he had begun to think it was all in his imagination and that Brak was dead. Along with his father. But in a matter of days, he found out he had been wrong. Both his father and his brother still lived.

"Brak!" He shot up from the floor in his cell and gripped the bars that kept him prisoner just as guards rushed into the cellblock to his left, bringing with them a din of commotion.

The scent of death hung like fog in the closed-in space, and metal clanged against metal as two cell doors slid open. He couldn't see them, but he could hear them, and now that he was lucid and no longer hanging by his last thread of sanity—thanks to his brother's ability to cleanse him—he realized that the two drecks who had been his neighbors since the day after he went into lockup were dead. Something—or someone—had killed them.

Brak.

But that wasn't Brak's purpose. Why would he kill?

The slow, measured *clack...clack...clack* of high-heeled boots made their way toward his cell, and when he glanced up, that bitch Cordray slinked around the corner. Her long, black hair was braided in about a hundred tiny braids that swished as she walked, and a black, sleeveless tank that shimmered and hung loosely over her large breasts showed off the multihued tattoos across her chest and down both arms. He growled and stepped away from the bars. He didn't want to be anywhere near her.

She stopped in front of his cell. Her eyes were such a bright blue, they cut through the darkness and practically glowed. "Hello, Trace. Hear or see anything interesting lately?" She tapped the nail of her index finger against one of the bars.

"No." He took to the shadows in the back of his cell and sat down on the floor in the corner but kept his eyes glued to hers.

She knelt down on her haunches. "Are you sure?"

"Positive." The word oozed from his lips like a lethal hiss.

Her eyes narrowed and her red lips curled into a tight smile. "You seem...better." She tilted her head to one side as if studying him. "The last time I saw you, you were a bit of a mess, Trace. Your skin mangled by your own fingernails..." She waved one elegant hand. "Bite marks up and down both arms..." She took a slow breath. "You were rocking like *Rain Man*. Now..." she nodded toward his pristine arms. "You look perfectly fine, not a scratch on you. I wonder, Trace, if this has anything to do with the two dead drecks down the passage. You wouldn't know anything about that, would you? By the way, who's Brak?"

Trace bared his fangs and hissed. He. Did. Not. Like. This. Bitch.

"Now, that's not very nice." She clucked her tongue as she raised her hand and curled her fingers in such a way as to appear she was holding the bar, but the silver glint of a razor caught his eye. She lowered her voice to a whisper so quiet no surveillance camera would pick it up. "Especially since I come bearing gifts."

The razor called to him. Brak had tamped down his power for now, but it was only a matter of time before he would need a way to keep his power at bay again. The razor would help. But why had she brought it to him?

Wary of her intentions, Trace crab-walked to the bars and reached for the tiny piece of sharp metal.

His gaze met Cordray's when their fingers touched, and he growled at her.

"Don't worry, asshole, the feeling's mutual," she whispered and released the slice of metal so he could take it.

He snarled and folded his hand around the blade. "Why the gift?"

"Because I refuse to see you go mutant this close to the king's family."

The dungeon was connected to the royal home by way of a series of underground tunnels, so her fears were founded.

"Why don't you just bring Micah to me and save yourself the trouble," he whispered back as he tucked the razor into his pocket. Micah could take care of Trace's needs. He would know just what to do to keep Trace's power at bay. "Better yet, release me to his care. He can lock me down inside AKM and take care of me there."

Cordray scowled. "Sorry. No can do. You'll just have to wait to kiss your boyfriend until after you're released."

Trace arched his eyebrow. "Jealous much?"

"You wish."

They were practically nose-to-nose at the bars of his cell as the guards down the way shouted out orders and made enough noise to drown out Niagara Falls.

"You're not my type." Trace sneered and stared her down as if she were prey.

"You got that right." She met his gaze without flinching, throwing a few eye daggers back at him while she was at it.

"You'll never be anyone's type. You're just a cold, frigid bitch."

Cordray smiled and showed her fangs. "Awe, flattery will get you nowhere."

They sat and glared at each other a moment longer, and then Cordray pushed away and stood up. "I'd love to stay and insult you longer, but I have a mystery to solve about how someone stole into our dungeon and killed two drecks and left not a...*trace*...of himself. You sure you don't want to tell me who Brak is?"

Trace rose to his full height and leveled her with an icy stare. "I have no clue what you're talking about."

"Uh-huh." She tapped her temple with her index finger and gave him a cozy grin. "I'll bet."

That bitch. She had dug into his mind and gathered everything she needed about his brother, and he hadn't even felt her, too busy fronting than to notice the sensation of crawling worms inside his head. A sensation he now felt cease as she pulled herself from his thoughts. How the hell did she do that, anyway? Not even Micah could drill through his mental defenses, and that guy saw all.

He lunged for the bars and shot his arm out with such speed Cordray couldn't get away. His fist latched on to a handful of braids and yanked her back. "You leave Brak out of this, or I swear to God, I will kill you first chance I get."

She hissed and snarled at him. "Do I look scared?"

"You should be." He yanked her closer. So close he could feel her blood coursing through her carotid...smell its lustrous scent. He needed to feed, and she smelled heavenly.

"Those drecks could have led us back to Bishop." She bit the words at him like an accusation. "Now they're dead before I could get more out of them. Your goddamn brother is to blame. He's interfered with a top priority royal investigation and will fry once Bain gets hold of him."

"You leave him alone. If he did this, he had good reason." Desperation tugged at Trace's heart. He couldn't let Brak suffer for what he had done. There had to be a good reason why Brak had turned to killing. He never would have done it otherwise.

"Oh yeah? Well, I can't wait to talk to him to find out what that reason is."

His right hand twitched. All it would take to protect his brother would be to close his hand into a fist, and he could crush her heart. Or her brain. Or her spine. He could kill her so easily in so many ways...right now...with nothing more than a thought.

Sudden fear shone in her eyes. She could sense how close to death she was. Well, goody for her. Now maybe she would understand just who she was fucking with and think twice before going all Lewis and Clark through his thoughts.

Even though the thought of killing her to shut her up was tempting, he couldn't. He just couldn't. The will was there, but the follow-through wasn't. For some reason he wasn't able to put a finger on, he knew killing her would be a colossal mistake, and not just because she had some tight-and-cozy relationship with the king, who held her in the highest regard and would surely execute Trace if he murdered her. No. There was something else. A feeling...a mental nudge of warning that said he would regret killing her on a scale so large he couldn't even fathom it.

He let go of her hair and shoved her away.

She spun, hit the opposite wall, and then stared back at him as if she couldn't believe he had let go.

After several long, terse seconds, Cordray finally huffed

and took a wary step forward. "Okay fine, asshole. Play this your way." She jabbed her finger at him. "I'll keep my mouth shut. For now. But when you're out of here, you and I will have a little date with your brother. If I'm not impressed, his ass is mine. So you'd better hope to God he impresses me." She spun on her heel and stormed down the passageway in those sexy stiletto boots of hers as if she was late for a pressing engagement, leaving Trace alone with thoughts of his brother, a razor...and a raging hard-on.

Fuck me.

How that female always managed to scare his power into oblivion and leave him in a state of amplified arousal was a mindfuck greater than the mindfuck Micah had worked on him at Mistress Diamond's scene party weeks ago. Now if he could just bottle that shit and dose on it whenever he needed a fix, he wouldn't need the goddamn razor in his pocket. And he wouldn't need to see her again.

Bitch.

CHAPTER 8

SWEAT POURED OUT MALEK'S BODY as he unloaded another volley of roundhouses, cross-jabs, and uppercuts on the four punching bags hanging in a quadrangle in the corner of the training center inside AKM. He'd been at it for over an hour, with no sign of letting up. His lungs burned, his muscles ached, but he couldn't stop. Not when The Voice still heckled him.

I told you she was dead.

Shut up.

But you had to go and think that image in your dining room was real.

Shut the fuck up.

If you would just accept that Carmen's gone, everything will be fine.

Fuck you. It will not be fine.

I'm not going anywhere until you get your head out of your ass or die, asshole, so deal with me. She. Is. Dead. And Gina is the solution.

"I said, shut up!" Malek flung himself at one of the punching bags, unloading enough aggression through his fists and legs that the leather, already duct-taped several times to hold the damn thing together, ripped apart.

Malek lowered his arms and backed away, watching sand spill from the tear like blood from a wound. Good. One enemy down, three to go.

Now I know you're losing your mind. You think a punching bag is the enemy.

Let's pretend it was you. Does that make you feel better?

The question is, does it make you feel better?

"Fuckin' A, it does." The grin that spread over Malek's face could only be described as psychopathic.

After his ghostly encounter with Carmen's hallucination this morning—and his subsequent meltdown—he had come into AKM before the sun rose, got about a minute of sleep in his dorm, then hit the training center. That had been hours ago. He had run twenty miles on a treadmill, rode another twenty on a bike, then hit the weights for an hour or so, went back to the treadmill, and then moved on to the punching bags.

His stomach was a nauseated, empty pit, but food was the last thing he wanted. The ache in his chest and the erection in his nylon sweats begged for only one thing, but Malek refused to relent. He would beat Gina out of his thoughts — and his body — if it killed him.

He took aim at the next heavy bag, ready to send another one to its demise, and attacked. Fists, legs, elbows, forearms. Malek used his whole body, unloading a physical onslaught that would have killed the Incredible Hulk from the sheer intensity alone.

You're an idiot. You'll never learn.

I thought I told you to fuck off.

And I thought I told you that you'll never get rid of me as long as you're behaving like a fool.

Well, then I hope you're ready to be disappointed.

It won't be me who's disappointed, pal.

I'm not your pal.

"You look like hell."

Malek spun midpunch, striking air. Micah stood in the doorway. What was that look on his face? Dismay? Confusion? Horror?

"Fuck off." Malek turned away. His shoulder-length hair clung like soaked, black ribbons to his face and neck.

"Nope, not gonna happen." Micah took a step in. "And I'd suggest you quit ignoring the other words in the English language. Hearing you tell me to fuck off every time I see you is getting old."

Malek glared over his shoulder at him. "Go fuck yourself. How 'bout that? Better?"

Micah shook his head and took a heavy breath. "When's the last time you ate, Malek? Huh? Or when you even slept?"

"That's my business."

"It'll be my business if you get yourself killed or jeopardize the team."

Malek waved him off then shot him the bird. "Not. Interested. And what team? There's just three of us, or haven't you noticed?"

"Four."

He popped his fist against the bag and scowled at Micah. "Four?"

"Lakota is joining us as of tonight."

Lakota. The bastard who had fucked Gina and tried to kill her. "Keep him away from me."

"Yeah, I thought you'd like that?"

"Oh? And why's that?"

Micah sneered in disgust and shook his head as if he held all the answers and thought Malek too dumb to figure them out. "You tell me, buddy. You're the one with the Gina fixation you keep denying, and Lakota did take her for a good fuck or two. That's not something that would bother her mate. Noooo, not at all. And I think deep down you know that." He tapped his temple knowingly.

See, even Micah knows the truth, asshole. The Voice just didn't know when to shut up.

Malek spun on Micah like a vicious lion and hissed, his fangs distended and his vision sharp as crystal. When he spoke, he sounded possessed. "Do not speak of her like that. She is mine and you will honor her!"

Only after he spoke—spurred by the immediacy of the moment—did he become aware of what he said. If he had been angry before, that was nothing compared to how he felt now.

And the Voice's cocky, in-your-face laughter inside his head only pissed him off more as Micah showed off a self-assured grin and knowing nod.

"Asshole! You tricked me!" He went for Micah. He would not be manipulated.

MICAH DROPPED INTO A DEFENSIVE STANCE as Malek flew at him. He had wanted to provoke Malek, but it looked like he had set off a cluster bomb inside the guy's head instead. Malek's reaction wasn't a surprise by any stretch, but his ferocious demeanor clearly was. The guy was pure rage, all reaction, no thought.

Micah ducked to narrowly avoid a fist to the throat and spun in time to catch the backhand coming for his head.

"Accept it," Micah said between clenched teeth. "She's your mate." He punctuated the statement with the butt of his hand as he thumped Malek's sternum with the force of a charging rhino. Malek tumbled backward into the wall.

But Malek wasn't done and shot toward him again, and this time he connected. His fist cracked against Micah's jaw. "NO!"

"Asshole!" Micah blocked the next swing and countered with one of his own, splitting Malek's cheek open. Blood flowed down the side of his sweat-soaked face and neck.

The two traded punches, kicked and shoved, rolled around on the floor, and jumped back up to go at it again until finally Micah had enough. This shit was going to stop right fucking now. With a maneuver that would have made Jackie Chan proud, he shoved Malek's arms behind his back, braced them with his fists, and bit halfway into the front of Malek's throat. His fangs dripped venom from their supercharged physical exchange.

Both growled low and deep, a deadly vibration of sound that stretched as the two postured for dominance. But Malek could growl all he wanted. Micah's bite was a potent message about who was in charge. A message that said loud and clear to Malek that if he didn't stop—and stop *now*—Micah would rip his throat out.

Malek froze, his head thrown back, and for several tense seconds, neither budged except to gulp in oxygen and growl at one another, both heavily exerted. Blood and venom mixed and trickled down Malek's neck until, finally, Micah bit down hard enough for his fangs to sink all the way in, and then quickly withdrew them and jerked himself away as he gave Malek a harsh shove.

Malek's hand shot to his throat, over the twin punctures that wouldn't heal like a normal bite, because Micah hadn't injected his venom deep enough to heal the wound. Micah wanted everyone to see the rank he had just pulled on Malek, to teach him and everyone else that his leadership was not to be tested.

"Get your head out of your ass, Malek." Micah pushed his sweat-dampened hair off his face, breathing heavily. "I've had enough of your shit."

Malek scowled back at him. His blood seeped through his fingers.

Micah felt as helpless as a worm in the middle of a busy street. This was Malek, who used to be his best friend. The two had been inseparable from the moment they met eons ago, and now Micah's heart was breaking. He didn't want to lose Malek, but he couldn't reach him, anymore. Malek was slipping further and further away, and all Micah could do was watch...and hurt. They might not be as close as they once were, but Malek was his brother. His goddamn brother! Micah had never stopped believing that, even though they came from separate bloodlines.

"Claim her and come back to me, brother," he said quietly. And with that, Micah wiped his mouth, turned, and headed toward the door.

"Just leave me alone, Micah. Leave me alone."

Micah stopped at the uncharacteristically soft timbre of Malek's voice, but he didn't turn around. "I can't."

"Why not?" This time, Malek's words held an edge of bite.

Micah looked at the floor. "Because I love you too much to stand by and do nothing while I watch you destroy yourself. Every day, the grave you're digging gets a little deeper, and every day I fear will be the one where I have to lower your lifeless body into that grave and bury you. And I..." Micah stopped and swallowed his emotion. "I refuse to do that, Malek. I refuse to let you die." He turned and fixed Malek with eyes that burned with unshed tears. "I refuse to let you die, do you hear me? I am willing you to live, and I will deplete every ounce of my will until either I win, or..." He frowned and had to fight to keep his tears from falling. "Or until *you* do."

MALEK STOOD ROOTED IN PLACE AS MICAH TURNED and left the room.

Or until you do.

He glanced into the mirror. A half-starved, sweat-drenched, bleeding-at-the-neck apparition stared back. A specter that looked eerily similar to him, but appeared alien.

What had just happened here between him and Micah? Well, for starters, Micah had clearly been pissed off. Enough to pull rank and imprint him with a physical mark to show everyone where he stood in the pecking order. Biting him like that was the equivalent of telling him to drop and give him fifty...in the pouring rain...with his face in the mud... and a fifty-pound pack on his back. Micah was the sergeant, and Malek was the grunt soldier. And now everyone would know it.

He dabbed his fingers at the punctures on his neck. They should have begun healing by now, even without Micah's venom. But instead, the wounds continued to weep crimson tears down to his chest, staining his white tank top.

His body's systems were deteriorating, which wasn't a good sign, and after his scuffle with Micah, at least he was aware enough to figure that out.

But he didn't know what to do to pull himself to the surface to stop from drowning. His shit needed fixed, but even though the answer seemed so easy to Micah, it wasn't as easy for Malek. Every part of him wanted Gina, but every part of him also wanted to repel her and stay attached to Carmen, and that was the side he wanted to remain faithful to. With Gina gone, it was easier to claim he didn't need her.

Yeah, but you could go find Gina. It wouldn't be that hard to do, you know.

You're back? Malek glared at his reflection.

I never left. His reflection glared back, and that just pissed Malek off. How dare he look at him that way.

Lucky me. Malek scowled and trudged across the room and grabbed a bottle of water from his bag. His wary gaze flicked back to his reflection. He needed to keep an eye on that guy in the mirror. What if he tried to jump him when he wasn't looking?

The Voice laughed inside his head.

What's so funny? Malek glared at the mirror.

You. Do you really think I'm capable of jumping you?

Definitely. You look stupid enough to try it. He took a drink.

Funny, but the guy in the mirror took a drink, too.

Laughter rang through his mind.

Are you mocking me, asshole? Malek glowered and took a menacing step toward the mirror. The guy took a step toward him, too. *You want some of this?* Malek seethed at the image that glared back at him.

More laughter. *You're a dumbass,* the Voice said.

Oh yeah?

Yeah.

How do you figure?

Because I'm you, asshole.

"No you're not," Malek said aloud, taking a wary step back.

Oh yeah, buddy. I sure am.

Malek backed away from the mirror, and his hand tightened around the bottle of water. What was going on here? Shit. Was he so far gone that he no longer understood fantasy from illusion? An ache shot from his chest to his balls, and he doubled over as the male in the mirror did likewise.

Damn! It was true.

"No." He gasped as his scrotum tightened painfully. He had been walking around with a hard-on for days, and now it felt like a major case of blue balls was getting good and comfortable down there.

More laughter rang through his mind and he clamped his fists over his ears, the bottle of water punching against the side of his head.

That's right, pal, you and I are stuck together, and you'd better hope I stick around a good long time.

Malek cringed and fell to his knees. *Why's that?*

Because the minute I leave is the minute you go six feet under, big guy.

MICAH STOOD OUTSIDE THE TRAINING CENTER, his back against the wall. His chest ached as he grimaced and heard every thought hammering through Malek's head. Malek was getting worse. At least before, he knew at some level that he and the voice inside his head were one and the same and acknowledged how crazy it was that he was talking to himself. But now? Now he saw The Voice as an outsider, not part of him.

If Malek survived the next twenty-four hours, it would be a miracle. Because all the will in the world couldn't save him, anymore. Malek was a dead man walking.

CHAPTER 9

JACOB PRESSED THE INTERCOM BUTTON for Brak's quarters in the basement. "Cynthia, is he back yet?"

Brak had been gone for over an hour. Something was wrong.

"No. He's still out-of-body," Cynthia's voice answered.

"Shit." Haslet shoved himself off the wall he'd been leaning against on outstretched arms.

"Hold it together, Haslet. We've got to get out of here." Jacob shoved more clothes in his duffel. This was no time to fall apart. They needed to keep their wits about them, pack up, and get out. And then burn the place down so that Brak's body went up in flames. That was the only way to guarantee their safety if Brak had figured out they had sold Maddox and could no longer hold him over Brak's head.

"He knows. I can feel it." Haslet paced and cursed under his breath.

"Shut up."

"Fuck you, Jacob! We have nothing to hold over him anymore." Haslet marched to the door. "I'm calling Bishop."

"Why?" Jacob zipped his duffel and dropped it on the floor.

"It's the only bargaining chip we've got."

He grabbed Haslet by the arms and shoved him against the wall. "No. We leave. We burn the place down and we escape. It's the only way to be sure."

Haslet shoved Jacob off of him. "I'm not willing to throw all this away, Jacob. We worked too hard. Brak doesn't know where we are. We've never given him anything of ours to enable him to find us. You know he needs a marker or some kind of totem before he can hunt someone down."

"Oh? And what do you think he's doing, Haslet? Taking a stroll through the park? No. He's looking for us."

"You don't know that." Haslet spun on his heel and started for the stairs. "Get a grip, Jacob. He can't stay gone forever. Sooner or later he'll need to return to his body, or he'll die. I'm calling Bishop. Let me see if I can work out an arrangement with him."

What Haslet said made sense, but it didn't ease Jacob's mind. He had a bad feeling about this.

CYNTHIA SWEPT HER GAZE FROM BRAK'S HEAD to his feet and back up again. Hope lit in her heart. Had he found a way out? Was he coming for the evil ones? Her mother, Brak's previous caretaker and a mystic, had foreseen this. *When Brak leaves and does not return, give him the keys to freedom,* she had said. *He will be able to free himself, and you with him.* Then she had given Cynthia two coins and nodded once, a harsh jerk of her head as if the coins were important.

She had carried those coins with her every day since, disguised as a pair of earrings. She'd had them melted down and remolded into simple, large studs, and each time she visited Brak for one of his jobs, she wore them in case that was the day to grant Brak his freedom.

Was it time? Had Brak's day for freedom finally come?

She waited another ten minutes and finally decided this was it. It was time to set Brak free.

With a smile on her face, she unfastened each earring, closed them in her loose fist, and said a quick prayer before uncurling Brak's fingers and placing the plain earrings in his palm.

She leaned forward as she closed his hand around the earrings. "Brak." She placed her hand over his and settled in close, her mouth next to his ear. "Brak. It's time. Time for your freedom."

Brak heard Cynthia's voice from what sounded like far away and realized she was talking to him.

Freedom?

Then he felt two small objects in his hand. They were small and round. Buttons? No. They were earrings.

Connecting with them, he catapulted into another traveling tunnel. He flew faster than the speed of light and crossed hundreds of miles in an instant until he landed inside a vast home in the middle of nowhere. Jacob passed in front of him, his expression worried.

From across the room, Haslet spoke on the phone. "What do you mean, you no longer have him? Where is he?"

Brak flashed to Haslet's side. Who was he talking to? And did the conversation have to do with his father?

Haslet's face paled. "Then the deal's off, Bishop. This was not part of the arrangement. You were supposed to keep Maddox—"

Bishop's voice shot through the phone, so loud Brak could hear him. "Do not tell me what I was supposed to do with something I had purchased, Haslet! I owned Maddox once you sold him to me. Do you think I like that his son found my lab and took him?"

"Of course not, but—"

"I lost my entire operation, you disgusting worm! And you dare to challenge me about your phantom's father?"

"You should have told us—"

"I owed you no explanations! I owned him."

"But we could have—"

"You could have done nothing. You made your choice. You sold Maddox to me for a handsome price. And now we're both out a valuable commodity. You'll have to deal with your own problems, as I must deal with mine. Consider our arrangement null and void."

The line went dead and Haslet slowly lowered the phone to the table, his face pale.

So, they had sold his father to a male named Bishop, huh? And this Bishop owned the lab where Trace had found him. And it sounded like Trace had worked his powers to destroy that wretched den of hell. Good for him. And now Brak would unleash a little wrath of his own.

Brak leaned toward Haslet. "You're dead, motherfucker." Brak had never been so angry, and pure hatred rushed through his normally gentle psyche.

Not bothering to be careful, Brak plunged both hands inside Haslet's body, grabbed either side of his ribcage, and pulled. Bones snapped like dry branches, and his heart and lungs ruptured as Brak smashed his hands together.

Haslet's limbs flailed briefly as his eyes flew open, and then his body fell slack and hung like wet laundry from Brak's invisible arms in a gurgling, sputtering heap.

"Oh my God!"

Brak turned to see Jacob's colorless face, his eyes so wide it was a wonder his eyeballs didn't fall out.

Let's see if I can help him with that.

Brak yanked his arms from Haslet's corpse and shot across the room as Haslet dropped to the floor. Before Jacob could flee through the front door, he closed his fist around Jacob's forearm. The vampire screamed like a terrified maiden as he recoiled and swatted his arm as if batting away wasps.

"No, please, no! I tried to stop him. I tried to tell him not to. I swear! Please don't kill me. Oh God, please!"

Brak didn't believe a word of what Jacob said. "You made me believe you had my father! You tortured us both and used me, threatening to hurt him if I didn't do as you told me to. And you don't even have him! You sold him like meat and kept me imprisoned." Rage burned Brak's soul as he shoved his right hand inside Jacob's skull and clamped down on his brain.

"No! Please!" Jacob cried out as he slapped his palms to his head. His fingers clawed as if trying to dig through his skull to tear Brak's hand from his brain. He squirmed, groaned, and screeched in pain, but Brak held on and squeezed. This was one death he wouldn't soothe away with tender words uttered in guilt. Brak would savor this kill for what the bastard had done.

Jacob's gray matter gave and squished through his fingers,

and the vampire's body jerked as his cranial synapses misfired and chewed through his nervous system from the cataclysm destroying his brain.

"Die, you fucking son of a whore."

Jacob's brain collapsed under Brak's palm, and then he lowered his grip to the cervical bones in Jacob's neck. Brak took hold and pulled, and Jacob's spine ripped from his body in a reenactment of a scene in the movie, *Predator*, where the alien ripped out the spine of his victim.

Predator was one of Brak's favorite movies. Only... he had always fancied himself the hero...like Arnold Schwarzenegger's character. Well, not today. Today, he was all angry, pissed off alien.

He threw Jacob's spine across the room and dropped Jacob's body to the floor as adrenaline surged through his ethereal spirit.

His servitude was over.

With a thought, he returned to his body, and his eyes snapped open. "I'm free."

"You're free." Cynthia's eyes lit as her entire face smiled.

Then Brak immediately rolled to his side and vomited.

CHAPTER 10

AFTER ARRIVING IN CHICAGO, Gina and Trevor took a cab to the Trump Hotel and spent the day inside the safety of their drapery-darkened rooms.

The Trump was where she had stayed before. When she'd hunted Severin. She had met Lakota there, too, in the lobby. Talk about reliving the recent past.

Around midmorning, as she debated the pros and cons for the tenth time about whether or not she should follow Trevor's advice and give Malek a chance, she had another panic attack. She had almost decided to revert to her original plan and forget about the whole letting-her-hair-fly-in-the-wind-while-she-ran idea when the first tremors fluttered behind her sternum. Before she knew it, her entire chest flamed with pain, and stabs of agony attacked her heart and lungs. She ended up with her head over the toilet as breakfast became nothing more than a memory.

Thankfully Trevor hadn't witnessed her gastronomic eruption and yet another unraveling so close on the heels of the previous one. Gina didn't need him giving her any more speeches.

After calming down enough to take a shower, she had ordered another breakfast—a much lighter one—slipped into her pajamas, and turned on a movie. With Neo and Trinity parading around in slick leather trench coats and carrying enough firepower to level a city, Gina contemplated her options again. Take a chance with Malek. Tell Malek to get lost. Take a chance. Get lost. It was like plucking petals from a daisy. Like she was playing Rock, Paper, Scissors with herself. Hell, maybe she should just flip a coin and make her decision that way.

As Neo flew up into the sky at the end of the movie, Gina closed her eyes and groaned. Fine, she would follow Trevor's advice. She wouldn't tell Malek to get lost—at least not at first. She would go to him, see how things played out, and if warning lights didn't go off, she would allow herself to test the waters. Just test them. She wasn't committing to anything, and she wouldn't until she gathered more evidence one way or the other.

If nothing else, her disastrous fail with Severin had taught her to get all the facts before making important decisions. And whether or not Malek was good mate material was about as important a decision as they came.

But one slip—just one red flag—and Malek was history. That was her compromise to herself—her out clause.

Now it was nightfall, and after taking yet another shower to wake her tired ass up, she put on black cargo pants, boots, and a black cotton sweater that zipped from her neck to midchest. She left the zipper open, not liking how constrictive the sweater felt around her neck when it was zipped up.

A knock came at her door, and after a check of her hair, which was more of a nervous habit and a way to disguise her distress than vanity, she opened up.

"You ready?" Trevor said, looking too dashing for a trip to AKM in his black pants and pullover that hugged every muscle in his chest and arms.

Her heart raced, and she tapped her palms together nervously. She was going back to AKM. A place where she was certain to have more enemies than friends. But if her problems were going to go away, this was where she had to start searching for answers.

Trevor grabbed her wrist and rubbed her pulse point. "God, your heart rate is through the roof. Calm down, sis. I'll be with you, okay? Nothing bad is going to happen."

She closed her eyes and took a shaky breath, then nodded abruptly. "I know. I know."

He pulled her against him and hugged her as he rocked her side to side. "I've never seen you like this," he said into her hair. "You're so nervous. When did you stop being such a tough ass?"

"Screw you." She gave him a light warning slap on the arm. "I'm still tough."

"Well, show me then." He squeezed her. "Let me see that badass female I've come to know so well."

But she couldn't. Not right now. She closed her eyes and spoke quietly. "She's taking a short break right now." She held him tightly, her fingers curled into claws that dug into his back. If she could just pull on his strength, she might be able to hold it together long enough to get through this first night.

Trevor chuckled. "Come here." He pushed her back into her room and closed the door then pulled her wrist to his mouth. "Maybe this will help calm you down."

He bit into her wrist and released his venom into her as he took her blood. Calm instantly swept through her, and she weaved forward and rested her head against his shoulder as euphoria fed her like a drug.

She sighed. Yes, this was much better. Tension oozed out of her neck and shoulders, and warmth flooded her belly. There was nothing sexual about the act, but by the very nature of euphoria, she felt her libido stir.

After another few seconds, he pulled away and the bite mark healed.

"Better?" he said, wrapping one arm around her and smoothing his palm up and down her back.

With her head still against his shoulder, she nodded. "Yes. Thank you. But Ms. Badass is still on break."

"Okay then." He grinned. "Well, maybe she'll be back soon."

Gina nodded. Getting her old self back was exactly why she was here. The persona of victimized weakling with bad aim and a panic problem didn't sit well with her. If she couldn't be the resilient, hard-ass assassin she had been before, then she might as well dig a hole, lie down in it, and pull the dirt over her own body. She couldn't live the rest of her life in her current condition.

Trevor held her a moment longer. Then he pulled away and took her hand. "Okay, let's do this."

They left the hotel and took a cab to the storage garage she had rented that held all the things she had left behind. Clothes, weapons, personal effects, and her Jeep.

She was still feeling loose and more or less relaxed as she got behind the wheel and started up the engine. "AKM isn't far from here."

Within minutes, they were pulling into the parking lot she had come to know so well during her nights of surveillance.

Trevor took her hand, squeezed it, and led her inside.

"May I help you?" the female behind the reception desk said.

Behind her was a locked door that led into the beast's belly. She trembled and Trevor gave her another reassuring squeeze before releasing her hand and pulling out his credentials.

"I'm from the Knights of Justice in Miami," he said, flashing a security card and a badge.

Even though the king no longer recognized the Knights as being a part of AKM, he still allowed them access inside AKM facilities around the world. Trevor and his team couldn't call themselves King's Men, but they could at least enjoy the benefits of being part of his posse of protectors.

Trevor continued, "We're here to see Micah Black. This is Gina Carano. Micah has requested her presence."

The female eyed her curiously and took Trevor's credentials. "I'll need to verify your status." She turned toward her computer.

"Of course." Trevor looked over his shoulder and gave her a reassuring smile, but she got the impression he just wanted to check on her and make sure she was still holding herself together.

She nodded shortly at him. She was okay. For now.

A moment later, the female slid Trevor's credentials back across the counter. "Welcome to Chicago, Mr. Knight."

"Thank you."

"Micah just started his team meeting, but I'll have someone come and take you back. It might take a couple of minutes, if you want to have a seat."

"That's okay. We're fine."

Gina paced away from the desk. A display of awards and accolades hung on the far wall, mostly glorifying AKM's more human pursuits. Even though AKM's primary objective was to monitor dreck activity, the agency fronted as a private security and detective service to blend in with human society. They also held a division of emergency responders. Enforcers assisted in bounty hunting, drug enforcement, criminal investigations, as well as in emergencies including entrapment and rescue, among other noble pursuits. At least, noble by human standards. Day walkers allowed AKM to operate around the clock, day or night, seven days a week.

When she had been an enforcer, she hadn't been involved much with the more human component of AKM's work. Her specialty was surveillance and elimination, and she had belonged to a special four-man team in Atlanta. Then Gabe died and, well, she saw where striking out on her own as a solo assassin had gotten her.

She crossed her arms over her chest and hugged herself, and Trevor took her wrist again and rubbed his thumb up and down her vein. "Ssshhh," he whispered. "Relax, Gina."

She gazed into his brown eyes, flecked with green and silver. "I'm trying."

He smiled down at her and winked. "Just remember I'm here."

And thank God for that.

After a few minutes, a mousy, dark-haired female with large blue eyes and wearing a faded, chunky sweater and long, flowing skirt—both of which looked like something out of the late 80s—entered the reception area. Shy didn't even begin to describe her.

"Mr. Knight? Ms. Carano?"

Gina had to strain to hear her, she spoke so softly.

"Yes." Trevor paced forward, and Gina followed.

"I'm Eva." The female ducked her head and looked down

at her feet, which bore simple, brown flats that looked worse for the wear. "Follow me, please."

She and Trevor fell into step behind Eva, who seemed to glide along quietly ahead of them, head down, arms in front of her, as if she was used to keeping herself invisible.

When they stopped in front of Tristan's office, Gina had to lean in to hear Eva speak.

"This is Micah's office," Eva said without turning around.

Gina exchanged glances with Trevor and frowned. "I thought this was Tristan's office?" When she was here before, this was where she had met with Tristan.

Eva was about to knock but paused and turned her head toward them, keeping her gaze on the floor. "Tristan is on leave. Micah took over for him."

"Oh." Unease filtered down Gina's spine, but she didn't know why. Maybe because Micah had been on her ass to return, and now that he was in charge, maybe that meant she wasn't in the clear for her actions against Severin and Lakota after all. Who really knew? But knowing Micah was in charge now did change the situation.

Eva knocked then opened the door. "I'm sorry to interrupt. Micah, you have guests." She shuffled aside, head down.

Gina took a step forward. Micah slowly rose from behind his desk as three sets of eyes fell on her.

"What the fuck is she doing here?" Lakota burst from one of the chairs, knocking it over in his anger.

Trevor jumped in front of her, while Severin and Micah lunged for Lakota before he could get his hands around her throat.

Well, shit. So much for a warm welcome.

And where in the hell was Malek?

CHAPTER 11

FOR A SECOND, Micah was shocked to see Gina standing in the doorway of his office. No call, no e-mail, no nothing, but there she was, and it felt like God was smiling down on him. In that instant, hope sprang eternal. Malek was saved.

And then all hell broke loose.

"Kota, no!" He and Sev practically tackled Lakota, each struggling to pull him back.

Damn, but that fucker was strong. Or maybe just supremely pissed off, which had a tendency to make weak men perform unspeakable acts of strength. In Kota's case, it was probably a bit of both.

"Fucking bitch! I'll kill you!" Lakota lurched forward again.

Whoever the guy was with Gina stiff-armed Kota and knocked him backward while Micah shoved Gina out the door. Micah didn't know who the new guy was, but right now it didn't matter. He was helping.

"Eva!" Micah pointed at the shy admin. "Shut the door. Keep her in the hall."

The startled female looked frightened as hell, but she ducked, grabbed the doorknob, and slammed the door closed.

Kota was beside himself. He clawed, growled, and pushed against Gina's friend as Sev joined the fray and helped contain him.

Micah wrapped his arm around Kota's neck from behind and cut off his air supply with a flex of his biceps. Kota grunted and grappled, wild and frenzied.

"Are you going to play nice, or do I have to knock your

ass out?" Micah flexed his arm again for emphasis, which pulled another pained grunt from Kota's throat. "You are not to touch her. Do you hear me?"

Kota resisted, clenching his jaw and trying to push Micah off.

"Is that clear?" Micah shouted. "If you so much as scratch her, I will break your fucking arms."

The fight slowly left Kota, and he finally gave a curt nod. But by no means was he cooled off.

Micah released him and shoved him at the new guy. "Hold him. Don't let go of him."

Kota glared back at him, but Micah didn't care.

"Why is she here?" Kota rubbed his neck and panted for breath.

"Because I invited her back. That's why."

"You what?"

"You got a problem with that?" Micah shoved his hair off his face and turned a lethal glare on Kota.

Severin looked lost as he slowly backed up to the couch. His eyes were wide, and his brow creased with confusion. "I don't understand. It was my decision to let her go. I didn't want to press charges and still don't."

Micah pushed his hair back again out of habit. "This isn't about you, Sev." He took a deep breath and turned his gaze toward the dark-haired guy with the quick reflexes and the stiff arm that would make any running back envious. "What's your name, and what are you doing here with Gina?"

"I'm Trevor. And it's a long story."

"Well, I'm dying to hear it, but not now." Micah brushed past him and nodded toward Kota, who was still locked in the guy's grasp. "Keep him on a leash."

"Fuck you, Micah." Kota growled out the words.

"Funny how everyone keeps telling me that. And funny how it's so not gonna happen." He opened the door to his office.

Gina and Eva stood across the hall. Both looked half-terrified. He could understand that from Eva, but from Gina? Fear wasn't something he associated with that female.

"Eva, please go get Malek and tell him he's late for our team meeting. And tell him not to test me, because if I have to go and drag his ass back here he'll have to carry his entrails with him."

Eva's face turned white, but she nodded and hurried off.

"Gina, please join us." He stood aside and waved her forward as he cast a sharp glance at Kota. "I swear to God, Kota, you'd better keep your head this time, or you'll have to pick it up off the floor after I kick it off your neck."

Shit, but he felt like a damn babysitter. He had newfound respect for Tristan if this was what being a team leader was like on a daily basis.

Gina set her jaw and, with only a slight hesitation as her gaze connected with Kota's, she slipped into the room. Sev ushered her to him and stepped in front of her as if prepared to be a roadblock should Kota hit the gas again.

"What's this about, Micah?" Sev asked, protectively holding his arm in front of Gina.

With a shake of his head, Micah took up residence between the two camps. Kota and Trevor on one side, Sev and Gina on the other. "In due time, Sev." He didn't want to go into all the shit about Malek right now. Besides, when Malek got there — *if* he got there — everything would become more or less clear, especially since Gina was rocking the scent of Trevor's venom, and he smelled of her blood. He had fed from her earlier, and wouldn't Malek just love *that* shit?

If not for the crowd in his office, he would have smiled, because little did Gina and Trevor know, they had just played perfectly into the situation. Malek's mated side wouldn't be able to tolerate the scent of another male on her. Hard telling what he would do when he got a whiff of that blasphemous act.

Shit could go critical again in the next few minutes, and Micah would have to be ready. He needed to hold the others back as soon as Malek entered the room and staked his claim over his mate.

"Tell Micah I'll be there when I'm ready." After the incident in the training center earlier, Malek wasn't in a rush to be anywhere near Micah.

At least his rampant thoughts had quieted after taking a short nap and eating a cup of cottage cheese that almost hadn't stayed down except by force of will.

The shy female that he vaguely recalled worked in administration as of a few weeks ago ducked her head. "I'm sorry, but he said that if you didn't come right now —"

"Fine, fine. I'm coming." He finished tying his boots and stood with a flip of his hair. His chest still ached and his balls did likewise, but after he hit up his favorite feeding ground later and took home another whore, maybe he would begin to feel better. Maybe tonight would be the night things turned around and he could get past his Gina fixation, as Micah called it.

An apologetic smile graced the shy female's face, and her mouth twisted as she nibbled the inside of her lip. She didn't seem comfortable around males, or maybe that was just her personality.

"What's your name?" He opened the door of his dorm and waved her out into the hall.

"Eva." She let him pass but kept her arms tucked in front of her. Her steps were light as she fell in step behind him.

"You work in admin, right?" It wasn't that he wanted to make small talk with her, but in a way, he felt bad for having been so short with her. It wasn't her fault Micah was a dick.

She walked just behind him and to his left. "Yes. Part-time. I also help in Dispatch."

Malek only half listened as they rode down the elevator. The ache in his chest thrummed back to life now that he was fully awake. By the time he was within ten feet of Micah's office, his whole body ached again, distracting him so severely that he didn't even notice that Eva wasn't beside him anymore. He turned, looked behind him, and realized they had passed Dispatch. He vaguely remembered her telling him good-bye.

Whatever. Good-bye, hello, get lost. Right now, he didn't care. He was in misery's grip again.

So much for thinking he was getting better.

Without knocking, he twisted the doorknob to Tristan's — ugh, Micah's — office.

"Okay, you can get the meeting started, asshole. I'm here now, no thanks to —" He cut off as his gaze lifted.

The scent of tension throttled him, as well as the smell of some new guy he had never seen before standing beside Lakota. Huh? What was Lakota doing here? Oh yeah, he was on the team now. How lovely. But who was the new guy with the short, dark hair? And —

His balls locked up as his gaze swept to the left and landed on Gina. She stood behind Severin, partially blocked by his large body and wide shoulders. As if in a tunnel, he honed in on her. His senses catapulted into the stratosphere, and his breath hitched so violently that he had to take a step back to keep his balance.

Micah backed up and took Lakota and the new guy with him as if he was clearing a path. Severin even seemed to feel the coming storm, because he stepped away and left Gina exposed. Her gaze met his, and she took a heavy, shaky breath. In an instant, he flew up on her with the speed of a bullet, so fast he hadn't even felt the floor beneath his feet. One moment, he was across the room, and the next his body was pressed against hers. He pulled to her as if she were the center of the universe and had a gravitational pull more powerful than the sun's.

Her breath caught as he pushed her back against the wall and dragged his nose up the side of her throat to her ear and inhaled. Pure Gina. Perfect and provocatively fragrant. She smelled faintly of vanilla and cloves. He pinned her between his arms and planted his palms against the wall on either side of her shoulders.

She trembled, and her shaky hands rose and pressed against his chest as she took several rapid breaths, as if she was terrified of him.

"Ssshh." He circled her ear with his nose and wrapped one arm loosely around her back. "Sssshhh."

She calmed and relaxed against him.

Everyone fell away but the two of them. Her palms on his chest felt like the touch of an angel, and the warmth of her body enveloped him like a cloud.

Gina, Gina, Gina. God, her beauty captivated him, and the sound of her breathy sigh was a siren's song.

"You're here. God, you're really here," he whispered against her ear. His lips played over her smooth, scintillating skin as he spoke.

He was drugged, intoxicated by her, hungry to feel her beneath him, holding him. She was his, now and forever. She had returned to make him whole. He couldn't get enough of her scent and dragged his nose across the front of her neck to the other side as he inhaled deeply so he could capture her aroma and hold it. Perfect...she was so perfect... her scent was unbelievable and —

Wait!

Malek's eyes burst open as his back straightened. What was that smell? Another male? Another male's venom tainted Gina's blood. When had another male fed from her? Who —? Malek growled low in his chest, and his hold on Gina tightened.

His dark, narrowed eyes turned on the unknown male who stood next to Micah and Lakota.

It was *his* scent inside Gina. *His* venom. *He* had taken blood from his female.

With another low growl, he pressed more firmly against Gina as if shielding her. Then he bared his fangs and hissed at that fucker as he pulled her farther back along the wall, into the corner of the room. He wanted distance between her and that *incubus* who had sampled her. He hissed again, making it clear who Gina belonged to. How dare that asshole partake of what belonged to him.

"Malek..." Gina's voice brought his gaze back around, and he instantly softened, under her command. Whatever she had been about to say caught in her throat, and her brown eyes locked to his, full of surprise.

Still, the simple passing of his name through her lips soothed him, and he gazed drunkenly at her delicate mouth before leaning in and rubbing the side of his face against hers with a sigh.

"Gina…"

She was here. She was his. And whoever that other male was, he held no claim on her. Malek's gaze steered back around, and he bared his fangs again in a silent snarl as he hid Gina from the other male's view. How dare he defile what belonged to him. Gina was his to feed from…his to hold…his to savor against his tongue and body. He wrapped his fingers around her wrist—the wrist that still bore the faint mark of a bite—and this time when he bared his fangs, it was to issue a lethal, low snarl of warning. No one was permitted to take from his mate, or they would answer to him. To make that point clear to her other suitor, he lifted her wrist to his mouth, and, while fixing the male in his gaze once more, sank his fangs in where the other had obviously bitten her. The message was clear. This one is mine.

Warm, vibrant blood flowed down his throat, and Gina's body trembled and fell instantly limp in his arms as she moaned and dropped her head back. Euphoria flooded her from his venom.

She tasted so good, so damn good. Not since Carmen had he sampled such exquisite blood. Not since the loss of—

He froze. What? Who?

Fuck!

How had this happened?

With a gasp, he released Gina's wrist and flung himself away as if she were the devil trying to claim his soul. Talk about an incubus. She was a succubus, here to steal him from Carmen. Well, damn her. He wouldn't let that happen.

"What is she doing here?" He stumbled backward until he fell against the far wall. His heart hammered against his ribcage.

The smug smile on Micah's face appeared surreal among the gaping, gawking stares of the others in the room, including Gina, whose mouth hung open as wordless gasps of surprise escaped her throat. She struggled to stay upright.

I told you she was your mate.

Shut up. He wasn't in the mood for The Voice's snarky I-told-you-so right now.

"Fuck. Me." Lakota shook his head. The guy looked like he was about to shit himself.

Severin only swallowed heavily and looked away as if uncomfortable.

Even the new guy seemed too surprised to speak as he met Gina's gaze and seemed to ask with his eyes what had just happened. She only stared back, her face flushed, still affected by his venom enough that she slumped to the floor, her legs bent to the side.

What had he done? How could he betray Carmen like that?

Gagging, he rushed from the room, making it to the restroom just in time before yacking up what was left of the cottage cheese he'd eaten earlier. So much for making the effort to keep it down in the first place.

When he left the stall, still wiping his mouth, Micah was there.

"You fucking asshole." He shoved past him and dropped his head down in front of one of the sinks and cupped his hands under the stream of cold water, and then lifted them to his mouth and drank.

"She just showed up here." Micah held out a paper towel as Malek stood.

He took the towel, wiped his hands, wadded it up, and tossed it in Micah's face. "Yeah, well, I know you had something to do that. But it won't work. I won't accept her. I won't." But, damn, he felt good. His chest no longer ached, and his balls felt like they were back to normal. Sort of. His dick was still hard, but he didn't want to think about the reason for that.

The shit-eating grin on Micah's face said it all. "Your

dick's hard because you want to claim her, and no amount of denial will change that."

"Fuck you, Micah. And get out of my head."

Micah chuckled, the sound of a guy who had him by the short and curlies and knew it. Micah reminded Malek of a bully who had just stolen the weak kid's lunch money *and* his Trapper Keeper.

"You're just pissed off because you let your Johnson out of your pants in there and showed your hand, and now everyone knows what's going on up here." Micah flicked his middle finger against Malek's forehead as if he were testing a cantaloupe. "And they don't need to have my special ability to poke around your thoughts to know it, either."

Malek ricocheted away from the tap on his head and glared sideways at Micah in the mirror. "Shut up. You don't know what you're talking about."

"Don't I?" Micah crossed his arms and leaned sideways against the wall next to the towel dispenser. "That's why you're so pissed off. Because you can't hide the truth, anymore." He nodded toward the door. "Everyone in that room knows what Gina means to you now. Secret's out, buddy. Can of worms. Open." Micah uncrossed his arms and gestured, mimicking an explosion with his hands.

The asshole seemed to be enjoying himself a little too much.

Not wanting to hear Micah's philosophical horseshit any longer, Malek spun for the door. "I'm out of here."

"Oh, no you're not. Not unless you're taking Gina with you."

"Why's that?"

"I'm assigning her to you."

"Assigning?"

Micah smiled like the Cheshire cat. Oh yeah, he *was* too pleased with himself. "Yep. You're her new trainer."

"Trainer? Fuck you. I'm not training her or anybody else."

"Yes. You are."

"Or what?" This shit wasn't going to fly. Micah couldn't

force him to take Gina under his wing.

Micah jerked him around and got up in his grill, nose-to-nose. "If you don't train her, Malek, I will hand her over to Lakota and let him do what he wants to her."

He growled. Gina would go nowhere near Lakota. Not on his watch. Lakota had been inside her. Had probably fed from her. And now he wanted to kill her. Talk about a recipe for bad medicine.

"You wouldn't." Surely Micah would never do something like that, so cruel and ruthless. Would he?

"Try me." Micah held his gaze, serious as shit, his navy eyes sharp with intent.

"You bastard." He was out of moves. After showing his hand and laying his mated dick out on the table, it was clear that no one but him would be allowed near Gina, and he had to face facts that Micah was right. Everyone knew that now. Nothing he said to the contrary would convince anyone that she meant nothing to him, because his actions had spoken more loudly than words. She was his, and whether he claimed her as his mate or not, the people in that room knew the truth.

"Yeah, well, I've been called worse." Micah shrugged then grabbed him by the scruff of the neck and maneuvered him out of the bathroom and back to his office. "Now, get in there and sit down. The team meeting isn't over, yet."

Gina was on the couch next to Severin, while *Incubus* over there had Lakota tucked into a chair in the corner. The four looked about as cozy as cats in the rain, their expressions icy and guarded.

He took up post behind the desk, in the corner where he could avoid Gina like she was infested with plague. Even so, it took all his self-control to keep from crossing the room to pull her into the shelter of his body. Without even looking at her, he felt every breath she took, heard every blink of her eyes, and was enthralled by her scent. The Voice was gone, at least for now, and for the first time in weeks, he actually hungered for food and sleep. Damn, just one drink of her blood, and look at how weak it made him.

Snap out of it. He couldn't let Gina win, not at the cost of losing Carmen forever. But her proximity combined with his wilted willpower made for one nasty opponent. While she had remained out of sight and out of mind, forgetting about her and focusing on Carmen had been easier. Now, his efforts of restraint had him feeling like a kitten trying to draw blood from an elephant with its itsy-bitsy claws.

"Who's the new guy?" Malek shifted his attention and glowered at the incubus sitting next to Kota. The male who had defiled Gina's blood.

Micah cut the guy a cursory glance as he circled his desk. "That's Trevor. And he was about to tell us how it is he hitched a ride back here with Gina." Micah settled into his chair, leaned back, and steepled his fingers in front of his chest. "And I'm practically creaming myself to hear *this* story."

"Look, it's my—" Gina's voice cut off when Micah's hand jutted out, palm toward her.

"No, I want to hear from Trevor," Micah said, keeping his eyes on the strange male. "What brings you to my world, Trev. You don't mind if I call you Trev, do you?"

"What if I do?"

"I'd tell you to get over it."

"Are you always like this?"

"Only to my friends."

The two locked gazes for several seconds until Trevor chuckled and looked away. "I'm not sure whether I like you or hate your guts."

Micah grinned. "I get that a lot."

"I bet you do."

"I like to keep people guessing." Micah took a deep breath, cleared his throat, and leaned the chair back so he could prop his booted feet up on the desk. "Okay, mine's-bigger-than-yours aside…seriously, who are you, and why did you come here with Gina?"

GINA LISTENED AS TREVOR RELAYED WHAT HAD HAPPENED in Florida with Searcy and Vaydon, but she couldn't take her eyes off Malek.

He had a partially healed laceration on his cheek, along with the remnants of a bite on the front of his neck that had clearly been given to him by someone in power. Most likely Micah from the looks of it. But why? Bites like that were only given in cases of extreme insubordination, but the Malek she remembered didn't have an insubordinate bone in his body.

But this wasn't the same Malek she had met a month ago. Something wasn't right with him. Malek had lost weight and looked perpetually pissed off.

At first glance, he definitely looked like a male in the grip of his calling phase without his mate. All the signs were there. He appeared gaunt and pale, and his clothes hung off him. He looked like he hadn't been eating or feeding. And he had the violent mood swing thing down pat.

There was only one problem. The mood swings and all the peripheral mental bullshit were supposed to stop once he was in the presence of his mate, not get worse. So if Malek was her mate, why wasn't he dragging her caveman-style to the nearest private room to claim her? Not that she was exactly eager for that to happen, given that barely twenty-four hours ago the last thing she'd wanted was to be mated. But she *had* said she would give him a chance. Still, Malek's behavior begged the question, was he or wasn't he mated to her?

On one hand, he had come into the office, stormed her, and taken her blood as if he owned her. On the other, after drinking from her and showing his pecker to every male in the room, he had then shot away from her as if disgusted. So, over here he acted like her mate, but over there, he acted like he couldn't stand her.

Gina was more confused now than ever. She had wanted to come here for closure. To tell Malek to get lost and forget about her. And then Trevor and his silver tongue ended up convincing her to run like those "running people" from Mexico—to leave her baggage, expectations, and preconceived notions about mates and abuse and her defunct womb behind and to give Malek a chance. So here she was. Chance being given. If he wanted her, she was his to woo. But instead of wooing her and beating his chest like Tarzan to her Jane, he stood with his arms crossed, shoulders hunched, gaze averted, as if she didn't even exist. Or worse, that she *did* exist, but that she was the last person he wanted to see.

And that shit hurt, whether she wanted to admit it or not.

"Dacians, huh?" Micah rocked back and forward, lowering his feet to the floor with a thud. "Interesting. And now you've led them to Chicago. Lucky us."

Gina finally turned away from Malek and glanced back at Trevor and Micah.

"I take it you don't get many Dacians in Chicago," Trevor said.

"No, we don't." Micah kicked back and grumbled unintelligibly under his breath.

Next to her, Severin shifted forward, elbows on his knees. "Excuse me, but what the hell is a Dacian?"

Micah spun in his chair and faced him. "That's right. You had a…um…unique upbringing and probably haven't heard about the first rulers of the vampire race, have you?"

The color drained from Lakota's face, and shame poured off him in sour waves. It didn't take a genius to figure out what he was thinking. As the absentee vampire father Severin never had, it would have been Lakota's job to educate Sev on the history of the race. With a dreck mother who didn't necessarily know the history or feel qualified to teach it, Sev had missed out on a lot that other vampires took for granted.

"First rulers of the race?" Severin frowned, obviously confused. "So, the throne hasn't always belonged to King Bain's bloodline?"

Lakota shook his head, clearly wanting to speak, but he

kept his mouth shut and let Micah tell the story.

"No. First were the Dacians. They were powerful and brutal, and were among the first clans of vampires, along with the Thracians, who are now extinct. Many clans have gone extinct, and of those, most were driven to extinction by the Dacians themselves. Except for the Thracians. They were like this with the Dacians." Micah crossed his fingers. "After the Dacians were ousted from power, it was thought they had been driven to extinction, too. But even though their numbers dwindled, they were able to slowly establish another colony, albeit a weakened one due to their small population. They don't mate like other vampire clans do, either. It takes them longer to repopulate, which is why we haven't seen much of them for a while. They went into hiding for centuries to rebuild their clan, but little by little, we've seen them venturing out into society again over the past hundred years or so."

"What makes them so special? I mean, why the concern that they're coming here?" Sev said.

Gina touched his arm and spoke before Micah could. "They're terribly violent." Her thoughts ran instantly to Armand. "Even half-bloods can be—"

"Half-bloods?" Lakota sat forward. "There *are* no half-blood Dacians, honey. Dacians are purists. Always have been, always will be, and they don't mix bloodlines. It's why everyone thought they'd gone extinct."

"Yes, there are half-bloods," she shot back. "And I should know."

"What the hell is that supposed to mean?" Lakota glared at her. "What? Are you the resident expert on Dacians now? Is that it?" He frowned and curled his lip as he looked away. "You know what? I'm sick of your shit, anyway."

Malek growled and everyone instantly calmed, knowing how dangerous he could be given what they'd all witnessed earlier.

"Shut up, Lakota," Micah said, keeping his voice even but firm. "You're just being antagonistic. You know as well as I do that even the Dacians took mates outside their clan, particularly with their allies, the Thracians."

"Yeah well, the Thracians are extinct, so they don't count."

Micah glared at him. "They even mated outside the Thracians, Lakota. Yes, it was extremely rare, but it happened, so shut up." He cocked his head to the side, and his navy eyes studied her.

Lakota held up his hands in surrender. "Fine. Shutting up." He sat back and huffed.

Micah rolled his chair toward Gina, and the compassion in his eyes nearly broke her. Why was he looking at her like that, with such sympathy, with such understanding? He touched her hand, and for the first time Malek's head spun toward her. His gaze blistered where Micah touched her as if he had felt it from across the room and wanted to cut Micah's hand off.

"Do you want to tell us how you know half-blood Dacians exist, Gina?" Micah said, his voice gentle. She almost couldn't bear his kindness. Outside of Trevor and her own parents, few looked at her with such sympathy, and she wasn't used to it, especially within this crowd. And after all the tough-ass e-mails Micah had sent her, he was the last person she expected to show her any big-hearted consideration.

Biting her lip, she squirmed under his gaze. Somehow he knew the truth. Somehow he had seen her past. How? Was there a file on her somewhere she didn't know about? Had Micah gone digging for information on her?

"Ssshh, Gina." He softly tapped the side of her head, beside her eyebrow. "I can see inside. I can't help it, and I'm sorry I can, especially now, but that's how I know."

Malek tensed and growled, but Micah ignored him.

Everyone in the room sat in silence, staring at her, except for Trevor, who bore a pained expression and kept his gaze on Micah.

"Leave her alone, Micah," Trevor said.

Gina held up her hand. "No, it's okay, Trev."

"Gina, don't," he said.

She shook her head. "I'm fine, Trevor."

Micah leaned closer. "You don't have to share it with anyone else, Gina," Micah said. "I won't make you. But it might do Wonder Mouth over there," he nodded toward Lakota, "a world of good to hear exactly how it is you know so much about Dacians." He cast a glance over his shoulder at Lakota. "And it might just shut him up, too, and give him a greater appreciation for you."

"Doubt it." Lakota quipped out the words with a roll of his eyes.

She regarded Lakota. His tone said he had no interest in what she knew, but his body language oozed curiosity, as did that of the others. Micah had put her in the spotlight, whether that had been his intention or not.

Panic threatened to take her in its grip, and that was when she knew she had to speak. She couldn't hold Armand inside, anymore. It was time to let him go. Tears burned her eyes, and her breathing turned harsh as she fought back the panic and pain.

Malek frowned from across the room. The look in his eyes was one of concern, but the firm set of his jaw bled contempt. What an odd mix. The guy didn't seem to know whether he wanted to help her or tell her to get lost.

She cast a glance back toward Lakota and steeled herself, setting her jaw. "I know half-Dacian's exist because…" She took a deep breath. "Because I was mated to one."

Severin's gasp, Malek's growl, and Lakota's indifferent snort were nothing compared to the burst of air that broke from her lungs a moment later. This was the first time in decades that she admitted aloud that Armand had been her mate, and a weight lifted from her soul. Was that all it took to purge herself of him? Did she just need to talk about him to rid herself of the pain and suffering?

A lightness settled over her heart. Until today, her family and Trevor were the only ones who had known about Armand. She had kept him her dirty little secret all these years.

Armand had caused her so much pain. He had beaten her,

taken her fertile womb, had almost killed her, and held her a prisoner of fear for so long she had been afraid to even utter his name after his death.

It was like the séance games human youth played. Turn off the lights, look in a mirror, and say Witchy-Poo over and over and over until, suddenly, the image in the mirror is no longer yours, but that of a witch you've called forth from the dark realm. Only in Gina's case, the name was Armand, and she had no desire to ever call him forth again, fearing that by talking about him as her mate, he would rematerialize and take his place in her life again, to pick up his torture where he had left off.

She glanced around, first at Micah, and then Trevor, and then Severin, Lakota, and Malek, whose gaze grew stormy with an emotion Gina couldn't identify. Hate, loathing, anger, malice? With the war raging inside him, she couldn't tell.

But one thing was clear. Every male in the room—except maybe for Severin—knew what she had gone through. They knew the kind of mate a Dacian male was, and only a Dacian female was tough enough to handle a Dacian male. Sure, Armand had only been a half-blood, but he'd been all Dacian when it came to genetics. And those genes had favored the more brutal, ancient clan.

Armand had told her more than once that he had wanted to take a Dacian mate. He was just as repulsed by his bond to her as she was, but even for all his toughness, he couldn't fight biology. When the mating call hit him, he had to answer.

She glanced at Malek, who averted his gaze.

Armand had reminded her every day with his fists how much he hated having her as a mate. It was his father's fault, he'd always said. His father had been a European vampire. His genes had given Armand his propensity to mate outside the Dacian clan, and Armand had cursed his father's name until the day he died for handing down such blasphemy.

The irony was that it was his mother's fault for giving him impure bloodlines. She had struck out in a rebellious fit of vengeance against her own mate. Gina never learned the whole story, but she had seduced Armand's father while he'd been in his calling with another female. How she did that was a secret she took to the grave, but her retaliation against her mate for whatever he had done to spurn her was what caused Armand to be born a half-blood. But Armand could never blame his mother for his impure genes. She was Dacian, so she was *perfect*. That left Gina to pay the price for his mother's betrayal.

"My God," Micah said, obviously seeing all that Armand had done to her. He looked sick. Angry but sick, as if he wanted to kill the guy before throwing up on him.

"It's over. It's done." Gina looked down at her hands, folded on her lap. They were trembling from the adrenaline rush created by voicing such a long-held and painful secret.

She had come to Chicago looking for answers to her panic attacks, not to absolve herself of demons. Armand's memory had left her cold, unfeeling, and empty for years, just like her womb. But now she didn't have to carry that burden, anymore. She could finally release him, and she felt lighter for having done so.

Her gaze lifted toward Malek again. This time, he didn't look away. He stared at her, and his emotions roiled within the dark brown depths of his eyes. A flicker of compassion passed over his face, and then flashed away as his features hardened and he broke eye contact.

Whatever was going on with him seemed to do with her, and he appeared to be at war over how to feel about her return. At first he behaved like a protective mate, then he hated her, and now he vacillated between both extremes, acting like he wanted to take her pain away but then give it right back a heartbeat later.

Micah squeezed her hand. "Thank you for sharing that, Gina."

She pursed her lips and glanced at Trevor, who offered her a tender grin and a reassuring nod. "I needed to," she said. She hadn't realized just how badly she had needed to open up about Armand until just now. This felt like a breakthrough moment.

"I know." Micah took a deep breath, patted her hand, and then rolled his chair back to behind the desk. "Okay, so…" He blew out a heavy exhale and slapped his palms on the desk with an air of finality. "We have Dacians either here in Chicago or on their way. I'll inform King Bain, but we'll need to be on alert. The king will probably send one of his own teams to the airport to monitor arrivals, but I'm sure we'll be asked to assist in the city. Who knows how they'll come here or how they'll travel while they are. Trevor." He pointed at him. "I want you to work with one of our CGI artists so we can get some pictures of what to look for."

Trevor nodded. "I have a few snapshots of them on my camera from my surveillance, too, if that helps."

"Yes. I want those pictures. In the meantime, I want you taking up residence here in the dorms. Sev will take you to get your things later. I'd locate you in our new underground facility, but it's not fully operational, yet, and it's too risky. Right now, all we've moved is part of the medical wing, as well as part of our Intelligence Department. One other thing." He looked around the room. "It seems the lab Trace and Io busted up last week in Arizona was using a lot of vampires from Chicago as test subjects, which means all those reports of missing vampires and day walkers we've been getting? Well, now we know where they were going. Which also means Bishop and Apostle have feet on the street here helping them collect lab rats."

"Wait a minute," Gina held up her hand. "What? Are you saying the drecks are kidnapping vampires and sending them to some lab in Arizona?"

"Were," Severin said. "They were. We busted it up."

Micah spun his chair around to face her again. "A lot's happened since you've been gone, Gina." He glanced toward Malek, who looked away, and then turned back to her. "We had a bit of excitement when drecks tried to kidnap Princess Miriam. Io and Trace ended up in a lab in Arizona when a vampire working with the drecks accidentally sucked them into his vapor tunnel with the princess. Trace pretty much annihilated the place, but they were holding vampires and day walkers in cells and were conducting experiments on them. Quite a few have died, but we were able to save others, and found out many of them were from Chicago."

"What were they using them for?" she said. This was messed up. And now she and Trev had dropped two Dacians onto the feeding grounds, as well.

"We don't know specifics," Micah said, "but whatever it was, they weren't trying to find a cure for cancer."

"Shit." She sat back. Whatever the drecks had cooking, she had a bad feeling it was only just beginning.

"My feelings exactly," Micah said to her with a wink. Then he leaned over, patted her knee once, and swiveled his chair back around. "Okay, so let's go. Let's get out there and see if we can't catch two Dacians and some drecks who've been stealing our people to turn them into guinea pigs. If you do, bring them back, and I'll question them personally." He grinned. "They won't be able to hide shit from me."

Trevor held out his hand. "Wait. What about Gina. If I'm staying here, where is she staying?"

Micah tossed her a cursory glance as if he'd forgotten about making accommodations for her. "It's too dangerous to keep her here after what happened before." He shifted his gaze toward Lakota. "Too many people want to hurt her after what she did to Severin. Isn't that right, Kota?"

Lakota grumbled and flicked a haphazard glance her way, but the bite seemed to have fled his bark after hearing about her ex-mate. Not that she needed any sympathy, but toning down his rabid dog routine was a nice side benefit to getting Armand off her chest.

Trevor sat forward on the edge of his seat. "Then I'll stay with her in the hotel."

A low rumble vibrated from Malek's chest, which he quickly tramped down when everyone turned toward him.

"No," Micah said, shaking his head. "Too risky. The Dacians will track you, if they haven't already, and I won't take the chance that either of you will be killed in my city. No way." He paused, and Gina got the distinct feeling that what he was about to say would cause an uproar. He turned and looked at Malek. "Gina will stay with you, Malek."

The air froze, and it felt like no one dared to breathe for half a second, and then…

"Fuck you, asshole!" Malek shoved away from the wall and got in Micah's face as Micah jumped out of his chair and met him head-on.

"You'll do it, and that's an order!" Micah said.

"I don't need a babysitter." Gina was on her feet.

"I'm not her guardian." Malek yelled over her.

The room exploded into mass chaos as everyone tried to shout over everyone else.

Severin jumped off the couch and took her hand as Trevor darted around the desk to run interference. "I'll take her home with me. Arion and I—" Sev began.

"Like hell you will!" Both Malek and Micah said at once, swinging around to face him.

Malek lunged forward, pushed Trevor aside as he tried to block him, and ripped Sev's hand away from hers before grabbing her and pulling her across the room. Away from everyone else.

"She's mine." The voice that growled out of Malek's throat didn't even sound like his. As if he were possessed by a demon. "Don't. Touch. Her."

Malek's behavior was beginning to scare her. He wasn't the same, gentle guardian he had been before. In fact, he looked more likely to hit her than protect her, even as he threatened to hurt anyone who came near her. The duality made her nervous. This was how Armand had been on his good days. He had pretended to be her protector, when in reality he had been her possessor. Big difference there. And she never wanted to be anyone's possession ever again.

What made things harder was how Malek bounced back and forth. Good cop one second, bad cop the next. He was giving her a headache. He was like a tennis match, the ball flying back and forth, back and forth. Game, set, match. She needed a timeout.

"Good. It's settled then." Micah turned to the others as if nothing had happened, leaving her in Jekyll and Hyde's grasp.

"What's settled?" Malek said, snapping out of whatever possessed stupor he had been in.

"Gina's going home with you."

Malek turned his gaze down to hers as if he had no idea how she'd gotten there, then frowned. "No. No way." He pushed against her.

She'd had enough of this shit. She batted his hands away and spun out of his grasp. "What's your goddamn problem, asshole?" She gave Malek a shove that sent him back against a filing cabinet. "Goddamn! You act like my mate one second and like you want to throw me in front of a train the next." If this was the way he was going to behave, then deal off. She didn't want him. He'd had his chance and he'd blown it, so it was time for Plan B. She jabbed her finger at his surprised face. "Let's get this straight, jackass. I don't want to be mated. Got that? I have no interest in being your doormat for you to wipe your feet on whenever you want to kick me around. Fuck you and your moody-assed bullshit." She gave him another shove and stalked away, hands on her hips, head down. Then she swung back around. "I thought you were the nice one. What the hell happened to you?" She threw her hands up and looked away. "You know what? Forget it. I don't care, anymore."

But she *did* care. That was the problem. And no matter what lies she said out loud about not being interested in mating, deep down, she wanted him. Even now, if he touched her, pressed his lips to hers, or even so much as gave her a look that hinted that he wanted her to scratch an itch on his cock…oh God, but she would take whatever he gave. And one look at Micah let her know he knew it, too. The guy was clearly trying not to smile.

As for the rest of the gawkers in the room, they stared in

stunned silence at her outburst. But no one seemed more shocked by what she'd said than Malek, whose expression swam between perplexed, pissed, and apologetic.

She stepped up to him, not ready to end her pent-up tirade. In fact, she felt like she was just getting started, and not even Micah's knowing smirk was enough to stop her. "You were so nice before, watching over me, not letting anyone get near me for fear they'd hurt me, and now you want nothing to do with me. Well, kiss my ass. I'm out of here." She spun, marched to the door, flung it open, and barged into the hallway.

If she didn't get out of there and find some less tense air, she was going to blow a fuse. Not only that, he had hurt her. Maybe everyone else in that room besides Micah would believe her lies, but she couldn't hide the truth from herself. Now that she had seen Malek again, she felt as drawn to him as a squirrel to a nut. And wasn't that a fitting analogy? Because Malek was seriously nuts. Even so, she felt as if an invisible thread connected her to him...as if she'd been following a trail of bread crumbs that led to him.

Lucky her.

Malek wasn't the male she remembered. What had happened to the sweet, protective male Malek had been before? He was anything but now.

She was stupid to have held even an ounce of hope that she could be someone's mate again. She had wanted so desperately to believe Trevor and give Malek a chance — to run free as Trevor suggested — but the more she was around Malek, the more upset she became. Because, damn it, he reminded her of Armand. She had been physically attracted to Armand, too, but he had been a monster. And now Malek looked like he was shaping up to be just the same. He didn't want her. He just wanted to *possess* her. Just like Armand had. To hell with that! She had been right to keep her distance, even from Malek.

So then why did each step she took away from him stab her heart with pain and fill her nerves with panic?

CHAPTER 12

FOOL! YOU FOOL! Go after her.

For once, Malek didn't have a nasty comeback for The Voice. In fact, every muscle in his body tensed as if preparing to run and chase Gina down.

Micah pointed to Sev. "Go get her. Trevor, go with him. Make sure she doesn't leave. Lakota, report to Dispatch and wait for me. I'm with you tonight."

Malek began to follow the others out, but Micah stopped him. "Not you." He grabbed his arm and pointed to a chair. "Sit."

He was not in the mood for this shit and refused to sit down. Instead, he paced to the far wall and leaned against it. "This is your doing. I know it. She didn't just show back up here. You made her come back. Why?" He could guess Micah's reasons and had a funny feeling he would be dead-on.

Micah shut the door and squared him up. "You know why."

Anger burned the inside of his skin. Micah was meddling where he didn't belong, forcing Gina like a hard wedge between him and Carmen to drive them apart. "You had no right." The words hissed out of him, tainted with outrage, and he pushed away from the wall, the picture of male aggression.

Micah stepped toward him, mirroring Malek's body language. "So what if I called her back? I told you I was willing you to live, didn't I? This is my will exerting force over yours. You got a problem with that?"

The two glared at each other, and Malek's unspoken *hell yes, I've got a problem with that* went without saying. "Well, I'm willing you to kiss my ass."

Micah ignored him. "You *will* take her home, and you *will* watch over her, and you *will* get your head out of your ass and take her as your mate, Malek."

"You can't force me."

"I won't have to."

True. If she was in his home, in such close proximity, he wouldn't be able to resist her. Even now, his cock practically wept to be inside her. If Micah forced this — and it looked like he was — he would have to find a way to resist her until he could get her out of his home. Somehow he would have to find a way to put her in someone else's care, because it was clear Micah was going to be a hard-ass on the issue, and putting her in harm's way was out of the question.

Damn Micah to hell for interfering like this and putting him between a rock and a hard place.

I know where you need to put your hard place.

Butt out.

"You have no right—" Malek started to say again.

Micah cut him off. "I have every right. I'm in charge. You got that? Or do I need to remind you again?" He gestured toward Malek's throat. "What I say goes, and I'm telling you to take her home and stay there with her until you're no longer a walking corpse."

"Asshole," Malek muttered under his breath. He might have to follow orders, but he didn't have to like them, and he certainly didn't have to leave Micah's office without making it clear how much he didn't appreciate being jerked around.

"Calling me names isn't going to get you out of watching over her."

"I know what you're doing, motherfucker." Malek leaned forward and stabbed a finger in Micah's direction, unable to keep his mouth shut any longer.

"Oh?" Micah opened his arms innocently. "I thought we'd already determined that."

"Yeah, well, I have a few choice words for you on the matter."

Micah chuffed. "You could start by saying thank you."

"Thank you? How 'bout fuck you? Mind your own goddamn business. This is my life, and if I want to fuck it up, that's my choice, asshole. You're messing where you don't belong. I'm fine. I'll *be* fine. I just need time, and your meddling isn't helping."

Micah walked behind his desk then turned, glanced down, and leaned forward, planting both fists on the desk's surface. "Where were you last night, Malek? What were you doing before you came in here this morning?"

Malek frowned and pulled back. His mouth moved, but no words came out, only air. Last night he had brutally fucked Trina and had contemplated setting up a St. Andrew's Cross in his basement while tripping down the stairs into hell.

"Is that your idea of fine, Malek?" Micah said quietly. "Huh? Buying whores every night, *brutally fucking* them, leaving them bruised and battered?" Micah stood upright, and his voice grew louder. "Is that what you're going to do with all this time you need to be" — he made air quotes — "*fine.*"

Outrage and humiliation dueled for supremacy. Knowing that Micah had seen his debased behavior and was now using it against him grated his nerves like barbed wire. "That's none of your damn business." He said it as if he could punch Micah with just a thought. Damn him. Micah had seen the degrading shit he pulled with his nightly buys. He had seen the way he abused them for his own pleasure, not that pleasure was easy to find with them. They weren't what he wanted and never would be.

"And, uh, how are those conversations coming with yourself? Huh, Malek? Have any good discussions lately?" Micah strolled back around the desk.

"Bastard." Rage and resentment skyrocketed in his veins at the invasion of his privacy. "You and your fucking mindfreak powers can go to hell. What goes on in my mind is none of your business."

"You're a loose cannon right now, Malek, so everything you are and everything you do is my business."

"Oh really?"

Micah pushed forward. "That's right."

"You son of a bitch," Malek said, chest-bumping him.

Micah's navy blue irises fired with anger as he surged

forward against Malek. "I've had enough of this. You need a wake-up call like no one I've ever known, so I'm forcing the issue that you've been too chickenshit for centuries to deal with. If you don't like it, that's too damn bad."

The two stood chest to chest, neither giving an inch.

"Go to hell, Micah! I don't need you telling me how to live my life and how to deal with my problems."

"Could have fooled me. You're long overdue to deal with Carmen's death. Get over it already."

"Oh, is that how you dealt with Katarina's death, Micah? Huh? By *getting over it*?" Malek made air quotes of his own and sneered.

Micah's eyes narrowed. Malek was pushing his luck, but he didn't care.

"You little asshole," Micah said, giving him a shove.

Malek shoved back. "Doesn't feel so good having the tables turned, does it?"

Micah seemed to grow a few inches taller as he swelled with anger. "At least I didn't internalize my pain and suffering, becoming a sterile, OCD, whitewashed version of myself who held entire conversations inside my head with some made-up little demon known only to me." Micah came at him like a pit bull in a dogfight. "I've seen what's inside there." Micah popped his index finger against Malek's forehead, forcing Malek's head to bounce back. "I've seen the fucked-up wasteland your insides have become because you refuse to accept Carmen's death. At least I accepted Katarina's." Micah stalked him now, bumping chests with him, forcing him backward despite Malek's attempt to resist. "I accepted that Kat was gone, and I lived in the seven realms of hell until I found Sam. You? You refuse to accept it, you little asswipe. Carmen. Is. Dead. *Dead!*" Micah seethed and breathed heavily, then lowered his voice to a lethal hiss. "Your salvation is waiting right outside that door." Micah pointed toward the hall. "But you're too stubborn to accept it and let yourself be happy."

"Screw you, Micah!" Malek had had enough and elbowed Micah's ribcage.

With a lightning back step, Micah cocked his arm and drove it into Malek's abdomen, and then slowly backed up as Malek fell forward, choking and gasping for air. It felt like every organ in his body had just been shoved up inside his chest and esophagus. Strong bastard! What had Malek been thinking going up against Micah like that? Oh, that's right, he hadn't been thinking.

"That's for Katarina, asshole," Micah said, wiping the back of his hand over his mouth.

Sucking up his pride even if he couldn't suck down enough air to breathe, Malek stood and faced Micah as square as he could with his liver taking up residence in his throat.

"Just butt out, Micah." A cough that sounded more like a croak shot from his lungs as just the simple task of inhaling seemed to be too much. "Just butt out."

"Fine, but you're still taking Gina home with you. You hear me?" Micah pushed his long sleeves up his arms as if he were mad at the fabric, then he lanced Malek with a glare so icy it was a wonder he didn't freeze. "Do you hear me?"

"I hear you, asshole!" Malek flipped Micah off.

Micah sat down and combed back his long, black hair with his fingers.

"Get out of here, Malek," Micah said, not even looking at him. "Before I kick your ass so hard you won't know whether you're shitting, pissing, or puking. I do not want to see you back here for twenty-four hours, and it's quite possible I won't even want to see you then."

Malek frowned. He really had hit a nerve with Micah by bringing up Katarina.

"What the hell am I supposed to do with her for twenty-four hours?"

Micah's head never moved, which made him look even more ominous when his gaze shot to Malek's. "I'd suggest you fuck her and get it over with, but things being such as they are, I doubt that's going to happen, so I don't give a damn what you do with her. Just do it where I don't have to see you. Got it?"

"Sure. Yeah. I got it." Malek could finally take a breath

again, and he turned and yanked open the door. "Maybe I'll see you in a week then."

"That'd be fucking spectacular," Micah said from behind him.

Asshole. Micah had no right to interfere and stick his nose up Malek's grill. Okay fine, he felt protective of Gina. Fine, he would even admit his body had betrayed him and struck up a bond between her and him. But that didn't mean he had to bend. And it didn't mean he wanted her or liked that she was his mate.

To the contrary. He hated it. Hated every goddamn second of wanting her in a way he hadn't wanted another female since Carmen.

Anger fueled his heavy march down the hall as he followed Gina's fragrant scent, so luxurious and intoxicating. But Malek wouldn't give Micah the satisfaction of accepting her.

Yeah, right. Too late, buddy. Once she's in your home and within arm's length, you're done for. You won't be able to hold back.

He shook off The Voice, determined to stay strong. If only he could convince himself he could, but in his heart he knew the truth. No male was strong enough to refuse the mating call and maintain his sanity, as he was beginning to discover. And that just pissed him off more, because this was a fight he couldn't win. He could posture and dig in his heels all he wanted, but in the end, the rational part of him knew he wouldn't be able to hold himself back for long if she was in his home. It was only a matter of time, and he would be on her and in her like a flower needed sunlight and rain.

Her scent led him to the break room, where he rounded the corner and glared first at Sev, then Trevor, and finally at Gina. "Let's go." He shifted so he was standing sideways in the door, head lowered, and his gaze directed back out into the hall. Jesus, but she smelled good.

"This is bullshit," she said, standing.

"You're telling me." His glare flicked askance in her direction, mostly because he wanted to look at her again, see her flawless skin, perfectly proportioned body, and striking face. She was beauty incarnate.

He had to get himself under control.

Trevor stood and joined her as she proceeded with caution toward him, but Sev had the sense not to test him and stayed behind.

Gina parked a few feet away, her arms crossed. She glared at him out of the corner of her eye. "Where are we going?"

"My place."

"Fuck that," she said. "I'm not going to be locked up all day in your home."

Trevor shook his head. "I second that."

Malek scoffed. "I third it, but" — He sucked his teeth and gave a nonchalant shrug — "those are my orders, sweetheart."

She scowled, and angry reluctance practically rolled off of her. "Great. I get to be locked up with Jekyll and Hyde. Fabulous." She rolled her eyes and started out the door.

He started after her, but Trevor grabbed his arm and yanked him back, all male aggression. Which settled about as well as an Ebola outbreak in New York City.

Malek flung off Trevor's arm and got in his face. "Don't touch me," he said between clenched teeth. "I'm not in the mood."

Trevor met him eye to eye. "Neither am I, asshole, and if you hurt her, I will hunt you down and kill you. Is that clear? She's my family, and I don't care what shit you've got going on in your head, but I won't stand by and let her get hurt by you or anyone else."

With an acid stare, Malek's narrowed eyes locked onto Trevor's. "Do I look like I care?"

"Not really," Trevor said, "which is why I'm giving you a warning."

"Save it." He shoved Trevor back and looked at Gina, who had stopped in the middle of the hall.

"Are you finished showing everybody how big your dick is?" she said. "Or should I take a seat and wait for you to prove to everyone how big and tough you are?"

Only she could say something like that to him and get away with it.

Feeling put in his place—and not liking how that felt one bit—Malek spun on his heel and marched past her. When she didn't immediately follow, he stopped, turned back, and said, "Today, sweetheart." It pained him to talk to her that way, but treating her like shit was the only way he could maintain control.

She glared at him, and then issued Trevor a final glance. "I'll call you later. *Conan's* in a hurry."

"Be careful," Trevor said, reaching for her hand.

Before he could stop himself, Malek shot toward them, knocked Trevor's arm away, and shoved him backward as his mated male instincts overrode conscious thought. Conan indeed. "She'll be fine, asshole."

Gina huffed and glared at him, then spun and stalked down the hall.

Malek regarded Trevor then Sev, and then turned and followed her.

In front of him, Gina was a petite firecracker, her steps quick and strong. She was angry, and that was good. If she was angry, she would stay away from him, and the farther away she was, the better. Otherwise, he would claim her by morning.

GINA WAS A LIT FUSE WITH ATTITUDE. Admitting to God and everyone that she had been mated to Armand had boosted her confidence. *Hey world! I was mated to a bastard and lived to tell about it!* Damn. Talk about empowerment. Maybe she should have talked more openly about Armand before now.

Or perhaps it was her growing irritation with Malek that had her so fired up. The guy had her in knotted twists over whether he was coming or going. And lucky her, now she was stuck with him. The crazy guy who claimed to be her mate but who seemed more likely to push her off the edge of a cliff and onto a bed of ten-foot razors. She sure had a way with the opposite sex, attracting what had to be the most undesirable males within the vampire race. Was this her lot in life? Was she to be the butt of every bad relationship joke known to man and vampires alike? Would she ever attract a *normal* male or forever be known as a jerk magnet?

"For God's sake, you're like a barbarian," she said. "I won't tolerate this shit from you." She tossed a look over her shoulder without slowing her gait. "You hear me?"

"Yeah, yeah. I hear you. Who can't?" He caught up to her, and they strode down the hall like pissed off assassins. They were both decked out in black, combat-ready gear. All they needed was Jason Statham and Sylvester Stallone, and they could be the cast for the next *Expendables* movie.

She ignored his verbal jab. "I've put up with enough shit from *males like you*, Malek. I won't have it, anymore. You don't have to like me, but you *will* respect me, or I'll lay your ass out. You got that? Don't think I won't. I—"

As she passed a heavy door on the right side of the hall, Malek latched onto her wrist and yanked her back around. "Slow down, Black Widow. You missed your turn."

She spun and flung his hand off her arm. "Don't touch me."

He opened the door and headed through. "No problem." The door began to hiss shut behind him.

She grabbed the handle and pushed the door open with such force it banged against the wall. Bastard. She glared at the back of his head before following him down a set of concrete stairs in a dimly lit stairwell. "And don't call me Black Widow." The door slammed shut behind her.

"Then don't call me Conan," he shot back.

"If the shoe fits!" She raced down the stairs behind him.

"Males like me, huh?" he said a moment later, referring back to her earlier comment.

"Yes, *males like you*."

His long, dark hair feathered off his face as he rounded the landing and took the next flight of stairs. "And what kind of male am I?"

She steamed after him. "An arrogant, barbaric asshole. One who thinks my only purpose in life is to take his shit and not fight back. Well, screw that. I've learned a thing or two over the years, and one thing I've learned is never to let a male like you make me feel like nothing. I'm not nothing, Malek." She slapped her palm on her chest to emphasize her point. "And I'll never allow you or anyone else make me feel like I am."

"I never said you were." He reached the bottom of the stairs, yanked open another door, and stormed out of the stairwell as if rushing to get away from her.

"You don't have to. Your actions speak for you, asshole."

He marched through the parking garage, barreling down an aisle of SUVs used by the AKM personnel. "What do you want from me, Gina? Huh? You want me to say I'm sorry? You want me to buy you flowers and treat you like you're something special? Huh? Is that it?" He wouldn't even look at her, keeping his gaze averted even as he tossed a glance over his shoulder at her.

"Eat me, Malek."

He bristled. "You would do well to stay out of my way, Gina, if you know what's good for you. Just stay out of my way or you'll get hurt."

Was he trying to scare her? If only he knew. After Armand, she was immune to being scared. Sure, because of Armand, she had lived in fear of mating again, but not because she was scared of males. Not at all. She was afraid of losing herself, of becoming just somebody's mate and no longer Gina. Of becoming a big fat nobody.

"You don't scare me, Malek," she said, staying with him stride for stride. "I've been there, done that. I've lived in fear and have been through the hell that went with it. Be scared of you? After what I've been through? Please." She scoffed as Malek's steps became more labored and his hands clenched into fists. "You're nothing compared to what I've been through. I've been treated like nothing...abused... tortured..." When had tears sprouted in her eyes? She tried to blink them away as she glanced down at his fists. "So go ahead and hit me. It's nothing I haven't been through before. I mean, hell...my first mate's idea of intimacy was closer to rape than making love."

Malek whirled around and grabbed her arms. "I am not him. I would never...I couldn't..." He stared at her, and confusion marred his features. "I would treat you like a..." He trailed off with a frown, as if he didn't know what he was saying or couldn't believe he was saying it.

"Like a what?" She was at once curious and wary, but anger still surged like fire in her veins. "Like a whore?" She arched one eyebrow. "A toy to play with whenever you felt the urge?"

He scowled and exhaled sharply as if she had punched him in the gut. "No. Why would you think something like that?"

"Experience," she said with a flippant sneer. "You are my mate, after all. Right? And from the looks of it, you'll be just like my first mate. All *heart*." She practically spat the bite of sarcasm at him. "Maybe I should—"

Before she could finish her thought, Malek pushed her against a concrete column. His Adam's apple bobbed up and down as if he struggled to hold back a torrent of pain, emotion, and obscenities. Ominous shadows darkened his eyes, which glistened with what appeared to be tears of his own, and he winced as his gaze met hers.

"I am...not...your mate." Every word strained out of his throat as if he fought himself not to say them. "Why...why would you think that?"

Was he serious?

"Just stop! Stop playing games with me. It's cruel." She pushed against his hold, but he pressed her back, not letting her go.

"What are you talking about?" He frowned and gasped, and his nostrils flared as if from exertion.

"You mated me. Stop denying it."

"No...I...no..." He looked confused and guilty, as if he'd hoped no one would notice the cat was already out of the bag.

"I heard you, Malek!" she screamed at him. Her frustration finally found an outlet. "In my cell! You thought I was asleep, but I was awake! AWAKE!" She tried to shove him back again, but he held fast. "You told me you'd mated me! Damn you!" She swung a fist at his arm but couldn't connect with the hold he had on her.

His brow furrowed and made the shadows around his eyes grow even darker as he looked down. "No...I..." His voice sounded small, tormented.

"Yes! Damn you! Yes, I heard you!" She broke down in earnest, trying hard not to cry, but unable to stop the shudder of a restrained sob that quaked her shoulders. There was so much pain...so much emotion to wade through.

Time stretched, and Malek kept his head bowed, his body tight. What was wrong with him? Why was he acting this way and denying the truth? Why wouldn't he say anything?

She glanced up at the blinking fluorescent light overhead and begged for her tears to stop. The situation was humiliating enough without her crying like a sissy girl.

Malek's voice was so quiet when he finally spoke that she almost couldn't hear him. "You weren't supposed to hear." His hold loosened, but now she was too spent to break away.

"Well, I did." She brought her gaze back down from the ceiling and wiped her fingers across her cheeks as she sniffed.

He took a pained step back and lifted his gaze to hers. Raw emotion roiled in the brown depths of his eyes with such ferocity it took her breath away. Something had shifted inside him in the last few seconds. He began to take another backward step, but as his breath hitched, he changed direction and surged forward, wrapped one arm around her waist, and pulled her to him.

"Oh God, what have I done? What have I done?" He buried his face against her shoulder.

Against every instinct that urged her to refuse him, she sank into the warmth of his body and breathed deeply for the first time in what felt like weeks. Without full awareness of her reaction to him, she slid her arms around his back and held on as if she would die without him. He was life. Her life. And every thread of her existence reached to bind her to him. It was as if a door had opened and she was being pulled through into his arms, unable to resist.

What was happening to her?

And why did she suddenly need Malek so damn much?

MALEK CHOKED BACK HIS EMOTION.

Somewhere between Micah's office and the thick concrete column he held Gina against, Malek's reserve had broken. Just that quickly, Gina had skinned him, cleaned him, and thrown him on the grill, making short work of all that remained of his denial that she was his mate.

In a blink, she had disarmed him. Only a mate held such power over a male.

Had it been Gina's ruthless verbal assault all the way down the stairs that had finally broken through his walls? Or the mention of her former mate and what he had done to her, which sparked Malek's need to protect her? Had it been her confession that she had heard his proclamation in her cell weeks ago? Or was it the simple truth that she was, in fact, his mate? And, as such, she had tremendous power over him?

How about all of the above?

What torment had she suffered at the hands of that half-Dacian bastard she had been mated to before? What had he done to her? And how had she survived? He pulled back, and his gaze ranged her face. Such beauty, such fire. She stole his breath, and he swayed from her heady scent. He would treat her like a queen. His queen. And he would revere and bow to her command every day, tend to her needs, care for her, and protect her with his life if he had to.

He couldn't move, couldn't breathe. In her bewitching way, Gina drew him in. She was a blossom, and he was the honeybee eager for her nectar.

But what he had said that day in her cell was still true. He wasn't worthy of her. She deserved more than he could give. As much as he wanted to be her everything, he knew he couldn't.

His resolve waned. He could no longer deny how much he wanted Gina, but he still couldn't have her. It would be unfair to claim her when he still clung to a ghost. Carmen still held him in the past. Carmen still possessed half his heart, which meant he couldn't give all of himself to Gina. And she deserved all of him, not merely a part.

Sacrifice replaced anger. Compassion replaced aggression. Gina had already suffered enough pain at the hands of another, and all Malek could offer her was more of the same. With his heart in two places, he would always pull her to him then push her away, just as he had done from the moment he saw her in Micah's office. She would be a Ping-Pong ball. Back and forth, back and forth. He would constantly fight himself to reconcile the two halves of his heart into one, and that wasn't fair to her. To try and make a life with her under such circumstances—to cheat her out of a full life with someone else who could give her his *whole* heart and not just half—would be selfish. Not only that, it was degrading and disrespectful to her.

What was happening between them could never be. He simply couldn't let her into his heart. Not because he no longer wanted to. Because, damn him, he did. But how do you let someone into your heart when half of it still lies with another?

In a blink, the reality slammed him with a pain more brutal than what he'd suffered so far, because this pain came with clarity of mind, body, and soul. He would always cause Gina pain. It was inevitable. Even if he claimed her as his mate, he would always hurt her. Why? Because a part of him—the part still attached to Carmen—would always drive Gina away.

Frowning, he looked down and stepped back. "I can't do this. I'm sorry, but this can't happen, Gina. No matter how much I don't want to, I will always hurt you." He turned, lowered his head, and walked away, a man defeated by himself.

CHAPTER 13

SEARCY STEPPED FROM THE AMERICAN AIRLINES JET and led Vaydon into the crowded O'Hare Airport.

They hadn't brought much with them—just a duffel bag apiece. Whatever else they needed could be found for a price. Even the items not available at the corner market, such as weapons and information. But really, they only needed one weapon to do what they came here to do, and it remained sheathed in a special compartment in Searcy's duffel. The ancient blade of his ancestors—a deadly weapon to those of his kind known as the Reaper's Blade, which had been in his family since eons before he was born. Now it belonged to him, and it had been far too long since the deadly alloy had tasted blood.

He and Vaydon made their way efficiently through O'Hare, noting a few vampires who gawked, gaped, and then backed away when they realized what they were. The color drained from their faces. Apparently, they had never seen Dacians and knew exactly who they were from the tales of the "ancient white-hairs" who used to rule the race. Searcy had to admit, their long, pale hair and silver eyes were a dead giveaway. Still, how nice to see his people respond with such fear and reverence. Even if King Bain sat on the throne, these vampires still knew who truly ruled the race, and before long, they would bow to him by rights, after he took his bloodline back to power and cast aside his usurper.

His first order of business after he ousted Bain would be to relocate the throne to a warmer climate.

"I hate the cold." Searcy stepped outside to a waiting line of cabs and minibusses.

Granted, for early spring, Chicago was unseasonably warm, but right off Lake Michigan at night, the wind had a bite.

Vaydon stood to his left, scanning the area. "This way."

Searcy fell into step with his son, and they eventually wended their way into a parking structure and projected themselves to the top floor.

Once there, Searcy tuned out all else, closed his eyes, opened his senses, and drew forth the marked scent of his prey, the two assassins who had led him to this cold, windy place.

He inhaled as if he could breathe in the whole city, then held his breath against his tongue. The filth, rotted fish on the shores of Lake Michigan, and the refuse sickened him, and he discarded anything foul, sifting further. Sex, drugs, even the essence of a freshly uncorked bottle of champagne somewhere nearby settled in. And then he weeded through the living beings, the smelly humans, even smellier drecks, and finally to the vampires, who always touched his senses last for some reason.

He exhaled, inhaled again, this time focused on those of his kind. The blood and venom of each vampire held a slightly different signature than all the rest. Ah, a mutant was about to be born in Chicago. How interesting that would be to see. But that would have to come after he caught his quarry. Further he filtered until finally…the weak, far away smell of his two little rabbits touched his senses.

Searcy opened his eyes. "They're here. But far away." He turned and found Vaydon standing in front of a tricked out Escalade with shiny chrome from wheel to wheel. "That our ride?"

Vaydon gave a half shrug. "Might as well travel in style while we're here."

The owner of such a fine vehicle probably thought he was being clever parking all the way up on the top floor of the parking garage, where only half the spaces were filled. Less chance up here of someone parking next to him and dinging his door.

Well, consider the door dinged. Because what was once someone else's was now his.

"Let's go."

Vaydon tapped the hood of the luxury SUV, and the doors unlocked and the alarm disengaged. Once inside, Vaydon started the engine with a thought, waited until Searcy was settled in, then backed out of the space, put the car in drive, turned up the radio, and pulled out.

Within days, that bitch and her sidekick, Mr. Clean, would be history. Then he would do a little sightseeing. Say, around the king's home.

GINA KEPT HER GAZE OUT THE PASSENGER WINDOW of Malek's truck. He hadn't said more than two words since they left AKM.

What had happened back in that parking garage?

In one swift moment, everything about him, as well as between them, had somersaulted and shifted as if they were two balls in a bingo tumbler. The back-to-back about-faces left her stunned, and she struggled to make sense of what had happened in all of two minutes. First, Malek had hated her, then loved her, and then sorrow so deep it had actually made *her* chest ache slackened Malek's whole body as he trudged away from her.

What had he meant by he would always hurt her? How? And better yet, why?

After pulling her feet from the cement, she had followed him to his truck, where he unlocked the passenger door, opened it, threw a shamed glance her way, and then walked around to the driver's side, climbed in, and started the engine.

Waves of hatred and animosity no longer pulsed off him like radio waves sending out a warning. Instead, a calm sadness seeped from every pore.

When she stepped into the cab, the heaviness in the air nearly knocked her out, and she'd had to open her window.

They stopped by the Trump to get her things and check out, and now they headed toward the suburbs in silent oppression.

The life seemed to have drained completely out of him, and she wasn't sure if she liked this new version of Malek better or worse than the angry one. At least when he'd been angry, he'd been alive. Now he just seemed…dead.

The thought made her heart suddenly race, and she feared she was on the verge of another panic attack.

No. No panic attacks. Not now. She glanced at Malek and her pulse instantly relaxed. How odd. She frowned and looked back out the window. She was damn lucky she hadn't fallen into a panic attack at AKM. In Miami, she would have had another attack by now, but since arriving in Chicago, she had only had the one brief episode that hadn't even been a full-on meltdown, more like a warning hiccup.

After several more minutes of silent driving, they pulled into the long, winding drive of what had to be Malek's home. He lived in a sprawling, single-story ranch style house on a wooded lot in what appeared to be an older, more established neighborhood.

His silence and despondent melancholy disturbed Gina, and she wasn't entirely sure of her safety in his care. Was he unstable? Suffering a form of psychosis? He had shown another side of himself in that parking garage, and now she was more confused than ever.

Cautiously sidestepping him, she entered his foyer and took a few steps into his living room. He barely had any furniture. A chair, a lamp, but not much else. The dining room table was loaded with books stacked at least a foot-and-a-half high.

"Looks like you need a bookcase," she said, trying to ease the tension.

Malek averted his gaze and shut the door as he pursed his lips. "Don't need one."

She turned back to all the books on the table and frowned.

There had to be at least four hundred paperbacks there. "Are you getting ready to make a donation to the local library?"

"No." He glowered, flipped his keys, and walked past her.

Welcome back, Mean Malek.

His arm grazed hers, and he paused just long enough to glance at her, his brown eyes firing with an emotion that was neither sorrow nor anger, but unadulterated, pure desire. The fiery heat blazed and charged the air between them with such force, her knees trembled and warmth flooded her belly. He swayed briefly, and his eyelids slid halfway closed.

Their connection was undeniable. Something was happening between them. Something strong and sexual. As much as she wanted to deny her attraction to him, she couldn't. In all honesty, she had wanted Malek from the first time she had seen him. Only now, as she was beginning to release Armand from her past, did she fully realize just how lonely she had been until she met Malek. He had awakened her, had given her a reason to live again. Truly live.

And clearly, one of the personalities playing peek-a-boo inside his head wanted her. The way he had stormed her in Micah's office and demonstrated possessive tendencies over her said as much, but now the purely masculine force within him confirmed it. No matter how hard he pushed her away, a part of him wanted to pull her close.

"Malek..." She reached for him.

For a moment, he closed his eyes, as if anticipating her touch, needing it, holding his breath. But as soon as the tips of her fingers grazed the healing laceration on his cheek, he jerked back and grimaced as if in pain. "No, Gina. I can't." He backed away, sad apology mixed with anger seeped into his expression.

Why was he fighting what his body clearly demanded? His behavior made no sense.

He disappeared into the kitchen as she looked around. Behind the dining room table, which was about to collapse under the weight of its heavy load, the wall sported a fist-sized hole, as if someone had recently mistaken it as Manny

Pacquiao and had gone for the knockout punch.

She looked over her shoulder at Malek's broad back and handsome profile as he stared out the window over the sink. The similarities between Malek and Armand continued to mount. Both liked to hit things. Although hitting a wall wasn't the same as popping a female in the nose, which Armand had enjoyed whenever he felt like throwing a fist, hitting inanimate objects was a gateway toward hitting living creatures. Her included.

Unfortunately, while the similarities piled up between Armand and Malek like the books on the table, so did her attraction toward Malek, which made no sense. Why would she feel enamored with someone who liked to hit? Did she have a thing for bad boys? If so, that was a bad recipe for future problems she didn't want or need. At some point, couldn't Malek just as easily hit her as the wall? Still, the attraction was irrefutable.

Maybe it was because Malek seemed more tortured than naturally aggressive. She got the feeling that he didn't like behaving this way…that he hated behaving like a Cretan, but that he couldn't help himself. Such an explanation made sense given the glimpse she'd seen of him a month ago, but what had happened to make him act like a monster with two faces? One that loved her and one that despised her.

He glanced out of the corners of his eyes in her direction. "Stop looking at me like that."

"Like what?"

"Like I'm some kind of puzzle you're trying to figure out." He squirmed and shifted, then turned and opened one of the cabinets. He grabbed a glass.

"Maybe if you'd stop acting like one, I wouldn't look at you like you are. But you have to admit, your behavior tonight has been erratic."

He flipped on the faucet and shoved the glass under the running water. "That's my business."

"Not when I seem to be your favorite target. Then it becomes my business, too."

He regarded her with a sideways glance as he pulled the

glass of water to his lips and drank. The heat in his eyes stirred desire low in her abdomen. Damn, but he was sexy. Too sexy for his own good. She needed to squelch that feeling right now if she knew what was good for her, though. Malek spelled nothing but trouble. Even so, at that moment, she wanted nothing more than to be the water in that glass.

Silence engulfed them as he downed the rest of the water and set the empty glass on the counter, never taking his eyes off her. For a moment, she thought he was going to come over and strip her naked and fuck her standing, but then he took a deep, shaky breath, tore his gaze away, and leaned against one arm as he propped his hand against the counter beside the empty glass. "Just...stay out of my way, Gina. Okay? It's for the best. Trust me."

The best for whom? Her? Him? And why did she suddenly want to go to him, slide her hands under his shirt, and show him how much pleasure they could give each other?

She quickly glanced away, swallowing hard as her breath deepened. This was nothing but his mating heat. Had to be. She couldn't be reacting to him this way on her own volition, because she chose not to. Mating heat was the only explanation. Right? So then, why didn't she feel the waves of heat pulsing off of him? Why did she feel like her desire was coming from within her, not *caused* by him?

Perhaps she should do what he said and stay away from him. Otherwise, she would do something in the next sixty seconds that would send them both into the nearest bed, and that was a path she didn't want to take. Not with any male, but especially not with Malek, who she feared would steal her heart if given a chance. And if he had her heart, he would wield the power to hurt her.

"Okay, so where's my room? I'll settle in and leave you alone." Yes, leaving him alone would be a super idea for the immediate future.

MALEK BARELY HELD HIMSELF TOGETHER. The last thing he

wanted was for her to leave him alone, but at the same time, it was *all* he wanted. Talk about a male divided. How do you reconcile two sides of yourself when they are so at odds with one another?

His skin still burned in the most wonderful way from where her fingertips had touched his cheek. He wanted her hands on him again. All over him. Everywhere. And he wanted his hands all over her.

God, being in this house with her during the lockdown of daylight was going to be hell.

"This way." He motioned toward the hall, and then led her to the end, where he opened the door to one of the spare rooms. "Bathroom's across the hall." He turned on the light inside the room then stepped back to let her go inside.

As she brushed past him, he closed his eyes and held his breath, doing all he could not to take hold of her and never let go. His dick wasn't helping, swelling inside his pants and aching for him to take what belonged to him.

I can't.

Yes, you can.

No. I won't do that to her.

Do what? She's your mate.

Fine. I get that now, okay. Happy? But I'm still mated to Carmen. I can't let Carmen go.

The Voice sighed, and Malek got the impression that it was covering its face and shaking its head in dismay.

True, he had crossed one hurdle, but he still hadn't crossed the other. Admitting that Gina was his mate was a moot point if he still couldn't let go of Carmen. And he didn't think he would ever be able to do that.

But knowing that didn't stop him from bringing his gaze up to watch Gina set her bags on the floor and turn around to look at him. The air crackled between them, aftershocks from the gentle caress just moments ago. That single touch had done something to her, too. He could smell it. Arousal wafted off of her like ambrosia, and his cock hiccupped.

This wasn't good. He needed to get away before he did something he would regret.

"If you need anything..." The words trailed off, and Malek could only shake his head as he dismissed himself and escaped down the hall, through the living room, and out the front door.

Out. He needed to get out and away from her. If he didn't, he would do just as Micah wanted him to do. He would fuck her silly into next week.

GINA HEARD THE FRONT DOOR OPEN AND CLOSE.

Had Malek just left? As in, left her alone in the house? What the hell?

She darted down the hall and threw open the front door in time to see the taillights of Malek's truck pull down the long, curving driving. Then his tires squealed as he hit the road and sped away.

What the fucking hell!

He was leaving her? Alone? In a strange house? *His* house? Under less than ideal circumstances? She had a pair of Dacian vampires gunning for her, she'd left her one ally — Trevor — back at AKM, had no idea where she was, and now the one guy who had brought her heart back to life and who was supposed to protect her had just abandoned her.

Her hands trembled.

Oh no.

Cold sweat broke down her back and across her forehead, and the trembling crept up her arms.

She slammed the door and locked it, which was a feat with her fingers suddenly shaking so violently she could hardly grip the bolt, then backed into the living room. Her whole body shivered, her teeth chattered, and the ache of fear welled inside her chest.

Oh God, oh God, oh God. No. Please don't let this happen to me now.

Her heart raced, bones rattled, and her chest constricted so she couldn't get a decent breath.

Pant-gasp-pant.

Shit. She couldn't breathe.

Bile rose in her throat, and nausea stabbed her belly as pain speared her chest. She was going to be sick. Turning on her heel, she sped toward the hall and into the bathroom, landing on her knees in front of the toilet just in time.

After what felt like an hour of retching, she fell back against the wall, and then rolled to the floor.

Not since this morning had she suffered a panic attack, even though she'd had every reason to have one with all the shit that happened at AKM. All day, she had kept her fear and anxiety at bay. She hadn't succumbed to the stampede of distress that had threatened her off and on for hours. The reprieve had been enough to make her think she was getting better, that she was somehow gaining control over the anxiety-induced invasions…that revealing her past with Armand had taken some of the edge off. She had thought that revealing and releasing her demons where that bastard was concerned would put an end to this shit. What was she missing? Hell, she had even come face-to-face with Lakota and lived. And even though she still held enormous guilt over what she had done to Sev, he had sat by her side tonight and protected her from his father as if he held no malice whatsoever against her. Just that simple gesture alone had gone miles to ease her guilt. Clearly, she had made big strides today, so why, after reclaiming some control over her life, was she now doubled over on Malek's bathroom floor, clutching her chest, with tears streaming her face, begging God to help her? Why was she suffering the worst panic attack she'd had yet?

Please, make it stop. Please, please, God. What more do I need to do?

She rolled to her hands and knees as pain stabbed her gut again, twisting inside her, stealing the rest of her breath.

If only Malek were here, everything would be fine. Everything would be—

Her whole body froze, and she gasped as if sucker punched. He was the answer. Malek was the key, but not in the way she had thought. She had thought that her panic attacks were a result of fear or a response to his declaration that he had mated her. That he was somehow the cause... that the thought he had mated her was the reason for them. But no. He wasn't the cause. He was the *solution*. That's what her body had been trying to tell her all this time—what it had been telling her last night after her failure with Searcy and Vaydon. Malek really *was* the solution. Her soul had chosen his, too, and the panic attacks were her body's way of telling her she needed him. That she had to return so she could be with him.

And hadn't this morning's panic attack struck immediately after she considered not taking Trevor's advice. When she had almost decided not to give Malek a chance. Her body's violent reaction had been telling her then that any thought against joining Malek wouldn't be tolerated.

Female vampires formed mating bonds to their mates just as males did, but their connections were usually much weaker, which was how they survived if they lost their mates. But once in a while, a female bonded more powerfully to her mate...to the extent that his absence created physical discomfort. That's what was happening to her. She was in a female suffering. Not only had she mated Malek, but she had connected to him on a deeper level than most females did to their mates. The fact she had tried to reject him for weeks had only made her suffering worse.

It all made sense now. Her debilitating panic attacks had started after she left Chicago—after she had left Malek. And not because he had mated her, but because *she* had mated *him*...because she needed him...loved him...yearned for him. He was her protector in every way. Hadn't she been okay the entire time she was around him? Even when her nerves were frayed and stripped bare—when she would have succumbed to her fear and fallen prey to anxiety under such stimuli only days ago—she had been okay as long as Malek was with her. It hadn't mattered that he had treated her like shit or that he seemed to be torn over his feelings for her. As long as he was with her, she was fine, but as soon as he was gone, her fear steamrolled back and unleashed with retroactive fury, ambushing her like a shark in chum-filled waters to leave her in a spent heap on his bathroom floor.

Now that she realized the truth, her chest eased, and she rolled to her back. For the second time tonight, she breathed more easily than she had in weeks. Earlier, in Malek's arms, she had taken her first real breath in forever, and now she felt like she'd come up from underwater. What a relief to be able to breathe again. Really breathe. Her lungs expanded to full capacity, and the tension that had set up shop in her neck vanished. And just like that, the panic subsided. The real trigger of her panic and anxiety was revealed, and now that she acknowledged the truth, it was as if a boulder lifted off her body, and she could rise again.

Her heart, body, and soul had fallen in love with Malek during the days he had watched over her in her cell, but she had been too guarded to see the truth. Just as he had mated her, she had, in her own way, mated him. Deep down, she had known that he was the one who could show her how to love again, but her mind had gotten in the way and failed to acknowledge her feelings and instead disguised them as fear and confusion, reminding her of all that Armand had done and all the pain he had caused.

Out of nowhere, harsh sobs burst from her chest. Tears flowed like rivers down the sides of her face as she stared up at the ceiling. The purge was on. Adrenaline broke inside her blood like a fever, and weeks of restrained emotions spilled from her in an exuberant rush, finally set free.

She laughed even as she sobbed, and she slapped her hands over her face and rubbed away the tears even as more replaced them. The release cleansed her and set her heart free, and each passing moment pushed her more fully into awareness.

She needed Malek. She needed him more than she needed food and water. He was her savior — the warrior who would guard her heart and save her even from herself.

Screw rationale. To hell with Armand's memory. And to hell with rejecting Malek as her mate. He belonged to her, goddamn it. He was hers, and she was his. She wanted him, and as soon as he returned home, she would tell him so. She would force him to face her and finish what he'd started back in her cell all those weeks ago, because now, more than ever, it was clear. She couldn't live without him. Not one more night, one more hour, or even one more minute.

Malek was the one.

CHAPTER 14

MALEK WAS CLOSE TO HIS BREAKING POINT. He had known for days that something eventually had to give, because he couldn't continue living like he was. Well, the time had come. Now what?

What do I do?

This time The Voice didn't answer. But really, what could it say that hadn't already been said a hundred times?

For all the progress he had made tonight by accepting that Gina was, in fact, his mate, it still felt like he had taken two giant steps back.

He had spent the past half-hour driving around the city, no destination in mind, not sure where he would end up until he looked up and realized where he had parked his truck. Four Alarm, the club where his team used to spend all their time off before Micah had mated Sam, Sev and Ari had mated each other, and before Io had found a mate in Princess Miriam. Now, he was the only one who seemed to spend time at Four Alarm on a regular basis, which was probably for the best given what he now came here for. There was no need for his teammates to witness how far he had fallen.

And wasn't it ironic that of all the places his subconscious could have taken him tonight, it took him here? How pathetic was he that he had nowhere better to go but to the place where he could get shit-faced drunk and buy whores?

He didn't want to go inside, but he didn't want to go home, either. Going home meant facing Gina, and facing Gina meant she would be in his bed within minutes of him walking through the door. And that would only bring them both more pain. With nowhere else to go, he pulled himself out of his truck and reluctantly trudged across the street and pulled open the door.

The doorman gave him a nod. "Full house tonight," he said.

What the doorman meant was that there were plenty of working girls there to choose from. Malek had built such a reputation for himself in the last few weeks that he couldn't even walk into the place without the doorman thinking he was there for anything but the hookers. Was this the kind of mate Gina deserved? Hell no. He was doing her a favor by skipping out. One day she would see that if she didn't already, and she would be grateful he was gone.

"Thanks." He passed through and mentally encouraged the humans sitting at his table to vacate the premises so he could sit at his usual post.

Within minutes, a waitress brought him a bottle of whiskey and a glass. His usual as of late.

How telling that the waitresses all knew what he drank without even having to ask.

Still, he accepted the bottle and handed over a bill. "Keep the change." Then he poured himself a glass, then another, and another, ready to drown himself. Maybe if he drank himself into a stupor, he wouldn't have enough strength or coordination left to steal Gina away to his bedroom when he got home. If he made it home at all.

LORENA ENTERED FOUR ALARM, ready to get her freak on with the first rough and tough male she could find. After taking a seat at a table by the dance floor and ordering a Disaronno, she settled back and took a quick inventory of the meat market. Lots of wimps — guys who thought they were tough, but who merely played wolves in sheep's clothing. The kind who, if they didn't care so much about styling their hair, manscaping their balls, and getting manicures, might have a set large enough to at least satisfy her. As it was, they were too pretty-pretty for her tastes.

She needed a rugged man. One who got off on giving pain as much as she got off on receiving it. A man who—

Well, well. What have we here?

Across the dance floor, sitting at the same corner table he had been at the first time she saw him and looking just as deadly delicious and ready for action, Malek was downing whiskey like he needed an IV of the stuff.

How fortunate was this?

Good for her she was dressed to impress in four-inch stilettos, skintight leather leggings, and a bustier that pushed her breasts into healthy swells and was cut so low as to barely cover her nipples. She fluffed her wavy, mahogany hair, slid off her leather jacket, and set her sights on her target. No one would take him from her tonight.

She grabbed her drink, slid out of her seat, and strolled around the dance floor, gliding her hand over the railing that encircled a cove of tables. Red, blue, and purple lights strobed the darkness, and as she neared Malek's table, his gaze lifted and met hers as if drawn to her.

She licked her lips and smiled as she closed the last few feet between them. "Hi there." She set her drink on the table and eased onto the red, leather seat beside him.

His drunken gaze swiveled and danced over her. Then he turned toward his dry glass and reached for the half-empty bottle of cheap whiskey. But his hand merely grazed the side, and he nearly tipped the bottle over.

"Here, let me." She picked up the bottle and poured him another glass, then lifted the glass to his lips. "This is what you want, isn't it?"

He blinked and one eyebrow ticked into a slight frown, but he nodded anyway and tilted his head back, opening his mouth as she poured the amber liquid down his throat.

He came back up, and his head bobbed left to right, then back again as he turned toward her. "Who are you?" He said it like he didn't really care about the answer.

She poured him another drink. "I'm Lorena. And I know

aaalll about you. Malek." She abandoned the glass, reached into his lap, and unzipped his fly.

Malek looked down as she slid her hand inside his pants, and his head bobbed as if he wasn't in full control of his reflexes. Her fingers encircled his impressively hard cock, which pulsed against her touch. He made a noise deep in his throat that sounded both like relief and pain, almost sad, as if he was on the verge of grief.

"You need me tonight, Malek." She leaned closer and stroked him, mistaking his moan as one of unspent need. "I'll take good care of you. And you can take good care of me." She drew her tongue up the side of his neck to his ear. "I like it rough. Very rough. And I hear that's how you give it."

He rolled his head toward her, and she stole a lingering kiss. One he didn't return, but no doubt only because he was so drunk. But that was okay. She didn't want him for his mouth. Well, maybe not entirely for his mouth.

"Home," he said. "I need to go home." He blinked heavily, his words slurred. "Gina. I need to go home."

Okay, so the guy couldn't get her name right. Gina. Lorena. It was a common mistake. But again, whether he remembered her name now or never, she didn't care. She had need of only one thing: his cock inside her and his hands around her throat as he gave her rough, hard, bruising sex that would leave her nearly broken and exhausted.

"Home it is," she said, pulling her hand out of his pants so she could zip him up. "Let's go."

Malek pushed past her and staggered as he stood up.

"Come on. I'll get us a cab." She hooked her arm around his and pressed in close.

Outside, she hailed a cab and maneuvered Malek into the back.

"Where to?" the cabbie asked.

"Home," Malek said.

"Like that helps." The cabbie rolled his eyes.

She looked at Malek, who only stared back as if she were some stranger. She couldn't take him to her place. She had too many items laying around that could incriminate her, and she couldn't risk letting an enforcer, even one as scrumptious as Malek, discover where her true allegiance lay. But he wasn't volunteering his address, so this could get tricky.

"I need an address," the cabbie said, sounding impatient.

"Hold on a sec," she told him, and began fishing around in Malek's pockets for his ID. Even vampires had to have ID to fit into the human world.

Once she found his wallet, she flipped it open and rattled off his address to the driver.

"If he pukes in my cab, he's going to pay the cleaning bill."

"He won't puke," she said, getting irritated with the guy. "Will you, baby?" She brushed her hand over Maleks' cheek, her gaze lingering on a partially healed gash that looked fresh. He must have been in a skirmish within the past hour. If the wound was older than that, it would have healed by now. Unless he was cranking a weakened system, which seemed possible enough with his gaunt, sallow features, now that she got a closer look.

Malek just stared at her then turned to look out the window.

"He won't puke," she said again to the driver. "Now, go." She was eager to get the party started with her prize.

The driver put the cab in gear and drove away from the club.

This was what she had been waiting for. A good dose of hardcore Malek. And now she was going to get it.

CHAPTER 15

LAKOTA ENTERED THE LOCKER ROOM of the training center behind Micah and tossed his filthy jacket over one of the benches. They all smelled like smoke. Not cigarette smoke, but rather the kind from a structure fire. The kind of smoke that stuck to your skin and hair — your very DNA — for days, clinging to every hair follicle and laying waste to the insides of your lungs. Good thing he wasn't human, or he would never breathe normally again.

"Motherfucking arsonist." Micah unlocked his locker and swung the door open with a clang.

Trevor, covered in soot, wandered in behind Severin. The guy was a mess. "You get this shit a lot in Chicago?"

Micah growled. "Quit bitching, Trev."

Lakota stared at his son as he wandered past without glancing at him. From behind, Lakota heard a faucet turn on. He turned and watched Trevor spit in a sink and rinse his mouth out. He paid the newcomer a split second of attention, and then glanced back at his son. Sev looked worse for wear, his face covered in soot just like the rest of them, but he wasn't a puss like that Trevor guy. He took the vile taste of smoke in stride, like a warrior.

Pride swelled inside Lakota's chest. That was his son. He had grown up to be a strong fighter and an even stronger asset to his team. Lakota only wished he could take credit for Sev's fortitude, but he had given up that right from the start, before Sev was even conceived.

He lowered his head and turned toward his locker.

After saying sayonara to Gina and Malek earlier, he and

Micah had teamed up to hunt down information on who was kidnapping and selling vampires to Bishop while Trevor and Sev struck out to see what they could find out about the Dacians.

They hadn't been out long when a call came in about a potential pre-mutant on the South Side, so he and Micah hightailed it that direction, only to be rerouted when word of a structure fire with entrapment came in. Micah had really wanted to go after the potential mutant, because with Dacians possibly prowling around Chicago, and drecks who were kidnapping vampires for lab experiments, the last thing they needed was a trifecta of trouble, especially one that included a mutant, the deadliest creature known to vampires aside from a mated male without his mate.

But members of Stryker's team had been closer to the mutant's location, and he and Micah had been closer to the fire, so decision made. It was fire patrol for them.

Micah pulled a towel and change of clothes out of his locker. He kicked off his boots and yanked his shirt over his head. "Fuck this shit. I'm taking a shower, finishing up some paperwork, and going home to bury myself in my mate for the next six hours. I've been here nearly three days straight."

Lakota sat down and glanced at Severin, who was unusually quiet.

Trevor took off his boots. "Anyone got a spare shirt and some shorts I can wear until I can get up to my room?"

Micah nodded. "Yeah. Follow me. We keep spares in back."

The two disappeared and their jabbering grew quieter as they walked away.

Lakota grabbed his towel out of his locker and stood back up. "How's things with you and Ari?"

Sev stiffened and grabbed his own towel. "Good."

"You happy?"

Sev looked his direction, but kept his gaze averted. "Yeah. We're happy."

Lakota nodded. It was good that Sev was happy. He deserved it, especially after the hell he had put that kid through by being such a bastard, absentee father all his life.

If only he could go back in time and do things differently. He wanted like hell to fix all the trouble and heartache he had caused, but it wasn't entirely his choice. Sev still avoided him when they weren't being forced together like they were now, and tonight was the most Sev had talked to him since he reentered his life, which wasn't saying much since he'd said only four words.

"I'm glad, son. I mean Sev. Sorry." Severin didn't like when he called him son, but it was so damn hard not to.

"No, that's okay." Sev waved his hand and sighed, then finally turned and met Lakota's gaze.

Shit, but sometimes it felt like he was looking in a mirror when he looked at Severin.

Lakota took a step toward the showers and shook his head. "No. I know you don't like it."

"Dad." Sev sounded impatient. Looked it, too, with his head cocked to one side and one eyebrow up.

But that wasn't what nearly caused Lakota to trip on thin air. Severin had called him Dad.

"Don't look so surprised," Sev said, as if reading his mind. "You are my dad, aren't you?"

Was this some kind of joke? Was he dreaming? He swore to God that if someone jumped out and shouted, "April Fool's Day," right now, he would kill them.

"Sure, I'm your father, but until now I didn't...you were...I thought..." Well, hell's bells, he was lost for words.

Sev held up his hand, saving him from tripping further over his tongue. "Look, I'm tired of hating you. It's exhausting, and I just want to get on with my life. And since you seem to be so keen on being part of it..." He took a deep breath and shook his head once. "What I'm saying is that I can see you're making an effort...*Dad*. Okay? And Arion and I have been talking, which has made me think, and..." He paused and stood. "Look, I'm not saying it'll be easy, and I'm not saying I'm crazy about the idea, but I'm willing to work on it."

This was more than Lakota could ever have hoped for, and it came as such a shock that he didn't know what to say.

Once again, Sev saved him. "On one condition. About Gina…"

Lakota bristled. Mood broken. "What about her?"

Sev held up his hands and gently arched one eyebrow. "I just want you to be nice to her."

"Nice to her? She tried to kill you, Sev."

Sev took an aggressive step toward him. "And I forgave her." The scowl on Sev's face showed how close he was to reverting back to the old, standoffish Severin with a cursory *fuck off* his way. "You weren't involved in what happened. You don't know the circumstances. She thought she was doing the right thing, and I don't blame her. I'd have done the same thing in her shoes. From her perspective, she was doing what she felt needed to be done." Sev huffed and began to walk away, but then stopped. "You should know better than anyone that a person can make mistakes and change their stripes. I mean, you *are* the person who raped my mother and made me a bastard, and now you claim to have changed. Or is that all just an act, *Dad*? Or should I go back to calling you Lakota? Or not talking to you at all? Because I can easily do that. No sweat off my balls." Sev fixed him with a deadly glare.

Point taken. Lakota still had much about his past to atone for, especially where Sev was concerned. He frowned back his emotions and looked away as heat flushed his face and a dull ache echoed deep inside his chest. "I'm sorry. You're right. I don't know the whole story."

Sev sighed. "I'm willing to give you a chance to make things right with me as long as you give Gina the same consideration, but I want to know Gina's safe around you."

Was Gina's safety that important to Sev that all it would take was him refusing to play nice with her to push Sev away again? He didn't want that. Even though Gina had tried to take his son from him, and she had trampled all over his heart in the process, he couldn't lose Severin over what had happened. Sev needed to know Gina would be safe around him. End of story. Lakota wouldn't lose this opportunity to be a part of Sev's life. Nothing was more important than that.

"Fine, Sev. You have my word. I won't hurt her."

Severin relaxed. "Thank you."

Really, how could Lakota not do what Severin asked? This was more of an opportunity to make amends with his son than he dreamed he would get. So, if excusing the actions and behavior of Sev's would-be assassin was part of what it took to get his son back, so be it. He would kiss her ass if that was what it took.

Micah reappeared with Trevor and cast him a questionable glance. "I really don't want to know what you two were just talking about, do I?"

Obviously, Micah had seen that last bit of his thoughts. He would need to get used to being around Micah with that mind probe shit of his.

He shook his head. "No. You don't. And with that, I'm taking a shower." He snagged his towel.

Sev joined him, and they walked into the shower room together. A first.

"You know, it wasn't just Arion who convinced me I should give you a break."

Lakota stopped outside one of the shower stalls and reached in to turn on the water.

Sev dropped his towel and turned on the next shower over. "Yeah, Mom wanted me to be nice to you, too."

Felice? She had gotten involved? "Oh?"

Sev nodded. "It was pretty important to her."

That made him smile. "How is your mom?"

Sev shook his head and looked away with a low growl that sounded more forced than natural. "Don't push your luck. *Dad.*" Then he paused and looked back at him with a half-smile. "You just be nice to Gina and you'll score major Brownie points with me. What she did to me wasn't her fault. Keep that in mind when you feel more inclined to stab her than help her fit in here. Understood?"

Sev fixed him with an icy stare that would have made lesser men tremble in fear, but it made Lakota proud.

"Like I said, you have my word."

Sev fought back a grin and as he stepped into his shower

stall. "Get cleaned up, old man. You stink."

As the shower curtain closed behind Sev, Lakota cleared the emotion from his throat. Not much got to Lakota, but tears stung his eyes. He wouldn't let them fall, though. He was too tough for that.

Micah and Trevor strolled in a minute later.

"What the fuck. Are you crying?" Micah said.

"Fuck you. No." Lakota rubbed his palm over his filthy face. "Fucking fire irritated my eyes. They sting like a bitch."

"Uh-huh."

A tight chuckle came from Sev's stall.

Lakota swiped his shower curtain aside and stepped into the stream of hot water. "Shut up, Micah. You too...*son*."

Lakota picked up his soap, ignoring the laughter coming from Micah, Severin, and that newbie, Trevor. Let them laugh at him. He didn't care. Because for the first time Sev had called him Dad.

And that was all that mattered.

CHAPTER 16

THE FEMALE WAS GLUED TO MALEK'S SIDE as he unlocked the door. Lorena, she said her name was.

Fine. If she wanted to play, he would play, because he sure couldn't dip into what he really wanted, which was a long, luxurious soak inside an ocean called Gina. And his balls ached so badly he needed to find release somehow.

When Lorena first came to his table at Four Alarm and introduced her hand to his dick, he had wanted no part of her. All he wanted then was Gina. His mind had been overflowing with thoughts of her.

And now, an instant after pushing open the door, Gina's scent rushed forward, flooded him, drenched him in warmth so soothing, he almost changed his mind about bringing Lorena inside. The sound of the shower in the spare bathroom told him Gina was in there, naked, water spilling over her pristine skin. He imagined his fingertips tracing the trails of water down her breasts, over her nipples. What did her nipples look like? Were they large or small? Dark or light?

"Oh, you have company?" Lorena sniffed the air and pushed up beside him, breaking him away from his fantasy before he could act on it.

"A coworker." *My mate.* He shut the door and shoved his keys in his pocket, feeling surer on his feet now that he was home and had a whiff of the female who ensnared half his heart.

"Mmm, will she join us?" Lorena pawed her hands up his chest, and her red lips curved into a coy grin.

Just the thought of introducing Gina to his debasement was enough to spark his anger and put full life back in his veins. "No." He glared at Lorena, whose eyes lit with lust against his reawakened emotional storm.

"Excellent. Because I don't feel like sharing." She took his hand and lifted it to her throat, opened his fist, and positioned his fingers around the slender column of flesh. "Now..." She grinned, and her gaze grew dark. "Hurt. Me."

Malek stared into her light brown eyes. But it was Gina's scent that invaded him. The shower beckoned, but he couldn't relent. Gina deserved better, and this whore deserved nothing. Which was really quite perfect, because he had nothing left to give. To anyone. All he had was pain and suffering, and if this bitch wanted that, she was welcome to it.

He gazed down on his hand around Lorena's throat. It looked good there, and he slowly lifted his fingers and closed them again in a tighter grip.

Lorena moaned quietly and her eyelids drooped closed. "Yes."

If he went to Gina, he would only hurt her. Gina meant something to him. Lorena, on the other hand, meant nothing. She *was* nothing. Just a vessel—a receptacle he could fill without harming Carmen's memory in the same way accepting Gina as his mate would harm everyone involved.

The difference was that Lorena wanted him to hurt her. He could give her the physical torture she seemed to crave, and so much the better, because that was exactly what he wanted to give to himself. By hurting Lorena, he killed two birds with one stone.

His gaze lifted to her face...to her eager expression of anticipation.

"Hurt me, Malek," she said on a low whisper.

She got off on the pain. He could use her as his outlet, pour all his suffering out on her, and she would never complain.

"You want pain?" he said, leaning down until his nose touched hers.

She nodded, practically panting. "Yes."

Her acrid arousal, sour and vile, fed his carnal debasement even more. Lorena was all he was worthy of now. Someone as nasty and decrepit as he was. Weren't they just perfect for one another?

"You don't know pain."

She closed her hand over his, still around her throat, and squeezed. "Then show me."

Oh, he would show her all right. He would take out all his frustration on her. If she wanted to be hurt, he would hurt her, because right now, all he was, was misery, suffering, sorrow, and distress. He had reached his final breaking point. Game over. His white flag flew in surrender. He could no longer fight himself. He wanted Gina but had no future with her. He still loved Carmen, but she was dead. So it was time to embrace the future he *did* have.

He swung Lorena around and shoved her toward the kitchen. The scent of her arousal stung deep, hard at his soul, and he prowled after her.

"I'll show you pain, Lorena." He pointed to the door at the back of the kitchen. "Downstairs. Now."

She panted and grasped the doorknob, threw the door open, and backed down the stairs, keeping her lust-filled gaze on his as he stalked after her.

Yes, whores like Lorena were his future. They were all he had left.

GINA HAD BEEN STANDING UNDER THE WATER for the last twenty minutes. The reality that she was ready to move forward rather than live in the painful past had left a smile on her face for the first time in forever.

She would never understand the phenomenon known as mating, or the tremendous power it held over those of her kind. The call to mate affected each vampire differently, but all to one end. To keep the race alive and thriving. Why she had tethered to Malek more strongly than other females bonded to their mates was a mystery. All she knew was that she had and that she was now a changed female. No longer was she broken and damaged. In fact, she had never felt more whole.

After another five minutes, she shut off the water, dried herself, and got dressed as she worked through how she would explain to Malek what had happened. Would she even need to explain? Perhaps she would just show him.

She grinned affectionately at the idea of surprising him in his bed. There was no way he would turn her away. As a mated male, he wouldn't be able to resist that kind of temptation.

Her mind was in midfantasy when the hair on the back of her neck bristled and she caught a whiff of—

What the hell?

With her senses leaping to high alert and sharp as razors, she yanked open the door and stuck her head into the hall. Was there a female on the premises? A foul, nasty...*aroused* female? And were those sounds coming from behind the door in the kitchen the sounds of...*sex?* Hard, body bruising sex?

Oh bitch, no way.

Her mated side lit up like a solar flare. Who did he think he was to give to another what belonged to her? This shit wasn't going to happen. Not now. She had finally realized what had been sending her head into the commode for weeks—that Malek was her life partner—and she refused to share him now that her invisible hooks had sunk in. Like she was going into battle, she charged through the kitchen, ready to kick some bitch ass. That was her male. *Hers!* If Malek was going to fuck anyone, it was going to be her, damn it! Not some secondhand slut. Not some stank ass, gum-on-the-bottom-of-her-shoe piece of trash.

She threw the door open and tore down the stairs into what had to be Malek's bedroom. From behind the door across the room, the sounds of sex grew louder.

"Harder. Fuck me harder!" the bitch said.

From the sound of something hard hitting the wall, followed by glass breaking and the intense way she grunted and screamed, "Yes!" it sounded like Malek had given the little home wrecker exactly what she asked for.

Little bitch! That was her mate in there!

Gina leaped from the foot of the stairs and landed in front of the bathroom door a split second before her booted foot shattered the damn thing off its hinges.

Malek had the bitch on the marble counter next to the sink, one hand around her throat, his pants around his ankles and hers on the floor. Her legs were over his shoulders, and the mirror behind her head was shattered. Shards of glass lay scattered around them. As soon as Gina busted in, their eyes swung toward her.

Knife meet heart.

"Gina!" Malek shot backward and struggled to pull up his pants while the female on the counter shrieked in protest.

Without wasting a second, Gina was on her. *What lovely hair you have. All the better to use as a handle and toss you across the room with.* She grabbed a handful of brunette waves and threw the bitch into the bedroom with the ease of a finger flicking a piece of lint off her blouse.

Ah, the power of unleashed mated aggression. It did a body good.

Before the cunt could stop rolling and get her bearings, Gina jumped on her, held her down with one hand, and used the bitch's face as if it were concrete and her fist were a jackhammer.

Bash! Bash! Bash!

She was just getting into a nice rhythm when arms wrapped around her and yanked her off.

Malek!

She elbowed him in the gut, swung around as he dropped her, and hissed at him. He might be her mate, but right now she was beyond pissed at what he had done. What was he thinking? His dick was hers and hers alone. If he was going to stick it anywhere, it was going to be inside her, not some random slut.

She was tackled from behind and landed face-first on the carpet, and the fight was on again. She grappled with the bitch and rolled over just in time to be coldcocked in the cheek.

"Stop, Lorena!" Malek grabbed her arm as she pulled it back to hit Gina again.

Lorena kicked him and sent him stumbling backward.

"Get off me, you bitch!" Gina freed one leg and shoved her heel against Lorena's chin until she fell backward. Then Gina was on her again.

She clawed, slapped, and pounded, wild with adrenaline and mated fury.

"Gina! No!" Malek dragged her off the half-naked bitch on the floor. "This is my fault, not hers!"

Gina didn't want to hear it. She was too pissed off. "Let me go! Get off me!" She flailed and broke free then spun around. Her fist shot out and cracked Malek in the chin. "You bastard! How dare you!"

Lorena jumped up and was about to tackle her again when Malek's arm shot out and caught her by the waist. "No!"

Gina glared at the two of them. She was angry, hurt, and pissed. Malek was just like Armand. Maybe he hadn't hit her, but his actions hurt nonetheless. He had left her alone to go God-knows-where, and then brought back this filthy tramp and fucked her right in front of her nose.

"Why?" Her eyes pleaded with him for answers, but he only stared back, speechless.

Malek hadn't laid a finger on her, and yet what he had done caused her more pain than any physical abuse Armand had ever subjected her to.

"Face it," Lorena said with a satisfied smirk. "He just doesn't want you."

Gina swatted her across the cheek, leaving bloody streaks where her nails broke the skin. "Bitch!"

"Sticks and stones, sweetheart." Lorena thrashed and tried to break out of Malek's hold, but he yanked her away.

What? Was he protecting Lorena? From her? Shouldn't it be the other way around? Shouldn't he be defending her honor instead of Lorena's?

Gina looked between them, disgusted and mentally shredded. "I hope you both rot in hell." She slapped Lorena again, hard enough to leave welts on her other cheek, and shot a glare so lethal at Malek it was a wonder he didn't go up in flames. Then she charged up the stairs two-at-a-time.

She needed to get out of there. No way would she stay there tonight after this. No fucking way.

Making sure her phone was in her pocket, Gina hit the front door and bolted as Lorena screamed a stream of profanities after her.

MALEK STRUGGLED TO PUSH LORENA back into the bathroom. She was livid, her body thrashing like she was a trapped wild animal.

"Get dressed." He shoved her away from him and turned for the stairs to go after Gina.

With a screech of protest, Lorena latched onto his arm and pulled him back around. "Finish what you started!"

"No!" He jerked his arm from her grasp and frowned at the crazed expression on Lorena's face. She looked almost manic. Not good.

"The bitch is gone. I'm here." She clapped her hand on her chest. "You owe me."

"I owe you nothing! Now get dressed and get out!" He hurried toward the stairs, but Lorena shrieked and jumped him from behind.

They fell to the floor. The bitch was a frenzy of physical strength, on the brink of violence as she struggled against Malek's defenses to unfasten his pants and take what he no longer wanted to give. At least not to her.

"I said NO!" He gripped her wrists and flung her to the side, but the bitch wouldn't give up. She rallied and attacked him again as he pushed off the floor and tried to scurry away, but she had hold of his ankle.

Goddamn! What had he gotten himself into with this one? He was wasting precious time. Gina was getting away. Not that she would forgive him if he went after her. What he had done was unforgiveable. He had taken another female in front of her—*his mate*. Damn him!

But this was what she could expect as his mate. Constant pain. A never ending supply of suffering as he struggled against his nature to pull and push her away. This was why she needed someone better.

Lorena leaped onto his back as he rolled and scrambled to get away. "You will finish me, Malek!"

For the love of God! What was this bitch's problem?

"Finish me!" She clung to him as he pushed to his feet, her arms and legs wrapped around him.

Enough! This shit was so done and over.

"I don't want you, bitch!" He grabbed her arms, bent forward, and flung her to the floor.

The whack-o actually moaned as if in pleasure. What the hell? But as quickly as she seemed to get off on the physical aggression, her eyes shot open, and she glared up at him. "What did you say?"

The furious atmosphere suddenly froze as if she couldn't believe he was rejecting her and needed a moment to gather her wits.

"You heard me." Malek turned, out of breath, and walked toward his dresser. When he glanced back at her, she rolled to her feet and stood. "I don't want you, Lorena. Now get dressed and get the fuck out."

Daggers shot from her eyes and she bared her fangs. "You asshole." She started for him.

He grabbed his gun out of the top drawer of his dresser and, within a fraction of a second, pointed it at her. That put her brakes on.

"Get. The fuck. Out!" Bringing this one home had been an epic fail on fifty different levels.

For several seconds, the two stood at a stalemate, and then Lorena wiped a streak of blood off her face, turned, stormed into the bathroom for her pants and boots, and got dressed in record time. She was still snapping buttons into place as she marched back into the bedroom.

"You'll pay for this." She whipped her jacket off the back of a nearby chair and shoved her arms through the sleeves. "So help me, you'll pay."

"Yeah, yeah. Goody for you. Now leave." Malek still had the gun trained on her.

Lorena spun and stomped up the stairs and out of his life. Hopefully forever.

He lowered the gun and sank to the bed, head hung. A dull ache set up house behind his sternum, and he rubbed his thumb up and down to try and ease the pain, to no avail.

What a mess he had made of things. Gina was gone, and maybe that was for the best. He should go after her, but what could he do or say to make things right with her? After what he had just done—which would be par for the course if they were together—there was no way she would forgive him.

Micah was going to be pissed, but so what. Micah could get in line, because it seemed that everyone Malek came in contact with lately ended up pissed off at him.

Damn it, but he just wanted the agony to end. He couldn't keep on like this.

GINA WAS TOO AGITATED to simply poof herself away from Malek's house, but her adrenaline needed an outlet, anyway, so she took off at Olympic record speed. Usain Bolt had nothing on her.

After running God knew how many miles in only a few minutes, her legs gave out and she collapsed on her knees at the side of the road. Her adrenaline high was crashing, and now her emotions tore through her. Daggers of ice lanced her heart. She would never be free, would she? First, Armand had held her captive and stripped away her soul, her very essence. And now she was in love with a male who would never love her back. Malek would never give himself to her, which meant she would never truly be healed. She was destined to go through life a prisoner of her past, with no hope for the future.

She dug her phone out of her pocket and punched up Trevor's number. He could come and get her, and they could leave. Go somewhere else. Anywhere but here.

That's when her hands started to tremble.

Shit. Not again.

Trevor's mobile starting chiming from the shelf in the locker as he tossed his wet towel in a bin against the wall. Micah sat a couple of feet away and was already half dressed. He hadn't even bothered to dry off. The guy really was eager to get home to his mate, and it showed by how quickly he yanked his sweater over his head.

Trevor fished his phone from the locker and frowned at the ID.

"Gina? Hey."

Micah's head snapped around, and his eyes narrowed.

"I need you to come and get me." She sounded agitated. Something wasn't right.

He instantly froze, on alert. "What's wrong? Where are you?"

"Side of the road. Two or three miles from Malek's house, give or take."

"What happened? Are you okay?"

"I don't want to talk about it. Just track my phone's GPS and come and get me. And hurry. Please." She sounded off.

"It's not Searcy or Vaydon, is it?" Shit! If they had found her, it was all over.

"No. Just come and get me. And don't tell Micah."

Trevor glanced over just as Micah frowned and stood up. He didn't look pleased. Whatever talents Micah had, they obviously included stealth mindreading.

"Too late," he said.

Silence answered him on the phone. Then she said, "Shit. He's right there, isn't he?"

Micah snagged the phone out of his hand. "Yes, I'm right here. Where are you?" Micah didn't sound happy.

After a couple of seconds, he said, "Where the hell is Malek?"

Another pause. "Stay put. I'll be right there. I'll find you. No.

Don't argue with me. I'll be there in less than five minutes." He handed the phone back to Trevor, sat back down on the bench, and yanked on his socks, grumbling under his breath about Malek and how "that bastard had better not have kept me from my mate today."

Trevor turned away and pulled the phone to his ear. "You still want me to come?"

"No," Micah said before Gina could answer. "You stay here."

He turned around to find Micah strapping on a pair of knives that would have made both Rambo and Crocodile Dundee envious.

"But..." Gina was his friend. He wanted to help.

Micah nabbed a Sig from his locker and holstered it under his arm, then turned intense, navy eyes on him. "I'll get her. You stay here. With your Dacian friends in town, I don't want to get stuck out there with both of you. She's bait enough."

Trevor spoke into his phone. "Did you get that?"

"Yes, I got it." Gina sounded irritated. "Just tell him to hurry the hell up." Her teeth chattered. She sounded like she was having another panic attack.

"Hold your panties," Micah said, lacing up one of his boots. "I'm hurrying."

"I'll stay on with you until he gets there," Trevor said. "Just calm down, Gina. Breathe."

"Okay, okay." She sounded breathless and shaky, like she was getting worse. This was a bad one.

"Are you okay, Gina? Don't lie to me."

"I'm f...fine. Just...shit!" Her breathing stuttered as if she was shivering.

"Gina?"

Sev appeared from the shower with Lakota right behind him. Micah turned toward them. "Sev, get dressed and get Malek on the phone. I don't have the patience to deal with him right now. You tell him to meet me at my apartment before sunrise. If he doesn't, and he keeps me from Sam today, so help me God, I will strap him into a chair and beat the living shit out of him until he finally breaks and accepts that he's mated Gina. Goddamn his stubborn ass! He's worse than a mule."

Sev and Lakota stopped dead. "Did we miss something?"

Gina yelled in his ear, and Trevor had to hold the phone away or risk temporary deafness. "You tell Micah that I don't want that bastard as my mate! Not after what he's done. That asshole! He can rot in hell! Fuck him!"

There was too much going on around him, and Trevor couldn't keep up.

Micah shut his locker and yelled toward the phone, "Gina, just hold on until I get there. I'll explain everything once I have you safe." He pointed at Trevor, then toward Lakota and Sev. "Trevor, fill them in after I'm gone." Micah stood, his jacket in hand.

"Wait, I'm not sure—"

"Just tell them what you know. I've got to go." Micah rushed out of the locker room and left Trevor with two blond males and a very pissed off Gina on the other end of the phone, who was still streaming out a trail of curses and obscenities.

"...motherfucker doesn't act like my mate. What kind of goddamn male fucks another female in front of his mate? If that asshole's mated me, then why is he acting like a goddamn fool? I don't—"

"Gina. Just slow down. Micah's on his way. I don't know what's going on, but Micah said he would explain everything when he gets there. Maybe he knows what's happening." Trevor sure hoped so, because he was lost.

Gina's breath came in tight bursts, and she continued rattling on, barely pausing, her words running together. "Trevor, I don't know what to do. He's the reason for my panic attacks...I had one as soon as he left the house. Right after he left...I had one...a bad one...I was lying on the floor...feeling like my chest was caving in...and it hit me. As long as I was around him, I was okay, but as soon as he was gone, I panicked. You see? Do you understand? Oh God, Trev. I'm so fucked. I'm so fucking fucked!" She broke down into hysterics.

"Gina, what are you talking about?" Her words flew at him at light speed, and he only comprehended half of what she was saying.

"I'm...in love...with him, Trevor!" She bit out the words as if struggling to speak. "Shit. Not now. P...please not now."

"Gina? Are you okay? Gina?"

Her breath burst through the line in tight gasps. "Another... panic...attack. Shit!" Then she grunted as if struck, and it sounded like she fell over.

Micah's voice reached him from the background. "Gina. I'm here. Shit!"

There were shuffling noises, then Micah spoke into the phone. "Trevor. I'm here. I've got her. I'm taking her to my apartment. Make sure Sev finds Malek and tells him to get his ass there pronto."

"Is she okay?"

"She's having some kind of seizure or panic attack."

The sound of retching in the background made it clear just how bad Gina's attack actually was.

"Fuck me," Micah said. "She's sick. I've gotta go. I'll take care of her."

The line went dead, and Trevor turned to see Sev and Lakota both staring at him, concern on their faces, which was odd for Lakota, given how he had treated Gina earlier.

"Well...?" Sev said.

"Come on. You need to get dressed. Micah needs you to get hold of Malek ASAP. I'll explain what I know while you dress."

He ushered them back to the locker bay and tried to wrap his mind around what was happening. If he hadn't heard it with his own two ears, he never would have believed it.

Gina was in love. Miracles did happen.

CHAPTER 17

MICAH HEFTED GINA INTO HIS ARMS. "Hold tight, Gina."

Damn, but this female had been through enough already. Where the hell was Malek? She needed him.

Her fingers dug into his shirt and put a death grip on the material. "Can't...breathe..."

"Ssshh. I know. Just hold on. I'm taking you to my place in the city." He hated going vapor, but under the circumstances, he had no choice. It was how he'd gotten here so fast, and it was how he would get her to his place even faster. With his mind, he attached himself to her and sucked her into the tunnel that projected them back to the balcony of his penthouse. Once he reanimated with her, he slid the glass door open and carried her to the bedroom and set her down on the comforter, picked up her arm, then stroked his thumb over the pulse point in her wrist. The glands in his mouth released their venom.

He hated taking her vein like this, especially given that it would piss Malek off, but he didn't have much choice if he wanted to help bring her back down.

As soon as he bit into her wrist, her body shuddered, stiffened, and then relaxed as euphoria took her.

How was it that he kept having to interfere to help his brothers claim their mates? First, Arion, who had nearly lost Severin because he'd been such a bonehead, and then he had helped bail Io's ass out of the fire with Miriam, and now he was about to surrender the cause with Malek. The guy simply would not take what was right in front of him. If only he would, Carmen's memory would slip away and fade into the past, where she belonged, which was what had happened with Katarina and Jackson after he had mated Sam. The natural progression of life would see fit to bring Malek full circle with Carmen's death and reopen him so he could fully commit to Gina. But the dumbass just wouldn't give in. Stubborn SOB.

He released Gina's wrist and placed her arm over her stomach as she squirmed through the lingering euphoria. "I'll be right back," he said.

She grabbed his hand. "Please, don't go."

"I'm not leaving. I'm just going to the kitchen to get you a glass of water. Then I'll get you a change of clothes and find you a toothbrush."

She closed her eyes and nodded, still a bit shaky.

He patted her hand then pushed off the bed and left the room.

Malek should be the one here taking care of her, not him. Malek needed to reassure her everything was all right. He was the one who should have taken her vein and calmed her. But he was MIA, screwing some random whore for only God knew what reason. He had seen inside Gina's mind as he bled her and knew what had happened during the past couple of hours. He saw her argument with Malek in the parking garage...the way Malek's demeanor had changed and how he fought not to take her...how he left her alone, and how she suffered only to realize she loved him...and how he had returned with another female named Lorena... how he had fucked her right under Gina's nose.

What was Malek thinking? Clearly, he had accepted the fact that Gina was his mate, but he still refused to close the deal with her. Until he claimed her sexually, the mating between them wouldn't complete and he would remain in hell.

Was Malek so thick that he didn't realize that?

He pulled a bottle of water from the fridge and poured it into a glass.

That female had endured enough. Until tonight, he hadn't known just how fucked up her past was. What she had done to Sev and Lakota were the least of her worries compared to what she had suffered at the hands of her first mate. How the hell had she pulled the short straw to get stuck with a half-Dacian? One who had beaten her so ferociously to render her womb barren?

The thought nearly made him retch, and unbidden tears stung his eyes. No female deserved what Armand had done to Gina, and if he hadn't already been dead, Micah would have hunted him down to do the honors for her. And he would have enjoyed the task.

It was times like this that he wished he couldn't see inside others' minds so easily, because seeing what had happened to Gina hurt his heart and made him ache in places reserved for Sam.

He took out his phone and dialed Sam's number.

"Hi, baby. You on your way home?" she said.

"No, not yet. Soon, though, okay."

Something in his voice must have revealed his pain, because Sam said, "What's wrong? Are you okay? I can tell something's wrong. Are you—?"

"I'm okay. I'm all right. I'll be home soon. I just wanted to"—he took a steadying breath—"I just wanted to call to tell you how much I love you. That's all. I love you so damn much."

Sam remained silent for a couple of seconds. "I love you, too, baby."

"I'll be home as soon as I can get away."

"I'll wait up."

"I'd like that." Because when he got home, he was going to show her just how much he loved her. Over and over and over again.

"See you soon."

"Soon." He hung up and returned to the bedroom with the glass of water and a toothbrush he dug out of the spare bathroom, wishing like hell he could show Malek what he was missing out on by rejecting Gina.

Malek could have with Gina what he had with Sam. He would never forget Carmen, just as Micah had never forgotten Katarina, but the pain of the loss would be gone, leaving behind only the good memories. The mystical tether would disconnect and free his heart, but Malek had held on so tightly to that string for so long, it was beginning to look like he would never be able to release it.

"Here, Gina." He helped her sit up.

She drank half the water, and then set the glass on the bedside table. "Thank you."

"Why don't you go brush your teeth and freshen up in the bathroom?" He gestured toward the master bath as he rummaged in one of the drawers in the bureau and pulled out a pair of Sam's Capri yoga pants and a tank top. "You can sleep in these. They should fit." Sam was tall and slender, while Gina was petite and had athletic curves, but the Capris would work better than a pair of Sam's flannel pajama pants, which would drape past Gina's feet.

She got up and took the clothes before heading into the bathroom. A few minutes later, she reappeared, smelling of mint Colgate. Water dripped from the ends of her hair from where she had splashed water on her face.

"Thank you again for helping me." She sat down on the bed and looked exhausted.

Then again, she had just had the mother of all anxiety attacks.

"Are you hungry?" He sat down next to her.

"No."

He nodded and took her hand. The two sat in silence for a long time.

Finally, Gina spoke again. "I know you saw in my mind what he did." She wouldn't look at him.

"Yes." No sense lying to her. "I saw everything. I'm sorry."

She sighed. The last of her strength drained out of her and she slumped forward. "I have to go away. I can't do this, Micah."

He put his arm around her and pulled her to him. "But you love him."

She lifted her gaze to his and shook her head. "It doesn't matter."

"Yes it does, Gina. It does matter. I saw that, too." He tapped her forehead and offered her a weak smile. "I saw firsthand what happens when you're not with him."

With a huff, she pushed away, stood, paced across the room, and then turned toward him. "I'll deal with it."

He stood with her. "Now you're beginning to sound like Malek."

"What's that supposed to mean?" She crossed her arms, but the gesture seemed more like self-protection than irritation.

He shook his head and stood akimbo. They were in such a mess. These two couldn't find their way to each other with a map and two flashlights. "Have a seat, Gina."

"No, I want to get out of here."

"Gina, don't push me. You need to hear about your *mate*."

She bobbed backward as if he'd pushed her. "He's not my mate. Not after—"

"Yes he is, and you know it, no matter what dumbass stunt he pulled tonight, he is your mate, and you are his. Now sit down and listen."

She huffed and rolled her eyes but sat on the bed. "How does a mate do what he did to me tonight, Micah? Clearly, you can see inside my thoughts, which means you can see what happened. How do you explain that?"

The images of what he had seen in her mind of Malek and the random bitch named Lorena fucking on his bathroom counter pounded inside his mind. He felt Gina's pain, saw her attack, heard her tell them both to burn in hell, and saw her run out the door.

He sighed and pulled up the easy chair that usually took up shop in the corner of the room, and then sat down, arms on his thighs. "Gina, let me tell you about Carmen."

"Who?" Her smooth brow creased in confusion.

"Malek's first mate, Carmen."

"Carmen?" Gina's frown twisted into an expression of realization. "He was mated before, too?"

"Yes, and I don't believe in coincidences. The fact that you were both mated before and have struggled to let go of the past is a sign."

She sighed. "A sign of what?"

"That you were meant to find each other and heal each

other's hearts."

She scoffed. "He doesn't act like he wants his heart to be healed."

He held up his hand. "Hear me out. He wants you. He wants you so badly he can barely stand it. Trust me."

"He has a funny way of showing it." She looked down and pretended to pick at a fleck of lint on the bed.

"That's because he's never dealt with Carmen's death, Gina. He's confused. He thinks he's disrespecting Carmen by wanting you. He's afraid he'll forget her, and that scares him."

"Why would he think that?"

"It's a guy thing." Micah leaned forward. "We mate deeply, as I'm sure you know."

She nodded.

"When we lose a mate, it can kill us."

Gina's throat worked as she swallowed, and she bit the inside of her bottom lip as her brow knitted into a pained expression.

"What we go through when we lose a mate is hard for females to fathom. When a female loses a mate, she only gets a taste of the loss we feel when we do—except you seem to have formed a much stronger mating bond than most females, hence your panic attacks. You share that little character trait with Princess Miriam, by the way. She formed a similar bond to Io, and it's a bitch to resist, isn't it?" His gazed pierced hers.

She glanced at her hands as if she had already figured that out.

"At any rate, something breaks inside us when we lose a mate, Gina. Almost as if part of our soul dies. We're no longer whole. We've lost a vital part of our existence, and for some of us, it's too much to bear. Many males die from that loss. I almost did."

Her expression tensed with awareness. "You were—?"

"Yes," he said. "I was mated before, too. And I lost her. I partially mated again last year, but...well...that didn't work out." He didn't need to talk about Jackson, who had been more of a deceptive blip than an actual mating. But the weird mating to Jack had reawakened his love for Katarina and nearly destroyed him. Thank God for Sam. She had saved his life. "My point is, when I met Sam, my mate now, I opened to her because I had already dealt with Katarina's death. I was ready to take a new mate, and Sam healed the part of me that needed to be whole again. I still remember Kat, and I still love her, but she is my past. Sam is my now and my future. She's the best part of me." He smiled fondly.

The awareness deepened in Gina's expression. "And since Malek has never accepted Carmen's death, he's not open. Is that right?"

"Exactly." Micah sat back, hands on his thighs. "You see, he's fought the truth ever since she died. I don't know how he did it, but every male reacts in his own way when a mate dies. And for Malek, his way was to internalize his feelings, box them up, and lock them away. Until you came along, he was a hollowed-out version of the male he used to be. He got the job done, but he lacked emotion."

"Because he buried all that with his memories of Carmen?"

He nodded. "Something like that, yes. Think about it. How could he feel anything else when all his feelings were tied up with his dead mate, who he refused to believe was actually dead. In his mind, she was merely sleeping."

"My God." She bowed her head.

Micah sighed. "He used to be my best friend, but we lost each other after our mates died." His gaze briefly wandered out of focus as he remembered the past, and then he blinked and brought himself back to the present. "I think he's finally begun to accept that she's dead, but he doesn't seem to understand that he can mate you *and* remember Carmen without dishonoring either one of you. He thinks that if he accepts you as his mate, he'll forget Carmen, or that he'll somehow be cheating on her. That's why he's doing what he is with the women he's been with, Gina. It's been a living hell being around him for the past couple of weeks, seeing what he's been putting himself through in an effort to deny what he feels for you. The hold you have on him scares the living hell out of him. If you could see what I see"—he tapped his head—"He fights himself over you. He wants you so badly that he's become two people."

Gina bit her lip and looked at her hands in her lap. "That explains his behavior tonight."

He nodded. "Yes. He's literally been Jekyll and Hyde. Two minds inhabiting one body."

She paled and looked almost sick. "And he's been like this for weeks?"

"Since just a few days after you left. He's gotten steadily worse."

"That's why you wanted me to come back." The lightbulb turned on over her head.

He nodded. "That's right."

"Why didn't you just say so in your e-mails?"

"Maybe I should have, but I thought it might have scared you away, not brought you back."

She considered that for a moment and nodded. "It might have. I don't know. I was pretty messed up myself."

"And now you know why." Micah had seen everything in her mind. How Malek had awakened her past, as well as how being away from him had sent her into agonizing anxiety attacks nearly every day.

"Yes, now I know why." She looked away again, stared out the window, then turned back with a sigh.

But there was more. Micah had also seen how Gina was more like Malek than she realized, and he needed her to see the truth. He got up and sat down next to her on the bed. "Gina, I know what Armand did to you, and I don't think you fully realize how badly it impacted you."

She turned and frowned at him. "What do you mean?"

He took her hand and closed his eyes against the pain that rolled through her mind. She was reliving the hell Armand had been. "Gina, you're so strong. Stronger than most females. To survive what Armand did to you"—he bowed his head—"I don't know how you did it, but…" He took a deep breath. This would be hard for her to hear. "Most females who endure what you went through would have become a sexual invalid. But you didn't."

Their gazes met, and he could see the guilt and fear in her eyes.

"You're like Malek, Gina."

She shook her head and began to protest.

Micah shushed her. "Yes, you are. You tucked away your pain and shoved it into the shadows of your mind. You never addressed it. Even now, you think on some level that you brought Armand's wrath on yourself. That somehow you're to blame. That you weren't good enough and deserved to be abused."

Tears welled in her eyes, but he felt her fight them back. For too long she had been a wall of strength, but she needed to let those tears fall. She needed to rid herself of the sorrow and hurt Armand had caused.

Micah squeezed her hand. "You began to see sex as a tool instead of a way to become emotionally close to someone. Sex became a means to an end. A way to get close to a target." His gaze drilled hers. "Like with Lakota. You charmed him with your body to get close to Severin, and you fulfilled your need for pleasure in doing so."

Her face strained in her effort not to cry, and her chin quivered.

"You haven't had a real relationship since Armand, have you?" Micah didn't need her to agree. He had already seen the truth in her mind. She had been alone since Armand. "One-night stands. Maybe a two-week fling here or there. Or a month. But as soon as a male began to get too close, you bolted. But now"—he shrugged—"you can't run anymore, Gina. Malek's your mate. If you run from him, both of you will suffer. He needs you. But more importantly, *you* need *him*. The two of you can heal each other."

For a long moment, Gina only stared at him as emotion rose and pulled at her soul, and then she flung herself at him as she burst into tears. Her arms flew around him as she buried her face against his chest and sobbed as years of guilt and fear poured out of her.

Micah held and rocked her as he brushed his hand over her hair "Ssshh. It's okay. I know what you're going through,

Gina. I went through it, too." He tried to soothe her. "You're strong enough to get through this, and Malek will help you. The two of you will help each other through this." He sighed and added under his breath, "Once he gets his head out of his ass." *And gets his ass over here.*

They sat like that for a while, Micah rocking her as she cried, until he said quietly, "You and Malek are so goddamn similar. You each internalized your painful pasts and hid from them. But while you turned sex into a tool, Malek became celibate. Well, until recently."

Gina pushed back and stared at him through bloodshot eyes. "Celibate?"

Micah grinned and nodded. "Yeah, well, he's making up for that now, isn't he?"

"Don't remind me." She sniffed and wiped her face with her hands.

"Do you want to know what Malek's idea of a good time has been since Carmen died?" Micah said.

She rolled her eyes. "Do I want to hear this?"

"Good point, but yes, I think you need to."

She grabbed a tissue from the bedside table and continued to dab her eyes. "Fine. Let's hear it."

He shifted back to the easy chair. "Until Malek met you, he hadn't touched another female since Carmen. Not a single one. That's how devoted he is as a mate. He refused to be with anyone else." He paused and slowly shook his head at what Malek had put himself through. "There's a strip club here in town called the Black Garter, and once a month he went there, paid for a private dance, watched, got himself sexed up, and went home alone to tend to his own needs. That's all the pleasure he allowed himself. And then he met you, and decades of sexual dysfunction boiled over as he struggled to accept what Mother Nature had done to him."

Gina sniffed again and took a heavy breath. "What are you saying?"

"I'm saying that despite what he did tonight, and as messed up as his mind is right now, Malek's heart is in a good place. He's a good male and a noble mate. Once he accepts he can join with you and not damage Carmen's memory, you will be the center of his world. He's thoughtful, considerate, and any female would be lucky to have him. He treated Carmen like a queen. He'll treat you the same way. I know he will."

Her expression still held an ounce of doubt, but she looked like she believed him. And was that hope he saw in her eyes?

"Okay, so let's say I believe you. What now? I mean, what can I do? He doesn't seem willing to accept me as his mate. Completely the opposite, in fact."

"He just needs a little push, Gina."

"A little push? Like what?"

Micah tilted his head to one side. Sometimes he couldn't believe he had to spell out what was so obvious. "Believe me, Gina. It won't take much for you to convince him. He's a mated male for God's sake. He wants you. Invite him in."

She pulled back and hesitated as his words sank in. "In? As in...?"

"Yes. As in...*in*."

She blushed and averted her gaze. "How am I supposed to do that?"

Micah sat back and arched an eyebrow. Really? Would he have to stay and guide Malek's pecker into home base, too? "He's a male, Gina. For you—his mate—it won't be hard to persuade him. Trust me. If you provide the right persuasion, he won't be able to refuse."

She shifted uncomfortably, looked away, then down, then back up.

Micah angled a questioning glance at her. "Are we on the same page then?"

Her eyes darted away, but she nodded. "Yeah, we're on the same page, but after what he did tonight, he's not going to get off so easily. I can tell you that much."

Micah grinned. Gina was feisty. Malek had his hands full with this one, but Micah had a feeling Malek would like having his hands full. Gina was perfect for him. And he was perfect for her. These two were going to be one hell of a power couple once they got out of their own way long enough to seal the deal.

Now, all they needed was Malek to cooperate and get there. Preferably before dawn. All this talk about Sam and mates made him homesick for the comfort of her embrace.

Blue balls didn't begin to describe the ache in Malek's scrotum. But that pain was nothing compared to the ache in his chest that threatened to consume him.

He had fucked up. He never should have brought Lorena home. He should have manned up and—

No, he had already decided Gina was better off without him. Going there would just bring more heartache. She needed more than he could give.

Malek sucked in his breath. Wait a minute. What had happened tonight? Why had Gina behaved the way she did?

He stood and paced, his face a study in confusion. Gina had busted into his bedroom like a female scorned. He glanced at his shattered bathroom door and recalled how she had attacked Lorena with the ferocity of a cyclone. Gina acted like a...oh God! Females didn't normally form such strong attachments to a male when they—well damn! Her link to him was just as strong as his to her. That's why she had attacked Lorena. She had been fending off competition for his affection.

Affection he had withheld from her. Affection she wanted. From him.

Awareness snapped inside his mind. Everything but Gina fell away. Even Carmen's memory. Suddenly Gina was the center of his universe, all-important, second to nothing and no one.

What had he done? He had caused her pain. Just as he was hurting now, she was likely hurting just as badly. She needed him.

His mate needed him, goddamn it! And he wasn't there to comfort her.

He tore up the stairs and through the kitchen. In that instant, an instinctual awareness as old as time crackled and ruptured through every cell in his body. Everything but the need to ease his mate fell to the background. How long had Gina been gone? Too long, but he could track her. He had to. He needed to find her and make this right. Knowing that she had bonded to him as he had to her, and that she was out there without him, miserable and hurting, half and not whole, ripped his heart to shreds.

He pulled the door open and nearly barreled into Severin, who was about to ring the bell.

Sev jumped back to avoid the collision, but grabbed Malek's wrist. "Don't you answer your phone, asshole?"

His phone. Maybe Gina had called him. He pulled free of Sev's hold and ran back downstairs to find his phone, turned off, on the dresser. Sev followed and parked at the foot of the stairs as Malek waited for the phone to turn back on.

"Malek?"

"Not now, Sev? I need to find Gina." Malek turned and started to rush past him, but Sev stopped him.

"That's why I'm here, dumbass. She's at Micah's apartment downtown."

Malek turned and grabbed Sev's shirt. "Why didn't you tell me?"

Sev threw off his hold. "If you'd answer your damn phone, you would have known a half hour ago, asshole."

"Is she okay? Is she hurt? Is—"

Sev held up a hand. "Save your questions for Micah. I'm just the messenger."

"You've got to know something, Sev."

"All I know is that she called Trevor and was really upset. And then I guess she had some kind of panic attack. Micah picked her up and took her to his place."

Malek turned and started back up the stairs as his phone dinged and showed six missed calls, all from Sev.

"Micah wants your ass there by dawn," Sev shouted after him.

But Malek was already out the door, on his way. Damn. He had left his truck outside Four Alarm. His truck couldn't get him there fast enough, anyway. He needed to project to

Micah's balcony.

As he turned to mist, he heard Sev chuckle and mutter from the front porch, "Go get your mate, dumbass. Don't worry. I'll lock up."

CHAPTER 18

GINA'S MIND SWAM with all that Micah had told her. Malek's behavior made more sense now that she knew about Carmen and what he had gone through for longer than she had been alive, but that still didn't excuse Malek's actions tonight. Okay fine, she was his mate. She accepted that. And what Micah said about the two of them healing each other might be true, but she sure as hell wasn't going to sit back and not let Malek know he had overstepped a boundary. Hell no.

"Come on," Micah said, "let's get you something to eat."

Gina nodded and cast aside her mental tirade. Her appetite had found its way back to her stomach, and she could use some food. Maybe an omelet. That sounded good. "Yeah, sure."

She followed him out of the room and down the hall, but before they reached the living room, Micah stopped so suddenly that she nearly plowed into his back.

What the…?

"It's about time you showed up," he said.

Gina frowned. Who was he talking to? Then she got a whiff of the male who had captured her soul.

Malek was there. He had come for her.

It took an act of God to remind her that she was pissed at the guy.

"Where is she?" Malek spoke from across the room.

Her heart skipped from just the sound of his voice, and she stepped out from behind Micah. "*She* is here." She scowled and wrinkled her nose as the stench of that *female*—and she was being polite—permeated her senses.

"Okay," Micah said with a glance her way as she crossed her arms and backed into the kitchen. "I can see that you two need to talk." He pointed toward her. "Gina, leave the knives in the block."

She glanced to the side and saw an impressive set of knives sticking out of a wooden stand and held her hands up as if she had no intention of drawing Malek's blood.

Malek's gaze fixed on her and never wavered. The guy looked seriously strung out.

Micah grinned sympathetically and sighed, and as he strolled past Malek, leaned in and said, "You should have showered before you came."

Malek's brow ticked as he glanced at Micah, and then he sniffed himself.

Yeah, big guy. Get a whiff of that bitch on your clothes, in your skin, in your goddamn hair. And you got pissed off because Trevor bit me. Hypocrite.

Micah must have picked up her inner dialogue, because he passed her a wary look before glancing back at Malek. "Good luck, buddy." He gave Malek a gentle pat on the shoulder. "You'll need it, but don't you dare leave this apartment until the two of you have worked this out."

With his gaze locked to hers, Malek said, "That's why I'm here. To make things right."

Micah patted his shoulder again. "Good man. That's what I want to hear." Then he stepped outside. A moment later, he was gone.

It was just the two of them.

And shit was about to get real.

Malek took a step toward her. "Gina—"

"I don't want to hear it." She spun and took off down the hall as if the kitchen were on fire.

"Gina, wait." Malek hurried after her. "Please listen to me."

She twirled and shoved him away. "Get away from me, Malek. After what you did tonight, just stay back." Who did he think he was to come here still smelling like that skank? The least he could have done was shower. But no, he had to bring her nasty smell here and add insult to injury. "I have to be the stupidest female on the planet," she said under her breath.

"I'm sorry, Gina. God, I'm so sorry."

But she wasn't ready to forgive him. She was still too angry and hurt. "Sorry? Were you sorry when you brought that whore into your house and fucked her under my nose? Huh?" Aggression burst from her like an explosion, and she shoved past him out into the hall again before spinning around to confront him as he charged after her. "You fucked another female in front of me, Malek! Is that how a mated male behaves? Is that the respect a female deserves from her mate?"

Why deny the obvious any longer? They were mates. She knew it. He knew it. It was time to cut through the shit and lay the cards on the table. One way or the other, tonight they would deal with the link that tethered them to one another.

"No, but—"

She batted him away and fled back into the bedroom. Adrenaline coursed through her. She had to keep moving. If she didn't, she would give in to the rising arousal he stirred in her belly simply from his proximity, even though he carried the reminder of his infidelity on his skin. "You *stink*. You smell like *her*." Her nose crinkled again as she paced to the other side of the room near the windows and crossed her arms. Then uncrossed them. She couldn't stand still. Nervous energy flirted with sexual hunger, and war raged within her body to distance herself from him, as well as throw him to the bed and take possession of what belonged to her.

He followed and reached for her hands, but she slapped him away. "Don't touch me. Get away from me, Malek." Even as she said the words, she wanted nothing more than his hands on her body.

Hurt and misery smeared his expression. "Please Gina, let me explain. I've been dying a slow death without you. I just didn't know—"

She held up her hands, dodged him, and shot back out of the room as he rushed after her. "You? You've been dying a slow death? I've been miserable for weeks, Malek, and all this time I thought it was because I didn't want to be mated. When all along it was because..." She fumed as she trailed off, angry with him for stealing her moment of realization from her earlier. When she had finally figured out the source of her anxiety and accepted the reality, ready to take her place by his side, he had abandoned her for another female.

In the living room, she paced and swatted him away as he reached for her again, and then hurried back to the bedroom. When she spun back toward the door, he blocked the exit. She was trapped.

"Gina—"

"Just shut up, Malek!" Under the bitch's scent, he smelled delicious. So inviting. "Males are nothing but trouble. Especially you! You're the worst kind of trouble I don't need!" But she did need him. And with every second that ticked by, her resolve to push him away cracked a little more. The side of her that had bound itself to him bullied its way through, pushing aside restraint and anger to feed her desire and make her too weak to hold back much longer.

He continued toward her with cautious steps, one arm slightly raised, his palm facing her, as if he were trying to capture a feral cat and didn't want to spook it. "I'm sorry, Gina. Please let me make this better." Anguish etched the lines of his face, and suffering roiled in the depths of his eyes. Malek was clearly in agony over what he'd done to her.

"Malek, don't. Just don't." She was faltering. He was here. Her mate was here. And no matter what he had done, the desire to go to him was more powerful than her anger. They were like polar atoms, one positive, one negative, drawn to each other to connect and form a brand new molecule. Something neither could do alone.

"Please, Gina..." Guilt wafted from him as he slowly closed the distance between them.

But she no longer had the strength to flee. Furthermore, she didn't want to. As much as she hated what he had done to her, and as much as she wanted to stay angry at him, she wanted to be with him more.

"Gina..." He took one last step toward her, and his warmth spread around her.

The two of them stood in silence for what felt like a long time, but he didn't try to touch her. It was almost as if he didn't want to break the fragile moment they had found together. One where she had to fit herself into a new reality she had fought for decades and only just now considered trying on for size again. But Malek fit like a favorite pair jeans. Had she doubted he would? After all, he was the other half of her, the greener grass on the other side of the fence, the brighter light without the rose-colored glasses to taint or cloud his image. Malek was everything that she needed to be complete. He was perfect, beautiful, and majestic.

"Look at me, Gina." With the tips of his fingers under her chin, he lifted her face.

Her fury was tapped out, depleted by expulsion, as well as by his presence. The mating bond was already doing its job, making them better individuals by fusing them into one. As she looked into his magical, dark brown eyes, her fears and pain evaporated, and she could almost feel his doing the same.

"I need you," he said.

Peace settled inside her, and her tension eased. Once again, she belonged to someone, but this time Mother Nature had gotten it right. Malek would be everything Micah said he would, and he would treat her like a queen. And he would be her king. Somehow she just knew this was true. They would be a mated force to be reckoned with, perfect complements for one another, a synergistic combination that made them exponentially stronger together than apart. And any male— or female—who attempted to put asunder what biology had linked through nature would learn the true meaning of defeat, because from this day forward, she and Malek were no longer two, but one. And nothing would tear them apart.

She closed her eyes. *My mate. My life.*

The two remained suspended in their surrender to one another for a heartbeat, and then Malek moaned a fraction of a second before hormonal heat wafted from his body through hers.

Oh my God! Mating heat. Strong, heady, and undeniable. She gasped and swayed against him, unable to steady herself.

He melted into her. "No more running from each other. No more denying the truth."

Her eyes lifted to his, and excitement and desire flared through her as he pulled her against him.

Another pulse of heat throttled her, and she moaned deep in her throat as her fingers clutched fistfuls of his shirt. She closed her eyes again and wavered as she fought for air.

He groaned and wobbled on shaky legs, a slave to his calling, which seemed to be beating the hell out of him now that he was near her. "Gina...God, I need you. I've always needed you. I just didn't know." As he whispered, his voice deepened to a dark and provocative roll of syllables until he groaned again through another swell of mating heat. The force of the surge caused his knees to buckle, and they staggered until her back slammed against the wall.

In an instant, she was back in his arms, and his nose pressed against the side of her neck as he purred through each labored inhale. "Gina, Gina...so beautiful." The warmth of his breath sent a shiver through her body. "I sat in that cell with you every day...watching you sleep... wishing I could take away your pain. And when I was given the opportunity to make good on my wish, what did I do?" His lips traced a seductive line to her ear. "I caused you more pain," he whispered. "I'm so sorry. I swear on my life I'll never hurt you again."

She couldn't speak, could hardly breathe, swept into the forces drifting and vibrating from his body, beating the air around them into a frenzy of erotic energy. His words lifted her, carried her, and caressed the deepest, most vulnerable corners of her soul. She had needed to hear him express himself this way...to tell her he was as much enraptured by her as she was by him.

His body called to hers again, and she couldn't stop

herself from answering. She rocked toward him and tucked her nose against the side of his neck. If only he didn't smell of another, the moment would be nearly utopian.

Flames lit in her core. Possessive flames. He was hers. No one else's. And if he was going to smell of anyone, it would be her, not that mutty tyke she had found him with earlier. She sprang to action and grabbed his shirt. "Micah was right. You should have showered, Malek." She yanked up the hem and drove her hands underneath to lift the shirt up his torso.

Need spurred her, demanded she mark him now for eternity, and she practically shredded his shirt as she tore it over his head and from his outstretched arms and tossed it to the floor.

In a blink, his arms were back around her. "You're so damn perfect." His voice held a lusty note of abandon, his hands molding to her body, tugging at the fabric of her top. Malek was a male losing himself to what was left of his calling, his mind of a single purpose. He needed to mate. With her. Now.

And she wouldn't stop him. Not anymore. Not ever again.

He wobbled drunkenly under her onslaught. In an instant, her fingers went to work on the zipper of his pants. Within seconds, he stripped off the last of his clothes as she whipped Sam's shirt over her head and tossed it aside.

"You belong to me, Malek." She snagged his arm and tugged him to the bathroom. "You're mine. From now on, I own you."

She turned on the shower as his fingers hooked the elastic waist of her pants. "I'm yours," he said.

In a blink, they were both naked and tumbling into the shower in a tangle of limbs.

"I'm yours," he said again, lifting her. His eyelids hung heavily over his lust-darkened eyes. "Only yours."

Cool water quickly warmed, and she threw her legs around his hips, ready to give herself to him. Malek *was* worthy. With Malek, she had a future, and after so much heartache, she finally believed that she *could* have it all. She and Malek would heal each other, and together they would put their pasts behind them.

"And I'm yours," she said. "Now claim me, damn it."

MALEK'S HEART HEAVED AND BURST WITH JOY. He needed her, craved her, was about to implode without her. As he sank into the depths of her body and joined them as one, he knew he had found what his soul had needed to come back to life. For the first time in centuries, his black-and-white world exploded with color, and before he could even thrust fully into Gina's warmth, he came.

So long—too long—he had fought his body's needs, and all the dysfunctional and dissatisfying sex he had tried to use to replace his true desire for her—*for Gina*—had served only to tie him in knots of torment.

And now, inside the haven of her body, all those knots released and sent him into a second orgasm immediately on the heels of the first.

He grunted and cried out through the agonizing rapture as her back slapped the tile wall. Life burst within him, but the pleasure caused such delirium he could hardly enjoy the moment. For too long, he had sought refuge elsewhere, and now, when he wanted to relish his savior and fully experience the sharing of their bodies, all he could do was hold on and wait for the unleashing to end.

This was what he got for withholding himself for so long... for seeking absolution elsewhere. All the whores and all the abstinence had led him into decay. What he had needed to be truly cleansed was Gina. And now he had her. If only his body would ease enough so he could catch up and engage.

"Gina!" His body shuddered as he came again. Fucking hell! What was happening to him? He couldn't slow down the rapid-fire bursts that continued to rip through his muscles. As soon as he came, another orgasm began to build. He had wanted to take his time, to explore and worship her, but he couldn't. His body wouldn't let him. "God, I'm sorry," he said between gasps. "So sorry."

"Ssshhh." Her lips pressed against his ear. "Take what you

need, baby. Don't stop." She held on as he took her to the floor of the shower.

He *couldn't* stop. She was a lock, and he was the only key that fit. With every thrust, he unlocked another treasure chest of pleasure. And in that pleasure, he saw his future. The past fell away, and all he was—everything in his world— was Gina.

He drove into her body again and again, unable to get enough now that he'd had a taste. Gina was exquisite. How had he refused this bouquet of perfection for so long? He had been crazy to deny his body's urgings.

Beneath him, her body rippled, and she gasped. "Don't stop...don't stop..."

Arousal—pure and feminine—spiraled and blended with his hormonal heat. She was about to come. Because of him. He was giving his mate the pleasure she deserved. Maybe not how he had wanted, but he would take it. The two of them anchored to one another and fed the give and take between them as the ultimate wave rose from the depths. This time when he came, she would join him, and their mating would be complete. She really would be his, and he really would be hers. Not that he wasn't already, because even now, Gina commanded every cell in his body.

With short, urgent strokes, Malek fed her fire, drew her release further into the open, and bathed in her pleas for more.

His fourth climax ripped through him as she cried his name and dug her nails into his back.

Claimed.

Malek was once more a claimed male.

For the last time.

CHAPTER 19

LORENA MARCHED INTO THE STRONG BREEZE that plowed between Chicago's skyscrapers. Tonight hadn't turned out at all as she had planned. For the second time in two days, she had lost Malek to another.

But the real bitch of it was that it looked like Malek had mated that cur who busted up her fun tonight. The connection between them even in the melee of flying fists had been unmistakable.

How could Malek have taken a mate? He didn't act like a mated male. Not even close. Bastard!

Gina, huh? Surely this wasn't the same Gina rumored to have swooped into town last month and blown a hole in the chest of an AKM enforcer. The same Gina wanted dead or alive for single-handedly shutting down Southeast cobalt production after a raid on a dreck facility went bad in Atlanta over a year ago. Bishop and Royce had been fuming for months trying to catch her. She had allegedly hunted down and killed over twenty cobalt distributors and dealers from that facility, and the price on her head was so high that dreck-friendly bounty hunters from all over the world had dropped other assignments to hunt her. So far, none had found her, but maybe that was about to change.

Perhaps the night hadn't been a total loss after all.

Still feeling spurned but at least more optimistic, Lorena made her way to the Underground, the place where seedier vampires dwelled and others escaped after the human bars announced last call. The Underground—or the UG, as it was known—was always open, even during the day, and she was sure to find an acceptable replacement for Malek here, as well as an opportunist or two she could join forces with to plot a means to an end where Gina was concerned.

Once she reached the UG's private entrance in a back alley, she took the stairs down into the guts of Chicago to a long, dark tunnel where a few lingering females leaned against the wall looking for one final sale before they packed it in for more personal pursuits. Drecks prowled the tunnel, as well, selling cobalt to those in search of a pick-me-up.

All walks of life came here. Even humans who were lured, unsuspecting, into the fray where their blood could provide entertainment for those who needed to feed.

Heavy bass from the main room echoed through the tunnel, and just ahead, a young vampire fell into violent tremors as the dreck who had just dosed him with cobalt capped his syringe and glanced over his shoulder at her.

His vivid blue eyes looked her up and down. Then he nodded and looked away as she passed. Everyone here knew who she was. At least those who mattered. She belonged to Bishop. She helped Bishop get what he wanted, which was more vampires for his lab experiments, and he gave her what she wanted, a chance to regain stature and power within the vampire race. And if they happened to fall into bed on occasion, so much the better. He was an inventive lover, and he never failed to leave her bloodied and bruised. He also didn't mind that she refused to be monogamous, which was an added bonus.

When she reached the heavy double doors to the main room, dented and scarred by years of wear, the doorman stepped aside and grinned.

"Hello, Lucan." Her gaze skipped down to his crotch. He was a favorite toy she enjoyed playing with when Bishop was away and no one else piqued her interest.

His hooded gaze ranged her appreciatively. "Lorena."

"Wanna play?" She sidled up next to him, pressing her breasts against the side of his abdomen. Lucan was a tall one, and built for aggression.

His lips spread into a devilish grin. "Only if you don't find the special visitors at the bar to your liking."

"Oh?" She arched one brow at him. Lucan knew her tastes, and while he certainly wouldn't mind taking her to his private chamber in the depths of the tunnel for a little one-on-one, he was blessedly patient and anything but possessive. If he was offering her an option other than himself, he knew she would find what she really wanted inside, not with him.

"Yes." Lucan's grin twisted, and he looked away. The devious twinkle in his eye, along with the way one side of his mouth curled mischievously, told her she was going to be very happy with the special visitors he had spied for her.

She playfully slapped his cheek a little harder than necessary. A gesture of endearment, and he knew it. "You're a dear, Lucan. Remind me to show my gratitude another time, won't you?"

His gaze smoldered. "You know I will."

Their arrangement was more one of convenience, as were all her liaisons, and she and Lucan kept each other happy during those times they both needed what others weren't providing. They looked out for each other, and in her line of work, if she could really call it that, having those who caught her back was a necessity.

With another playful slap, she pushed through the doors into the churning atmosphere of The Underground. Darkness invaded every corner, with dim red and blue lights barely illuminating the scene. Electronic trance pulsed from speakers around the large dance floor, where half-naked bodies undulated and pressed together.

A quick scan of the bar, and she located what Lucan had referred to. Two warrior-sized males with long, pale hair sat with their backs toward her.

Dacians.

Tingles shot out from her belly, and her knees went weak. Dacians! Two of them. Here. Bless the stars that shine! Getting kicked out by Malek was beginning to look more and more like a stroke of good fortune than a devastating blow.

As the last remaining Thracian vampire, Lorena hadn't dreamed she would ever see another Dacian.

In the ancient past, around the time the Pharaohs began to rule Egypt, Dacians had been the only vampire race worthy to mate with Thracians, and even though Dacians were notorious for maintaining pure bloodlines, they made an exception for the Thracians, who were as physically demanding and ruthless as they were.

Their two clans made strong allies, and Thracians had supported Dacian rule during the great uprising when Bain's ancestors overthrew them and stole the throne.

That had been before Lorena's time, but her people had rued the day Dacian rule ceased and a new regime took over and spent the next two millennia hunting and exterminating anyone of Dacian or Thracian descent as new vampire colonies continued to thrive.

Those who didn't go into hiding suffered in glorified witch hunts until both clans neared extinction. Then the drecks rose against the vampires and diverted their attention, thus ending the bloody vampire revolution, but not before the Dacian and Thracian clans were so weakened that extinction seemed imminent.

Lorena eyed the two striking males. Although she had heard recent rumors that Dacians hadn't gone extinct as previously thought, she was still surprised to see two of them here.

The two males glanced around the crowded, darkened room and appeared as though they were looking for companionship. Unlike with Malek, she needn't worry she would lose these fine specimens to another. Dacians didn't like to mix with what they referred to as lesser vampires, or even humans. Not to say they wouldn't do so to get their jollies, but once they saw her and realized she was Thracian, they would take to her like the captain of the football team took to the head cheerleader.

As if on cue, the taller of the two swiveled his head around and met her gaze. Something in his body language said he was in charge.

She smiled and descended into the belly of the club as the gaze of the second male turned and joined that of the first.

Moving like an alley cat in heat, she slid up between them and waved down the bartender.

"Disaronno. On ice."

A palm fell over her ass and glided up to the small of her back. "I thought Thracians were extinct," the taller one said.

How impressive that he recognized her bloodline so quickly. She turned toward him. His silver, hooded eyes held his interested appraisal of her.

"I could say the same thing about Dacians," she said. "But then...here we are."

"And how interesting is that?" The second male leaned closer, and his arm slid around her waist.

These two seemed intent on sharing, which was fine by her. The more, the merrier.

The bartender brought her drink, set it down, and faded away.

"How about we find someplace dark, boys? Someplace where we can"—she looked back and forth between them—"talk."

Talking was the last thing on her mind, but like others in the room, she wasn't opposed to fucking them both right there among the other patrons. Some nights in The Underground became more or less an orgy, anyway. Perhaps this could be one of those nights, but she wouldn't share these two with anyone. They were hers now.

"Lead the way," the taller one said.

Both followed like lethal predators ready to mark their territory as she led them away from the bar toward a darkened cove split off from the main room.

"What are your names?" She set her drink on a table in the corner. At the next table over, a female had her face in the lap of a male who stared down at her with glazed eyes as she bobbed up and down.

This place was like Studio 54 in its heyday. Sex, drugs, and disco. Only now it was club and trance music.

"Vaydon." The shorter of the two sat down and pulled her onto his lap so she faced him.

"I'm Searcy." The other slid in beside them.

"My name's Lorena."

Vaydon's arms tightened around her and Searcy pushed closer, bringing his mouth to her ear. "We're pleased to meet you, Lorena."

She grinned against Vaydon's strong hold and the way Searcy eased around behind her as he pushed the table out of the way so he could close her in with his arms stretched out against the wall on either side of her. "I want you to fuck me hard," she said, in heaven, panting and ready to be stripped down and laid bare.

"Oh, rest assured, Lorena. You'll be fucked hard. But first." Searcy gripped a fistful of her hair and yanked her head back. "Tell us how it is that you smell of our prey. Her scent clings to you. And while your body is something to be desired, we didn't come to Chicago to fuck. We came here to kill. And while we'll make an exception for one as fine as you, make no mistake, you are not our priority. Is that understood?"

Anger and frustration rose like a tidal wave. She was not going to be thwarted a second time tonight. No way! And what did they mean that the scent of the one they hunted was all over her. Who? She reared back to screech an angry howl at him, but Searcy clamped his hand over her mouth and Vaydon drove the tip of a blade under her chin.

These two were serious.

And they were seriously turning her on.

"Don't make us hurt you, Lorena. It would be a shame to mar such rare, exquisite flesh, but we will if we have to." He bit her earlobe, and she nearly came from the pain as his fang pierced the tender flap of skin. "Now, tell us...where did you come in contact with our prey, and then we will reward you with what you want."

Searcy removed his hand from her mouth, and she practically panted the words, "I don't know who you're talking about. Who are you after?"

Vaydon slid the blade down her neck between her breasts, and she moaned. "The assassin who tried to kill me. She's petite. Has dark hair. Smells like vanilla and cloves. We know she's here, and it's clear you were with her recently.

Or someone who was very close to her." He pulled her more securely onto his lap and ground his erection between her legs. The thrill of pain mixed with pleasure obviously excited him, too. "Where have you been tonight, Lorena?"

"Yes, just where *have* you been? And who have you been with?" Searcy reached around and cupped her breasts.

The sensory overload was off the charts, but not so much that she couldn't put two and two together. "You want Gina."

"Gina?"

"Yes. She's mated to Malek, a member of the King's Men. A real whore." She spoke on a breathless moan and ground her pelvis against the hard ridge in Vaydon's lap, close to coming.

Searcy's grip on her breast tightened and she gasped as a burst of pleasure erupted low in her abdomen like an explosion of bees. "Ah yes. Gina. But..." He licked her neck. "What was that about a mate? Mated males can pose a problem."

She reached around with one hand and held onto the back of Searcy's head as she gyrated her hips again and moaned. "He won't be a problem. He's weak."

"Even a weak mated male is strong, sweet thing," Vaydon said.

She barely heard him, lost in pleasure. But one thing was clear. Lorena had found what she sought by coming to the UG. Searcy and Vaydon could give her what her body needed, and they were the perfect partners to help her claim the bounty on Gina's head. "No. He's been in suffering...hasn't been feeding..." She thought of the wounds on Malek's face. "He isn't healing."

Searcy hummed thoughtfully. "Not healing, is he? Well, that makes a difference."

Lorena nodded and rubbed herself with more urgency against Vaydon's erection. "I'll help you. Let me help you kill her."

If these two wanted to kill Gina, she would gladly help. She owed that bitch for taking away her fun. And a third of the bounty on her head would be a nice bonus.

SEARCY WAS SURPRISED TO SEE A THRACIAN in Chicago, let alone one as beautiful as Lorena. And from her reaction to him and Vaydon, she, like her ancestors, enjoyed receiving rough treatment as much as he enjoyed giving it. The giving and receiving of pain between their clans in days of old, when the world of vampires had been different, had always been a common bond between them.

Her eagerness to help hunt down their quarry impressed him, too. Fealty still existed between their races, and he would reward her well for being quick to offer her assistance. But first things first.

"Tell me more about Gina, Lorena." He stepped back and growled as the name struck a chord in his memory. He suddenly remembered where he had scented Gina before.

Over a century ago, his spurned sister, angry with her mate, seduced a common male in his calling. How she lured him away from his mate remained a mystery, a secret she had taken to her premature death, but the offspring she birthed had grown to be an impressive half-breed. A male named Armand.

Gina had been Armand's mate. And a treasonous one at that. She had killed Armand.

Self-defense, the royal court had decreed. Self-defense, his ass. They could call it what they wanted, but by his definition, she had murdered Armand. He had been her mate. As such, he had rights over her body and soul to do whatever he wished with her. If that meant beating her to within a brink of death, so be it. That was his right. If she was too weak to survive, that was her fault, but for her to kill him under the guise of self-defense was ludicrous.

He had helped his sister lay Armand to rest in their sacred burial grounds, back into the earth where he belonged, but he had never gone after Gina. But now that bitch had come for another of his blood, and he had double the motivation to see her dead.

Searcy wouldn't make the mistake of letting her get away this time. He caressed the handle of the ancient blade sheathed beneath his trench coat, its alloy a deadly combination of metal and primitive magic cast by wizened yet powerful Dacian priestesses older than time. The weapon had been in his bloodline for millennia, since his forefathers ruled the race.

He spun back toward Vaydon. "Release her."

Vaydon's brow creased with confusion, but he did what he was told and lowered the blade and let go of her.

"No. Don't stop!" Lorena grabbed the knife and tried to pull it back to her throat as she dry-humped his son. Her scent indicated she was within seconds of coming.

Searcy stepped forward, grabbed her wrist, and pulled her off Vaydon's lap. "You'll get what you want, but first we need information."

She writhed and reached down as if to massage herself to orgasm, but Searcy grabbed her wrist, eliciting a frustrated growl from her.

He tightened his hold. "I said you'll get what you want. Now talk. Then Vaydon and I will make sure you're well taken care of, Thracian."

"Promise me." Her legs continued to scissor. She was lost to her lustful needs.

"Oh, rest assured, Lorena. I give my word. Vaydon and I will fuck you breathless and leave you black-and-blue by nightfall."

She shivered and grinned like a deranged mental patient, but the promise that he wouldn't leave her hanging high and dry seemed to calm her, and she slid away from Vaydon and settled onto the seat next to him. Her guarded brown eyes watched him closely as he pulled up a chair, pushed the table toward her, and sat down across from her.

"This female. Gina. You will take us to her," he said.

"Now?"

"No. It's too close to sunrise. At nightfall." He looked at Vaydon and explained, "She is the one who killed Armand."

Vaydon's eyebrows rose on his forehead, and understanding crossed his features. "I see."

Lorena crossed her arms. "Who's Armand? And what's in this for me?"

Ah, a female after his own heart, but he expected nothing less from a strong Thracian female. "Armand was my nephew. And what would the lady like? Besides a day with us, because that's a given, isn't it?" Yes, he would have this female, and if she pleased him, perhaps an arrangement could be made.

Lorena sat forward, alert and cunning, her sharp mind obviously working over her options. "I know this Gina bitch isn't your only interest in Chicago."

She was smart. Searcy leaned back, amused, if not a little turned on. "And what makes you say that, Lorena?" He tossed a brief, sideways glance toward Vaydon, whose lips curled on one side.

She glanced between them. "Your line used to rule the race, did it not?"

Searcy nodded, and his grin grew wider. "It did."

"And King Bain lives in Chicago."

He and Vaydon exchanged glances again. "Your point, pretty thing?"

She leaned forward in such a way that her arms pushed against the outside of her breasts, mashing them together to show off the healthy cleavage boosted by her tight-fitting bustier. "You wish to make a play for the throne. To take back what's yours."

He mirrored her body language and leaned over the table so that their faces were only inches apart. What a spirited, rare female. Beautiful, intelligent, and a likely stick of dynamite in bed, or wherever she chose to fuck. He reached out and let the tip of his index finger trace a line around the generous swell of one breast. "What if you're right? What is it you want?"

She grinned and pushed forward against his touch. "I want to be your queen when you take back the throne."

That got Searcy's attention, and one eyebrow jacked upward as his finger stilled on her skin. "That's a hefty asking price, Lorena."

"Yes, it is. But I can help you."

"How?"

"I know people. Powerful people. Influential people."

"Such as?"

A self-assured smile spread over Lorena's face as she leaned closer. "Let me tell you about my friends Bishop and Premier Royce, Searcy. I'm sure they would love to see you come to power."

"Oh? At what price?" There was always a price, but since the Dacians had never been bothered by the drecks, Searcy wasn't opposed to a mutual arrangement between their races that could prove mutually beneficial. Under the right circumstances, of course.

Lorena's lips brushed his, and her lovely dark eyes sparkled as she met his gaze. "The disbanding of All the King's Men, for starters," she said. "After that, I'm sure the five of us can find common ground to work from." She glanced at Vaydon.

The disbanding of AKM? How sweet an idea. Searcy would love nothing more than to put the head of that beast in the guillotine and chop it off.

His lips teased hers as he spoke. "Tell me more...my future queen. I'm dying to hear about your...*friends.*"

"Of course." Her wicked lips curled into a lovely smile. "Let me just make a quick phone call first."

Searcy sprawled in his chair and stared at her ass as she shimmied away from the table, her phone in hand. He could appreciate a female like Lorena. Cunning, statuesque, thirsty for both pain and power. A woman after his own heart. The perfect consort for both he and his son, and a perfect candidate to be the mother of their future progeny.

Dacians weren't afflicted with the abhorrent calling that made males from other vampire clans slaves to sexual congress, as well as to their females. Instead, a Dacian male chose his mate when his fertile time came, which occurred every hundred years. Dacians didn't mate for life, so it was common for many females to bear the young of one male if he chose to procreate. Because it was *his* choice. He could either give a female his seed or not. As long as he didn't, he remained fertile, but once he did, he had to wait another hundred years to procreate again, which was why Searcy and Vaydon had held on to their fertility for the past several hundred years. They hadn't found an adequate female to bear their young.

One look at Lorena, however, and it became clear. He and Vaydon both would give her their seed.

He glanced at Vaydon and raised one eyebrow. Vaydon grinned back. No doubt he was thinking the same thing Searcy was. But he would not overstep his bounds. Vaydon knew he would have to wait until she bore Searcy's young before she bore his. The rank and file between father and son was firmly cemented.

With a soft chuckle, he let his gaze drift back to the beauty with the black heart. She grinned and nodded as she spoke and glanced back at him out of the corner of her eye. When she disconnected and dropped the phone from her ear, she slinked back and crawled into his lap.

"Bishop has agreed to meet with you," she said, winding her hands around to the back of his neck.

"How lovely." He gripped her hips and pulled her against his hard cock.

"And he's given us permission to use his private suite for the day." She ground her crotch against him.

"Even lovelier."

"Shall we leave then?"

Oh, he would ride this female hard by nightfall. So hard she would forever be branded by his mark. "Absolutely."

Tonight, pleasure.

Tomorrow, Gina's head on a spear.

After that, the throne.

It was time for vengeance.

CHAPTER 20

BISHOP STARED REFLECTIVELY AT HIS PHONE by his plate. What an interesting conversation that had been. Lorena had found new friends. Friends with a fascinating background and designs on usurping the throne from the vampire king, as well as on exterminating those pesky fleas, All the King's Men.

Interesting.

Imagine all he could do without AKM thwarting his efforts. And if he could get his hands on their blood or venom, even better. They may not be mongrels, but from the sound of it, Lorena's two friends could benefit from his lab work, especially if they were as rare as she claimed. He could clone them. Or if they could provide him with a Dacian female, he could harvest her eggs, their sperm, and grow them into an army. Of course, he would have to add in a little of his own special sauce to ensure compliance among the test tube younglings, but no one would have to know. Or maybe he could just use their genes to splice with that of drecks and create a new race of half-breeds that exhibited all the best each race had to offer.

The possibilities were endless.

With a lick of his lips, he picked up his fork and knife and cut into his barely cooked steak. The red, marbled meat glistened, and he practically drooled. His thirst for blood had grown stronger in the past twenty-four hours. Which reminded him. He had a pretty vampire guest at the cabin who needed to feed.

He glanced up at Apostle, who ate quietly on the other side of the long, rectangular table. "You're quiet this morning, brother."

Apostle cleared his throat, shifted uneasily in his chair, and kept his gaze on his plate, but didn't reply.

"Are you still angry about that whole stabbing thing?" he said, setting his utensils down. He dabbed the corners of his mouth with his white cloth napkin, and then waved over his servant.

Apostle glared at him. "More like that whole you've-changed-my-DNA-against-my-will thing."

Bishop waved his hand. "Pshaw! Oh that? That's what you're angry about?"

The servant stopped beside Bishop and waited to be addressed.

"What do you mean, 'oh that'?" Apostle slammed the butt of his knife against the varnished wood of the table. "You've changed me into one of them, Bishop! You've turned me into a *mongrel*. A goddamn mongrel. They're the enemy, for Chrissakes! I don't want to be one of *them*. I want nothing to do with those beasts. And now you've made me into one. Goddamn you!" He tossed his fork and knife onto the table and erupted from his seat. "How dare you perform your psychotic experiments on me without my permission! How fucking dare you!"

"Enough!" Bishop slammed his fist on the table, making his plate hop like a jumping bean.

Apostle fumed, his jaw set. But just a hint of fear shone in his eyes. Fear of what Bishop would do to him if he didn't guard his tone and bite his tongue. Good. Apostle should be afraid. Very afraid. Bishop held no qualms about doing more to Apostle than just setting his altered scorpions on him and restructuring his DNA, and Apostle knew it.

"Sit! Down!" Bishop wouldn't tolerate this insubordination, not even from his brother. *Especially* from his brother, who should have bigger balls than this.

After several long, terse seconds, Apostle finally faltered and lowered himself unsteadily back into his seat. *Good little doggy.*

Bishop waved the servant closer, and he knelt down. "Find

a human for my guest in the cabin. She needs to feed." He dismissed the servant and looked back at his brother. "You still don't understand, do you?"

Apostle's eyes narrowed. "I understand that you're delusional."

"Ah-ah. Watch yourself with me, Apostle."

Looking away, Apostle acquiesced. "Fine. What don't I understand, Bishop?"

Bishop pushed back from the table, pulled out one of his beloved Sobranies, settled the filter between his lips, and lit it. No matter how much his body changed, he would always enjoy the succulent richness of his tobacco.

As he smoked and left a cloud of sweet richness behind him, he paced to the window that overlooked the plain flatness of his new facility's grounds. Northern Indiana was nothing like the rocky landscape of Arizona, but he would have to get used to it. This was where he had to work now. But at least northern Indiana was closer to his suppliers. That was about the only benefit, though.

"You don't understand that to win this war, we have to become our enemy," Bishop said. "The secret lies in making them weak, as well as in making us stronger." He turned, one hand in his pocket while the fingers of the other settled around his brown cigarette. "Cobalt is our way of making them weak, you see." He leaned against the edge of the table beside Apostle and looked down on him. "Our blood, our venom. It weakens them."

A frown settled on Apostle's brow, but Bishop couldn't tell if it was because he didn't understand, didn't want to, or that he was just disgusted, in general.

"You see, brother, we've been going about defeating the vampires all wrong. We've always thought our weakness was just that. A weakness. All we needed was to change our perspective." He took a drag on his cigarette and blew the smoke in Apostle's face. "Turns out our weakness is also *their* weakness...which in turn makes it our strength. Kind of like the enemy of my enemy is my friend."

"What are you saying?" Apostle waved the smoke away.

"Are you simple?" Bishop huffed and shook his head. "Cobalt is made of our blood. It's made with our venom. Hence the name."

"Yeah, duh. I get that," Apostle said. "What I'm not getting is your point. What's this have to do with turning me into a goddamn half-vampire?"

Apostle would never understand. He was too much of a purist. Too averse to change and progress in favor of keeping with the way things had always been. Too devoted to winning the war against the vampires by remaining in the past, stuck in the same methods, the same rank and file, using the same weak tactics with no regard toward advanced ideas. Bishop should have cut Apostle loose the moment he returned from Chicago after Deacon was killed.

"God, you're such a simpleton." Bishop rolled his eyes. "We've turned what made us weaker than the vampires into what now makes them weak, while we take what makes them strong and use it to make us stronger. Don't you see?" He huffed and glanced across the room. "Of course you don't. You want to think we can match against them as we are—as we *were*." His gaze burned back into Apostle's. "*As we were*, Apostle. But we can't. As normal drecks, we can't compete. They will always be stronger than we are—*were*. But now, by using cobalt, we can make them weak with our blood and venom while we take theirs and make ourselves stronger. We are becoming the dominant race now, Apostle. Don't you see? Can't you taste it? It's right there…just within our grasp."

"You're deranged." Apostle shrank away from him. "Cobalt can get the job done without us having to become the enemy."

Maniacal laughter rang through the dining room. "Maybe in the short-term."

Question marks hovered in Apostle's expression, and Bishop laughed again. "You should see your face, my brother. You look positively stymied." He settled his hand—the one holding his cigarette—on the table, and a trail of smoke rose like a snake from the burning tip. "You see, Apostle, that's what all the experiments have been leading up to. This is why we've worked so hard to pump cobalt into the vampire masses." He lifted his hand, took a drag off his cigarette, blew out the smoke, and settled his hand on the table once more. "Did you really think we simply wanted to get them high all this time? Did you really not realize there was more to cobalt than that?"

"Of course not. I've always known its purpose was to make them weaker, but I thought...I didn't..."

"Well, spit it out, Apostle."

What a dolt. Apostle simply wouldn't do. Perhaps he should toss him back out into the streets as a dealer, or maybe he should just kill him now. Clearly, Apostle wasn't going to work out in the New World Order, where drecks took over and turned the tables on the vampires. No more subservience. No more playing second fiddle. The drecks would hold the power, and the vampires would be nothing.

As Apostle looked away with that silly, confused expression on his face, Bishop crushed the burning end of his cigarette against his cheek. Apostle cried out and snapped away, slapping his palm over his cheek as Bishop pushed away from the edge of the table and laughed at him.

"The vampires fall at our feet for cobalt. They buy it, snort it, shoot it up, and within months they will learn its true purpose." He sauntered away, turned, looked back at Apostle. "We're about to embark on a magnificent campaign, Apostle. One that will see mass numbers of vampires die. The new cobalt cocktail will have a special ingredient, dear brother. One that will rain death on the vampires. We've almost perfected it in the lab. It's only a matter of time. And after it's perfected and distributed bit by bit throughout our network of dealers, our time will come. Mongrels will explode into mutancy, as will full-bloods. Those who don't will suffer brain damage so severe they'll be nothing more than vegetables. King Bain and his dogs, All the King's Men, will have their hands so full trying to contain the mass chaos within their race, they won't even see us coming. They will be helpless to stop us, because we will no longer be simply drecks, but drecks with vampire strength...vampire abilities.

Bain's *brave, powerful* soldiers will be no match for our altered, equally powerful drecks. They will strike us, and we will heal ten times faster than they will. They will be weak, and we will be strong." He raised his fist and thumped the air.

Apostle only stared at him as if deaf and dumb.

Bishop lowered his fist and sighed, disappointed, frustrated, and out of patience. "You're an imbecile, Apostle. You don't have half the stomach Deacon had for what has to be done. Deacon had balls. He spearheaded the operation. He was eager to begin his alteration. You?" Bishop sneered. "You're a coward. A waste. A complete and total letdown. I gifted you with the power to heal, and you spit on me for it. You turn up your nose at progress...at ruling the world, humans included. We can have it all, Apostle, and yet you adhere to antiquity. You cling to the belief that we can continue to live as we've always lived and somehow find a way to overcome. You accept that mediocrity is enough. That it's okay to always be held under their thumbs as if we are merely their servants and not worthy of more." He flicked his spent butt to the floor and crossed his arms as he bent over Apostle, whose palm still held his cheek. "I refuse to accept that, Apostle. I will not be held down any longer. And neither will Premier Royce. We will overthrow them, and after the phone call I just had, it looks like we now have an unlikely ally who will make our cause all the more successful." *And be my ticket to overthrow Royce, if all goes well.*

"Who?" Apostle's voice was weak, defeated...disgusting.

"A vampire named Searcy, and his son Vaydon. Ancients, from what I'm told. Ancients with a penchant for inflicting pain and suffering...ruthless and ready to join forces to oust King Bain's ass from that pedestal of power he hides behind."

Apostle gulped and stared. Just stared. Horror in his eyes.

Bishop chuffed and lowered his head. Trying to explain things to Apostle was useless, and he didn't want to waste any more precious breath on his idiotic brother.

"Clean yourself up," he said as he flicked his hand

dismissively and spun for the door. "I can't stand the sight of you."

APOSTLE STARED AFTER BISHOP as he practically slithered from the room.

Bishop was fucking nuts. Certifiably crazy times a hundred.

He took his hand away from his cheek and stared at his palm. He had always known that cobalt was a mechanism to weaken vampires, but he hadn't realized just how much. He hadn't known the full extent of what the drug would be used for.

Not that he cared about killing hundreds or even thousands of vampires. So much the better, as far as he was concerned. But Bishop's methods of going about it seemed like nothing more than toying with Mother Nature, who had a way of getting pissed off and turning the tables on those who tried to jack up the natural order of things.

Bishop was messing with fire. He was a modern-day Dr. Frankenstein. A mad scientist motivated by the lust for power. A psychopathic lunatic with a well-funded lab, where he could jack around with whatever madness he could think up.

Any way Apostle looked at it, Bishop's quest was a folly waiting to blow up in his face. Maybe he could win the short-term battle and strike a healthy blow against the vampires. Maybe Bishop would even succeed in defeating King Bain and deal a harsh setback to AKM, but in the long run, Apostle's instincts told him these games Bishop and Royce were playing would grow teeth, horns, a forked tail, and then turn on them with a vengeance.

Had they not learned that lesson from the humans? Look at all the failures humanity had stacked up when trying to mess with Mother Nature. For every human problem solved by science, two more seemed to be created. Like antibiotics. They seemed like such a great idea, but overuse and medicinal abuse now rendered many ineffective, and superbug bacteria were growing more and more uncontrollable. And now Bishop was traipsing down the same path. What kind of superbugs would *his* experiments and scientific research produce? Could he be sealing the fate of the drecks and not even be aware of it? All in the name of *progress*?

And who were these ancients he spoke of? Searcy and Vaydon? All Apostle really needed to know was that they were vampires, and vampires were not to be trusted. As far as Apostle was concerned, forming an alliance with vampires, no matter how aligned their motives were with theirs, was just another form of going against Mother Nature. He refused to partner with vampires. Screw Bishop and his whack-job ideas.

Apostle left the dining hall and headed toward his room. As he passed a mirror in the hallway, he stopped and stared in astonishment to see that the cigarette burn on his cheek had already healed.

God, he was a freak of nature now. No longer dreck. Not a vampire. A fucking freak.

He looked away from the mirror and kept his head down as he walked the rest of the way to his room and shut the door behind him.

The writing was on the wall. His time here was limited. If he didn't get out on his own, he would end up dead. He could feel it. Maybe Bishop was the genius, and maybe Deacon had been the progressive thinker, but Apostle had always been the warrior. His instincts were finely honed from centuries on the front lines while Bishop and Deacon had stayed safely tucked in the background. Consequently, he could smell danger from a hundred miles away.

And right now, danger came with the scent of smoke from a brown, gold-tipped cigarette.

CHAPTER 21

FOR THE FIRST TIME IN WHAT FELT LIKE A MILLENNIUM, Brak stepped outside. Open air. He was free. Finally, blessedly free.

After killing his keepers and coming back to his body to vomit all over himself—which he always did after expending his energy to kill—Cynthia had cleaned him up as she always did. Then he had fallen into a heavy sleep for several hours, totally drained. When he awoke, his things were already packed, and she told them they were leaving. At first, he didn't understand. Freedom had become such a foreign concept that the knowledge didn't fully register that he no longer needed to stay imprisoned. That basement enclosure had been his home for so long that the idea he could leave and make a new home somewhere else didn't sink in until Cynthia pulled him toward the small door she used to exit his chamber.

He ducked and followed her through to emerge into a wide hallway that led to a set of stairs. Panicked voices echoed down the stairwell, a lot of shouting, along with hurried footsteps.

"The staff is arriving," Cynthia explained.

Once upstairs, he found Jacob and Haslet where he slaughtered them. He had been this close to his physical body when he killed them. Somehow, knowing that felt strangely surreal.

Those in the room—guards and caretakers, perhaps—froze when they saw him. Terrified didn't begin to describe the fear that gripped their expressions. They all seemed to know who and what he was.

"I'm leaving." His deep voice was a compassionate rumble. His vocal chords were still raw from how violently ill he had become after returning to his body. "You're all free now."

Then he had turned and followed Cynthia to the door.

Now he stood outside, face turned skyward, a smile spread across his mouth, eyes closed.

A soft breeze blew over his skin, and he sighed. Something so simple to those who lived with the freedom to enjoy it every day was the epitome of pleasure to him. A small miracle created to hold him rapt as air swirled and caressed him. He opened his eyes and glanced down at the ends of his long hair as they lifted and swayed gently in the breeze. As he glanced toward Cynthia, a gust of chilled air tickled his skin with goose bumps, and he laughed as he lifted his forearms and stared in awe at his prickled flesh.

"What's so funny?" Cynthia smiled.

He showed her his arms and grinned from ear to ear. "Goose flesh."

She glanced at his arms then met his gaze again, one eyebrow arched, her face screwed into an amused expression. "Okay, Brak. No more fresh air for you."

He laughed and leaped off the porch. His guitar, which was slung by its strap across his back, bounced against him, and he spun around to drink in his surroundings.

The house sat on a hill that overlooked a tree-filled valley to the east, and the glow of coming dawn yellowed the horizon. To the west was another valley, filled with more trees, and the waning moon hung low in the sky.

"Where are we?" he asked.

"West Virginia." Cynthia joined him and slid her hand inside his. Her kind, brown eyes dazzled with delight as she watched him. "You're like a big kid discovering Oz in the middle of Willy Wonka's chocolate factory."

He had seen those movies and grinned. "Yes, this is all very fantastical to me." He inhaled deeply. "And fascinating."

"Just wait until you see the city."

Excitement shot down his spine, and goose bumps erupted again all over his body. "Will it be like I've seen on the Internet?"

She laughed. "Better. And worse."

"Worse?" He sounded taken aback.

With a squeeze of his hand, she smiled up at him. "You'll see."

The door opened behind him and they turned to see one of the home's caretakers dart out. She carried a suitcase, duffel bag, and an umbrella. When she saw them, she faltered then stopped. "Thank you, sir. Thank you." She bowed her head, hesitated for a heartbeat, and then hurried off to a small car parked in a row beside the house.

"What was that about?" he said.

Cynthia caressed his arm. "She's grateful to you. You freed her."

"She's human." He watched the young woman throw her bags in the car and climb into the front seat.

"Yes." Cynthia sounded sad. "Haslet's blood slave...and slave for other things."

"What other things?" Brak frowned, getting a sense he knew what Haslet had used the pretty human for.

Cynthia paused before speaking, clearly uncomfortable. "Brak, she was his sex slave."

Anger rose within him and darkened his mood. He looked to the trees in the west, up to the moon, and across the lightening sky before dropping his gaze to his booted feet. "It's good I killed them. They did not appreciate what they had."

Cynthia nodded and pulled his gaze around to her with her fingers on his cheek. "Yes, Brak. It's good you killed them. They were evil. Bad, bad people. You've saved lives today. You should be proud."

He looked away. Killing never made him feel proud. Trace was the death dealer. He was supposed to be the giver of life.

But together he and Trace were more powerful than anyone could fathom, and discovering that Trace still lived filled him with indescribable joy. Together, they became the best and the worst of each other. Balanced. Synergistic.

How Trace had survived this long without him blew his

mind, because, of the two of them, he carried the more detrimental power. A power that required constant vigil…a function Brak had been made to temper.

But his powers had been abused for decades by those bastards who had held him prisoner. He had been forced to kill, and kill, and kill some more, and each time he did, his soul wept and sickness overcame him. Even now, he still felt weak. If not for the exhilaration of freedom, he would still be passed out in bed, and would remain there for days. And Cynthia knew it, because it was her job to tend to him through his recovery.

"Brak?" She touched his cheek, and he turned his tired, sorrow-filled eyes toward her.

She was his friend. So kind and giving. She had given up her life to tend to his. Just as her mother and grandmother before her.

"Brak," she said again, "I know what you're thinking, but don't. They were bad people. In a way, you gave life today to those who have been held prisoner by them the same way you were held prisoner."

He nodded and took a heavy breath. She was right, but it didn't make him feel better about what he had done. In the heat of the moment, he had thrived on their deaths, greedy for them, hungry to feel their life squeeze out of their bodies. But now that time had passed and he had returned to normal, what he'd done made him feel like a monster.

"I'm ready to go," he said, his earlier fascination now gone.

She issued a tight nod. "Okay." She led him to another of the cars beside the house, helped him load his guitar and bags into the backseat, and then held the front door open so he could climb inside. It was a tight fit until she bent down, slipped her hands between his knees to the underside of the seat, and did something to make the seat slide back.

"Better?" she said.

"Yes." He looked down and tried to figure out what she'd done to increase his leg room.

She shut the door, and he glanced up and stared out the window at the house. His prison. He would never come back here. This time in his life was over, and it was time to find his brother and father. Rebuild what was left of their family. Catch up on all that had happened.

"Where are we going?" Cynthia asked as she climbed in beside him and started the engine.

"We?" He glanced across the seat at her.

"Yes. I'm going with you."

He shook his head. "I can't take you away from your family, Cynthia."

"It's my choice. Besides, you'll need me. You don't know how to live in this new world."

True. He had learned much from the Internet, but once he reached civilization, he was sure he'd have questions. Lots and lots of questions. He needed a guide. That Cynthia wanted to be that guide warmed his heart. She was a touch of the familiar in a land of strangers, and he was comfortable with her. "Thank you," he said.

"You're welcome. Now…where are we going?" She worked her feet against the floor of the car and moved a lever, and the car began to move backward.

Riveted by how her movements affected the car's movement, he watched but remembered finding Trace in that dungeon cell.

"Chicago," he said. "I want to go to Chicago."

"Chicago? Why there?" Cynthia shifted the lever raised from the floor between them again, adjusted her legs, and then the car surged forward.

"My brother's there." He clapped one hand down on the inside of the door and gripped his seat with the other. He had never ridden in a car. The only time he had been transported between facilities, he had been drugged and slept through the entire trip.

"Brak? Just calm down. It's okay." She laughed at him. "I'm a good driver. You're safe."

He licked his lips and nodded briskly, but stared wide-eyed out the window.

She laughed again. "You should see yourself. And I'm not even going that fast, yet."

"This isn't fast?" The trees began to blur as she pulled down a long, paved drive.

"No. Just wait until we hit the highway."

"Highway?" Yes, having Cynthia along as his guide was a good thing. He already felt like a bird without wings, and the house he'd called home for the past forever wasn't even out of throwing distance.

And so began his adventure back into the world.

CHAPTER 22

MALEK STOOD IN AWE OF THE PETITE FIRECRACKER in front of him. Gina was his. They were together now, and for the first time in forever, he didn't feel half alive. He was whole again.

Tom Cruise's famous line from *Jerry Maguire* ran on a repeating loop through his mind, and he grinned.

"What are you smiling about?" she said as she skimmed a layer of suds from his chest.

"You ever see *Jerry Maguire*?" He enjoyed the feel of her hands on his body as she continued to rinse away the soap she had lathered him with.

"Of course." Her eyes narrowed as if she had an idea where his mind was.

"You—"

"Don't say that cheesy line." She rolled her eyes and laughed.

He laughed with her. "Why not? It's true." He brushed the backs of his fingers down her cheek. "You complete me, Gina. You really do."

Her cheeks turned red as she averted her gaze and watched her hands slide up and down his torso. "You've lost too much weight, Malek."

The change of subject wasn't unexpected. He got the feeling Gina wanted to keep the mood from growing too serious...that maybe she was stalling or had something on her mind she wasn't ready to discuss. No worries. She could take all the time she wanted, because now that they had consummated their mating, all they had was time. Time enough to say and do everything they could possibly imagine to one another.

"I'll gain it all back," he said.

"You should eat." She reached around to shut off the water, but he stopped her.

"Later." First he wanted to return the favor. "Your turn." He grabbed the bottle of lilac-scented soap he was sure belonged to Samantha and poured a generous drizzle into a lavender loofah.

This was his female, and it was high time he started treating her like the reverent creature she was.

He worked the soap into thick suds that dropped to the shower floor in dollops, and then slowly massaged the soaped-up loofah over her shoulders, across her collarbones, and down to her breasts. Bathing her was a privilege, one that was as much a visual feast as an honor, and he drank in the way the white, soapy foam slid down the curves of her breasts, clung briefly to her puckered nipples, and then dropped to the shower floor.

"You're like a piece of living art," he said quietly. "So beautiful and perfect."

"And apparently pretty possessive of my male," she teased. "Let's not forget *that*."

"Yes, let's not." Malek smiled then turned her around and began washing her back. "That's how I knew, you know," he said a moment later.

She looked over her shoulder. "Knew what?"

"That you needed me as much as I needed you." He set the loofah aside, rinsed her back, and then grabbed the shampoo and poured some in her hair. "You coming into my bedroom and attacking that..." He was too ashamed to say out loud what had happened.

"It's over now. She's the past. I'm the present and the future." She turned to face him again.

"Yeah, well, seeing you fight for me like that..." His fingers massaged the shampoo into her hair. "It woke me up. It made me realize you had chosen me, too, and that I needed to fight just as hard for you as you had for me. I thought I had been doing the right thing by pushing you away, but I was wrong.

God, was I wrong. I just didn't want to hurt you, but when I saw that I was, anyway, it killed me. I had to find you...fix things. Accept you...us."

"I was wrong, too, Malek. I didn't want to be mated, either." She looked away and fidgeted. "I've been having these panic attacks." Her eyes met his again. "Really bad ones ever since I left Chicago. I thought I was having them because of what you said to me in my cell about mating me. That fear of being mated again—not just to you, but to anyone—was causing them." She took a deep breath. "But I was wrong."

Emotions passed back and forth between them, and his fingers stilled against her scalp. "Wrong?"

"Being away from you was so hard on me." Her gaze bore into his. "All this time, I had those stupid panic attacks because I needed to be back here. With you. Right where I am this very second." She pressed against him. "Because, Malek, you complete me, too."

Malek's fingers were still buried in her hair, covered in shampoo, but he tucked her against him with his elbows. "Is that what finally brought you back to Chicago?" He tugged her hair so that she leaned back into the shower of water.

She closed her eyes. "Yes and no. Trevor and I fucked up our hit on Searcy and Vaydon—well, *I* fucked it up." She glanced down guiltily. "But we had to get out of Florida fast, and I thought if I came back here and told you to kiss my ass, I'd get better."

He smiled. "Kiss your ass?"

She smirked. "That was the plan."

"And what changed your mind?"

"Trevor."

That was unexpected. "Trevor?"

She nodded. "He told me some silly story and convinced me to give you a chance."

Malek suddenly liked Trevor a whole lot more. "Smart guy, that Trevor."

She rolled her eyes at him. "You say that now, but earlier—"

"Hey, I'm allowed to be a little moody. I'm a newly mated male."

"That you are." She pecked him on the lips then dipped her hair back into the water again.

Once her hair was rinsed, he turned her back around and applied conditioner. He loved tending to her, bathing her, taking care of her like this. "I thought Micah forced you back because of me."

Her hands joined his and helped him massage the conditioner into her scalp. Their fingers mingled and danced, and as she leaned forward to let the water rinse her hair again, she linked their hands and pulled them around her. God, but she was incredible, with silky skin and smooth curves that nestled perfectly within the angles of his body.

She let go of his hands and brushed her wet hair back as she turned to face him again, still rinsing her hair. "Micah kept e-mailing me about coming back, but never told me why. But I assumed it was because of you."

"And now you're here."

"Now I'm here." She said it with an air of finality. As if they had reached the end of one journey and were about to embark on another, more enjoyable one.

Their bodies pressed together, and his calling started toward its next crescendo. This time, he would take the time to savor her.

He bent her body back and ringed her neck with his palm. Water splashed onto her breasts and stomach. What an erotic sight.

"You have the most unbelievable neck." He caressed the slender column and drew his fingers down between her breasts, and then pulled her back into his arms.

Who would have thought a shower could be so sensual? But then, Malek had a lot of missed time to make up for. He had never showered with a female...had never experienced the luxuries of modern-day lovemaking. He hadn't been with a female—truly *with* one—since Carmen.

Funny. Even thinking about Carmen didn't awaken a shit storm of guilt or oppressive frustration. Her memory still lingered, but he no longer wanted to cling to her. All he wanted was the female in front of him. His Gina. His spirited, sexy mate.

Water dripped off the ends of her hair and clung to her eyelashes, and rivulets ran down her face and off the tip of her nose. She was adorable and sexy and alluring. All the things a female should be.

And she was his.

He lifted her into his arms, and her strong legs locked around him. Her arms hugged his shoulders. He turned off the water.

Shower over. Time to love her again.

He carried her out of the shower and back to the bedroom, where he climbed onto the bed and settled her on the blankets before he eased himself onto her.

"I love you." His lips brushed hers, and she pulled him down into a simmering embrace.

Malek craved Gina. She was oxygen, absolutely necessary to his survival, and he had waited much too long to breathe. But he breathed now, and with each full inhale and cleansing exhale, his body calmed a little bit more from the nightmare of the past several weeks—hell, the past several centuries, if he was being honest with himself. The nearness of her—his mate—unfurled each coiled muscle, pulled to their limits for so long that the pain had become a way of life. No wonder he had been wound so tightly. Because, literally, he had been.

Not now, though. Now he loosened and sprawled. The soothing caress of her nearness chased the tension away, and he sighed as his body relaxed.

Gina's warm hand, so perfect and gentle, glided up his stomach and over the subtle swell of his pec, and he bowed his head against her and slid his nose up her shoulder to her neck. A quiet purr broke in his chest.

How had he denied her before? He must have been insane.

Oh wait. That's right. He had been. But now he saw how crazy he had been to refuse their bond. With her now, so close, touching her, smelling her, breathing in the air that skimmed the surface of her body, he knew he was home, and he purred again.

Her pulse quickened at the sound. He felt it course furiously beneath the skin of her neck, where his nose rested. The thu-thump of her heartbeat pulsed against his lips, which he pressed directly over her vein. He lived now for that vital pulse, and his fangs throbbed with the need to feed.

A wave of hormonal heat vibrated out of him and called to her. It was time to renew their connection. Time to continue what they had started in the shower, hopefully without as much urgency so he could cherish each moment and savor the experience. Her body answered and rippled from her head to her feet as she moaned.

Keeping his lips pressed against the sexiest part of her—the pulse in her throat—Malek rocked against her body. Another purr broke in his chest as hormonal heat surged out of him once more. He was captivated...enraptured.

If he had thought the fire they started in the shower was hot, it was nothing compared to the blaze that now crawled through his spine...down...down...to wrap around his scrotum and tingle the inside of his cock. His four previous orgasms cowered like chumps at what built within him now, which felt more like the Goliath of all releases to stomp all the puny Davids that had come before.

Heat continued to rise as she slid her arms around his back and pulled him to her. Her breasts mashed delicately against his chest.

"I want you," he whispered against her neck, his voice restrained and raspy.

She turned her face into his and kissed his cheek below his ear. "Then take me."

Unwilling to break the connection between his mouth and her throat, he latched on with his teeth, hooked one arm on the inside of her thigh, opened her, and settled more snugly between her legs. His engorged cock rubbed against home base, and he grunted from the pleasure that shot through his groin and down both legs.

Their energy spun, twined, and intensified with each breath and soft caress. Gina was a female worth savoring. She was a beauty to worship, and only he had the right to do so. Now that they had claimed each other, he was helpless against her.

He had worried that he would blemish Carmen's memory by taking Gina, but he'd been wrong. Exercising his mated right with Gina didn't make what he'd had with Carmen disappear or cast aside her memory. Carmen was still there, in his heart and mind, but now he accepted the truth. She was gone. Not in spirit, just in body. He could still love Gina without dishonoring Carmen, and he could still remember Carmen without withholding even a piece of himself from Gina. There was room for them both in his heart, not one or the other as he had thought. He could have his past and his future and never diminish the love or power of either.

As his hips settled between Gina's legs, there was no more guilt. No more suffering or anguish. Gina was all that existed, and his heart opened fully to welcome her as she prepared to welcome him into her body once more.

"Oh, God." He purred again as he shifted and rolled against her. Pure desire opened like the jaw of a lion, too long denied and ready to devour them both. His voracious appetite stole his breath. He didn't just want her, he hungered for her.

"I need you, Malek." She trembled.

"I'll never hurt you again." He kissed and laved her nape with his tongue as he kneed her legs farther apart, his body primed and ready to feel her bliss again. Her wet, short hair felt soft and smooth as satin against his fingers, and he wrapped his other arm underneath her body as he slid his cock against her welcoming slickness. But still he didn't enter her, content to take his time and let the inferno build.

She sighed. He groaned.

She panted. He purred.

Back and forth, they traded a symphony of breathy moans and gentle gasps, each more erotic than the one before, tainted with rising need.

Pulling her hair, he encouraged her to turn her head so he could admire her succulent neck, erotica incarnate. No expanse of flesh had ever been more inviting, not even Carmen's, and he would have to take a moment each day to worship the elegant slopes and curves that called for him to drink. He would adorn her with jeweled necklaces and low-cut blouses so that he could delight in her most striking feature and sneak a quick, unobstructed taste whenever the mood struck him. If he had his way, she would never wear a turtleneck again.

With his tongue, he outlined the subtle taper that extended from her jaw then swept out to her shoulder. What a magnificent expanse of skin. So supple. So smooth.

And her taste...perfection.

"God, your neck is sexy." He nibbled and suckled, creating a trail from ear to shoulder, then from right to left so he could sample every inch. Gina's was a neck to adore, treasure, and bow down to. Just the thought of biting her nearly made him come, and he wasn't even inside her yet.

Her inner thighs caressed his hips as she wrapped her legs around him and slid her feet to the inside of his knees.

A tangle of limbs and pulsating heat, they writhed skin-against-skin, and he ground his erection against the heart of her. She kept one arm wrapped around the bunching muscles of his back and held his face to her neck with the other. "Don't stop. I like that." Her words came out as a breathless whisper, and she stretched, pulled her damp hair away, and bared her throat. "More."

Bless her. She wanted him to feast exactly where he wanted to remain. And he had no intention of stopping, not now that his fractured psyche had glued itself back together to connect his disjointed personalities into one again.

He thrust against her, and the shaft of his cock glided smoothly between her nether lips, riding up and over her clit. So good. She was wet and ready for him, hot and wanton, and her throaty groan blistered his flesh.

He would never take for granted another day. Each moment was a gift, and each day would be another to remind him of his fortune. Now that he had found her and embraced all that she was, he was the richest male in the world. He would never forget that again.

Keeping his mouth on her neck, he pressed his nose and

lips against her skin as each thrust demanded more. With each advance, she lifted her hips to meet his, breathing out incoherent, monosyllabic exclamations every time their bodies rocked toward the headboard. She squirmed beneath him, gasped in need, and her breasts crushed against his chest as she arched her back and moaned.

Her body was a pleasurable oasis. The temperature rose, heat flooded him, and his muscles contracted in a way he hadn't felt in centuries. Restraint ebbed as unbridled desire flowed, and he rocked more forcefully against her. He pulled back farther, drove the length of his cock between her slickened lips with more power. The point of no return fast approached—if not already passed—and just as their moans reached desperate levels, the head of his cock breeched her as he began another upward thrust.

They both froze, and neither dared to breathe for a heartbeat.

Malek lifted himself on his arms and looked into her eyes, which sparkled with anticipation as she heaved for breath, her chest rising and falling heavily. So beautiful. So precious. *Mine, mine...all mine. Forever.*

With parted lips and pleading eyes, she pushed her fingers into his long hair and lifted it away from his face. Her tongue peeked out and wet her lips. "Please don't stop. Please...I've needed this for too long." Her hand, tense and trembling, cupped his face.

She looked as if she feared he would pull away again, just as he had hours earlier in his home, when all he had wanted was to go to her. Instead, he'd fled and sought comfort in another.

Not anymore and never again. She needn't worry that he would run scared and abandon her. Those days were over and his fears no longer held sway over him. With her, he was complete and had found his place. There would be no more retreat...no more running away. His heart was hers to rule for the rest of his life. His body was hers to find her own pleasure in, and to bring to ecstasy with her touch.

"Sshh." He turned into her hand, kissed her palm, turned

back to meet her gaze again, and then nudged his way farther inside. "I'm where I belong...where I want to stay forever."

Gina's brow softened as relief washed through her expression, and her eyelids drifted to half-mast as a plaintive moan flowed from deep within her belly, followed by an erotic sigh as she shifted under him and held him more tightly.

This was home. With her. Now. For the rest of his life.

He sank all the way in, and they both bit out a staccato exhale as they succumbed to one another.

Refuge.

Gina's body was a refuge, and he found solace within her sleeve of perfect warmth and sanctuary. Like taking a breath, each deliberate stroke gave Malek life.

New life. Because he hadn't truly lived since Carmen's death. He had merely gone through the motions, taking in oxygen simply because his reflexes forced him to breathe, eating to squelch the hunger in his belly, taking blood for the same reason. But all this time, what he had been doing couldn't be called living. He had existed, but he hadn't lived. But now, he could actually hear his own heartbeat. It pumped hard and strong, ready to burst with love. He breathed not because he had to, but because he wanted to take in her essence and let her scent invade every microscopic crevice inside him. And his appetite for food and blood burst back to life, and not just for sustenance, but to enjoy with all five senses.

He wanted to feast on life. On Gina.

Anchored to her as if she kept him from setting adrift, he advanced and retreated with an ease that was only diminished by the urgency with which he held her and assaulted her neck with his lips and tongue.

This is what I wanted. This is who I needed.

For the first time in weeks, and unlike the rushed, frenetic climaxes he'd had in the shower, his orgasm got out of the easy chair it had taken up residence in and prepared to give him hell.

He buried his arms between Gina and the mattress. Her skin tasted exquisite. Surely her blood would taste just as fine. Every part of him wanted to sink in his fangs, but he held back. Not yet, not yet. But soon.

Each forceful exhale rode the rising crescendo of muscular tension that pulled his body taut. The energy built inside him as if he were a stick of dynamite with a lit fuse, and with each inhale, his senses flooded with more of her irresistible scent, which fueled him, fired his desire, and coiled him into a tight ball ready to explode.

The way her nails dug into his back as her arms tightened around him was perfect, because he wanted her to hold him close, keep him there, and never let go. Her hips raised and rocked in rhythm against him with an urgency that only served to take him closer to the edge with each long, measured stroke.

Oh fuck.

There comes a time while making love that a male simply has to forget about everything else...about taking his time... about giving his partner pleasure...about being gentle. And Malek had reached that point. His body took over for him, pushing away conscious effort to speed toward the destination culminating in the center of his soul.

His hips slapped rapidly against her inner thighs, his abs screamed from exertion, and his legs tightened into ramming rods. He was about to come, and he was ready to feel the full force of his orgasm's brutality. Beyond ready. He had gone unsatisfied far too long, and the consolation comes of weeks past were no longer welcome. The rushed, explosive bursts in the shower had been breathtaking and satisfying, but he didn't just want to lose his breath. He wanted to lose his mind. He wanted to lose himself and feel his muscles shred in ecstasy.

With an urgent groan, he tightened his grip, his body contracted, and with one last, smooth thrust, he blew apart.

"Oh God!" His abdomen tightened and released through each successive pump of his erection as he emptied himself into her, grunting hard through wave after wave of release.

It wasn't until a moment later that he realized Gina's body had fallen into rapid contractions beneath him. Her entire body seemed to have fallen into orgasm as his name shuddered from her lips.

Malek lifted his gaze to find her head thrown back, her eyes closed in rapture, her pink lips open as she sucked in her breath and cried out again as another wave of shuddering bliss overtook her. Her short, dark hair spilled over the white pillowcase, tousled, damp, and utterly adorable. *She* was adorable, so precious and perfect.

Unable to hold back, he closed his mouth over hers, breathed her, tasted her, feasted on her full lips as she answered in kind. Back and forth, they traded tongues and teeth. Their combined orgasms drew out and left them shivering and battered until finally he stilled above her, pulled his mouth from hers, and bowed his forehead against the top of her shoulder, spent and breathless.

What they had just shared had been beautiful and perfect.

He had needed this, and apparently, so had she.

Closing his eyes, he buried his face against her neck once more, his body crashing as his orgasm waned.

Happy now? The Voice said quietly, sprawled in exhaustion.

God yes. I've found where I belong.

It's about time. My work here is done.

With that, The Voice was gone. It was just him. Him and her. Gina. His life-giving mate. He was finally able to say good-bye once and for all to his beloved Carmen.

Rest in peace, my love. But my place is here now.

He had a feeling Carmen was gazing down on him, smiling, happy to see him whole and alive again.

Good-bye, Carmen. Thank you for loving me, but it's time to let you go.

CHAPTER 23

BRAK BLINKED AGAINST THE SUNLIGHT as he woke up. Even with the sunglasses Cynthia gave him, the brightness hurt his eyes.

"What time is it?" He adjusted the seat, which Cynthia had shown him how to recline when they'd stopped for breakfast, and sat up, squinting. He rubbed his fingers over his sleep-crusted eyes under the dark lenses.

"It's almost one o'clock. I thought we'd stop for lunch and a quick restroom break. I need to pee."

"So do I." Maybe he shouldn't have had that second cup of coffee at breakfast, because he was about to burst. He wasn't used to being away from the comforts of his cell like this, where he could drink as much as he wanted without worrying over when the next bathroom break would come.

He tried to ignore the discomfort of his bladder and gazed out the window as the scenery flew past.

It was a wonder he had fallen asleep at all, but after he had gotten used to the speed of the car and its gentle rocking motion and the lull of the engine, exhaustion, along with a large breakfast of pancakes, eggs, bacon, and milk—and a decanter of decaf—had taken him under. He had slept for the past five hours. Then again, what he'd done the day before had drained him. He needed sleep to recover and recharge his power.

"Where are we?" He looked out the window at the more densely populated landscape. Buildings jutted skyward in rows. Apartment buildings. He had seen pictures of them on the Internet. Lines of houses and industrial-looking shopping centers sprawled on either side of the highway. Shiny glass buildings loomed ahead, and a line of traffic was encroaching on his right, entering the highway. Cars and tractor-trailers closed them in on all sides.

He jarred to attention, suddenly claustrophobic and panicked.

"Sshh, sshh, Brak." Cynthia reached across the seat and took his hand. "We're outside Indianapolis, just north of the city."

He stared in fear as a car entered the freeway and pulled up alongside them. If he opened his window, he swore he could have reached out and touched it.

"The cars are so close." He looked in the mirror beside him, then out the front window and to the left, past Cynthia.

"They're not as close as they look, sweetie. Just relax. I do this all the time. I won't let them hit us."

She was so confident, calm, and relaxed. Would he ever be so calm in the driver's seat of a car like this? The last time he was free to roam where he pleased, the fastest transportation had been a horse. And traveling in comfort meant riding in a carriage, which had been a privilege of the upper class. Roads had been worn dirt paths or maybe cobblestone in the bigger cities, where structures had been built of wood, laid brick, or stone, not steel and glass. He had lived in a one-room thatch hut with an underground chamber where his father slept. Everything was so different now. What if he couldn't live in this new world he had missed out on as it grew up around him?

The car slowed and Cynthia veered onto what he knew by now was called an off ramp. "What are you in the mood for, sweetie?" she said in her Southern drawl.

"What do you mean?" He was on sensory overload. There was so much to see, he didn't know where to look first.

"Food," she said. "Aren't you hungry? I'm famished."

Multiple lanes of traffic fed north on what looked like another highway, more crowded than the one they'd just left. "Sure." He was hungry. He could eat.

"How about Bob Evans." She pointed ahead to the right.

He really didn't know a Bob Evans from a hole in the ground. "Okay."

"They have good food, sweetie. Kind of like home. Biscuits and gravy, fried chicken, good stuff. You'll like it."

He hadn't eaten much other than what Jacob and Haslet had seen fit to provide him back in West Virginia, but he trusted Cynthia. If she told him the food was good, he believed her.

"How far are we from Chicago?" he said.

"Just a few more hours. We'll be there before nightfall." She turned onto the cross street and into the parking lot for Bob Evans. "If you think the traffic here is bad, just wait. You ain't seen nothing yet."

He glanced back out toward the highway, at all the cars lined up bumper-to-bumper at the stoplight they'd just gone through. Chicago was worse than this? What was he in for? Not that it really mattered. As long as he got back to Trace and his father, he would endure traffic a hundred times worse than this.

What was left of his family was all that mattered. That and finding new purpose now that he was free.

CHAPTER 24

WHEN GINA AWOKE, her body ached in all the right places, and for all the right reasons. Malek had made love to her for hours, obviously in what had to have been the final stages of his calling.

Clearly, Micah had been spot-on. Malek had not only been suffering the loss of Carmen, he had also been locked in the pull of his calling. No wonder he had behaved like a guy badly in need of an exorcism one minute, and an angel the next. Malek had been in a mental wasteland of torture and confusion for weeks, torn between extremes. How had he denied his body's urgings for so long without going irrevocably insane? It was nothing short of a miracle he had held himself together as long as he had.

He had more than made up for his otherworldly powers of restraint this morning and into the afternoon before collapsing into a sleep so deep not even a lightning strike inside the room would wake him.

He had taken her every way imaginable. In the shower, on the bed, once on the kitchen counter when they went in search of food and found each other again instead, and then in bed again three different ways.

After that, exhaustion had claimed them, and they tumbled into slumber, arms around each other.

Gina slowly looked over her shoulder at her new mate, curled behind her and cradling her body against his. He was her protector, even in his sleep. And wasn't that a change from what she had received from Armand, who had been more likely to make her sleep on the floor than to hold her securely while they slept. She had been silly to fear that other males—especially Malek—were like Armand and would treat her the same way he had.

Malek looked peaceful, dead to the world. When was the last time he had slept? Really slept? From the looks of it, he hadn't rested in a long while.

When her stomach rumbled, she grimaced at the intrusion. She might as well get up and find something to eat. This could be her only chance, because she might be wrong about Malek's calling coming to an end. When he woke up, he might kick off round two of their marathon.

Carefully, she slipped out from under his arm, pulled on a robe she found in the bathroom, and quietly closed the bedroom door as she stepped into the hall. Her cell phone sat on the kitchen counter, and she picked it up to see a notification that Micah had called and left her a message. She pulled up her messages and played his back.

"I'm hoping that the fact you aren't answering your phone is a good sign." She smiled to herself. Yes, it was a good sign. "Whether it is or not, I want you and Malek to stay at the apartment tonight. We've been receiving multiple reports from all over the city that two Dacians are in town. Sounds like your friends have made it here. You should be safe there for the time being, but we're working on a plan. You've got my number. Call if something comes up."

The message ended, she disconnected, and then she invaded the kitchen to make a quick meal of eggs and toast. She ate as she wandered around his living room. Micah had a lot of books and CDs, along with some impressive artifacts and works of art. The guy lived well. His apartment looked nothing like Malek's house, which was rather plain and sparse. She pulled one of the books off his shelf, set her dirty dishes on the kitchen counter, and went back to the bedroom.

Malek was still sleeping, on his side, his head burrowed into one of the pillows so that his dark hair fell partly over his face.

Damn, even asleep Malek was sexy as hell.

Taking care to be quiet, she changed into another pair of

Sam's yoga pants and a tank top. She and Malek needed to do a load of laundry for Micah and his mate...maybe even buy them a new bed. This one was ruined. Micah would never be able to use it again unless he didn't mind being reminded of what she and Malek had done here.

The thought made her smile as she carefully climbed back into bed, pulled the covers over her legs, and turned to the first page of the book.

She was still reading a couple of hours later, long after the curtains and blinds had whispered open on their tracks. She was seeped in the book when she felt eyes on her. Turning toward Malek, she found him awake, motionless, staring at her.

"Hi," she said, and bit her lip as she grinned.

So much had changed between them in the last twenty-four hours, and part of her still feared he would revert back to the Malek he'd been before. Would he snap at her again? Push her away? Or had that phase fully passed?

"Hi." He blinked, and his shapely, full mouth curved into a tender, subtle smile.

That was a good sign.

"How long have you been awake?" She set the book on her lap.

"A while."

"Why didn't you say something?" She brushed a strand of his hair back and tucked it behind his ear.

He closed his eyes, shifted, and crept closer. "I was watching you read."

She set the book on the nightstand, scooted down, and lay so she faced him. Hardly a foot separated them.

They lay like that for a while, staring into each other's eyes and letting the quiet encapsulate them. Neither spoke, as if both wanted simply to exist with one another. That same feeling as before, as if a million unspoken words hung over them, swelled and drifted like a cloud, and its presence became more obvious as the minutes ticked by.

"Carmen liked to read," he said quietly, sticking the pregnant balloon with the proverbial pin.

"Is that why you have all those books on your dining room table?" She had assumed as much after what Micah had told her, especially in light of the odd exchange between them when she'd asked about the books after entering his home.

"Yes. And I have an entire room in my basement filled with them, too."

His talking about Carmen was a good sign. It meant he was ready to move on. For him to open up to her about Carmen spoke volumes about how he felt now. Toward her. Because she knew from what Micah had told her that Malek had never spoken to anyone about Carmen. Not even him, and he had been Malek's best friend at the time.

"Maybe we need to get some bookcases and turn one of the rooms in your house into a library," she said.

Malek scooted closer and smoothed the tip of his index finger down the side of her neck and into the small hollow at the base of her throat. "I'd like that." Gratitude shone in his eyes as his smile widened. "You wouldn't mind?"

She shook her head. "No. As long as you don't mind if I read them. I love to read."

His finger trailed up and down, tracing the tendons in her neck. "I don't mind. I think Carmen would love knowing someone is enjoying them, and that I found someone who loves to read as much as she did."

"I'm sure she would. She sounds lovely."

He took a deep breath, blew it out. "She was."

"Tell me about her." If he was going to heal completely, he needed to get all of Carmen out of his system.

"Are you sure?"

"Yes. She was a part of your life. An important part. Don't hide her, anymore."

Moisture glistened his eyes. "I love you," he said.

This was the first time anyone outside of family had said those words to her.

"I love you, too. I've loved you since I met you. It just took me a while to figure it out."

He puffed out an impish breath and looked down. "Me, too. Obviously."

"Obviously." She caressed his cheek, and his soft stubble scratched her palm. "So, tell me about her, Malek. What was Carmen like?"

He kissed her palm. "Carmen was human."

This came as a bit of a surprise. Micah hadn't mentioned that earlier. Still, it wasn't uncommon for a vampire and human to mate.

"I met her during the late Middle Ages, during one of the short-lived truces between wars back then. She had long, auburn hair." He gestured, pulling his hand down through the air to signify long hair. "It was naturally curly, so when she wore it loose, she looked like a seventies flower child." He chuckled. "But it was very soft. I loved touching it. Like I love touching yours." He pushed his fingers into her hair. "But yours is softer. Your hair feels like satin, so smooth and silky." He paused, combed his fingers through her hair a few times as if hypnotized, and then settled back on his pillow again. "I wanted to change her. Make her immortal. I even petitioned the king, but he denied my request. It wasn't until much later, after she died, that the king changed the law and allowed males to change their human mates. But by then it was too late. Carmen was gone." He said it more matter-of-factly than emotionally. He definitely had crossed over to acceptance regarding Carmen's death.

"How did she die?" She took his hand and squeezed.

He smiled sadly. "I had turned to farming with the war over. She and I had a small cottage and a field where we grew wheat, barley, and corn. It made for long nights. We had humans who shared the land and profits with us, and they tended the field during the day, while I worked with the other vampires at night." He paused. "Just before dawn, I returned home." Another pause. "I smelled death before I reached the door. I rushed inside only to find her lying on the floor, her body bent at an awkward angle. She'd had a stroke while on the step stool putting away some preserved fruit on a shelf. The fall broke her back."

Gina frowned and looked down, fighting back tears even though Malek seemed to be holding it together. "God. I'm sorry."

"Ssshh." He brushed his hand over her cheek. "It's okay. I can finally think about it now. I can talk about it and finally let her go. Before you, I couldn't do that."

"But...that must have been awful for you."

"At the time, yes. And until I met you, it was."

"Even after you met me," she said. "I awakened that memory for you."

"Only so that I could deal with it and move on...to you...to my life with you." He brushed the backs of his fingers down her arm.

"What about children?" She wanted to think he and Carmen had young, because then at least she wouldn't have to fret over being unable to provide that for him. "Did you and Carmen have young?"

He shook his head. "She couldn't have them." His hand drifted unbidden to her stomach, and his palm flattened against her belly, almost as if he was checking for the life signature of a child. After making love for hours, he surely expected to find a growing life inside her.

He wouldn't find one.

"Malek..." She squirmed and pulled his hand from her stomach. "Don't."

His brow wrinkled. "What's wrong?"

"I just..." Damn it, but she didn't want to cry. What would he think of her when she told him she was barren? Would he be disappointed? She wasn't sure she could bear that. Malek deserved a child, which was something she could never give him, no matter how much she wanted to.

Unable to meet his gaze, she lowered her head and hid from him before the first tears could fall.

"Gina, talk to me. I don't want to invade your thoughts to see what's wrong."

How easily he could, and how sweet that he wouldn't. Armand had never given her that consideration. He had stolen into her mind whenever he felt like it, raping her thoughts just as he raped her body whenever the urge took him.

"Baby, please." Malek caressed her cheek down to her chin,

where he placed two fingertips below her jaw and slowly eased her head back up until their eyes met.

He leaned in and kissed away her tears before brushing his lips over hers. "Tell me what's wrong, Gina."

But when she opened her mouth, no words came out. Why was telling him about her past so hard?

He reached behind her and shut off the light, throwing the room into darkness. "Is that better?" he said.

Actually, it was. The lights of Chicago still fed light into the room, but the darkness made her feel safer.

She nodded. "Yes."

For a long moment, nothing was said, and Malek didn't push her. He let her get to her confession in her own time.

She took a deep breath. "I can't have children, either, Malek." Saying it aloud was harder than she thought, and she covered her face with her hands as a sob erupted from her throat. "I can't give you a young."

Strong arms wrapped around her and pulled her into his body, and he gently rocked her.

But Gina was inconsolable. She cried and poured a lifetime's worth of guilt, pain, and sorrow into her tears. Like Malek, she had never mourned what Armand had done to her, just as Micah said. She had tucked Armand away like an old sweatshirt that didn't fit anymore but that she couldn't give away. In her mind, he had become a talisman of regret, shame, and guilt, and she had used him to shield herself from her emotions, as well as from others.

How perfect she and Malek were for one another. They possessed such similar pasts, only with different circumstances. Both had tried to tuck away what had caused them the most suffering, thinking that by doing so they could forget the past and carry on. Only the plan had backfired. What they had tried to forget had never gone away. It had sat, watching and waiting until the time was right, and then the past roared back to life, ready to be heard and dealt with, not to be ignored anymore.

"Ssshh." Malek's hold tightened.

The world fell away in his arms. Her fears quieted. These

were the consequences of his love...knowing he was there to catch her, hold her, kiss away her tears if need-be. Through his touch, she felt his commitment to her. Only a day ago, Malek had been distant, but now he embraced his station as her mate and let go of his past. And he was stronger for her because of it.

There was a lesson to be learned from him. Maybe it was time she learned it and did for him what he had done for her...and reveal her past. All of it.

She pushed back, wiped her face, took a deep breath, and kissed him. "There's more," she said.

His arms loosened as if he instinctively knew she needed to stand on her own in that moment. "I'm not going anywhere."

"I know, but it's hard. I've never told anyone this." She suspected Micah knew most of what had happened, but him seeing her thoughts wasn't the same as her consciously talking about them.

"What about Trevor. You two seem close."

She shook her head. "Trevor is a longtime family friend, but he only knows some of what happened. I never told him everything."

"Why not?"

"I don't know." She dropped her gaze. "Like you, maybe I thought that by not talking about the past, it would go away. Just disappear on its own."

"That bad?" Malek's hand skimmed up and down her hip, soothing her.

"Yes."

He stroked her wrist, down to her hand, and then lifted his hand to her face and smoothed his fingers over her brow. "Take your time. When you're ready, I'm here."

She smiled and blinked heavily as his fingers caressed her face again and again, so gentle and loving. His thumb arced around her eye as he tenderly cupped her cheek.

Finally, she opened her eyes and looked at him. "I was mated before, too, as you know."

"Yes," he said softly.

"His name was Armand, and as I said at AKM, he was

half-Dacian."

Malek's fingers curved and tightened their hold on her. Understandable. All males had a soft spot when it came to hearing about other males their mates had been with.

"He was cruel, ruthless...abusive."

A growl rumbled from Malek's chest.

She shushed him, placing her fingers over his lips. "It's okay. I'm okay. At least, now I am."

He grabbed her hand and pressed her fingers more firmly to his lips, kissing them. He drew the tips into his mouth, and she smiled. Malek really was a gem, a diamond that had only needed polishing a couple of days ago.

"I met him in 1938," she said. "My parents were hosting some kind of party. We lived in Boston at the time. He was a guest. He asked me to dance. I didn't want to, but I didn't want to be rude, either. Within minutes, I knew something was wrong. At the end of the party, he stayed behind, and I remember that he wouldn't let me leave the room. 'She's mine, now,' he told my parents. Everything happened so fast after that. I wasn't even allowed to pack. He grabbed my hand, pulled me out the door against the protests of my family, stuffed me in his car, and drove me away. I was too stunned to even cry.

"As soon as he got me home, he raped me, but it wasn't seen as rape since he was my mate. But I know what I know, and what he did to me was rape."

Malek threw off the covers and practically leaped from the bed. "I'll kill him!" He paced to the window, hands on his hips, his naked, too-thin form silhouetted against the backdrop of the city. As she sat up, she noted that they really needed to get him back on a blood-healthy, calorie-rich diet. Until he began feeding in earnest again, on both food and blood, he would be weakened and slow to heal, which the still unhealed cut on his cheek and bite on the front of his throat proved.

"He's already dead." She scooted to the edge of the bed and let her legs hang off the side.

Malek turned around and looked at her as if he sensed what

she was about to say. His shadowed gaze grew concerned.

She folded her hands in her lap and looked down. A moment later, he kneeled in front of her and placed his hands over hers.

With a sigh, she met his gaze. "I became pregnant," she said. Then she huffed ironically. "Imagine my horror. I was going to give birth to a quarter-Dacian young, the product of being raped by my own mate. I swear shit like this can't be made up." She quieted as she allowed the long-hidden memories to flow.

Malek squeezed her hands. "What happened?"

"He beat me for being terrified of what I was carrying inside me. He didn't even care that it was part of him. The fact that he had mated a non-Dacian sickened him to begin with, which was why he treated me the way he did. It didn't matter that he was merely half himself. He hated that he wasn't full-blooded. And lucky me, I was the one who received all his misdirected anger." She sneered with sarcasm. "The beating was so severe I almost lost the baby and died. But miraculously, we both survived." Her words were laced with irony and contempt. "That time, at least." She closed her eyes as what happened next entered her memories. "I couldn't go on living like that, being abused every day, verbally, mentally, and physically. At one time, I had been happy and full of life. Armand took all that from me. In less than six months, he stole every shred of hope from my soul. I was steeped in depression and ready to die when I made a decision to take back my life or die trying."

Malek remained silent, on his knees in front of her, rapt and attentive.

She offered him a wan smile. "I waited until he was asleep, rolled over, pulled the knife out from between the mattress and box springs that I had hidden there earlier, turned around, raised it..." She paused, seeing that day in vivid detail. She could still see the silver of Armand's eyes as they flashed open and he lunged for her. "Before I could stab his heart, he woke up. I didn't know about how males attached themselves to their mates during sleep, but

I learned that day." She looked down. "He attacked me. Hit me so hard that I flew across the room and into the dresser, dropping the knife. He was on me so fast. He tore off my clothes, threw me down, and practically ripped me open as he took me." She stifled a sob, remembering the pain. "Sex was power to him. It was how he controlled me. 'Bitch! You little bitch! You think you can kill me?' he said. He took me with such force that my body slid across the floor with each thrust. And in a way, that was what saved my life, because I knew he was going to kill me after he took me one last time.

"As I cried out, screamed for help, and struggled to get away, my hand smacked down on the handle of the knife. Desperate, I grabbed it and stabbed him in the back of the shoulder. He pulled back, and I saw my chance to escape. I scampered backward, kicking at him as he tried to grab my feet. I stood up, tried to run, but he was already on his feet and pulled me back by my hair." She lifted her hand to her hair. "It was longer then." She half shrugged. "He tossed me across the room, against the armoire. It shattered and I fell backward and slammed into the wall. He stalked toward me, pulled the knife out of his shoulder, held it in front of him. I knew I was dead. I tried to crawl away, but there was nowhere to go. I was trapped. That's when I saw his handgun out of the corner of my eye. In hysterics, I grabbed it. I'd never touched a gun before that day. Just as he reached me and lifted the knife, I swung the gun around and pulled the trigger." She closed her eyes and saw the shower of blood. "The bullet went through his mouth and into his skull. He died instantly, just as he fell forward and the knife plunged into my belly." She raised her palms to her stomach.

Malek gently lifted her hands away, kissed her knuckles, and then bent forward to kiss her stomach. Tears balanced on the rims of his eyes when he looked back up at her. His tender show of affection both touched and soothed her.

"For a long time, I just laid there, bleeding, splattered with his blood. I knew the baby was dead, but I was glad. Isn't that horrid of me?" She searched his gaze. "I was actually happy I'd lost the baby, because I didn't want any part of him inside me." She swallowed a quiet sob. "It wasn't until later, after the doctors removed the fetus, that I realized the attack had rendered me barren." She took a deep breath, blew it out. "How's that for irony? I was happy to be rid of his unborn child, and then I found out that not only had I lost his baby, but also the ability to have a baby altogether." She wiped her fingers over her cheeks. "I guess that was God's way of punishing me for being glad the baby was killed."

Malek took her face in his hands and rose up on his knees. "No. Don't think like that, Gina." He shook his head. "God would never punish you for something like that. You'd been through a lot. You were justified to feel the way you did. You did nothing wrong, and you didn't bring this on yourself. Do you understand?"

She hadn't known how badly she needed to hear someone tell her that until just now. Malek absolved her of guilt and lifted the burden she had carried for far too long, and her love for him blossomed more deeply because of it.

"I laid there for so long, Malek." She pulled his hands from her cheeks and threaded their fingers together. "I was in shock, battered, in so much pain. But then my survival instinct kicked in, along with the reality that I was free. I actually started laughing. It hurt like hell, but I couldn't stop. I was almost manic with laughter, because I was finally free. I was with Armand for only six months, but those months felt like decades."

"I know the feeling."

She smiled. "Yes, you do, don't you?"

He kissed her knuckles again.

She took a deep breath, ready to tell the rest of her story. "After realizing I was free, I pulled out the knife, kicked him off me, crawled out of the rubble to the phone—we were one of the privileged families who had a phone at the time—and called my parents. They contacted the authorities." Her gaze dropped with guilt. "I lied to everyone but my brother Gabe. I didn't tell them I had intended to kill him. I told them he had attacked me in my sleep. It was easy enough to convince everyone that he was the one trying to kill me. I was bloodied, bruised, stabbed, and had clearly been sexually assaulted. Examination showed my flesh had been torn and all evidence supported my claim. But I knew if I told them the truth, I would be punished for murder, because that had been my intention. I had wanted to kill him, and I hadn't cared about the consequences. The fact that he fought back and beat me so badly is the only reason I wasn't punished. Armand's death went down as self-defense, and I was found not guilty. I really was free." She quieted and kept her gaze on Malek's hands, which covered hers once more on her lap. "That was the day I became an assassin, if I'm being honest. It started that day."

After a moment of silence, Malek squeezed her hand. "Your secret's safe with me." He paused. "If you ask me, the bastard deserved everything he got. If you hadn't killed him, I would hunt him down now and do the deed myself."

She glanced at him and smiled. "I know you would. And that's one reason why I love you so damn much."

Malek was everything a true mate should be. Loving, warm, and most of all, protective.

She sighed and smiled. "It felt good to finally tell that to someone."

He rose to his feet and bent over her, nose-to-nose, hands on either side of her hips on the bed. "Thank you for telling *me*." His lips met hers and held, unmoving, connecting them to each other.

After a long, easy moment, he broke away, lifted her feet off the floor, and rotated her legs around onto the bed. "Let me join you."

She rolled into the center of the mattress only to be pulled back against him a moment later as he pressed behind her.

His strong arms, albeit thinner than they had been a month ago, encircled her.

"You need to eat, Malek."

"Later." He nuzzled the back of her neck. "Right now I just want to hold you." His lips traced side to side at the top of her spine, sending a chill through her body.

"That feels nice." Malek was the antithesis to everything

Armand had been. Kind, loving, gentle, attentive, compassionate, patient, giving—

"*You* feel nice."

—complimentary.

His lips explored the back of her neck and shoulder, peppered soft kisses up, down, and all over. Minutes passed, his affections increased, and his hands worked themselves under her top as he nipped the side of her neck. "I love how brave you are. So strong." His hands skimmed her everywhere. "You're such a warrior, and God that's a turn-on."

"You say the sweetest things."

A low rumble that sounded like it might have been a chuckle under different circumstances vibrated into her back. "You have no idea."

"Oh?"

He snuggled closer and his lips did naughty things to her skin. "Huh-uh."

"Care to fill me in?"

He shook his head. "Later." The fingers of one hand tickled a heated path to one breast, while his other hand dove beneath the elastic waist of her pants.

She sensed that he wanted to mark his territory. Even though Armand was dead, Gina had a feeling that talking about him had fired up Malek's need to let any competition for her affection know he had already staked his flag in her heart. Mated males were like feral beasts. Once they took a mate, all others got the message loud and clear: Hands off! They didn't take kindly to the thought of other males getting too close, even if the male in question was deceased.

But she liked *his* hands right where they were. With a moan, she writhed in his arms, reached around, and dug her fingers into his hair.

The air in the room shifted and charged with mutual affection and sexual energy. With no more secrets between them, their hearts and souls opened, and a lightness invaded her senses that yearned for him to brush away the crumbs of her past and cap off the moment by showing her what lay in her future.

His fingers tickled their way lower until they parted her, and then his palm slicked all the way down as his finger slid inside.

"You're so wet for me," he whispered against her neck, grinding his erection against her bottom.

All she could do was nod and part her legs so he could explore deeper.

"How did I refuse you for so long?" He dipped his head against hers and inhaled as if trying to breathe her in. "I was insane."

"So was I." Making love to Malek was just that. Two people in love, sharing themselves in a mutual dance of passion and respect. Never had she felt anything like this, and she never wanted it to stop.

He rocked behind her with light, easy thrusts. His actions spoke more fluently than words about how he felt for her. He wanted her, but he wouldn't force himself on her, either. She dictated the pace.

She looked over her shoulder, pulled his face to hers, and fused her mouth to his. He lavished languid tugs against her lips. "I love a female with a gun," he said between kisses. "It's so sexy." He nipped playfully at her chin.

Only Malek could make her laugh at a time like this, after she had just confessed her darkest secrets, and while he was putting such sweet moves on her, no less. But this was why he was perfect for her. With a simple statement, mixed with a playfulness she hoped to see more of, he broke through what was left of her pain and pushed it away. Her resulting giggle felt therapeutic, almost like she had just awakened from a nightmare and realized she wasn't in danger.

"You're so different," she said, still giggling as he peppered small kisses up and down her neck.

"From...?" He licked her earlobe.

"Before."

"You mean when I was a moody bastard too hung up on the past to see what was right in front of me?" He tugged at her tank top. "Or when I sat dumbfounded and silent in your cell, too enthralled with you to do more than stare? By the way, you're still wearing too many clothes."

"Malek!" She burst into laughter as he wiggled his hand under her top and wrapped one leg around her hips, grinding against her backside as he pushed up her shirt. "Mmm." She moaned and laid her head back against his shoulder as he cupped her breast. "And both. You're different both from when you were a bastard, and when you watched over me in my cell."

"Mmm, I thought you were the most beautiful thing I'd ever seen." His hand slid to her other breast, causing her nipple to pucker against his palm. "Of course, that was before I went temporarily insane."

"Of course." She shimmied out of the tank top and tossed it aside.

"But now you're back." His lips brushed over the skin of her neck as he spoke, and his playfulness quickly transformed back into a desire so intense it wrapped around her like an erotic blanket.

She writhed out of Sam's pants. "Yes. I'm back." Butterflies lit in her stomach, the mood quickly intensifying as he shifted, reached down, and grasped the inside of her thigh then lifted her leg.

"My sexy assassin," he whispered against her ear. "And you're all mine." He grazed his teeth against her neck.

"And you're mine." Like him, she would never let him go now that she had found him.

The tip of his tongue danced up and down the side of her neck as he slowly rolled her to her stomach and lay on her back. "I'm going to buy you a different necklace for every day of the month," he said, thrusting into her, hitting her just right.

"Oh?" She gasped as he locked his fingers with hers, pushed her arms under the pillow, and drove farther inside.

He released her hands and glided his down to her hips, where he gripped her as he rolled against her again. Amazing friction burned between them as he breathed against her nape. "Yes. Ones that glorify this exquisite neck." He purred and pumped his hips forward and back in a series of gentle, shallow surges. "And when I make love to you, that's all you'll be wearing."

That was when the loving got serious. She kept her head on the mattress as he lifted her hips, bent over her, and took her in the most primitive manner since the dawn of man. And when she climaxed, he joined her and sank his fangs into the side of her neck, shuddering behind her. As she broke into euphoria, she came again. It didn't matter that she couldn't give him a child. He loved her, anyway.

Armand was no more. She could finally send him to the trash bin of her mind.

She belonged to Malek now. And unlike Armand, Malek would take care of her, cherish her, and love her for a lifetime.

CHAPTER 25

AFTER A SATISFYING, if not bruising, day of hard fucking, Lorena's limbs felt as loose as slack rope.

Mmm. How lovely.

She slithered against the red satin sheets in Bishop's private suite in the Underground and closed her eyes to revel in the tight soreness of her thighs and shoulders, the dull throb in her neck, and the luxurious sting of dozens of scratches down her back. And her breasts felt like they'd been cranked through an antique clothes wringer, shoved between two rollers meant to wring the water out of freshly laundered clothes.

Searcy lay on his stomach to her right, and Vaydon sprawled on his back to her left. Her two virile Dacians could fuck. They had held her down, choked her, brutalized her body to within an inch of delirium. Oh the things they had done to her! She had never felt more satisfied. Not even with Bishop. But wouldn't he make a fine addition to the games for three on one. The thought made her giddy.

With her eyelids barely parted and a drunken grin splattered on her face, she rolled her head to look at Searcy. What an innovative fuck buddy he was. Vaydon was exceptional, as well, but Searcy held a slight edge in the hardcore department.

She was insatiable, but she could only milk a cow so long before the udders emptied and there was no more milk to give. And she had milked Searcy and Vaydon dry.

No matter. There would be another day to ride them like the broncos they were. Besides, the three of them had a big night tonight. They had a bitch to kill. Getting a few hours of sleep in the afternoon had been a wise call. That way, they could be good and frosty on the hunt. She didn't think they would have a problem finding Gina and taking her out. Malek appeared too weak to protect her against two Dacian warriors and her. She couldn't count herself out. She wanted a piece of this action. The look on Malek's face alone would be worth the effort of tagging along.

What had she seen in Malek? Because now that she had found two prize stallions who effortlessly gave her everything she needed and more, Malek seemed so much like small potatoes. At least one good thing had come from her brief interlude with him. He had given her a powerful bargaining chip to dangle in front of Searcy. Without Gina, Lorena might not have won them over, and if she hadn't won them over, she would be in Lucan's bed right now. And while Lucan was an adequate lover, he didn't even compare to these two. She looked between Searcy and Vaydon, and an almost demented sense of joy bubbled inside her belly like it was Christmas Day and she had gotten everything she had asked for and more.

Stretching like a large feline, she groaned quietly, relishing the residue of pain in her body. Then she pushed herself up and slid to the foot of the bed between her two male suitors, pushed herself to her feet, and padded barefoot and naked to the bathroom.

Mascara-smeared eyes stared with satisfaction at her from the mirror, and her mahogany hair was a tousled disaster, tangled and strewn about like she had just spent a month in a jungle with no comb. Bruises in the shape of fingers ringed her throat and stamped her shoulders and arms like faded tattoos.

Brands. Like the ones ranchers burned into the hides of their cattle. She was branded now. Theirs. Searcy's and Vaydon's. And she caressed the marks with adoring fingers, gazing at them with hooded eyes. Heat flooded her saturated core.

Searcy appeared in the doorway behind her, his silver

eyes sleepy but alert. He met her gaze in the mirror, and one corner of his mouth ticked upward with the devil's smile. Without a word, he stepped up behind her and quietly shut the door.

"You will take me to Gina tonight," he said, slowly raking his nails down her raw back.

She trembled, and wicked, lusty fire shot through her. "Yes." She would do anything for him. Anything at all.

He licked his lips and his quicksilver eyes flashed like mercury, deadly and poisonous. "But first..." He pushed behind her and spread the cheeks of her ass. "A little wake-up call."

He breeched her tight opening, raw from the day's savagery, and thrust sharply inside. She cried out, slapped her palms down on the vanity, and nearly fell into rapture from the pain.

She didn't need a wake-up call, but she sure felt like she was dreaming.

MALEK STOOD ON THE BALCONY of Micah's apartment. Spring was in the air, and just as with the seasonal new beginning, a sense of newness ran in his veins. Had this been how Micah felt when he met Sam? As if the proverbial planets had aligned and the heavens had opened to rain God's light down on him?

Man, he so had to eat crow for Micah now, didn't he? But so what? He had what he needed. What he wanted. He chuckled to himself. He and Micah had gone at each other like brothers fighting over the top bunk...times one hundred. And, as usual, Micah had been right. He was always right. At some point, Malek would have to stop doubting his oldest friend, who had been with him through just about everything a guy could go through, both good and bad. Now that he was sane again, trusting Micah would be a lot easier, because there were no more voices in Malek's head to contradict Micah's wisdom.

His hands rested on the banister, and he gazed out over the city, a perpetual smile on his face. What a difference a day made. Just one day ago, he had still been fighting his feelings, trying to justify why he was no good for Gina, even after admitting to himself she was indeed his mate. And now he had fully taken her in, joining with her in body and blood. He lifted his hand and ran the tips of his fingers over the almost imperceptible mark where Gina had taken his vein. The tiny indentations felt good on the side of his neck, like they belonged there. Which they did. She owned his body as he owned hers, and she could bite him wherever she wanted, whenever she wanted to.

A day.

Hell, not even a day. He had relented and accepted his station by her side in an instant.

Would the vampire phenomenon known as mating ever make sense to him? To any vampire, for that matter? A mated male, especially one who was newly mated or without his mate, was like a damn pinball, completely at the whim of biological forces he couldn't see. And those forces shattered his entire being, body and soul. They fractured his mind, knotted his sanity, and thrust him beyond rational thought... all to force him to either take his mate or die. Then as soon as he claimed his mate, all the fallen, scattered dominoes of his psyche shifted back into order in an instant to leave him scratching his head at how he could have been so stupid.

Malek wasn't the first male to behave like an idiot times ten while in the throes of mated need, and he wouldn't be the last. He was just thankful he had awakened from his dance with mated insanity in time to make the connection that Gina was his future, while Carmen—may she now rest in peace—was his past. For the first time in more than ten human lifetimes, Malek was at peace and whole again.

Sure, Carmen still hummed in the back of his mind, but she was a pleasant presence now, not a painful memory. Guilt no longer jarred him, and he no longer fooled himself about where she was. She wasn't washing his clothes in the stream in the woods, and she wasn't tending to the fields or sleeping. She was dead. And although her death was tragic, she had passed over into the other realm a long time ago, where her spirit lived on, and where she no doubt watched over him.

In the distance, lightning flashed, still too far away to worry about, but close enough to know a storm was coming. Not that he needed the lightning to tell him that. The low clouds racing to the north and east, along with the unseasonably warm, humid gusts that blew out of the south, told him as much.

The wind blew his hair off his face, and he breathed in as he closed his eyes, refreshed in body and spirit. Cleansed. Ready to move into his future with his new mate.

Gina had glued his broken spirit back together. He was ready to live again. No, that wasn't exactly right. It wasn't that he was ready to live. He just simply craved life. A life with Gina.

He sighed and gazed out at the dark horizon beyond the lights of Chicago as another flash of lightning faintly lit the sky. A finality and sense of peace settled over him. "Good-bye, Carmen," he whispered. "I can finally say good-bye to you, but I'll never forget you."

His past was over, and as Gina walked quietly up behind him and wrapped her arms around his waist and pressed her lips against the back of his shoulder, he placed his hands over hers and pressed against her, feeling his future in her embrace.

"I want to take you home," he said quietly.

"I am home." She squeezed him harder. "With you, anywhere is home."

He smiled as he looked down at her slender hands, her fingers curled into his shirt against his abdomen. She had such small, delicate hands for an assassin. "Good point." He caressed the backs of her fingers, and she opened her loose fist so he could glide his fingers in between hers. "I'll clarify. I want to take you to my *house. Our* house, if you'll have it."

She rested her cheek between his shoulder blades. "Yes. With a little decorating, of course."

He chuckled. "Of course." His house definitely needed a feminine touch to make it a warm, cozy space. "And we'll need lots and lots of bookcases."

He felt her smile against his back. "Yes. Lots of bookcases."

"And the kitchen needs to be remodeled." He liked this, the two of them talking about their plans for the future.

"Your kitchen isn't so bad," she said.

"But there's nothing of you in it. I want you in every room, Gina. So that when I'm home, everywhere I look, I'll see a piece of you."

She remained silent, but her arms tightened around him as if she refused to ever let go, both physically and mentally.

After a moment, he turned his head to the side and said over his shoulder, "Is that all right with you, *piccolina?*" Somehow in the past several hours, waxing poetic in various languages while making love to her, he had nicknamed her after the Italian word for petite, and she had instantly taken a liking to it.

She nodded. "It's perfect, *tesoro.*" And she had nicknamed him after the Italian word for treasure, an Italian term of endearment.

He was *her* treasure. That's what he would be from now until eternity claimed him.

"*Mi hai salvata,*" she whispered. You saved me.

If only she knew, she was his savior as much as he was hers. Without her, he would have died within the week. He had been on the fast track to a coffin six-feet under, just as Micah had predicted. Gina had saved his life.

"*Non più di quanto tu abbia salvato me, amore mio.*" No more than you saved me, my love. "*Piccolina mia.*" My petite.

She pulled back as he turned and wrapped one arm around her. With his other hand, he caressed the backs of his fingers over her cheek. "*Sei tu a tenere il mio cuore, adesso.*" You are the one holding my heart, now.

She smiled up at him and kissed his fingers. "*Ti amo.*" I love you.

"*Ti amo. Adesso andiamo a casa e perdiamoci l'uno nell'altra.*" I love you. Now let's go home and get lost in one another.

She nodded once, and her cheeks flushed as she smiled and took his hand then led him inside. He still had to get his truck from where it was parked across the street from Four Alarm, but after that, he was taking Gina home, where they would stay tucked away for a few days. No one but them, lost inside each other.

He had a lot of time to make up for.

CHAPTER 26

NINETY MINUTES AFTER THE QUICK and devilishly divine wake-up call in the bathroom, Lorena, Searcy, and Vaydon made their way out of the UG. They had a job to do. But first, they needed fresh blood. After their all-day sex marathon, where they had shared blood with each other but taken no new blood in, they needed to replenish themselves. A good feeding from a healthy human was like Red Bull. It gave you wings. Plus, it was always beneficial to feed before a hunt. They would be at their peak, with no risk of blood hunger to distract them from their target.

Finding adequate donors inside Four Alarm was easy enough. A quick scout of the terrain, and the three of them stole their prey into the back alley, where they took their fill of blood, wiped the humans' memories of the encounter, and slipped away.

Searcy and Vaydon marched along on either side of her as they exited the alley and crossed the street.

"Take us to Gina now," Searcy said, his voice gruff, his body tight.

"As long as she's still at Malek's house, you'll have her within the hour. *My king.*" She shot him a pointed, come-hither glance.

An air of entitlement and power flowed out of him, and he looked pleased by her fealty. "You'll make a fine queen, Lorena."

"And a fine consort," Vaydon added, not to be left out.

Searcy grinned at his son. "You have a keen eye, Vaydon." Lorena was about to hail a cab when Searcy pulled to an abrupt halt. "Who's truck is this?" He paced toward the black truck parked at the curb.

Lorena hesitated, turned, and joined him. With a sniff, she picked up Malek's scent. It was stale and faded, but his aroma surrounded the driver's side door. And hidden just under the masculine undertones she had come to know during her brief interlude with him, a softer, fainter, more feminine scent lingered. Gina. No doubt, hers was what caught Searcy's attention.

"This is Malek's truck," she said, scooting closer.

Vaydon inspected the bed and peered inside the passenger window. "His scent is old. It's been at least twenty-four hours since he was here. Do you think he will come back for it?" He glanced down at the truck again.

"I don't see why not." She looked from Vaydon to Searcy and back again. "He could be on his way now."

Searcy snapped his head around to her. "Go. Now. Check his home. Vaydon and I will wait here. If he and that bitch are there, contact me. If not, come back and join us here, and we will await his arrival. If Gina isn't with him, we will follow him until he leads us to her."

Lorena nodded briskly. "Of course." She grabbed Searcy's wrist before he could turn and head off into the shadows. "Just one thing. Do what you want to that whore, Gina, but leave Malek to me."

The corner of Searcy's mouth crept upward, the sinister sneer one of pleasure. "Consider him yours, pretty thing. Now go." He spun away, and he and Vaydon disappeared into shadow, and then were gone, likely to high ground where they could keep watch on Malek's truck.

Lorena ducked into an alley, willed herself into vapor, and shot to Malek's home. After appearing in the backyard, she rushed to the back door, then around to each window so she could peer inside. The house was dark and quiet. Too quiet. Even if Malek were sleeping in his basement bedroom with his darling little matey-poo, she would have felt them, heard them, smelled them on the premises.

The house was empty.

Low thunder rumbled in the distance as the wind picked up. Ah, yes, it was a lovely night for a storm.

With one last glance inside another window, Lorena ducked into the cover of the trees in his expansive backyard and projected herself to the flat-topped roof of a building near Four Alarm. As soon as she spotted Searcy and Vaydon on a nearby roof, she vapor-tunneled and landed in a crouch between them.

"They weren't there."

"Had they been?" Searcy said.

"No. Not recently."

"Then perhaps they're on their way here." Vaydon stood and disappeared.

Lorena scowled at the empty air where Vaydon had just been. "Where did he go?"

"To scout the area. If they're coming, Vaydon will find them." Searcy crouched with one knee on the roof, the other bent and supporting his hand, as he leaned forward and pushed his fingers against the filthy surface of the building. He lifted his nose and sniffed the air, and his long, silvery-blond hair swirled like Medusa's tentacles on a gust of wind.

Lightning flashed just as Vaydon reappeared. The wind caught his hair, as well, and it whipped over his face. The two looked like gods. Powerful warlocks ready to slay dragons.

Lorena's blood raced, spiked with adrenaline and the lust to punish the one who had spurned her.

Vaydon slowly dropped into a crouch beside her. "They're coming from the north."

"How close?" Searcy regarded him as the first drops of rain began to fall.

"Not far. A mile, maybe two."

Two pairs of silver irises sparkled against another flash of lightning, and a violent gust of wind blasted them as the storm bore down.

"We move. Downwind." Searcy stood and punched his pointed finger toward the east. "I don't want to take a chance they'll smell us out."

Lorena and Vaydon stood, and the three of them leaped

and projected themselves toward the east to another rooftop about a half mile away. There they would lay in wait.

By morning, Malek's mate would be dead, and soon thereafter, so would he.

A smile crept over Lorena's face. Paybacks really were a bitch, weren't they, and she owed Malek in spades.

By the time the cab reached Malek's truck, the storm had hit in earnest. Brilliant lightning lit the night sky, and cracks of thunder split the air. It was the perfect night to hole up inside and go a whole lot of nowhere.

Gina waited for him to pay the fare, and then she bolted out into the downpour behind him. The rain fell in such torrents that by the time they reached the truck, they were soaked through. The truck beeped as the alarm disengaged, and she practically leaped inside as Malek catapulted into the driver's seat.

What a surprise to hear her own laughter, and an even bigger one to hear Malek's. Until now, she had never heard him laugh, and the sound was rich and honest, full-bodied and spirited.

He leaned toward her, beaming, his face bright with happiness, and pulled her into a spontaneous kiss. God, she loved this side of him. So open and giving, and surprisingly young at heart.

"You have a beautiful laugh," she said, breathless and love struck. Had it really only been a few days since she had sworn she had no interest in being his mate? Now, she couldn't imagine her life without him. Trevor had been right, and he was sure to gloat the next time she saw him.

"So do you." He caught his breath and gazed in wonder at her.

The way he stared at her in complete adoration made her feel like he was seeing her for the first time all over again. His gaze danced from her eyes to her mouth then up to her hair as if he couldn't believe she was actually there.

"Pinch me," she said, feeling weightless.

He laughed. "What? Why?"

"Because I must be dreaming."

They both broke into laughter again as he started the truck. "You can't be dreaming, because if you are, then so am I. And I refuse to accept that this is a dream, *piccolina*."

"Then take me home and get these wet clothes off me and show me how awake I am." She leaned back as rain dripped from her soaked hair into her eyes and down her cheeks, and she skimmed her fingertips from her neck down to between her breasts.

His gaze followed her hand and turned smoky. The button-down sweater she had borrowed from Sam's closet hugged her chest, and she already knew her nipples protruded against the soaked fabric.

"I see your point," he said.

An instant later, he had the truck in drive and the wipers on full blast. Even so, it was hard to see out the windshield.

After a couple of minutes, it was clear the storm had intensified and they weren't going to get anywhere fast. Sheets of monsoon-like rain pelted the truck, along with pea-sized hail.

With a coy giggle, she glanced across the seat and lifted her hand to the top button of the light sweater. "Oh, Malek," she sang.

His gaze flicked sideways at her, and arousal fired to life as his eyes landed on the button as it popped free and revealed a hint of cleavage.

"We're not going to make it home, are we?" he said at a stoplight. He leaned toward the windshield and glanced around as if looking for a place to park.

"I don't mind a quickie in an empty parking lot." She reached across the console and squeezed his thigh. He practically jumped the red light as his foot hit the gas. Luckily the light turned green an instant later, and he proceeded through the intersection.

"Damn, female." He took a heavy breath.

"This rain *is* coming down awfully hard." She released

another button. "Oops."

His breath hitched when he glanced to find even more of her breasts exposed. "Fuck this. You're killing me here." His gaze shot back around, and he strained to see out the windows.

A couple of minutes later, he parked the truck in a shadowed, mostly empty lot under the 'L.' They weren't the only ones looking for a little public privacy, though. About twenty yards away, an SUV with fogged windows was parked, and shadowy figures moved and rocked against each other in the front seat.

"Come here often?" she said as she slipped another button free.

"Never." He reached for her. "But many do." He winked and pulled her onto his lap and slid his warm hands under her sweater. "I never thought I'd be one of them, though."

"First time for everything." She pressed her groin against the hard length inside the sweatpants he had borrowed from Micah's closet.

"We patrol here every night. Lots of action." His hands eased around to her back and pulled her down.

"Oh?"

He nodded.

"Do you think one of your buddies might happen by and see us?" She brushed her lips against his, not worried in the least.

"Let them."

She grinned against his mouth. "Exhibitionist much?"

He chuckled and kissed her. "No. I just don't care."

"Why not?" She burrowed her hands under his shirt.

"Because I've never been so goddamn happy."

The storm had intensified, and rain and hail pounded the roof of the cab. Lightning flashed every couple of seconds, and thunder boomed like explosions in a war zone, but it was all peripheral noise compared to what was happening inside the cab. The only storm that mattered was the one that roiled under her, whose hands now gripped her breasts and squeezed, whose hips rocked against her with an urgency she felt all the way to her bones.

Was this really happening? Had she finally found love? Had luck really smiled down on her for once? Never before had she known such joy. And to think she had fought this. How foolish.

"God, pinch me," she whispered against his ear, winding his wet hair loosely around her fingers.

"I already told you," he whispered back, "you're not dreaming."

"I don't believe you." She rotated her hips around in a slow circle, making him moan.

She wanted to believe him. She really did. But bad luck had followed her through her entire life. Everything good that happened to her seemed to come with an out clause, where good fortune bailed out and left her hanging with the short end of the stick. Armand, Gabe, what she had done to Sev and Lakota, her defunct womb. So many aspects of her life had been tainted with bad luck and ill fate. Could she really count on good fortune to smile on her for once?

"*Piccolina*, you're not dreaming." He spoke softly against the side of her neck. "We're together now. It's over. The past is over. It's just us, and we have our whole lives to look forward to." He kissed her skin. "Nothing bad is going to happen anymore. Trust me. I'll take care of you."

She smiled, closed her eyes, and let herself fall into his reassurances. Maybe he was right. It was time to look forward to a better, happier time with him. "Make love to me, *amante*."

"God, yes." His mouth pressed against her skin, and his hands lowered to the waist of her pants. "Forever."

He had just begun to push against the elastic waistband when something landed with a deafening crash in the bed of the truck and shook them so violently she knocked her head against the roof. Malek's hands shot out and grabbed onto the dash on either side of her.

"What the fuck?" He spun and looked out the back window as he let go of the dash and pulled her against him.

Gina glanced over his shoulder and saw the silhouette of

a man through the fog and rivulets of rain on the glass.

Oh no. This could only mean one thing. The Dacians had found her. How had she forgotten about the Dacians? How could she have put her fledgling mating with Malek in danger like this?

The male leaped and landed on top of the cab, and the roof caved, and she cried out as she tried to figure out what to do.

She and Malek were trapped.

"Get down, Gina!" Malek palmed the back of her head and held her close as he ducked to the side.

He reached toward the glove box, but before he could get to it, the driver's side door whipped open and cold, strong hands grabbed her by the back of the neck and forearm.

"No!" Malek's hands flailed as he tried to keep hold of her, and suddenly, she was the rope in a game of tug-of-war. Malek and her assailant grappled to keep hold of her as rain pelted her face, stung her eyes, and drenched her exposed torso. But for all Malek's mated strength and retaliation, the weeks of suffering had taken their toll. He was too weak to hang on, and when Vaydon leaped from the roof of the truck and put a choke hold on him, her hand slipped from his grasp.

"Malek!"

One second she was reaching for him, and the next she was airborne. Head over heels, she tumbled in open air like a ragdoll.

"No!" Malek roared as she crashed into the wet pavement and rolled until she came to a stop in a deep puddle.

Every muscle protested, and when she tried to push off the pavement, pain bolted through her leg. She screamed and fell back into the puddle as she clutched her fractured knee.

"Not so tough now, are you? *Gina*."

As the burn of broken bones trying to mend themselves flared to life, she glared up into the mercurial, vicious gaze of one nasty Dacian. Searcy. Behind him, Vaydon held Malek by the throat, and even though he was in full-on mated male aggression, he was no match for Vaydon in his weakened state. And she had no weapon to defend herself.

Searcy knelt down in front of her. His long hair was soaked and plastered to his face, and the ends whipped in the wind. He reached out and ran his fingertips down her jaw to her chin, where he took hold and lifted her face into the driving rain. "I know it sounds cliché, but...we meet again." He paused, and unbridled fury darkened his eyes. "Armand's *murderess*."

Lady Luck hadn't smiled on her, after all. Once again, what was briefly good and perfect in her life turned to dust. Without a miracle, she was as good as dead.

MALEK STRUGGLED AGAINST THE HOLD the Dacian had on him. Why couldn't he break free? He was a mated male, for God's sake. He should be stronger than this.

A third pair of boots thunked down on the rain-splattered pavement, timed perfectly with an ominous crack of thunder and flash of lightning. As large, heavy raindrops pounded his face and eyes, he looked up into the familiar face of the female he had taken home from Four Alarm the other night. Lorena.

"Well, well, well." She took two measured, hip-swaying steps toward him and kneeled down. "If it isn't the sheep in wolf's clothing." She tilted her head to one side as her expression shifted into mock concern. "What's wrong, Malek? Not strong enough to break out of Vaydon's meager little grasp? A tough, mated male like you?"

Across the parking lot, Gina growled at Lorena's back. "Get away from him, you bitch."

A tinkling of malicious laughter rang from Lorena's throat, and she looked over her shoulder. "I could say the same to you, little one. But then...you're already way over there. And Malek's here. With me." She caressed his cheek, but he jerked his face away.

The second Dacian clamped a hand down on Gina's throat just as she lurched to attack. The sounds of choking were like death in Malek's ears, and he fought to wrench free. His mate was in trouble, and she was hurt. He could feel the pain in her body from here. Gina needed him. Now!

Lorena's laughter grew louder, joined by another clap of thunder. "You already have your hands full, Gina. Perhaps you should worry more about what Searcy is going to do to you than what we're going to do to your pesky little boyfriend." She turned her gaze back to his.

And that's when he realized...Lorena was a Thracian. He had missed that before. But now, with his clear mind, he caught the unmistakable whiff of the ancient clan and identified it for what it was. Not only were the Dacians not extinct, but neither were the Thracians. This didn't bode well. Not for the king, AKM, and especially not for him and Gina. He had to get free. He needed to save his beloved from disaster.

Overhead, the 'L' rumbled by as he pulled against Vaydon's grip. But it was useless. He couldn't break free. He was too weak. The weeks of suffering had drained him, and he wasn't strong enough to be the mate Gina needed him to be to save her life. But he wasn't going down without a fight, because if he fought, the odds were better they would kill him, too. And he needed them to kill him if they killed her. Because he couldn't live without her. He *wouldn't*.

With a fierce growl, he strained toward Lorena. "I'll kill you if you hurt her."

The inner corners of her eyebrows lifted as her lips pouted in fake sadness. "Awe, you're no fun." The expression faded from her face as she leaned closer. "I smell her on you, Malek. The little whore. You were about to fuck her, weren't you?"

Fury boiled in his veins and he doubled his efforts to break away from Vaydon and strike Lorena down. "You will not speak of my mate in such a manner." A lethal hiss spit through his rain-drenched lips. If he could kill just one of them before they killed him, the encounter would be a success.

"And if I do? What? What will you do to me, Malek?"

His hair hung over his eyes, and rain poured in rivers down his face and streamed off his chin. When he spoke, his voice rumbled with deadly malice. "I will kill you."

She laughed. "That would be a neat trick, Malek, seeing

that you're not even strong enough to break free of Vaydon's grasp."

He tripled his efforts, and for a moment, he gained the upper hand. Vaydon grunted and strained behind him and nearly lost his grip. The sudden fear in Lorena's eyes thrilled him. All he wanted was to get to her, kill her, make her pay for what she had done to Gina. And then he would turn his wrath on the Dacians. But just as he was about to wrench free and lunge for her, Vaydon kneed him in the back and took him down to the pavement again.

Motherfucker! His cheek pressed against the wet pavement, and Vaydon's weight crashed down with an elbow between his shoulders. He cried out as pain throttled his spine, and then he was hefted like dirty laundry from the ground, locked in Vaydon's hold once more.

The amused smile that crossed Lorena's features burned with contempt and confidence. "You see, Malek. It's useless. You lose, and now you'll pay."

Behind her, Searcy rose to his feet and dragged Gina by the hair into a kneeling position. "Lorena. Hold her."

Malek's breath came in rapid bursts and sprayed water away from his face with each urgent exhale. Time was running out. He could feel it ticking away in slow motion, like shattered glass blown from a window, but suspended in weightless animation.

Lorena kept her eyes on him. "I want you to watch, Malek. I want you to see as we take away the one thing that is most important to you."

No. He couldn't lose Gina. Not like this. Not at all. He had only just found her. If he lost her, he would die.

Lorena sashayed to where Searcy held Gina down on her knees execution style. Gina clawed at his arms and hands, but he ignored her struggles as a horse would a gnat.

His eyes met Gina's and locked. She was his mate. He had promised her not ten minutes ago he would take care of her and that everything was fine. And now he had failed to keep his promise. What kind of mate was he that he couldn't keep her safe?

With a sad, defeated shake of her head, she dropped her hands to her sides. She looked resigned to her fate.

Urgent gasps broke from his lungs as Lorena took Searcy's place and yanked Gina's head back, forcing their connection to break. He couldn't see her eyes, anymore. The windows of her life. Desperation rankled his muscles, but he couldn't break free. He could only watch. He had failed.

Searcy took a step forward and sneered at him. "Pitiful. You're a pathetic excuse for a vampire, Malek. I will soon put an end to your kind, but for now..." He turned back toward Gina. "Now I will avenge my nephew's death, as well as your harlot mate's attempt on my son's life." He pulled a sheathed knife from his coat and slipped the blade from its leather scabbard.

Malek recognized the knife at once. He and the others called it the Reaper's Blade. A knife made of ancient alloys and magic, its one purpose was to kill vampires not of Dacian descent. There was no remedy. No way to reverse its effect. Once it broke a vampire's skin, death was certain within hours.

Gina curled her lip at Searcy then spat at him. "That's what I think of your nephew, as well as you and your son, you bastard."

"Feisty to your last breath, aren't you? I'll enjoy your death... for Armand's sake, as well as for mine and Vaydon's. I don't need ones like you lurking in the shadows when I take back the throne." Searcy paid a cursory glance over his shoulder at Malek. "That's right," he said. "Your king's time has come to an end. As has yours and hers." He turned back toward Gina.

Time slowed. Malek saw the blade lift, saw Gina's head fall back as Lorena pulled her hair. That exquisite neck, so pristine and smooth, lay bare to the glint of the knife as lightning lit the sky. Thunder cracked angrily as if Mother Nature decried the separation of two souls she had taken such care to bring together, especially after the efforts expended to get him and Gina out of their own way to let their love flow.

He no longer felt the rain batter his face, no longer heard

the thunder as it boomed. Malek's sole focus was Gina. As if trying to hold on to her last moments of life, all he saw was her. All he heard were her breaths.

And then he heard her whisper, "Malek...I love you."

A moment later, the ancient blade sliced a crimson trail from the side of her neck, diagonally across her sternum, to the inner swell of her breast.

Slow motion. Everything drew out as if in slow motion.

Her scream of agony erupted like the howl of a banshee as the poison broke in her body.

"GINA!" He strained, and the muscles in his arms tore as he fought to break free.

Vaydon grunted behind him but kept hold, practically pulling one of his shoulders out of its socket.

Lorena shoved Gina's head forward and released her hair as Gina spasmed and clutched her chest. Searcy wiped the blade on his pants and stepped to the side as Gina fell face-first in a puddle. With a self-satisfied sneer, he glanced toward Malek. The pompous expression on his face said it all. He had won. Gina was as good as dead.

Malek's brain snapped, and the world popped back into real time, no longer in slow motion. Gina's body rested in a flowing river of puddled water that rolled toward a drain, and she convulsed as rain continued to pound her from above. As if to add insult to injury, Searcy reared back and kicked her in the abdomen. She flew back from the blow, but didn't even have the strength to cry out as she merely rolled back onto her stomach. Searcy discarded her and strolled toward him as Lorena's laughter mingled with the rain and thunder in a mockery of sensory onslaught.

"Motherfucker! I'll kill you! I swear to God, I'll kill you!" Malek's tears mixed with the rain that ran down his face.

Searcy resheathed the Reaper's Blade and tucked it away as he stepped up and knelt down in front of Malek. "You cry for her." He scoffed, smearing his fingertips over Malek's face. "Weakling. You disgust me."

Malek glared at him, then up at Lorena, who joined them with a sickening grin on her face. "Why?" he said.

He wanted to wipe that satisfied smile off her face with his boot.

"Why what?" she said. "Why did you kick me out of your bed?" Her brows lifted innocently. "Or why did I seek revenge on you for doing so?" She shrugged and fondly tucked Searcy's wet hair behind his ear. "And while I was at it, I secured the future of my own personal interests."

Malek gulped back a cry of mourning as he looked at Gina's shivering form lying in the puddle. Was that what this was about? Had Lorena really turned Gina over to the Dacians because he had kicked her out of his bed? Was she so psychotic that his refusal to fuck her had led to Gina's inevitable death?

"Awe, the lightbulb comes on," Lorena said, pleased with herself. She crouched beside Searcy and stared at him. "Now you will learn how I felt, Malek. Now you will see how it feels to lose what you only just found." She paused and gave Searcy a little pat, as if she were petting a dog. "But unlike you, I've found a suitable replacement. You never will...and you will die. Just as she will by morning." She bobbed her head in Gina's direction.

Malek couldn't deny the truth in Lorena's words. Once Gina was gone, he would never find another.

"Kill me," he said. "Please kill me." Even as he said it, he knew they wouldn't.

Still, Searcy's arrogant burst of laughter struck him more deeply than if he'd stabbed him. "No. You will watch her die. You will suffer as Armand suffered in his last moments at *her* hands." He pointed over his shoulder toward Gina.

"Armand beat her. Abused her. He tried to kill her, you bastard!" This was Malek's last gasp.

"He was her mate!" Searcy's voice boomed. "He had every right to do what he pleased with her!"

They were crazy. All of them. Trying to reason with them was like trying to hold on to a greased glass. It no longer mattered, anyway. The only thing that did was getting to Gina and making her last hours as comfortable as he could.

The sound of squealing tires brought their heads around.

The humans in the SUV had apparently gotten a whiff of what was going on and decided it was time to split, no doubt wanting to avoid being witnesses to a murder. But the intrusion seemed to bring an ounce of sense back into Searcy's maniacal brain.

"Let's go." Searcy stood and leered down at him. "Your fate is sealed, weakling. As is the fate of your friends at AKM. In time, they will all suffer for their betrayal." He snapped his fingers at Vaydon, who released him with a violent shove that sent his face into the wet pavement.

By the time he righted himself and looked up, they were gone. He pushed to his feet, rushed to Gina's side, and fell to his knees.

"Oh God! Gina!" He lifted her from the puddle and smoothed the grit and water from her face.

Her body contracted every couple of seconds as the poison continued to break through her system. "Ma...lek."

"Ssshh. I'm here. I'm here now. Stay with me, *piccolina*. I'm here."

"It b...burns."

"I know, baby." He brushed her soaked hair off her face, leaned down, and kissed her forehead.

He knew by morning she would be gone, but he had to try. He couldn't give up. He owed her that much for failing to protect her.

"You're going to be okay. You're going to live, baby."

Denial pushed forward again, just as it had with Carmen. He refused to accept that Gina was dying. No way was he going to lose another mate. Fuck that! Gina would live, damn it. She had to.

Sorrow filled her eyes. "No, *tesoro*. No." She shook her head as her body contracted again and again.

Her hand crept toward his. She was too weak to move. He took her delicate hand in his, lifted it to his cheek, and pressed her cold palm against his face.

"I won't let you die, Gina. I'll find a way."

A wan smile lifted the corners of her mouth. "Too...late... for that."

No! The word echoed through his mind. *NO!* She was his life. He had only just found her. God couldn't take her from him already. Not so soon. They had a whole life ahead of them. Only an hour ago, they had chosen the colors for their new kitchen during the cab ride back to his truck. Lavendar walls with eggshell, antique brushed cabinets. With recycled flooring. Gina believed in the green movement. They had even shopped for bookshelves on her phone so they could pull out all the books he had bought over the years and build a library.

This wasn't happening—couldn't be happening.

"No!" With a burst of life, he hoisted Gina's limp body into his arms and rushed her back to the truck. After getting her settled into the passenger seat, he jumped behind the wheel, turned the key, gunned the engine, threw the truck in gear, and like the humans before him burned rubber as he spun the truck around and headed toward AKM.

Somebody there had to be able to help. One of medical staff had to have developed a cure for the Reaper's Blade. They must have!

"Hang on, Gina."

As long as she breathed, he had a chance. Not much of one, but even a fraction of one percent was something.

FIRE BURNED THROUGH GINA'S VEINS and blistered her cells. She could almost feel her tissues turning black and withering away on a hot breeze like some homemade dirigible over a bonfire, its edges burning, deteriorating, until all that was left was ash.

Poor Malek. He thought he could save her. Or maybe he only hoped he could. She didn't have the heart to tell him again that it was too late for that. She was already a walking corpse. In time, the poison would be too much for her heart to bear, and she would succumb.

Ironic, wasn't it? Only a month ago she had attempted to kill Severin and rob his new mate, Arion, of the joy they had found with one another. She had failed—thank God. But where she had failed, Searcy succeeded. She and Malek had just found each other and after only two all-too-brief days, their mating was coming to an end. Talk about karma coming back around to the power of ten.

It was her fault. She had brought all this on herself the moment she vowed blood vengeance for her brother's death. No…she had sealed her fate long before even that. The second she pulled the trigger and blew Armand's skull apart, she had set the wheels into motion to lead to this moment. Her demise had been inevitable from the instant she murdered Armand.

Malek would never survive this, so the blood on her hands only grew darker and more profuse. In effect, she had killed herself *and* Malek that day. Like some train on a winding track that led downhill, she had set them both on this course toward death, and now they careened out of control, the end of the tracks coming at the edge of a cliff that would send them both tumbling to their agonizing deaths.

An assassin, huh? Really? Well, if she was, she was lousy at her job. What kind of assassin fucked up so badly that she killed everyone important to her? Even herself.

"I'm s…sorry," she said, too weak to turn toward him. Fresh tears dripped from the lower rims of her eyelids. "S… so sorry."

His warm hand clasped hers. She was cold. So damn cold. Even so, she didn't want him touching her. If he knew she had brought all this pain and suffering to him, he would surely push her away.

She was a fool to think she deserved to take a mate like Malek. Only a few short hours ago, everything had felt perfect, as if they had saved each other and healed one another's hearts. Maybe in his way, he had healed hers, but what she had done to him was unforgiveable.

Because she hadn't healed him.

She had sealed his death warrant.

CHAPTER 27

BRAK LOOKED OUT THE WINDOW of his hotel room. The storm was beginning to wind down.

When was the last time he had witnessed a thunderstorm? Forever ago, it seemed like. For the past forty-five minutes, he had stood rooted in place, gazing out at the lightning, breathing in as thunder ripped the air, as if by engaging all his senses he could more fully experience the wrath of Mother Nature.

He and Cynthia had arrived in Chicago a few hours ago, found a hotel, and had grabbed dinner. Room service, Cynthia called it.

His loaded cheeseburger tasted nothing like anything he'd ever eaten. Much better than their lunch at Bob Evans, and far tastier than any burger he'd ever cooked for himself.

"You ready?" Cynthia said from behind him.

He turned and nodded. "Yes." He wanted to see Trace and needed to find out what had happened to his father. He had so many questions, he didn't know where to begin.

With kind eyes, Cynthia took his hand and led him toward the door.

"Do I look okay?" he said, catching his reflection in the mirror.

Everyone in this new world looked so different. Not like the people he viewed on the Internet. Did he fit in with this new world he had missed out on? Was he dressed the way he should be?

"You look fine," Cynthia said. "Very handsome. Very... normal."

He wore a white Henley tee that buttoned a third of the way down, along with a pair of tan, linen pants with a drawstring waist and a pair of brown sandals. He had showered, and his long, brown hair fell in damp waves well past his shoulders.

"Are you sure?"

She smiled at him. "Positive. Now come on. Let's go find your dad and brother. I doubt they'll care what you're wearing and will just be happy to see you."

He grabbed the information for AKM off the dresser, including a map he had printed before leaving his prison in West Virginia, and followed her into the hall and down to the parking garage.

It wouldn't be long now and he would be back with his brother.

Malek didn't bother with parking in the underground garage once he got to AKM. He pulled up to the back door, hauled Gina out of the passenger seat, held her against him, and hurried inside to the medical wing.

"Help! God, someone help me!"

The nurse at the front station took one look at the blood still oozing like acid from Gina's neck and chest and immediately jumped to action. Within sixty seconds, doctors and medical staff poured into the entryway. Someone lifted Gina from his arms, but he refused to let go of her hand as they settled her on a gurney and wheeled her to the trauma unit.

"What happened?" one of the doctors asked as a nurse began strapping down tubes and inserted an IV in Gina's arm. Another began cutting off her soaked clothes, while a third held a white, warmed blanket at the ready to cover her.

"We were attacked by Dacians. One of them had the Reaper's Blade." Malek squeezed Gina's hand. "Is she going to be okay?"

"Reaper's Blade?" The doctor's eyes grew wide.

Surely, the doctor had heard of the Reaper's Blade.

"Yes. You have a cure for the poison, right?" He gripped the doctor's white coat with his free hand. "Surely, we have a remedy that will save her!"

By now, the doctor's face had grown so pale he looked translucent. "No, Malek. I'm afraid such a remedy doesn't exist."

"Something! Anything! You can't let her die!" The futility of his request began to sink in. He was whistling to the wind.

The doctor put his hand on Malek's shoulder. "I'm sorry, Malek. There's nothing we can do but make her as comfortable as we can."

All he could do was stare at the doctor. Just stare and shake his head while his mind searched for a way to save his beloved Gina. Nothing. He got nothing. The cause was lost.

"We're ready to move her to a private room," one of the nurses said, obviously aware from the conversation that there was nothing they could do for her in the trauma unit.

The doctor led them to a quiet room in the back and transferred her to a bed.

"You can lie beside her if you like, Malek," the doctor said softly. "In fact," he cleared his throat awkwardly, "I would encourage it...after we get you in dry clothes, of course." He paused. "I'll have the nurses bring in a pair of scrubs you can change into."

The lump in Malek's throat prevented him from speaking, but he jerked his head in acknowledgement.

"Should I get Micah?" The doctor was fully versed on who reported to whom.

Malek bobbed his head in a tight nod again and averted his tear-laden gaze. He was about to break down on a colossal scale and didn't want any witnesses.

As if reading his mind, the doctor cleared his throat again, turned, and quietly left the room.

As soon as the door hissed shut, Malek fell to his knees beside the bed and let loose an outpouring of emotion unlike anything man had ever seen. Tears gushed down his cheeks, and harsh sobs racked his chest and shoulders with uncontrollable spasms, and the pain of nearly a thousand years erupted from his soul in what felt like a nuclear explosion. How could so much pain and suffering be contained inside his body...inside such a small space?

But there was no denying how horribly he suffered now. He was truly lost. Or, rather, he would be by morning. Because as soon as Gina passed over, his life would end. One way or another, he was dead.

How stupid he was. So damned fucking stupid! He had fought mating Gina for weeks. What if he hadn't? What if he had succumbed that first day...that very moment in her cell when he knew in his heart he had mated her? If he had simply given in and claimed her...if he had completed the mating between them the moment he knew she was his, he never would have taken to whoring, he never would have been at Four Alarm the other night, and he never would have met Lorena. And if he had never met Lorena, she would have had no cause to join forces with the Dacians and lead them to Gina, and Searcy would never have had the chance to put his evil blade to Gina's sacred blood.

This was his fault. His selfish pride and refusal to let go of the past had killed her. He had killed his precious, beautiful mate.

How much time did he have left with her? Already, she labored to breathe.

Where was the nurse with dry clothes, damn it? He wanted to be in bed beside her. He wanted to hold her as long as he could before she was gone. Couldn't they hurry up and get him what he needed so he could be with her, for God's sake?

The door flew open.

Malek lifted his head and looked up at the horrified face of his oldest friend. Micah's expression was one of shock, dismay, disbelief.

"Oh my God," he said, his gaze jumping to Gina and then back to him. "Oh my God. Malek."

For the first time in forever—and most likely the last—Malek needed his friend. He needed Micah and his strength now more than he ever had.

Slowly, he rose to his feet. "Micah..." He blinked and took

a deep, shaky breath. "God, Micah, I'm so sorry."

All their fighting, and all the awful things they'd said to one another fell away as Micah rushed forward and yanked Malek into a firm, body breaking hug.

"Don't you apologize for a damn thing, Malek." Micah gripped him so hard it hurt, but in such a good way. "You have nothing to be sorry for, you hear me. Don't you apologize to me or anyone else, you got that, brother? More than anyone else, I know what you were going through. I get it. Do you hear me?"

"You were right. You were right about all of it." He knew this was his last chance to say everything he had to say to Micah before his mind fell into the permanent wasteland of suffering and loss. "I love her. I have since I met her. I thought I could deny it, but I couldn't. I've been such a fool, and if I had only listened to you..." A sense of desperation pounded through his veins, and he felt panicked. There was so much to say...so much to convey before there was no more time left.

Micah pushed him away and tapped his temple with a shake of his head. "You don't need to tell me anything, my brother. I see it all. Right here. I see everything."

Which meant Micah saw what he wanted to do as soon as Gina passed. "I can't live without her, Micah. And I won't go through the hell I just went through over Carmen again. I won't."

For a long, tense moment, nothing was said as the weight of reality sank in, and then Micah sighed in defeat. Tears bloomed and glistened in his eyes, and his jaw clenched in a hard line as he fought to hold his own emotions in check. This was good-bye, and Micah knew it.

"I want you to pull the trigger, Micah. I want you to be the one to do it, because God knows, you won't miss."

Micah's chin quivered, and his mouth worked hard as he blinked and looked away. He sniffed heavily before running his palms down his face to wipe away his tears. "Fuck," he bit out quietly between his teeth. "Don't ask me to do that. Please don't ask me to do that." He sniffed again and looked back at Malek, his eyes bloodshot with his efforts to restrain his grief.

"Please, Micah. Please. Do this for me. This one last favor."

Micah regarded him, clearly losing the battle to keep his composure. After a moment's hesitation, he bowed his head and clasped Malek's hand like the brothers-in-arms they were. "You can count on me. You need me, and I'm there. Just like old times."

"Just like old times." A choked sob broke lose as Malek pulled Micah in again and the two embraced. Two friends who had lost each other for too long, to finally find one another again at the end.

After a long moment, Micah pushed back and wiped his face again as he took a deep breath and nodded toward Gina, who lay in a drugged sleep. "Go be with her, Malek. Spend what time you have with your mate." He spoke softly, his voice thick with compassion.

"I can't. Not until they bring me dry scrubs." And why oh fucking why was it taking so long for them to do that?

Micah stepped back and pulled off his sweater. He handed it over before stripping out of his pants and holding them out. All he had on were his boxer briefs and a black T-shirt. "Take them. You need my clothes more than I do right now. I'll wear the scrubs."

The gesture was enough to break Malek's hard exterior just a little bit more. Here was his commander and friend, someone who had put up with a lot of shit from Malek for the past several hundred years, and particularly in the last few weeks, and the guy would still literally give him the shirt off his back to help him. Micah's actions humbled him.

Malek cleared his throat and glanced down at the floor as he shoved off his soaked pants and began pulling Micah's on. "I don't deserve a friend like you." He pulled off his drenched shirt and pulled Micah's warm sweater over his head.

"Fuck that," Micah said. The words came like a term of endearment. "We were always there for each other, and that hasn't changed. You had my back, and I had yours, and I'm still there for you. When you need me, I'll be ready."

Malek looked up to find Micah grinning sadly at him.

"We're *brothers*," Micah said. "And we'll always be brothers, no matter that we came from different parents."

Unable to speak, Malek gave a humble nod. The two clasped hands and forearms, and Micah gripped the back of Malek's head with this free hand and pulled their foreheads together.

"Brothers," he said again quietly, staring him dead in the eyes.

Malek blinked, because he couldn't speak through the lump in his throat. This was a conversation he and Micah had needed to have for a long time. How unfortunate that it came under such morbid circumstances.

"I love you," Micah said, and then kissed his forehead. "You're my blood. I don't care what anyone says."

"I love you, too, old friend." Malek gave him one final embrace and broke away with a glance back at Gina, who was still passed out from whatever the nurses had given her.

The nurse chose that moment to come in with the scrubs. She stopped abruptly when she saw Micah standing in his underwear. Without missing a beat, Micah turned, grabbed the green scrubs from her hands, and pulled on the pants, dismissing the nurse with a look. She scuttled out, and Micah turned back toward him as he cinched the drawstring around his waist.

"How do I look?" he said, and then pulled the shirt over his head.

"Like a saint."

Micah grinned and wiped his face. "Don't blow smoke up my ass."

Malek gazed with longing at his friend. Within hours or even minutes—who really knew how much longer he had?— he would never see Micah again. They would never again fight alongside one another, draw blood together, or catch each other's backs. The end was here.

The emotional silence in the room weighed on them both, but true to form, Micah was the one to break it. "Go." He nodded toward the bed. "Be with her. I'll keep the others out for a while."

"Others?" Were the other members of the team waiting to see him?

"Yes. The whole team. They want to see you." He cleared his throat. "Pay their respects."

Of course. And he owed it to them to allow them in. After all they'd been through with one another, he couldn't depart without saying his own good-byes to them, too. "Okay, yeah. That'll be good. But, yeah, just give me a while first. I need... time." Time. Something he didn't have much more of.

Micah nodded, and then turned and left him with his beloved.

He carefully climbed into the bed with her and pulled her against him. "*Piccolina?* I'm here. I won't leave you." He brushed her damp hair off her chilled forehead. She was no longer feverish. Not a good sign. Her body was giving up the fight.

She moaned weakly and turned into him, but she was so feeble he had to help her even with that. "Malek?" Her breathy voice was almost inaudible.

"Sshh, *piccolina*. I've got you now. I'll take care of you." He bit back tears, determined to stay strong for her, to live in the moment until the very end. "I'll never leave you again."

Never. And he meant it. Because as soon as she passed, he would follow her. To join her even in death and live for eternity with her in the afterlife.

CHAPTER 28

BRAK TOOK A NERVOUS BREATH and pulled open the door to the AKM facility where Trace worked, and where he would find Trace's closest friend, Micah. He had seen as much during his brief encounter with him in that dungeon cell. Which still didn't make sense. Why was Trace being held prisoner?

"Can I help you?" the girl behind the desk said.

He looked down at Cynthia, and she nodded for him to go ahead.

Why was this so hard now that he was here? He should have been jumping for joy, eager to finally be free and about to be reunited with Trace and his father. But so much time had passed. The world was a strange, foreign place. And he didn't know what to expect once he was face-to-face with his brother. What if Trace had learned to live without him? What if he didn't need him? What if he wouldn't be happy to see him? What if…?

Shit, but this was silly. Why wouldn't Trace be happy to see him? Brak was being irrational, letting his insecurity get the better of him.

"Sir?" The girl behind the desk cocked her head and gave him a quizzical look, as if she recognized him from someplace.

Resolved to just get it out there, Brak took a deep breath and said, "I'm here to see my brother."

The girl's confused expression deepened. "Who's your brother?"

"Traceon Benyon."

She shot back and stood in a blink. "Oh my God." She covered her mouth with one hand. "That's why…you're his...I didn't...he never..."

"I know he's being held in a cell," Brak said, taking an eager step forward. "Is he here? Where is he? Why is he being held prisoner? Did he do something wrong? Is he in trouble?" Now that he'd pulled the seal off the dam, he couldn't stop his questions from flying.

The girl stammered unintelligibly and pressed a button on her phone.

"Yes?" A male's voice came through the speaker.

"Micah, I need you up front, please," she said.

"What is it? We've got an emergency back here."

This was Micah. Trace's friend. Brak leaned over and looked down at the phone. "Is that Micah Black?"

"Yes—" The girl began to speak, only to snap her mouth closed as Micah replied.

"Who the hell wants to know?" The voice on the phone held an edge of aggression.

"You're Trace's friend?" Brak craned toward the phone as if Micah would sprout from it.

Silence.

"Micah? Micah! Are you the Micah who's friends with Traceon Benyon?" Brak was nearly frantic.

"What the fuck? I'm on my way up."

There was a click followed by silence, and the girl behind the desk finally cracked a small smile, her eyes wide with wonder. She took a tentative step forward. "Are you...? You're his twin?" She stared up and down at his hair.

Brak frowned in dismay. "Yes. He's my twin. Why?"

Her smile widened and she blinked rapidly several times. "You're just so...different. But the same. I just...I can't believe he has a brother."

Cynthia shifted uncomfortably beside him as the door flew open and a dark-haired male wearing surgical scrubs burst through.

"Who the hell...?" Micah stopped dead and his dark navy eyes narrowed under thick, black eyebrows that creased into a frown as he looked Brak up and down.

"You're Trace's friend." Brak recognized him from the

images he had seen inside Trace's mind.

"And you're...oh my God. How is this possible?" Micah jacked his hands up on his hips and looked away. He appeared frustrated. "Well goddamn. I can't believe this. But it makes sense."

What was Micah going on about? "Is he okay? He's in prison. Why?"

Micah turned back and held up his hands. "He's fine. He's okay."

"Where—?"

Micah cut him off. "I know you've got questions. I can hear them flying at me from your thoughts. But we've got an emergency in back, and I need you to give me some time. Come with me and I'll set you up in my office, and as soon as I can, I'll tell you everything. As long as you do the same for me." He fixed him with a hard stare. "I have a lot of questions of my own about your brother."

Cynthia took his hand, and he glanced down. She smiled up at him with a nod, as if to encourage him that they were doing the right thing.

He looked back at Micah. "Of course."

Micah ushered them through the doors into a long hallway and led them to an office. "You can stay in here for now, and as soon as I can, I'll be back."

"Thank you," Cynthia said, tugging him toward the couch against one wall.

Brak hated waiting, but what choice did he have? "Thank you."

Micah stalled at the door. "I'll get back as soon as I can. I'm so sorry about this."

With a shake of his head, Brak held up one hand. "It's okay. I understand." They had shown up unannounced. Maybe he should have had Cynthia call first.

Micah turned and hurried away, leaving them alone.

"Are you okay?" She stroked his forearm with her fingertips.

He lifted his nose and sniffed the air. Something was wrong. "I'm fine." He pulled away and poked his head out the door, inhaled again.

"Brak?"

He frowned and tilted his head. "Oh no."

"What? What is it?" Cynthia stepped behind him.

Brak pulled back into the room and closed the door. He looked down at her, his expression grave. "Someone's about to die here."

MALEK KNEW GINA ONLY HAD MINUTES LEFT. She was fading rapidly, but he had hoped to have longer with her. This was too soon.

He trailed his fingertips down the side of her ash-colored face and across the seam of her bluish lips. "You're so beautiful," he whispered. A lone tear trailed from his eye, but he didn't bother to wipe it away. "The moment I laid eyes on you, I thought you were the most beautiful female I'd ever seen. You were so perfect, so full of fire." He grinned and brushed his thumb across her eyebrow. "I'd never met anyone like you. An assassin, and a beautiful one at that." He bent down and kissed her eyelid. "I will always love you, Gina. Always and forever."

A soft knock came at the door, and a moment later Micah peered inside. Malek could see the crowd of bodies behind him. Even Lakota was there, but he didn't care. Not anymore. A strange sense of peace had fallen over him, as if every ounce of energy was preserved to will Gina to cling to life as long as she could before the inevitable end.

"Can we come in?" Micah said.

Malek waved his hand and nodded. "Yes. It's time. It won't be much longer now." How he could be so calm, with his mate on the brink of taking her last breath, was nothing short of a miracle, but he had walked through hellfire and skirted the edge of psychosis to find his way to Gina. Maybe he had already paid his dues and this last gasp of lucidity was God's way of giving him a reprieve.

Micah held the door open, and everyone on his team filed in, including Io, who had shirked the final day or two of his calling to be here, and Arion, who technically was no longer a member of the team. Lakota stood to the side, more or less an honorary team member, as did Gina's friend, Trevor, who choked back a sob.

"I'll get them back for this," Trevor said as he stepped up to Gina's side of the bed. "For both of you." He reached across and clasped Malek's hand. "I promise. I will make them pay. I will hunt those bastards down and avenge you both."

Malek didn't tell him not to. He knew it wouldn't do any good. "Thank you." He shook Trevor's hand solemnly. "And thank you for bringing her to me. She told me it was you who convinced her to give me a chance."

Trevor cleared his throat and bowed his head, jaw clenched. "I'm sorry things didn't turn out—"

Malek held up his hand. "Don't be sorry. I had two beautiful days with her because of you. I was dead before you brought her back, and at least I was able to live for forty-eight hours with her in my arms. I wouldn't trade that for anything. Every second was worth it to have this time with her." He caressed Gina's chilled face.

Sev and Ari took Trevor's place as he stepped back, head bowed. An unspoken promise passed among the three of them. Ari wouldn't say it out loud, but Malek read in his eyes that he would come out of retirement to join Trevor in avenging him. The firm resolve in his intense, tawny gaze said as much, and Sev seemed more than down with that plan.

Malek bowed his head to them, they clasped hands, and without a word, they stepped back.

Io came next and placed his fist over his heart. "For you and your mate, I'll see that you're avenged. I swear it."

Even Tristan had been allowed off house arrest to come and pay his last respects. Tears sparkled in his blue eyes as he bumped fists with Malek. "I can't believe it's going to end like this," he said.

Other than Micah, Tristan was the one he had known the longest. The three of them had been there at the beginning. They were among the first to join the king's new guard when he created All the King's Men. Now the trio would become a duo as Malek stepped into the afterlife with Gina.

"Everything has to end," Malek said, ready to die.

"Not like this." Tristan shook his head and moved aside.

Lakota hung back, even as Micah gave him a nudge.

"Kota, come here. You're part of this team now, too." Malek met Lakota's gaze and nodded.

With hesitant, difficult steps, Lakota approached the side of the bed, bowed his head, and then broke down as he fell to his knees. "God, I'm so sorry," he said as he grabbed Gina's hand. "I'm so sorry. I forgive you. I forgive you for what you did to me...to Severin." He struggled to speak as his shoulders slumped. "You have to know that. Both of you." Lakota looked up and met Malek's gaze.

Lakota's reaction was unexpected, and Malek sensed there was more to Lakota than he first imagined. Whatever had happened in his past, it'd had a profound effect on him. Or maybe learning about Gina's past had awakened painful memories of his own history. From what Malek had heard, Lakota had been a bastard in another life, and now he sought forgiveness for his sins, which included his actions toward Gina.

The others coughed, cleared their throats, looked away, or wiped their hands down their faces, all of them shattered by Lakota's outpouring, as well as by the somber mood in the room.

Malek glanced at Micah. "Trace?"

Micah shook his head. "I tried, but I couldn't secure his release."

Damn.

"Well, you make sure to tell him—" Malek cut off as Gina tensed and shuddered, and his heart stopped.

"Gina?" He sat up and pulled her against him. She didn't move, didn't make a sound. "Gina? *Piccolina?*" He placed his fingers on her neck, at the place where her pulse should be. Nothing. He felt nothing.

No. Not yet. It's not time. It's too soon. He still had things to say to her. He needed to tell her that he loved her one more time. Her lifeless body draped in his arms. No breath, no heartbeat, nothing. He pressed his lips against her pulse point. If life still clung to her—even a little—he would surely feel it through his lips.

Nothing. She was gone.

He inhaled, held his breath, and tears broke in his eyes. And then the air ripped with agony as he roared to the heavens. "NOOOO!"

Gina was gone. His life was over.

He turned pained, urgent eyes toward Micah. His heart was already breaking apart, fracturing, splintering his insides, and spreading like black poison from his chest.

"Micah!" He needed to go. To meet his end. Now. Now! Before it was too late and he lost his sense of reality and sanity. Before he turned mutant from the intense anguish.

Micah rushed forward and took his hand. "I'm here. Let's go, brother. I've got you."

Malek turned toward Gina one last time. "I'll be with you soon. Wait for me, *piccolina*." He bent, kissed her cold lips, lingered for a heartbeat, and then allowed Micah to drag him away.

Pain broke through his limbs, and his chest erupted with sharp stabs as if blunt pickaxes pounded him from the inside out. The room swam as Micah dragged him away and rushed him down the hall toward the weapons center.

"Hurry," he said. "I'm...oh God...I'm losing it."

From somewhere that sounded far away, he heard Micah curse through ragged sobs. "I'll get them back. I swear to God I'll kill those motherfuckers with my own hands. Put my own fucking blade to their throats. See how they like that. Motherfuckers."

Malek grinned as his mind split in two.

Welcome back, he said to The Voice as its presence reignited.

Some welcome.

It'll be over soon.

Thank God for that.

CHAPTER 29

BRAK COULDN'T SIT STILL and paced in Micah's office. Someone needed him, and he didn't require the shattered cry of a male obviously in the throes of loss to tell him that.

"I have to go." He threw the door open and started down the hall in the direction where death hung like fog.

"Brak! What are you doing?" Cynthia hurried to catch up as he sniffed the air and turned down another hall.

He was a bloodhound on a mission to seek death's imprint and obliterate it. "Someone needs me. Now. Before it's too late." He could help. He had been born to help. This was what his power was meant to be used for. This was his true purpose.

He pushed through a set of double doors into what had to be a medical unit.

"Wait! You can't go back there!" The nurse tried to stop him, but he pushed past her. His only goal was to find the person who needed him now.

"I can help," he said flatly over his shoulder as he forged onward. He sniffed, looked in each room, and sought the Grim Reaper as it reached to claim another soul.

This one. He stopped in front of a brown door and gently pushed it open.

In his periphery, he saw several males in a state of mourning, but his focus was on the female lying lifeless in the bed.

One of the males stepped toward him. "Who are you?" His hair was short and dark, and Brak sensed he was a close friend of the deceased.

From behind, Cynthia followed and urged the clean-cut male back. "He means no harm."

Murmurs fell on his ears, but Brak was already in the zone. The energy his mother had gifted him spun into a vortex. It coursed through and around him, preparing to work in the way Mother had intended.

Taking his place beside the bed, he closed his eyes and fell into a trance. He saw the female's body in his mind's eye as a network of energy and light. Only hers was fading as her spirit departed for the other world. But there was enough of her essence left to work with, and he could save her.

Slowing his breath, he hovered his hands over her body and fed life back into her as he glided them up to her head and back down, past her chest, over both arms, her torso, her hips, and down both legs to her feet.

Her womb was barren, and she had suffered a broken knee recently, which had partially healed. Both were easy fixes, but her primary infliction was that she had been poisoned. So much poison was inside her. Almost too much for him to cleanse. *Almost.* But whoever had done this to her had failed. He would make sure of that. This female would not die today. Not on his watch.

After repairing the damage to her womb and knee in the blink of an eye, he suspended his right hand over her torso while he pushed the ethereal essence of his left hand into her chest and around her heart. As he drew the poison out through her belly button, he rhythmically pumped her heart, manually stimulating her circulation. Within seconds, he held the poison in his fist, focused his concentration, and turned it into harmless vapor. He would be ill when he finished, but it didn't matter. All that mattered was bringing this female back to life.

With the poison destroyed, he sent his right hand into her throat. With one touch of his index finger on her trachea, air surged into her body and lungs as if he were performing CPR. Which, in his own way, he was.

He pumped her heart and continued to force air in and out of her lungs, until—

The female's entire body jerked as she sucked in a blast of air, and then coughed violently as she gasped ragged draws of breath in and out of her lungs without assistance.

Brak broke the connection and woke from his trance as he staggered backward, suddenly too weak to stand. He had done it. For the first time in longer than he could remember, he had saved a life instead of taken one. The poison had been powerful, but no match for his strength, which now faded from the magnitude of what he'd done. Sickness roared into his stomach. Just in time, he spied a waste can, fell to his knees, leaned over it, and vomited.

Within seconds, Cynthia was beside him, stroking her hand up and down his back. "You did it. You saved her, Brak."

"What the hell?" someone said behind him.

The others in the room burst into action, a mass of movement and disbelief.

"How did you...? Who are you, man?" A male with long, blond hair knelt beside him.

All Brak could do was turn away and throw up again.

The room was a cacophony of noise. What he had done sent everyone into exclamations of celebration and relief until the female stopped coughing, caught her breath, and asked in a raw voice, "Where's Malek?"

Brak could have heard a pin drop as the din abruptly quieted.

"Oh fuck," the guy with the blond hair said.

Oh no. This wasn't good.

MICAH WIPED HIS EYES for about the hundredth time, but his fucking tears wouldn't stop coming. He couldn't do this if he was crying. He needed clear vision. He didn't want to risk missing, which would destroy him. One shot. He had only one shot.

To his credit, Malek was holding it together, although his restraint was clearly taking a toll. That insane voice in his head was back, and Malek was having one hell of a conversation with it. None of the jabbering made any sense, but he got the impression that was the whole point. Malek was simply trying to bide time, and blathering a load of nonsense with his inner demon seemed to be his way of doing that.

Micah checked the clip again, took a deep breath, and slapped it into his Sig. He never thought he would have to kill one of his own, let alone the one guy he had thought of as a brother for almost as long as he had been alive. But life had a strange way of playing out in unexpected ways, and now all Micah could do was honor his promise not to let Malek suffer anymore.

He chambered a bullet and took several deep, steadying breaths as the Sig hung at his side.

Malek stood in front of him. His head moved back and forth as he took on both sides of the conversation with himself, totally lost. Game over. Checked out.

"I love you, man." Micah lifted the gun and pointed it at Malek's head.

Malek stilled and met his gaze. Clarity shone back at him for the first time in five minutes. Was that relief he saw in his friend's eyes? "I love you, Micah. Thank you. Take care of Sam."

Micah almost lost it all over again at Malek's words, and he nodded tightly, blinking back tears again. He swallowed his sorrow and looked at the ceiling, willing the tears to stay away. "God, forgive me."

Just as his finger began to depress the trigger, the door to the weapons center burst open.

"STOP!" Severin barged inside.

Images Micah couldn't reconcile with reality blasted him from Sev's thoughts, and he snapped the gun back and pulled his finger off the trigger. "What the hell?" He couldn't believe what he was seeing from Sev's mind. Trace's brother had…somehow he had brought Gina back to life. Was this for real?

Sev stepped aside as Trevor carried Gina into the room. She was still weak, and her coloring was still pale, but mother of all miracles, she was alive.

How the hell...? He and Brak definitely needed a little one-on-one. There was more to Trace's brother than he first realized.

"Malek?" Gina's voice sounded frail, but her spirit was strong.

Malek turned toward her voice, blinked rapidly as if coming out of a trance, and frowned. "Gina?"

Tears fell down her cheeks. "Trevor, put me down, please." She struggled to get out of Trevor's arms and dropped her feet to the floor with a wince.

Her knee was swollen, and she looked like she might fall over, but she managed to stay upright and limp across the room with Trevor's help.

"Am I dead?" Malek held out his arms. "Are we together again?"

Gina shook her head as Trevor helped her into Malek's arms. "I'm not dead, *tesoro*."

Malek's brow furrowed. "Yes you are. I was there. You stopped breathing."

Micah saw inside Malek's mind. He thought he was in the afterlife or hallucinating. Micah set down his Sig and went to Malek's side. "No, Malek. You're both alive."

"But...the Reaper's Blade?" Malek struggled to grasp what had happened as he looked between him and Gina. "You died in my arms. I was holding you. I felt you leave me."

"It's a miracle," Micah said as he backed away to join Sev and Trevor. "I'll explain later...after I get a few answers of my own." He *really* needed to get that face time with Brak. "Fellas," he said as he clapped Sev and Trev on the shoulders, "let's leave them alone."

Malek still looked dazed as Micah and the others turned for the door, but just as he was about to grab the door's handle, the dam burst. Malek's splintered mind fused back together with such force, Micah felt it like a slap on the back, and he glanced over his shoulder at the most beautiful sight he'd seen since mating Sam. Malek had Gina in his arms, his face buried against her neck.

"You're alive? You're really alive?" he said, as if he still couldn't believe it.

Gina laughed through her tears as he took them both to their knees and hugged her to him. "I'm alive, baby. I'm really alive."

Micah had seen a lot of strange shit in his long life, but he had never seen someone come back from the dead. Until now.

When he turned around, Sev and Trevor were grinning from ear to ear.

"Some stranger came in and saved her," Sev said. "He was all Jesus-looking. Long, brown hair, white shirt, loose pants, sandals. I have no idea what he did, but whoever he is, he saved Gina's life."

Micah ushered them out and closed the door. "That would be Brak," Micah said.

"Brak? Who the hell is Brak?" Sev fell into step beside him.

Micah sighed and hit Sev with a hard glance. "Brak would be Trace's brother, Sev."

Sev nearly tripped over his own feet. "You're shitting me!"

"Nope."

"Well, fuck me."

"You said it."

Goddamn. Trace had a brother. A goddamn brother. And apparently the guy was just as powerful as Trace, but in his own way.

How 'bout that?

MALEK PRESSED HIS LIPS TO GINA'S FOREHEAD. "I thought you were gone. I thought I'd lost you, *piccolina*."

"I know, but you didn't. I'm here." She breathed against his Adam's apple as he held her close and rocked her.

The warmth of her body seeped into his. She was warm. Not cold as she had been ten minutes ago. Life surged through her again, and with each second, he felt it grow stronger. She was reanimating right before his eyes, as he held her, as he breathed in the vanilla scent of her hair. "How?"

She shook her head. "I don't know. One second I was walking toward a bright light, and the next I was back in my body, gasping for air as a tall, strange male stood over me. I don't know who he is, but he brought me back. He saved me. Somehow, he saved me."

Malek pulled back and met her wistful, confused gaze. He didn't know who the mysterious male was or where he'd come from, but it didn't matter. "Whoever he is, I'm indebted to him. He gave you back to me. He saved my life as much as yours."

She blinked and nodded. Her eyes glistened with tears of happiness. "Maybe Lady Luck is finally smiling on us."

Lady Luck. Until now, that bitch had all but abandoned them both. "Maybe she feels we've been through enough."

"I hope so, because I'm done with her shit."

He chuckled and pulled Gina against him. "I love you. God, I love you."

She was alive and safe, and they were together.

Gina gently pushed away and searched his eyes. "What were you doing, Malek? What was going on in here when Trevor brought me in? Micah had a gun in his hand, and it looked like...I thought he was about to..."

Malek looked down at her lovely, elegant hands and threaded his fingers between hers. "I couldn't live without you, *piccolina*."

There was a pause, and then, "Was Micah going to kill you?" She spoke softly.

With a nod, he met her gaze again. "Yes. I didn't want to live without you, so I asked him to." He shook his head and fought back tears. "I couldn't live without you, Gina. Do you understand? I only just found you. You made me whole again, and I—"

She cut him off with a kiss. Her soft lips pressed against his mouth and flooded him with life. What was once cold now warmed, and what had been broken now fused back together. All from the tender brush of her lips on his.

When she pulled away, she arched one eyebrow. "Don't you ever do anything as stupid as that ever again, baby. Or

I'll kill you myself. Is that clear?"

He licked her taste from his lips and smiled as he caressed her cheek with the backs of his fingers. Even after dying and coming back to life, she was still full of fire. Gina was the polar opposite of Carmen, but he couldn't imagine himself with any other. His biology had chosen well. "Crystal clear." He kissed her again then spoke against her lips. "And don't you ever stop bossing me around."

"Now you're just asking for trouble, *tesoro.*" Her eyes twinkled.

"I expect nothing less from you, *piccolina.*" He trailed his fingertips down her neck.

"Oh? Why's that?"

He buried his face against the side of her neck, inhaled, held her precious scent on his tongue, and then exhaled. "Because you've been nothing but trouble since I met you, and, oh baby, I've loved every second of it."

She giggled, and the sound was like butterflies flittering through silver chimes. "Except for that whole suffering thing, right? I'm sure you didn't enjoy that."

"Well, except for *that.*" He smiled against her skin. "Otherwise, I wouldn't trade a single moment."

Her fingers combed through his hair, and she kissed his temple. "I love you," she whispered.

If only he could crawl inside her skin, because he couldn't hold her close enough. "I love you, too."

For a long moment, nothing was said, and then Gina whispered. "Take me home, Malek. Take me home and be my mate for the rest of my life."

Home. The word held new meaning, because she *was* his home. He dwelled within her now, and she dwelled within him. No matter what happened from here on out, nothing would change that.

"For the rest of mine," he said and picked her up.

Once he found a ride out of there, he planned on starting the rest of his life with her, in *their* home, in their bed, and in every way imaginable.

Now and forever.

CHAPTER 30

MICAH MADE HIS WAY BACK TO THE ROOM where Gina had died only minutes ago—and then was brought back to life—to find Trace's brother lying on the bed. His pallor looked nothing like it had when he greeted him up front. The guy was grey and transparent. Someone had taken off his shirt, and his blood vessels showed through his skin like red and blue lines on a roadmap.

"What's wrong with him?" he asked as the door swung shut behind him and Sev. Most of the others had left the room and stood in the hall, but Lakota had stayed behind. He held a waste can at the side of the bed.

The woman who came with him, Cynthia, glanced up as Brak rolled to his side. Lakota quickly stepped forward with the trash can, and Brak vomited into it. It looked like he had been vomiting a lot.

"Whatever he pulled from the woman made him very ill," Cynthia said.

Shit. No kidding. "Is he going to be okay?" Micah stepped to the side of the bed. If only he could do something to help. However Brak had done it, he had saved lives tonight. Gina's, Malek's…and a little piece of everyone on Micah's team, who now stood outside in the hall and had looked as helpless as he felt.

Cynthia stroked her fingers over Brak's brow as he rolled to his back and shivered. "Ssshhh, sweetie. It's okay. I'm here." She met Micah's gaze. "This is normal. He always gets sick when he returns to his body. But he's especially ill this time. What was wrong with the woman?"

"She was cut by the Reaper's Blade."

Cynthia frowned. Micah could see from her thoughts that she had no idea what the Reaper's Blade was. Micah wasn't surprised since she was human.

"The Reaper's Blade is deadly to vampires," Micah said. "Once it breaks skin, no matter how small the cut, death is inevitable."

Cynthia nodded and turned her gaze back toward Brak, whose teeth chattered. "He's burning up."

Micah grabbed a towel from a nearby shelf, tore it in half, and shoved the pieces toward Sev. "Wet these." Then he glanced at Lakota, who still looked unnerved from earlier. "Kota, go tell the nurse to bring me a bowl of water and ice."

Lakota set down the trash can and disappeared out the door, and Sev returned with the towels. "I don't understand. If they have this…Reaper's Blade…can't they just use it and kill us all?" he said softly.

Poor Sev. The guy really had missed out on a lot.

Micah took the towels and pressed them to Brak's forehead and neck, then looked over his shoulder at Severin. "The blade can only be used once every twelve lunar cycles. The magic requires the moon to regenerate its power or some shit, so the Dacians reserve the blade to be used only for the most notorious of those they've marked for death. So the legends say."

He turned back toward Brak and dabbed the towel on his face. This was Trace's twin. His best friend's flesh and blood. He was going to tend to Brak as he would Trace and make sure he survived whatever was happening to him.

"I see," Sev said. "So, now that they've used the blade, the playing field is level. Is that what you're saying?"

Micah liked the tone in Sev's voice that said the lightbulb was turning on.

"Exactly." With a nod, he picked up on the thoughts of the others in the hall. They seemed to have come to the same conclusion Sev had and were ready to hunt those fuckers down. If they were going to strike, the time was now, because the Reaper's Blade was about as ineffective against them as a cat scratch…and would be for the next twelve full moons. Brak moaned and brought Micah's attention back down. "He'll get better, right?" He looked at Cynthia.

She shrugged. "I don't know. I've never seen him so ill." Her voice was filled with worry. "This is really bad."

"How did he do that, anyway?" Sev asked. "How did he heal Gina like that?"

"It's his gift," Cynthia said with a sad smile as she caressed his cheek. "He was made to heal." Bitterness crept into her voice. "But those who enslaved him before used him for evil. They made him kill." She pulled Brak's hand to her lips as tears welled in her eyes. "But you're free now, sweetie. You're free. So you have to get better, you hear me? You have to enjoy your freedom and not be sick. Your brother needs you."

Brak moaned again softly and blinked his eyes open to meet Micah's gaze. "Trace. Is he okay? Is he safe?" His voice croaked quietly.

Micah nodded. "Yes. He's safe."

"But…prison…?"

Micah shook his head and rubbed his thumb up and down Brak's pulse point to calm him. "He's okay. He helped a friend, but had to break the law to do so. He was sentenced to a short time in custody, but he's due out in a few days. You'll see him then."

Brak shivered but grinned. "You're a good friend…you and Sam."

How the hell did Brak know about Sam? "Yes we are." Trace practically lived with him and Sam now. The three of them had a special friendship that grew stronger every day, and Sam yearned for Trace to be released from the king's dungeon as much as Micah did. They needed him as much as Trace needed them.

Micah realized Brak was reaching for his hand and clasped it as he pressed the compress against Brak's forehead.

"Thank you for taking care of my brother," Brak said. He sounded a bit stronger.

"The honor's mine." Micah met Brak's weak grin with one of his own. "Are you going to be okay?"

The color was beginning to return to Brak's skin, but Micah could feel how weak he still was.

Brak nodded once. "Just need to rest a few days."

Cynthia sighed with relief, smiled, and patted Brak's other hand. "He's always so tired after he goes out of body like that, but I was hoping it wouldn't happen now that he doesn't have to use his power to kill, anymore."

Kill? Cynthia had mentioned something about that earlier. What did she mean? Brak's mind was too much of a mess right now for him to get anything that made sense, and all he could see in Cynthia's thoughts was Brak lying on a bed like he was hypnotized, and then awaking to get sick like he was now, only not as bad. Micah really wanted that one-on-one with Brak, but it would have to wait until he was well. He wouldn't put Brak through the twenty questions until he had recovered.

Brak rolled his head on the pillow to look at her. "It depends on what I do, Cyn. This was bad. The female was full of poison. If I had merely healed a broken bone, I would simply feel nauseous and need a nap."

"You do too much," she said, caressing his face.

He closed his eyes and sighed. "It's why I was made. It's what I was born to do."

Micah glanced at the face that looked so much like Trace's and frowned. If Brak had been made—*born*—to heal, what had Trace been born to do?

Given the extent of Trace's power, he had a feeling he already knew the answer to that question. And the emotional pain Trace had to bear from his mixed-blood gift was the equivalent to the illness Brak suffered from his.

He squeezed Brak's hand, and then let go. "You stay here and rest, Brak. I'll make housing arrangements for you." AKM had available homes and apartments all over the city, some waiting for tenants, others being used for various purposes. He needed to find Malek and Gina a new place to live now that his current residence was compromised, so while he was at it, he'd line something up for Brak and Cynthia, too. He didn't see that they were mates, but clearly they were important to one another and needed to stay together.

He stood and turned toward Cynthia. "I'll have them bring in another bed for you so you can stay with him. And I'll make sure someone brings you extra blankets and clean clothes…and cleans up the mess." He nodded toward the waste can.

Cynthia smiled at him. "Thank you, but I'm used to this."

He winked at her. He knew she was used to it. He saw inside her mind and knew what she had endured to see Brak through these episodes.

For a human, she was strong.

She would fit in well here.

CHAPTER 31

MALEK'S HAND CREPT UP THE BLUE TOP the hospital had given her. "You look good in scrubs," he whispered against her lips. She looked good in everything.

Color filled her cheeks. A welcome sight after how pale she had been not even two hours earlier. Her eyes darted to the front seat, to Severin, who had volunteered to play chauffeur and take them home. Arion sat beside him in the passenger seat. Clearly, the two were trying to remain invisible, but who was he kidding? He and Gina had been making out in the backseat like horny teenagers since they left AKM, and the atmosphere in Sev's Challenger was murky with arousal, especially since it had become clear his calling wasn't quite over and pulses of hormonal heat were echoing from him every five minutes or so.

Before letting him take Gina home, Micah had made it clear he would have to move. Since Lorena and the Dacians thought Gina was dead—and, as a consequence, Malek—no one saw any harm in letting them spend a day or two in Malek's current residence to ride out the last of his calling, but remaining there long-term was out of the question.

No worries. He had all he needed in his arms. He could leave everything else behind and start over fresh anywhere as long as Gina was with him.

A gentle pulse of heat rippled from his body as Sev pulled up his driveway, and everyone in the car moaned.

The car stopped by the walkway to the porch, and as he pushed open the door and tumbled out with Gina, he caught a glimpse of Sev and Ari. They looked beyond desperate to be alone with one another, and he had a feeling they would get about as much sleep in the coming day as he and Gina would. Which would be not much.

He hoisted Gina into his arms.

"I can walk," she said with a playful shove.

"Ssshh, you." Malek kissed her then turned back toward the car. "Thanks, Sev."

"No problem." Sev nodded and then looked across the seat at Ari. His expression practically melted the windows.

Malek carried Gina to the front door as Sev started back down the drive.

"You sure have a way about you," she said.

"What do you mean?" Now that they were alone, another beat of heat surged from him close on the heels of the last, and she lolled her head back and moaned.

That luscious neck lay bare to his gaze, and it took all his willpower not to pull her up and sink his fangs into her flesh.

"I mean Sev and Ari," she drolled. "They looked like they were about to shed their skin in that car."

He set her down to dig out his keys, and she wrapped her arms around his waist and assaulted his neck. Her sharp fangs scratched his skin and sent quivers through his muscles. Holy hell, he was about to burst. With a murmured curse that gave way to a groan, he looked skyward as his knees trembled and almost gave out.

Have to get in. Have to unlock the door.

He fumbled with the keys as Gina continued molesting his neck. By some stroke of luck, he finally got the door unlocked, backed her inside, kicked the door shut behind him, and didn't even wait to get her downstairs to his bedroom before he began tearing away her clothes.

Hormonal heat pounded out of him like high tide rolling in, and the fire of a thousand candles consumed them both.

"You belong to me," he said as he picked her up and tossed her over his shoulder as if he were a caveman taking his clubbed-over-the-head woman to his cave.

She cried out and laughed as he smacked her bare ass and hauled her through the kitchen to the stairs that led to the basement.

Once downstairs, he stopped at the foot of his bed and playfully flung her off his shoulder to the mattress.

"Malek!"

She bounced, and in a heartbeat Malek was on her, over her, lavishing her body with his tongue, his lips, his hands.

Inch by glorious inch, he licked his way up the insides of her thighs, pushing her legs open, until he took a taste her sweetness. Her fingers drove into his hair and gripped his scalp as she murmured something he couldn't understand through a rush of breath.

Her flesh was soft and smooth, silky, musky, delicious. And he feasted and suckled her swollen nub until she shuddered and gasped his name.

Even before her orgasm waned—the first of many he planned on giving her in the next twelve hours—she sat up, gripped the back of his shirt, and tugged it over his head as he unfastened the pants Micah had loaned him and shoved them off.

No words passed between them. They weren't needed. Everything that mattered was revealed in her eyes, her touch, the way she nipped his neck as she pulled him down on top of her. All his love spilled from his pores, through the tips of his fingers as he gripped her hips, from his tongue as he laved her nipple. She was heaven, the stars, his whole damn universe.

And when she guided him inside her, the planets aligned in a celestial cataclysm that resonated with perfection.

"Gina…" His body drove into hers over and over, open and receptive, giving her all he was and taking all he needed.

"I'm yours," she said, breathless.

He lifted up on his arms and looked down on his life, his love, his world. When had making love ever felt so wondrous? When had he ever known such bliss?

As his body tightened, his gaze fell to the slender column of her neck, and like a drunk staring at a glass of scotch, everything else in the room vanished. He couldn't take his eyes off her neck. Blood…thirst…he needed to feed. His fangs ached and distended, and with each hungry thrust into her body, he panted out a grunt borne of another hunger.

Gina's palm wrapped around the back of his neck and pulled. She knew what he needed. "Feed from me, *tesoro.* Take what you need."

He let her pull him down, let her place his face in the curve of her neck as she rolled her head to the side and held him in place.

So good, so fragrant, so fucking hot.

His breath came in tight bursts. He was close, and so was she.

"Malek...please...now."

Instinct took over, and as she crested, he sank his fangs in deep. Blood spilled over his tongue. Her blood, so perfect and warm. She shattered in euphoric pleasure as her body quaked with release. An instant later, as his own orgasm broke through his flesh and her blood mixed with his, he grunted and clamped down even more forcefully on her neck like a lion to his lioness in the midst of mating frenzy.

Gina was his to love, cherish, honor, and protect for all eternity. No other would ever hurt her again. He would make sure of it, because any who threatened her would answer to him, and once he got his strength back, he would be a force from hell to any who threatened her.

Too long he had been alone, but no more. His beautiful assassin had returned. She had come back for him, and he would never let her go again. Ever.

CHAPTER 32

THREE DAYS LATER, and already moved out of Malek's old home, Gina joined him and the others inside Micah's office at AKM. Micah, Io, Severin, Lakota, Trevor, and even Arion—who had supposedly retired from enforcing—were there, chatting among themselves. Malek kissed her cheek and excused himself to talk to Micah. She gazed after him. He already looked ten times better than he had a few days ago. The wounds on his neck and cheek had healed, and he had already gained back a few pounds.

"Hey you," Trevor said after pulling her aside. "How does it feel to have the wind in your hair?" He smiled and ruffled her bangs.

With a glance over her shoulder at Malek, she grinned. "It feels damn near perfect."

She and Malek has spent a whole day getting him through the last of his calling, which she hadn't minded one bit, and then helped pack up his belongings with a team Micah sent over. Malek didn't mind moving. He told her that as long as she was with him, he would happily live in a one-room shack if he had to. As it was, the house Micah found for them was anything but a shack, and the security system was rock solid. The king himself would be safe there.

They still had a few things to unpack, including all the books Malek had stored throughout various rooms in his old home, but they had all the time in the world to get to that.

"Gabe would have loved to see this, little sis." Trevor's multihued eyes twinkled with fondness.

"I know he would." She hugged him. "Now, what about

you, Trev? Gabe would love to see you happy again, too, you know. Are you going to take your own advice and run with the wind in your hair, too?"

He chuckled. "Been there. Done that. It didn't work."

Trevor had dated his Knights of Justice partner, Talon, for two years before they broke up.

"So, you're just going to give up?" She playfully punched his shoulder. "After your pep talk about me taking another chance on love? Was that all just bullshit, Trevor?"

He laughed and held up his arms in surrender. "No, it wasn't all just bullshit, but I'm not going to force it, either. I learned my lesson the last time."

"Talon really loved you, you know."

"I know, but we just didn't work out."

What he meant was that they had never mated. Trevor wanted a mate. He was ready to feel that connection with a special someone. He wanted what Gina now had with Malek.

"Give it time, Trev. If it can happen to me, it can happen to you." And wasn't that the truth? Never in a million would she have thought she would take another mate.

Before Trevor could answer, Micah stepped behind his desk. "Okay, let's get going."

Malek joined her and took her hand as they sat down beside Sev on the couch. Everyone in the room looked determined, primed, ready to kick some ass.

"We found our unwanted guests," Micah said.

Malek squeezed her hand just as she did his. For the past two days while she and Malek got settled into their new home, the others had burned the midnight oil and pulled out all the stops to find Searcy, Vaydon, and Lorena—quietly so as not to tip their hand—and developed a plan.

"I've met with King Bain, and he wants us to send a message—a *loud* message—but not kill them. And if we can obtain the Reaper's Blade, he wants us to." Micah turned toward her. "Gina, you're lead. Malek, you and I are secondaries. The rest of you will take up posts around the location to make sure they don't escape and be at the ready if we need you." He pulled up a map on his computer and projected it on the far wall as Lakota turned off the lights. "Here's the plan..."

THREE HOURS LATER, Gina lurked in the shadows, wearing black on black with a crossbow slung over her shoulder. Malek and Micah were right behind her. And hopefully Lady Luck had shown up as an ally this time, as well.

The three crept into the back door of the row house where Lorena was rumored to live, and where Searcy and Vaydon were staying.

Sounds of hard, brutal sex came from upstairs. What sounded like a bed banged violently against the wall as garbled cries of pleasure and harsh curses echoed through the upstairs hall.

She looked over her shoulder at Malek and Micah, who nodded once to let her know he wasn't picking up any thoughts from anyone downstairs. He held up two fingers. Only two were here. Damn. Two wasn't as good as three, but was better than nothing. And since the king only wanted them to send a message and not kill them, two was fine.

With the coast clear on the lower level, they started up the stairs, and Gina pulled her crossbow down to the ready, securing a long, metal-tipped arrow against the bow.

The sounds of sex grew louder as they reached the landing and fanned out. Gina led the way down the hall to the bedroom where all the action seemed to be taking place. A quick peek through the cracked door revealed that Searcy was nowhere to be seen, but Vaydon had Lorena pinned to the bed by the throat with one hand, the other holding her ankle up in the air, her leg stretched out at what had to be a painful angle. Still, Lorena seemed lost in oblivious pleasure, as did Vaydon.

They had to move fast. Vaydon would pick up their scent within seconds.

Gina ducked back against the wall and held up her index

finger then made a fist. She was going in.

Both Micah and Malek nodded, hands on their weapons. And what impressive weapons they were. Micah had a long, steel blade that looked like a freak of nature, as if someone had given growth hormones to a regular knife and said, "Go my child. Go forth and be lethal." Malek held a beast of handheld firepower that would make Dirty Harry say more than just "Go ahead, make my day." Shit, that piece would probably give ol' Clint an orgasm. This was a gun you pointed at someone and said, "Bitch, who's your daddy?"

Gina peeked inside the room again to find that Vaydon had released Lorena's leg and now had both hands wrapped around her throat, fucking her in earnest.

She gave her boys a look, nodded, stepped away from the wall, and with a quick step forward, she leaped and disappeared into vapor, blew through the thin slice of open air between door and jamb, and shot into the air.

A split second later, she reappeared above the pair on the bed, almost suspended in midair, legs tucked up under her, crossbow aimed at the center of Vaydon's lower back.

She released the arrow and flew down, landing with her feet on either side of Vaydon's torso as the arrow shot clean through them both, pinning them to the bed. The bed jolted from both her landing and their sudden convulsions of pain, but Gina was back in her element. Deadly and vicious, and monumentally pissed off and ready to level her own kind of justice on those who would have killed her and Malek. With a hiss, she lunged forward and grabbed a fistful of long, white-blond hair and pulled Vaydon's head back as he let loose a scream mixed with anguish and lust. His body shuddered. Obviously, he had been about to come as the arrow penetrated his back, and now let loose his orgasm.

Lorena screamed as her body fell into orgasm, as well.

"Man, you guys are fucked up." Gina's face wrinkled in disgust. "Whack jobs."

Micah appeared and pressed his Godzilla-sized blade against Vaydon's throat. "I know it's not the Reaper's Blade," he said with a devilish grin, "but it'll get the job done better than that puny knife of yours." He glanced at Gina. "As you can see for yourself, Gina's alive and well."

Vaydon and Lorena both hissed and snapped their fangs at him, but they weren't going anywhere. Not with an arrow holding them down.

An instant later, the muzzle of Malek's gun pressed against Lorena's head, and he leaned in close. "Hello again. Surprised to see us?"

Lorena regarded him through angry, shocked eyes, pinned under Vaydon and held to the mattress. Then she shot an acid glare up at Gina.

Gina gave Vaydon's head a healthy yank so she could look down at the bitch. She tsked and feigned concern. "You don't look happy to see us, Lorena."

Vaydon growled and thrashed, but Micah knocked his arm away and pressed the blade farther into his throat, bringing his resistance to a halt.

"I'm only sorry Searcy isn't here." Gina crouched behind Vaydon. "I guess we'll have to leave our little message with you, bitch."

"Fuck you." Lorena spat blood at her.

Malek hissed and jabbed his gun against Lorena's temple. "I want you to watch," he said, repeating what they'd said to him in the parking lot four nights ago. "And I want you to be reminded forever of what we're capable of." He slithered in close. "We can find you anywhere, anytime we want, and you and your boyfriend here will become the poster children for what happens to anyone—Dacian, Thracian, or otherwise—who threatens us, the king, or the throne. So pay close attention. You lose." Malek stood and nodded once at Gina.

With her hand still fisted in Vaydon's hair, she yanked back his left arm with her free hand. He protested and snarled, but Malek darted around the bed and grabbed hold of Vaydon's hand so he could help her hold his arm away from his body.

Lorena began panting, desperate to break free. But she was trapped. There was nowhere to go and no way to free herself.

Gina exchanged glances with Micah who said with deadly malice, "Consider yourselves warned." With the deadly grace of a ninja, Micah drew his blade from Vaydon's throat, spun, and swung the razor sharp edge through Vaydon's forearm, through not just muscle and tendon, but bone, too.

Vaydon shrieked as blood sprayed the floor. His body convulsed with pain.

Lorena screeched a litany of obscenities at them as Vaydon's blood splattered her body. "I'll kill you! You'll pay, you filthy whore."

Malek dropped Vaydon's severed hand to the floor.

"Awe, don't worry, Lorena. We didn't forget about you." Gina pulled a small, dagger-shaped knife from her boot and pressed the tip against the skin below Lorena's eye. "We wouldn't want you to feel left out." She swiped the blade down her face in a diagonal.

Lorena screamed and tried to slash her with her nails, but Gina slapped her hands away.

"Salt water," she said to Micah.

He tossed her the bottle of water they'd brought with them. She caught it, popped the top, and poured half the contents on Lorena's face before dousing the stub of Vaydon's arm with the other half.

Their mingled screams of pain split the air as smoke rose from their wounds and sealed over in ugly, black scabs. They would forever be maimed, and within days, everyone in the vampire community would know not to fuck with the King's Men...or their women.

Gina hopped off the bed and turned back to lash Lorena with a vicious backhand. "Let's see how Searcy likes you now. Maybe if he puts a bag over your head, he can fuck you and not be reminded of how you and his son let three 'weak vampires' get the better of you, or that he's not as infallible as he thinks."

Lorena's face would be scarred forever, and Vaydon would never grow back his arm. They would forever be maimed... marked as a reminder to Searcy and anyone else of what traitors risked by going against the king, which was the only reason Vaydon and Lorena weren't dead right now. King Bain wasn't a fool, and he was more ruthless than many gave him credit for. He knew the best way to quash an uprising was to show others what could happen to them if they did. Lorena and Vaydon would serve his purposes well.

Malek stepped to her side, a powerful presence both in body and in mind. Not only had she found a mate in him, but also a true partner.

"You give Searcy a message for us, bitch," she said to Lorena. "You tell that bastard he fucked with the wrong assassin, and if he wants to kill me and mine, he'd better bring more than that pathetic knife of his and two pieces of shit like you and his son. You tell him that if he wants to live, he'd best leave Chicago, because I've got more where this came from. If he wants to play, we'll play. And we'll win. You got that?"

Lorena's breath came in angry, wicked bursts.

Gina smacked Lorena's cheek as Vaydon scowled at her. "That's a good little bitch."

Malek popped Vaydon in the jaw. "If you ever come near us again, you're dead." Then he leaned over Lorena, cocked his head, leaned closer, and whispered, "Still feeling spurned that I kicked you from my bed, sweetheart? Because this…" he circled his index finger in the air to indicate what had just gone down. "This is nothing compared to the hell I will rain down on you if you come near either of us again." Then he leaned even closer until his lips almost touched Lorena's ear. "I *will* kill you if you try to hurt my mate again. Not even the king will be able to stop me. And now that I'm feeding again, not even your Dacian studs here will be able to hold me back. And you know it." The last he almost spat at her as he stood back up and took his place beside Gina.

Pride rose in Gina's heart for her mate. Yes, he was perfect for her. Strong, deadly, and magnanimous in the most powerful way. Gina had no doubt that Malek would move mountains to keep her safe.

"Let's go," Micah said. "Our work here is done."

She and Malek joined him and made for the exit as he

radioed the others and checked to make sure the coast was clear. It was.

"This isn't over!" Lorena screamed from the bedroom. "Do you hear me? You bitch! This isn't over!"

"Yeah, yeah, yeah. Blow it out your ass, psycho." Gina stepped out onto the back porch and projected herself back to the AKM parking lot. A moment later, Malek appeared beside her and took her hand. Within an instant, Micah showed up and led them inside.

"Nice work," Micah said. "I was impressed."

"So was I." Malek's tone said he was impressed in more ways than one. In fact, he sounded downright turned on.

"You two get out of here," Micah said over his shoulder in such a way that she knew he had picked up on Malek's vibe as she had. "I'll debrief and let the king know how things went."

"You sure?" Malek said.

"Absolutely. Now go home." Micah stopped outside his office, turned, and looked at Malek, and then down at their joined hands. "Damn glad to have you back, brother."

"Damn glad to be back."

Micah pulled him into a brotherly, one-armed hug. "Everything's coming together."

Malek nodded and hugged him. "Yep. You. Me. Arion's back, at least temporarily. And Trace is getting out in less than twelve hours."

"Yep."

Gina remembered Trace from the night she shot Severin. She had picked up bits and pieces about what had happened to him since she'd been gone.

"You going to pick him up?" Malek said.

Micah gave a jerky nod. He looked antsy. "Yep. Soon."

"Say hi for me."

"Oh yeah, because I'm sure that'll be the first thing he'll want to hear." Micah laughed, but it didn't sound genuine, and he shoved his fingers through his hair.

"How's his brother? Brak?" Gina said. She knew now that Brak was the one who had saved her life, and she owed him everything.

Micah shrugged. "He's better. He and Cynthia are settled in for the time being, just waiting for Trace to be released."

"Has he seen his dad, yet?" Malek said.

Micah shook his head. "They've moved Maddox to the new facility, and I've been too busy dealing with our 'little problem' to get him over there. Now that Operation Kick Ass is over, I'll try to take him as soon as I get Trace situated at my place." Micah fidgeted again, like he was strung out or something. Then he waved them off. "What are you two still doing here? Get home. Make love to each other or something." He spun and went inside his office.

Five minutes later, Gina sat in the passenger seat of a borrowed SUV as Malek drove them out of the parking lot. "What was that all about in there?" she asked. "Micah seemed tense talking about Trace."

Malek made a face as if he wasn't sure where to start. "Micah and Trace...they have a special relationship,"

"Oh? How special?"

"They keep the details pretty hush-hush, but it's obvious they're close."

"As in...?"

He shrugged. "I really can't say, but knowing Micah, I wouldn't want to place bets it's strictly platonic."

"But he's mated."

Malek hit the highway toward their new home. "I stopped trying to figure out Micah a long time ago. He doesn't seem to be like the rest of us."

"How so?"

He took her hand from across the console and pulled it to his lips. "What's with all the questions about Micah? You're going to make me jealous." He was teasing her.

"I'm just trying to get to know my new teammates is all." She was now officially a member of Micah's team. The announcement had been made yesterday.

Malek settled her hand on his lap and layered his over it. His thumb caressed her knuckles back and forth, back and forth. "Micah's just different. It's hard to explain, but you'll see. If you're around him enough, you'll figure it out."

"You two were close once." This was nice. The two of them talking about their lives with one another like a married human couple.

"Yes, we were. Hopefully, we can be again. We were like brothers from the moment we met when we were kids." He chuffed. "And our lives have mirrored each other's ever since. He took a mate, I took a mate. His mate died, my mate died. His mate couldn't bear young, and my mate couldn't bear young. And a few months ago, he mated again, and now I've mated again. Only this time, he's the one who mated a human and I'm the one who mated a vampire." He lifted her hand and kissed her fingers but kept his eyes on the road.

"Can his new mate bear young?" she asked softly. If Micah's and Malek's lives mirrored each other's so closely, if Sam was fertile maybe she would be, too? And how insane was that? She already knew she was barren.

"I don't know." He squeezed her hand reassuringly as if to comfort her. As if he knew why she was asking. If anything, he probably hoped he and Micah didn't replay history again so that Micah could have a child with his new mate. "Sam was newly transitioned when he had his calling, and she had almost been killed by dreck venom, so her body was probably too weak to accept a child. We'll have to wait until his next calling to find out."

They drove the rest of the way home in silence, his hand over hers on his lap.

Once home, Malek led her to the kitchen.

"I'm going to grab a shower," she said.

"Okay, *piccolina*." He kissed her. "I'll make us some dinner." He kissed her again and slipped his arms around her waist. "What are you in the mood for?"

"You," she said without hesitation.

He grinned against her mouth. "I can arrange that."

She kissed him, and then slowly pulled out of his arms. "I'll be right back."

"I'll be here." He winked and started digging inside the

fridge.

She was in and out of the shower in less than ten minutes and smiled at the dainty nightgown loaned from Tristan's mate, Josie. Until she could return to her old home in Atlanta and pack her own things, she would have to make do with what she could borrow or buy.

After combing her hair and dabbing a drop of vanilla perfume behind each ear, she dressed in the red, lacy negligee and checked her reflection. This getup would torture poor Malek. But everyone deserved to be tortured once in a while, and she had a feeling he wouldn't complain.

The aroma of steak and asparagus wafted down from the kitchen, and she checked her reflection one last time. In so many ways, she still couldn't believe she was here. She felt like she was dreaming...and she didn't want to wake up.

MALEK PAN-SEARED TWO NEW YORK STRIPS and put them in the oven with butter, and then blanched the asparagus. Then he opened a bottle of red wine, poured two glasses, took a sip, and turned his gaze to his abandoned vest over the arm of the new easy chair in the living room.

Micah had gone all out getting him into this furnished behemoth of a home. He and Gina had already discussed what would stay and what would go, but the one thing that was definitely staying was the built-in bookcases that took up walls in both the living room and the den.

But that wasn't all Micah had done for Malek. He set his wine glass on the counter, peeked over his shoulder to make sure Gina wasn't coming, and then fished out the velvet case inside one of the pockets in the vest. Micah had stashed it there for him before he and Gina arrived at AKM this evening. He cracked open the lid and licked his lips as sixty diamonds arranged in a wreath sparkled up at him.

This was the first of many necklaces he planned on purchasing for Gina, and Micah had helped him buy it so he could surprise her with it tonight.

He carefully lifted the wreath from the case and slipped it inside his pocket just as Gina's scent announced she was on her way.

When she appeared from the back hallway, Malek's heart flipped and he groaned. "You look..." Red satin and lace looked good on her. Very good. And her subtle vanilla fragrance sent shivers down his spine.

She stepped forward and ran her fingers down the front of his shirt, over his chest. "Amazing? Stunning?"

"Breathtaking," he said.

Her perfect smile beamed. "You're not so bad yourself, handsome. Maybe a little overdressed, but still a looker."

"Overdressed?"

She nodded.

"And I bet you have a plan to correct that, don't you?

She nodded again. "I've always got a plan."

"So do I." A pleased grin spread over his face.

Her eyes narrowed. "What are you up to?"

He brushed his fingertips over the fabric covering her nipples, which responded and formed tight peaks against the shimmery satin. "Nothing. I just think you're a little *under*dressed. That's all."

The way she leaned in and pressed herself to him filled him with warmth and pulled a moan from deep within his chest. She brushed her lips against his ear and whispered. "If I were any more underdressed, I'd be naked."

Her arms wrapped around his shoulders, and her lips played naughty wonders over his skin. If he wasn't surprising her with her first necklace tonight, he'd more than willingly let her continue, but that would have to be for another time.

"That's a thought, *piccolina*, but maybe you'll like my idea better." With his hands on her hips, he turned her around to face the counter and nibbled the back of her neck.

"What are you doing?"

"Hush." He slipped the necklace from his pocket and kissed a trail down the side of her neck. "Close your eyes," he said between kisses.

"Malek—"

"Shush. Close them." She sighed as he pulled back slightly and unfastened the necklace's clasp. "Are your eyes closed?"

She grumbled good-naturedly, and he could almost see her rolling her eyes. "Yes, they're closed."

Slowly, he draped the wreath around her neck. "For you, *piccolina*." He fastened the clasp. "Open your eyes."

She looked down an instant before she gasped. "Malek!" She spun and met his gaze. "Oh my God." Her fingertips caressed the diamonds as she glanced back down at the small fortune around her neck.

"I told you I was going to buy you a necklace for every day of the month," he said. "This is number one." He pinched the red satin at her hips and slid it up her torso. "And do you remember what else I told you?"

A smile spread over her face. "The steaks are going to burn, *tesoro*."

He arched one eyebrow and grinned. "No changing the subject. Now...do you remember?"

Her hands glided up his chest and over his shoulders as she bit her lip and nodded. "You said you would make love to me."

"And...?" He worked the negligee farther up her body.

She lifted her arms so he could take it off. "You said that all I'd be wearing was one of those necklaces."

"Uh-huh." He nodded, lifted the skimpy nighty over her head, and tossed it behind him. She wore nothing underneath. "And what are you wearing right now, baby?"

Her fingers already worked the buttons of his fly. "A necklace."

"*Only* a necklace," he said as his pants fell to the floor. He stepped out of them. A few seconds later, his shirt joined them, as did his boxers, socks, and shoes.

"What about the steaks?" Gina said as he lifted her and she wrapped her legs around his hips.

"Hold on to me," he said.

She laughed and gripped his shoulders as he quickly shut off the oven, pulled out the steaks, and dropped the pan onto the stove with a clang.

"They need to rest before I slice them, anyway. Now, where were we?" He wrapped his arms around her and carried her out of the kitchen.

"I think we were about to christen necklace number one," she said.

"Mmm, yes, I think you're right."

He carried her downstairs, laid her on the bed, and christen the necklace they did.

Twice.

GINA SETTLED INTO THE MOUND OF PILLOWS that rested against the leather, cushioned headboard of their new bed and smiled as she fingered the necklace Malek had given her. No one had ever given her such an opulent gift, and the diamonds brought out the long-repressed female inside her. For the first time, she could see herself putting on an evening gown, a pair of heels, and doing up her hair for an evening out rather than to manipulate a target. Always before, her appearance had been meant as a way to work her way in, project a certain image, and get close to her victims. Now, she simply wanted to look good for Malek.

It was all about Malek now.

This new direction in her life appealed to her. She had gotten her assassin mojo back, the panic attacks had stopped, and for the first time, she felt a sense of clarity and purpose. Her past was now in perspective, and her future was falling into place. The only thing that would have made her life perfect was to have Gabe back. But even that bitter pill was easier to swallow now that the rest of her life was getting back on track.

"Dinner is served." Malek appeared at the bottom of the spiral stone staircase that led to the basement. He held a tray with two plates and two glasses of wine.

"Thank God. I'm starved." She crossed her legs under the covers and sat up.

Malek set the tray on the bed and slipped out of his

sweatpants as she took their glasses of wine and set them on the nightstand. This appeared to be a clothes-optional dinner. No shirt? No shoes? No pants? No problem. And that was fine by her. She liked feasting her eyes on Malek's naked body.

A moment later, he joined her, took a piece of sliced steak in his fingers, and held it out for her to eat. "I had to heat it back up," he said. "How is it?"

She chewed and swallowed. "Delicious."

They ate in silence, but Malek kept sneaking kisses as he fed her bites of food from his own plate.

As he lifted yet another sliver of steak toward her, she shook her head and gently pushed his hand away. "No, *tesoro*. You need to eat more than I do right now." He looked better than he had several days ago, but he still had about ten pounds to gain, from the looks of him.

He set his plate aside and snuggled against her, his arm over her torso. "I'm good. I want to take care of you."

"You do take care of me." She set her plate on the nightstand and slid down to lie beside him.

"You need to eat, too," he said. "You almost died a few days ago." His fingers skimmed up and down her stomach.

She grinned. "You're just making excuses, baby. I'm fine."

"Excuses?" He pretended to be affronted. "Me? Never." He burrowed closer and nuzzled her neck as his palm caressed her torso.

She giggled. "What am I going to do with you? Are you always going to be like this?"

"If by 'like this' you mean hopelessly, totally, and ridiculously in love with you, then yes. I will always be like this." He nibbled and teased her skin.

Angling her head so he had better access, she closed her eyes and let herself be swept away again. Malek was an incredible lover. Attentive, tender, both gentle and fierce. And inventive. Apparently, he had always harbored an interest in the Kama Sutra and tantric sex, and now he wanted to explore both with her. If the little trick he had done to her earlier—which had given her an orgasm that had nearly blown her toes off—was any indication, she would like studying the Kama Sutra and tantric sex with him. Very much.

Suddenly, Malek's entire body jerked to a standstill. A moment later, he lifted himself on his elbow and stared at his hand on her abdomen.

She opened her eyes. "What? Malek, are you okay?"

His startled expression scared her. What could he sense? Was something wrong? Maybe Brak's nifty magic had only been temporary, and she was dying again...and Malek could feel it. Maybe—

"Gina..." He lifted his wide-eyed gaze to her as a slow smile spread over his face.

"What? Malek, you're scaring me."

He blinked and gently shook his head, and she swore she saw the hint of tears in his eyes.

"Malek, tell me." She placed her hand over his on her stomach.

After a heartbeat of hesitation, he leaned into her and pressed his mouth to her ear. "You're pregnant, *piccolina*."

What? How? It wasn't possible.

Gina's head snapped around and their gazes locked. "No," she said. "I'm barren. I can't be...it's impossible."

Sincerity and undeniable truth shone back at her as his hand pressed more firmly into her stomach.

"Malek?" How did this happen? How had her womb been rendered fertile when she knew without a doubt for decades that she would never bear children?

"You're pregnant, Gina," Malek said. "I can feel the baby's life force. I'm absolutely positive."

"But how...?"

He shrugged. "I don't know, baby. Maybe Brak did more than just bring you back to life. Maybe he healed your entire body."

For several long moments, Gina processed this change of events. Was Lady Luck trying to make up for all the years of screwing her over? The news that she was pregnant was almost too good to be true, but Malek seemed certain. Even now, he stared in awe at his hand as he wriggled his fingers against her tummy with a proud grin on his face. It was the kind of grin that made her heart flutter. He looked so proud…so happy…and very pleased with himself.

This was what every mated male wanted. This was why they endured the brutal pain-pleasure of the calling. The sole purpose of their freaked out mated biological servitude was to reach this end. To create a child.

And whether she understood the how and why, it was clear Malek had succeeded.

"I'm pregnant?" She placed her hand over his again, beginning to believe him. "Really?"

Malek nodded and smiled. "Yes." Then he pulled his hand away, reached behind him, picked up a piece of steak, and lifted it to her mouth. "Now, what was it you were saying about me needing to eat more than you do?" He waggled the piece of meat against her lips as if encouraging her to open up. "Because it seems you're now eating for two, baby." The steak pressed against the seam of her mouth. "Come on. Open up."

She sighed. "You're going to be cocky about this, aren't you?"

He arched an eyebrow. "Who? Me?"

Taking the bite of steak, she rolled her eyes at him, and he rested his chin on her chest and watched her eat.

"You're far too proud of yourself." She combed her fingers into his long, soft hair.

"Yep."

The way he said it, as if he should be wearing a cowboy hat, made her laugh.

"I'm going to feed you," he said, and then kissed her. "And I'm going to take care of you." Another kiss. "And I'm never going to let anything bad happen to you ever again." He lifted himself and settled on top of her.

"Right back at you." She pulled him down, held him close, and whispered. "But don't you fucking dare dote on me, or we'll have a problem."

He chuckled and eased himself inside her. "I can't make

you any promises on that, *piccolina*. I *am* a mated male with a baby on the way, after all. It's my job to dote."

"You're going to be trouble, aren't you?" She wrapped her legs around his hips as he rocked into her.

"No more trouble than you'll be." He nipped her shoulder. "You're trouble with a capital T."

"Mmm." Gina was where she belonged, right where she wanted to be, and with the male she wanted to be with for the rest of her life. "And don't you forget it, baby."

He grinned against her neck. "Don't *you* forget it."

"Now you're just being bossy."

"Absolutely."

God, she was so in love. "Shut up and make love to me." She gave his ass a gentle slap.

"Now who's being bossy?" But he gave her what she asked for and drove into her again.

"I love you," she said, holding on to his shoulders.

"I love you more."

In so many ways, her life was just beginning. Right now. With Malek. What more of a beginning could she ask for than to have a new mate and a child? In a way, the idea scared her, but in another, more powerful way, the thought of having Malek's child thrilled her beyond words. He was hers, and she was his, and together they were perfect... evenly matched in every way. And together they would raise their child to be the best of them both. Malek would make an excellent father. In her heart, she knew without question that he would. And even though she had no idea how to be a mother, as with everything else in her life, she would figure it out and get through. Now that she had found Malek, anything was within reach.

"Gabe," she whispered. "Or Gabby."

Malek murmured against her neck as he made love to her. "What, love?"

"I want to name our baby Gabe or Gabby."

He lifted on his elbows and looked into her eyes, already breathless. "Gabe or Gabby will be perfect. I love it."

Tears bloomed in her eyes and she smiled, but all she

could was nod, unable to speak. She pulled him down and kissed him, holding him close, relishing the feel of his body inside hers.

As he lifted her once more into the heights of pleasure, she finally believed she could be happy. Malek had taught her that. And he had taught her that even a badass assassin like her could find love and not be weakened by it. If anything, she was stronger. And anyone who messed with him or her future child would have to answer to her. Because as fiercely as Malek promised to protect her, she was just as fierce about returning the favor.

Theirs might not have been the most perfect courtship, but their union was and always would be perfect.

Gina had finally found a mate worth living for. And she was stronger because of him. And when Malek growled and sank his fangs into her neck as he came, she knew he was stronger because of her, too.

Through each other, they had found their way back from despair to become who they were born to be—who they were *meant* to be. An assassin and a warrior. And now mates and future parents. Forever in love, forever one soul, and for an eternity.

DID YOU ENJOY READING THIS BOOK?

If you did, please help others enjoy it, too:

Recommend it.

Review it at Amazon, iBooks, or Goodreads

If you leave a review, please send me an email at donya@donyalynne.com or message me on Facebook so that I can thank you with a personal e-mail.

ABOUT THE AUTHOR

DONYA LYNNE is the bestselling author of the award winning All the King's Men Series and a member of Romance Writers of America. Making her home in a wooded suburb north of Indianapolis with her husband, Donya has lived in Indiana most of her life and knew at a young age that she was destined to be a writer. She started writing poetry in grade school and won her first short story contest in fourth grade. In junior high, she began writing romantic stories for her friends, and by her sophomore year, she'd been dubbed *Most Likely to Become a Romance Novelist.* In 2012, she made that dream come true by publishing her first two novels and a novella. Her work has earned her two IPPYs (one gold, one silver) and two eLit Awards (one gold, one silver) as well as numerous accolades. When she's not writing, she can be found cheering on the Indianapolis Colts or doing her cats' bidding.

For more information on Donya's books or just to say hello, visit her on Facebook or swing by her website.

www.facebook.com/DonyaLynne

www.donyalynne.com